Praise for Elizabeth Bear

"Elizabeth Bear is awesome."

—John Scalzi

"Bear is an amazingly impress~~____~~ ~~_____~~ ~~____~~ ~~____~~ ~~____~~ems to write great work that wins awards—and deserves them—at an astonishing rate, over a huge variety of speculative fiction subgenres."

—*The Agony Column*

"Elizabeth Bear is one of the best writers in genre today. Period."

—*SF Signal*

"Bear's tales are not only ingeniously mysterious but also richly textured with details."

—*Publishers Weekly*

"Elizabeth Bear is talented."

—*Entertainment Weekly*

"Bear's . . . elegant storytelling should appeal to fans of Charles de Lint, Jim Butcher, and other cross-world and urban fantasy authors."

—*Library Journal*

"Bear makes the rest of us look like amateurs."

—Peter Watts

"Bear holds nothing back, and everything that she pulls into her story just gleams with that special wonder of discovery."

—*The Magazine of Fantasy and Science Fiction*

"[Bear] does it like a juggler who's also a magician."

—Matthew Cheney, *The Mumpsimus*

"Bear's ability to create breathtaking variations on ancient themes and make them new and brilliant is, perhaps, unparalleled in the genre."

—*Library Journal*, starred review, on *All the Windwracked Stars*

SHOGGOTHS IN BLOOM

Elizabeth Bear

SHOGGOTHS
IN
BLOOM

Elizabeth Bear

PRIME BOOKS

For Scott.
This is the first one.

CONTENTS

Introduction
By Scott Lynch

So, a hard science fiction writer, a fantasist, a consulting futurist, a sociological essayist, and a speculative fiction critic walk into a bar . . .

Which is less hectic than it sounds. It turns out they're all the same person.

Let's try another. An archer, a rock climber, a kayaker, an anthropologist, a gamer, a gardener, and a very talented amateur chef/mixologist—

Ah, you're ahead of me this time. Yep. All the same person.

A pair of Hugo Awards, a Drabblecast Annual Story Award, a John W. Campbell Best New Writer Award, a Locus Award, and a posse of nomination trinkets and ribbons arrange themselves on a shelf . . .

Okay, those are clearly inanimate objects, so they can't be a person. But they've all got her name on them.

Elizabeth Bear is the sort of writer who keeps the trophy and ribbon manufacturers of the world gainfully employed.

I could never be accused of neutrality on the subject of Bear. Before we were friends, I appreciated her work. Once we became friends, we found that it didn't suit us, so we became close friends. Once we became close friends, we eventually realized that it wasn't working out, so we were forced to start dating. As I type this, somewhere on the irresponsible side of a sweltering summer midnight in central Massachusetts, she's asleep on a couch about a dozen paces away, breathing gently, surrounded by shelves of books. She wrote a daunting number of them herself.

I could gush. That is to say, I could keep gushing. I could go on an Ellisonian bender and spit adjectives and superlatives until the sun comes up and my face hits the keyboard. When Paula Guran asked me to write this introduction, she handed me a double boon: the chance to laud a woman I love, and the chance to associate my name with the most powerful collection of her short fiction yet assembled. The former is a privilege of personal circumstance, but when you read the collection you'll see why the latter is something other writers might well begrudge me . . . with knives and brass knuckles and sugar in my gas tank.

Elizabeth Bear is the sort of writer who might get me murdered by my peers. I would die happy.

I'll tell you a little bit about what you'll find here, but I'm not handing out keys. Oh, no. No keys, no Cliffs Notes, no maps or flashlights for Elizabeth Bear stories. Talk about the fastest possible way to ruin the whole damn point. You need to make your own keys, sometimes slowly, and find your own doors, sometimes painfully. Throw yourself on these things, and mind the spikes and brambles, and be aware that you might need to make a few attempts. You might rebound entirely from some of them. There's no baby food prose here, no pat punchlines at the ends, no Obvious Spokesbeings who walk out into the spotlight and Tell You What It All Means in the worst tradition of the middle-school book report, or the platonic ideal of the half-assed science fiction story.

This is never to say that Bear doesn't have a point. All of these works have points. Huge points, important points, melancholy and rueful points. But her Relevant Portions of the Text are never conveniently circled and underlined. She doesn't light up her Themes and Messages so that they're visible from any distance. Skim these stories and you're lost. The only way in or out of this particular fictional country is to pay attention.

Elizabeth Bear is the sort of writer whose works are like found objects. They don't come with instructions.

Her personal eclecticism projects into her work like a beam of light passing through mist and foliage, casting peculiar shadows and spiraling off into alternately disquieting and entrancing patterns. Here are stories of murder and criminal investigation, stories of broken hearts, stories of communication and miscommunication, stories about drinking and exile and sacrifice, both voluntary and involuntary. Here are stories of lost dreams and broken lives and people moving forward, always forward, however slowly and painfully, however twisted their paths.

Bear is a proven survivor, and she writes about survivors. But it's a curious thing, how many of her survivors are also casualties, and how many of her casualties are also survivors.

Elizabeth Bear is the sort of writer who doesn't play zero-sum games with the important stuff.

Here you'll find myth and mythic resonance, fantasies both subtle and epic in tone. Here you'll find the hardest sort of hard science fiction, speculations about the loneliness and unbridgeability of the space between the stars, knowingly hard-edged projections of possible futures. Yet you won't hear the tinny hum of any comforting old-time propaganda behind it all. No unstoppable over-people, no Competent Men with buzz cuts and slide rules, no pat on the back with a jolly reassurance that the universe is waiting patiently for us to pave it and mark out subdivisions.

Bear's universe is an altar, and the mere act of living is the sacrifice. We lay ourselves out, hot metal on a cosmic anvil, and the fateful hammer comes down. Sometimes we come out harder, sharper, stronger. Sometimes we simply get smashed and discarded. Yet once smashed, we still move forward, always forward, however slowly and painfully, and eventually, inevitably, we put ourselves beneath the hammer again. That's Elizabeth Bear right there . . . and this is as close as I'm going to swing to giving you a possible outline of one of those keys I mentioned.

Bear's universe isn't a simple inheritance, waiting tamely for our pleasure. But gods and powers and entropy be damned, that's no excuse for not flinging ourselves at it anyway. To be smashed, and disappointed, and discarded, and then to stand up and do it all over again.

Elizabeth Bear stories can be uncomfortable in the same way life itself can be uncomfortable.

You're getting older. You're losing things. The strength you have now can never last, no matter how hard you work to sustain it. It seems like there's less room for air in your lungs all the damn time. You might as well breathe deep even if it hurts. You might as well run, even if it makes your feet sore. You might as well throw parties. You might as well make mistakes. You might as well heave yourself gamely onto the altar of the universe and see what happens, even if you're bound to get smashed. The alternative is to be dead. So you might as well.

You really might as well, so long as you're here.

Bear's stories won't conceal sweet lies like soporific venom. They won't ever, ever try to pretend you can have something for nothing. They won't tell you there's a grand design and anyone or anything to watch over you as you stumble through it. But somehow they're like anti-matter for cynicism. They're what nihilism has nightmares about. Just because there's no grand and assured meaning behind the pain doesn't mean there's no personal reason to take it anyway, to fight through it, to go down burning in it if we must.

Elizabeth Bear is the sort of writer who always reminds you that you get a fighting chance.

No more, and no less, and sometimes it's not enough. Invariably it's not what you hoped it would be.

But she'll tell you to fight anyway, all the way to the end.

These, her stories, are full of sympathy for the unsympathetic. Of quiet and personal justice for the downtrodden. Of tiny victories of kindness and comprehension over anger and prejudice. Of the living choosing to carry hard and bitter burdens for the sake of a future they'll never see. These are tales of reinvention after disaster. Tales of the lost and wounded and forgotten making new missions for themselves in the worlds they have to live with. The worlds they do live with.

The worlds they keep on fighting in, and fighting for, all the way to the end.

Tideline

Chalcedony wasn't built for crying. She didn't have it in her, not unless her tears were cold tapered glass droplets annealed by the inferno heat that had crippled her.

Such tears as that might slide down her skin over melted sensors to plink unfeeling on the sand. And if they had, she would have scooped them up, with all the other battered pretties, and added them to the wealth of trash jewels that swung from the nets reinforcing her battered carapace.

They would have called her salvage, if there were anyone left to salvage her. But she was the last of the war machines, a three-legged oblate teardrop as big as a main battle tank, two big grabs and one fine manipulator folded like a spider's palps beneath the turreted head that finished her pointed end, her polyceramic armor spiderwebbed like shatterproof glass. Unhelmed by her remote masters, she limped along the beach, dragging one fused limb. She was nearly derelict.

The beach was where she met Belvedere.

Butterfly coquinas unearthed by retreating breakers squirmed into wet grit under Chalcedony's trailing limb. One of the rear pair, it was less of a nuisance on packed sand. It worked all right as a pivot, and as long as she stayed off rocks, there were no obstacles to drag it over.

As she struggled along the tideline, she became aware of someone watching. She didn't raise her head. Her chassis was equipped with targeting sensors which locked automatically on the ragged figure crouched by a weathered rock. Her optical input was needed to scan the tangle of seaweed and driftwood, Styrofoam and sea glass that marked high tide.

He watched her all down the beach, but he was unarmed, and her algorithms didn't deem him a threat.

Just as well. She liked the weird flat-topped sandstone boulder he crouched beside.

~

The next day, he watched again. It was a good day; she found a moonstone, some rock crystal, a bit of red-orange pottery and some sea glass worn opalescent by the tide.

"Whatcha picken up?"

"Shipwreck beads," Chalcedony answered. For days, he'd been creeping closer, until he'd begun following behind her like the seagulls, scrabbling the coquinas harrowed up by her dragging foot into a patched mesh bag. Sustenance, she guessed, and indeed he pulled one of the tiny mollusks from the bag and produced a broken-bladed folding knife from somewhere to prize it open with. Her sensors painted the knife pale colors. A weapon, but not a threat to her.

Deft enough—he flicked, sucked, and tossed the shell away in under three seconds—but that couldn't be much more than a morsel of meat. A lot of work for very small return.

He was bony as well as ragged, and small for a human. Perhaps young.

She thought he'd ask *what shipwreck*, and she would gesture vaguely over the bay, where the city had been, and say *there were many*. But he surprised her.

"Whatcha gonna do with them?" He wiped his mouth on a sandy paw, the broken knife projecting carelessly from the bottom of his fist.

"When I get enough, I'm going to make necklaces." She spotted something under a tangle of the algae called dead man's fingers, a glint of light, and began the laborious process of lowering herself to reach it, compensating by math for her malfunctioning gyroscopes.

The presumed-child watched avidly. "Nuh uh," he said. "You can't make a necklace outta that."

"Why not?" She levered herself another decimeter down, balancing against the weight of her fused limb. She did not care to fall.

"I seed what you pick up. They's all different."

"So?" she asked, and managed another few centimeters. Her hydraulics whined. Someday, those hydraulics or her fuel cells would fail and she'd be stuck this way, a statue corroded by salt air and the sea, and the tide would roll in and roll over her. Her carapace was cracked, no longer water-tight.

"They's not all beads."

Her manipulator brushed aside the dead man's fingers. She uncovered the treasure, a bit of blue-gray stone carved in the shape of a fat, merry man. It had no holes. Chalcedony balanced herself back upright and turned the figurine in the light. The stone was structurally sound.

She extruded a hair-fine diamond-tipped drill from the opposite manipulator and drilled a hole through the figurine, top to bottom. Then she threaded him on a twist of wire, looped the ends, work-hardened the loops, and added him to the garland of beads swinging against her disfigured chassis.

"So?"

The presumed-child brushed the little Buddha with his fingertip, setting it swinging against shattered ceramic plate. She levered herself up again, out of his reach. "I's Belvedere," he said.

"Hello," Chalcedony said. "I'm Chalcedony."

By sunset when the tide was lowest he scampered chattering in her wake, darting between flocking gulls to scoop up coquinas-by-the-fistful, which he rinsed in the surf before devouring raw. Chalcedony more or less ignored him as she activated her floods, concentrating their radiance along the tideline.

A few dragging steps later, another treasure caught her eye. It was a twist of chain with a few bright beads caught on it—glass, with scraps of gold and silver foil imbedded in their twists. Chalcedony initiated the laborious process of retrieval—

Only to halt as Belvedere jumped in front of her, grabbed the chain in a grubby broken-nailed hand, and snatched it up. Chalcedony locked in position, nearly overbalancing. She was about to reach out to snatch the treasure away from the child and knock him into the sea when he rose up on tiptoe and held it out to her, straining over his head. The flood lights cast his shadow black on the sand, illumined each thread of his hair and eyebrows in stark relief.

"It's easier if I get that for you," he said, as her fine manipulator closed tenderly on the tip of the chain.

She lifted the treasure to examine it in the floods. A good long segment, seven centimeters, four jewel-toned shiny beads. Her head creaked when she raised it, corrosion showering from the joints.

She hooked the chain onto the netting wrapped around her carapace. "Give me your bag," she said.

Belvedere's hand went to the soggy net full of raw bivalves dripping down his naked leg. "My bag?"

"Give it to me." Chalcedony drew herself up, a-kilter because of the ruined limb but still two and a half meters taller than the child. She extended a manipulator, and from some disused file dredged up a protocol for dealing with civilian humans. "Please."

He fumbled at the knot with rubbery fingers, tugged it loose from his rope belt, and held it out to her. She snagged it on a manipulator and brought it up. A sample revealed that the weave was cotton rather than nylon, so she folded it in her two larger manipulators and gave the contents a low-wattage microwave pulse.

She shouldn't. It was a drain on her power cells, which she had no means to recharge, and she had a task to complete.

She shouldn't—but she did.

Steam rose from her claws and the coquinas popped open, roasting in their own juices and the moisture of the seaweed with which he'd lined the net. Carefully, she swung the bag back to him, trying to preserve the fluids.

"Caution," she urged. "It's hot."

He took the bag gingerly and flopped down to sit crosslegged at her feet. When he tugged back the seaweed, the coquinas lay like tiny jewels—pale orange, rose, yellow, green and blue—in their nest of glass-green *Ulva*, sea lettuce. He tasted one cautiously, and then began to slurp with great abandon, discarding shells in every direction.

"Eat the algae, too," Chalcedony told him. "It is rich in important nutrients."

When the tide came in, Chalcedony retreated up the beach like a great hunched crab with five legs amputated. She was beetle-backed under the moonlight, her treasures swinging and rustling on her netting, clicking one another like stones shivered in a palm.

The child followed.

"You should sleep," Chalcedony said, as Belvedere settled beside her on the high, dry crescent of beach under towering mud cliffs, where the waves wouldn't lap.

He didn't answer, and her voice fuzzed and furred before clearing when she spoke again. "You should climb up off the beach. The cliffs are unstable. It is not safe beneath them."

Belvedere hunkered closer, lower lip protruding. "You stay down here."

"I have armor. And I cannot climb." She thumped her fused leg on the sand, rocking her body forward and back on the two good legs to manage it.

"But your armor's broke."

"That doesn't matter. You must climb." She picked Belvedere up with both grabs and raised him over her head. He shrieked; at first she feared she'd damaged him, but the cries resolved into laughter before she set him down on a slanted ledge that would bring him to the top of the cliff.

She lit it with her floods. "Climb," she said, and he climbed.

And returned in the morning.

Belvedere stayed ragged, but with Chalcedony's help he waxed plumper. She snared and roasted seabirds for him, taught him how to construct and maintain fires, and ransacked her extensive databases for hints on how to keep him healthy as he grew—sometimes almost visibly, fractions of a millimeter a day. She researched and analyzed sea vegetables and hectored him into eating them, and he helped her reclaim treasures her manipulators could not otherwise grasp. Some shipwreck beads were hot, and made Chalcedony's radiation detectors tick over. They were no threat to her, but for the first time she discarded them. She had a human ally; her program demanded she sustain him in health.

She told him stories. Her library was vast—and full of war stories and stories about sailing ships and starships, which he liked best for some inexplicable reason. Catharsis, she thought, and told him again of Roland, and King Arthur, and Honor Harrington, and Napoleon Bonaparte, and Horatio Hornblower, and Captain Jack Aubrey. She projected the words on a monitor as she recited them, and—faster than she would have imagined—he began to mouth them along with her.

So the summer ended.

By the equinox, she had collected enough memorabilia. Shipwreck jewels still washed up and Belvedere still brought her the best of them, but Chalcedony settled beside that twisted flat-topped sandstone rock and arranged her treasures atop it. She spun salvaged brass through a die to make wire, threaded beads on it, and forged links which she strung into garland.

It was a learning experience. Her aesthetic sense was at first undeveloped, requiring her to make and unmake many dozens of bead combinations to find a pleasing one. Not only must form and color be balanced, but there were structural difficulties. First the weights were unequal, so the chains hung crooked. Then links kinked and snagged and had to be redone.

She worked for weeks. Memorials had been important to the human allies, though she had never understood the logic of it. She could not build a tomb for her colleagues, but the same archives that gave her the stories Belvedere lapped up as a cat laps milk gave her the concept of mourning jewelry. She had no physical remains of her allies, no scraps of hair or cloth, but surely the shipwreck jewels would suffice for a treasure?

The only quandary was who would wear the jewelry. It should go to an heir, someone who held fond memories of the deceased. And Chalcedony had records of the next of kin, of course. But she had no way to know if any survived, and if they did no way to reach them.

At first, Belvedere stayed close, trying to tempt her into excursions and explorations. Chalcedony remained resolute, however. Not only were her power cells dangerously low, but with the coming of winter her ability to utilize solar power would be even more limited. And with winter the storms would come, and she would no longer be able to evade the ocean.

She was determined to complete this last task before she failed.

Belvedere began to range without her, to snare his own birds and bring them back to the driftwood fire for roasting. This was positive; he needed to be able to maintain himself. At night, however, he returned to sit beside her, to clamber onto the flat-topped rock to sort beads and hear her stories.

The same thread she worked over and over with her grabs and fine manipulators—the duty of the living to remember the fallen with honor—was played out in the war stories she still told him, though now she'd finished with fiction and history and related him her own experiences. She told him about Emma Percy rescuing that kid up near Savannah, and how Private Michaels was shot drawing fire for Sergeant Kay Patterson when the battle robots were decoyed out of position in a skirmish near Seattle.

Belvedere listened, and surprised her by proving he could repeat the gist, if not the exact words. His memory was good, if not as good as a machine's.

One day when he had gone far out of sight down the beach, Chalcedony heard Belvedere screaming.

She had not moved in days. She hunkered on the sand at an awkward angle, her frozen limb angled down the beach, her necklaces in progress on the rock that served as her impromptu work bench.

Bits of stone and glass and wire scattered from the rock top as she heaved herself onto her unfused limbs. She thrashed upright on her first attempt, surprising herself, and tottered for a moment unsteadily, lacking the stabilization of long-failed gyroscopes.

When Belvedere shouted again, she almost overset.

Climbing was out of the question, but Chalcedony could still run. Her fused limb plowed a furrow in the sand behind her and the tide was coming in, forcing her to splash through corroding sea water.

She barreled around the rocky prominence that Belvedere had disappeared behind in time to see him knocked to the ground by two larger humans, one of whom had a club raised over its head and the other of which was holding Belvedere's shabby net bag. Belvedere yelped as the club connected with his thigh.

Chalcedony did not dare use her microwave projectors.

But she had other weapons, including a pinpoint laser and a chemical-propellant firearm suitable for sniping operations. Enemy humans were soft targets. These did not even have body armor.

She buried the bodies on the beach, for it was her program to treat enemy dead with respect, following the protocols of war. Belvedere was in no immediate danger of death once she had splinted his leg and treated his bruises, but she judged him too badly injured to help. The sand was soft and amenable to scooping, anyway, though there was no way to keep the bodies above water. It was the best she could manage.

After she had finished, she transported Belvedere back to their rock and began collecting her scattered treasures.

The leg was sprained and bruised, not broken, and some perversity connected to the injury made him even more restlessly inclined to push his boundaries once he partially recovered. He was on his feet within a week, leaning on crutches and dragging a leg as stiff as Chalcedony's. As soon as the splint came off, he started ranging even further afield. His new limp barely slowed him, and he stayed out nights. He was still growing, shooting up, almost as tall as a Marine now, and ever more capable of taking care of himself. The incident with the raiders had taught him caution.

Meanwhile, Chalcedony elaborated her funeral necklaces. She must make each one worthy of a fallen comrade, and she was slowed now by her inability to work through the nights. Rescuing Belvedere had cost her more carefully hoarded energy, and she could not power her floods if she meant to finish before her cells ran dry. She could *see* by moonlight, with deadly clarity, but her low-light and thermal eyes were of no use when it came to balancing color against color.

There would be forty-one necklaces, one for each member of her platoon-that-was, and she would not excuse shoddy craftsmanship.

No matter how fast she worked, it was a race against sun and tide.

The fortieth necklace was finished in October while the days grew short. She began the forty-first—the one for her chief operator Platoon Sergeant Patterson, the one with the gray-blue Buddha at the bottom—before sunset. She had not seen Belvedere in several days, but that was acceptable. She would not finish the necklace tonight.

His voice woke her from the quiescence in which she waited the sun. "Chalcedony?"

Something cried as she came awake. *Infant*, she identified, but the warm shape in his arms was not an infant. It was a dog, a young dog, a German shepherd like the ones teamed with the handlers that had sometimes worked with Company L. The dogs had never minded her, but some of the handlers had been frightened, though they would not admit it. Sergeant Patterson had said to one of them, *Oh, Chase is just pretty much a big attack dog herself*, and had made a big show of rubbing Chalcedony behind her telescopic sights, to the sound of much laughter.

The young dog was wounded. Its injuries bled warmth across its hind leg.

"Hello, Belvedere," Chalcedony said.

"Found a puppy." He kicked his ragged blanket flat so he could lay the dog down.

"Are you going to eat it?"

"Chalcedony!" he snapped, and covered the animal protectively with his arms. "S'hurt."

She contemplated. "You wish me to tend to it?"

He nodded, and she considered. She would need her lights, energy, irreplaceable stores. Antibiotics and coagulants and surgical supplies, and the animal might die anyway. But dogs were valuable; she knew the handlers held them in great esteem, even greater than Sergeant Patterson's esteem for Chalcedony. And in her library, she had files on veterinary medicine.

She flipped on her floods and accessed the files.

She finished before morning, and before her cells ran dry. Just barely.

When the sun was up and young dog was breathing comfortably, the gash along its haunch sewn closed and its bloodstream saturated with antibiotics, she turned back to the last necklace. She would have to work quickly, and Sergeant Patterson's necklace contained the most fragile and beautiful beads, the ones Chalcedony had been most concerned with breaking and so had saved for last, when she would be most experienced.

Her motions grew slower as the day wore on, more laborious. The sun could not feed her enough to replace the expenditures of the night before. But bead linked into bead, and the necklace grew—bits of pewter, of pottery, of glass and mother of pearl. And the chalcedony Buddha, because Sergeant Patterson had been Chalcedony's operator.

When the sun approached its zenith, Chalcedony worked faster, benefiting from a burst of energy. The young dog slept on in her shade, having wolfed the scraps of bird Belvedere gave it, but Belvedere climbed the rock and crouched beside her pile of finished necklaces.

"Who's this for?" he asked, touching the slack length draped across her manipulator.

"Kay Patterson," Chalcedony answered, adding a greenish-brown pottery bead mottled like a combat uniform.

"Sir Kay," Belvedere said. His voice was changing, and sometimes it abandoned him completely in the middle of words, but he got that phrase out entire. "She was King Arthur's horse-master, and his adopted brother, and she kept his combat robots in the stable," he said, proud of his recall.

"They were different Kays," she reminded. "You will have to leave soon." She looped another bead onto the chain, closed the link, and work-hardened the metal with her fine manipulator.

"You can't leave the beach. You can't climb."

Idly, he picked up a necklace, Rodale's, and stretched it between his hands so the beads caught the light. The links clinked softly.

Belvedere sat with her as the sun descended and her motions slowed. She worked almost entirely on solar power now. With night, she would become quiescent again. When the storms came, the waves would roll over her, and then even the sun would not awaken her again. "You must go," she said, as her grabs stilled on the almost-finished chain. And then she lied and said, "I do not want you here."

"Who's this'n for?" he asked. Down on the beach, the young dog lifted its head and whined. "Garner," she answered, and then she told him about Garner, and Antony, and Javez, and Rodriguez, and Patterson, and White, and Wosczyna, until it was dark enough that her voice and her vision failed.

In the morning, he put Patterson's completed chain into Chalcedony's grabs. He must have worked on it by firelight through the darkness. "Couldn't harden the links," he said, as he smoothed them over her claws.

Silently, she did that, one by one. The young dog was on its feet, limping, nosing around the base of the rock and barking at the waves, the birds, a scuttling crab. When Chalcedony had finished, she reached out and draped the necklace around Belvedere's shoulders while he held very still. Soft fur downed his cheeks. The male Marines had always scraped theirs smooth, and the women didn't grow facial hair.

"You said that was for Sir Kay." He lifted the chain in his hands and studied the way the glass and stones caught the light.

"It's for somebody to remember her," Chalcedony said. She didn't correct him this time. She picked up the other forty necklaces. They were heavy, all together. She wondered if Belvedere could carry them all. "So remember her. Can you remember which one is whose?"

One at a time, he named them, and one at a time she handed them to him. Rogers, and Rodale, and van Metier, and Percy. He spread a second blanket out—and where had he gotten a second blanket? Maybe the same place he'd gotten the dog—and laid them side by side on the navy blue wool.

They sparkled.

"Tell me the story about Rodale," she said, brushing her grab across the necklace. He did, sort of, with half of Roland-and-Oliver mixed in. It was a pretty good story anyway, the way he told it. Inasmuch as she was a fit judge.

"Take the necklaces," she said. "Take them. They're mourning jewelry. Give them to people and tell them the stories. They should go to people who will remember and honor the dead."

"Where'd I find alla these people?" he asked, sullenly, crossing his arms. "Ain't on the beach."

"No," she said, "they are not. You'll have to go look for them."

But he wouldn't leave her. He and the dog ranged up and down the beach as the weather chilled. Her sleeps grew longer, deeper, the low angle of the sun not enough to awaken her except at noon. The storms came, and because the table rock broke the spray, the salt water stiffened her joints but did not—yet—corrode her processor. She no longer moved and rarely spoke even in daylight, and Belvedere and the young dog used her carapace and the rock for shelter, the smoke of his fires blackening her belly.

She was hoarding energy.

By mid-November, she had enough, and she waited and spoke to Belvedere when he returned with the young dog from his rambling. "You must go," she said, and when he opened his mouth to protest, she added "It is time you went on errantry."

His hand went to Patterson's necklace, which he wore looped twice around his neck, under his ragged coat. He had given her back the others, but that one she had made a gift of. "Errantry?"

Creaking, powdered corrosion grating from her joints, she lifted the necklaces off her head. "You must find the people to whom these belong."

He deflected her words with a jerk of his hand. "They's all dead."

"The warriors are dead," she said. "But the stories aren't. Why did you save the young dog?"

He licked his lips, and touched Patterson's necklace again. "'Cause you saved me. And you told me the stories. About good fighters and bad fighters. And so, see, Percy woulda saved the dog, right? And so would Hazel-rah."

Emma Percy, Chalcedony was reasonably sure, would have saved the dog if she could have. And Kevin Michaels would have saved the kid. She held the remaining necklaces out. "Who's going to protect the other children?"

He stared, hands twisting before him. "You can't climb."

"I can't. You must do this for me. Find people to remember the stories. Find people to tell about my platoon. I won't survive the winter." Inspiration struck. "So I give you this quest, Sir Belvedere."

The chains hung flashing in the wintry light, the sea combed gray and tired behind them. "What kinda people?"

"People who would help a child," she said. "Or a wounded dog. People like a platoon should be."

He paused. He reached out, stroked the chains, let the beads rattle. He crooked both hands, and slid them into the necklaces up to the elbows, taking up her burden.

Sonny Liston Takes the Fall

1.

"I gotta tell you, Jackie," Sonny Liston said, "I lied to my wife about that. I gotta tell you, I took that fall."

It was Christmas eve, 1970, and Sonny Liston was about the furthest thing you could imagine from a handsome man. He had a furrowed brow and downcast hound dog prisoner eyes that wouldn't meet mine, and the matching furrows on either side of his broad, flat nose ran down to a broad, flat mouth under a pencil thin moustache that was already out of fashion six years ago, when he was still King of the World.

"We all lie sometimes, Sonny," I said, pouring him another scotch. We don't mind if you drink too much in Vegas. We don't mind much of anything at all. "It doesn't signify."

He had what you call a tremendous physical presence, Sonny Liston. He filled up a room so you couldn't take your eyes off him—didn't *want* to take your eyes off him, and if he was smiling you were smiling, and if he was scowling you were shivering—even when he was sitting quietly, the way he was now, turned away from his kitchen table and his elbows on his knees, one hand big enough for a man twice his size wrapped around the glass I handed him and the other hanging between his legs, limp across the back of the wrist as if the tendons'd been cut. His suit wasn't long enough for the length of his arms. The coat sleeves and the shirt sleeves with their French cuffs and discreet cufflinks were ridden halfway up his forearms, showing wrists I couldn't have wrapped my fingers around. Tall as he was, he wasn't tall enough for that frame—as if he didn't get enough to eat as a kid—but he was that wide.

Sonny Liston, he was from Arkansas. And you would hear it in his voice, even now. He drank that J&B scotch like knocking back a blender full of raw eggs and held the squat glass out for more. "I could of beat Cassius Clay if it weren't for the fucking mob," he said, while I filled it up again. "I could of beat that goddamn flashy pansy."

"I know you could, Sonny," I told him, and it wasn't a lie. "I know you could."

His hands were like mallets, like mauls, like the paws of the bear they styled him. It didn't matter.

He was a broken man, Sonny Liston. He wouldn't meet your eyes, not that he ever would have. You learn that in prison. You learn that from a father who beats you. You learn that when you're black in America.

You keep your eyes down, and maybe there won't be trouble this time.

2.

It's the same thing with fighters as with horses. Race horses, I mean, thoroughbreds, which I know a lot about. I'm the genius of Las Vegas, you see. The One-Eyed Jack, the guardian and the warden of Sin City.

It's a bit like being a magician who works with tigers—the city is my life, and I take care of it. But that means it's my job to make damned sure it doesn't get out and eat anybody.

And because of that, I also know a little about magic and sport and sacrifice, and the real, old blood truth of the laurel crown and what it means to be King for a Day.

The thing about race horses, is that the trick with the good ones isn't getting them to run. It's getting them to *stop*.

They'll kill themselves running, the good ones. They'll run on broken hearts, broken legs, broken wind. Legend says Black Gold finished his last race with nothing but a shipping bandage holding his flopping hoof to his leg. They shot him on the track, Black Gold, the way they did in those days. And it was mercy when they did it.

He was King, and he was claimed. He went to pay the tithe that only greatness pays.

Ruffian, perhaps the best filly that ever ran, shattered herself in a match race that was meant to prove she could have won the Kentucky Derby if she'd raced in it. The great colt Swale ran with a hole in his heart, and no one ever knew until it killed him in the paddock one fine summer day in the third year of his life.

And then there's Charismatic.

Charismatic was a Triple Crown contender until he finished his Belmont third, running on a collapsed leg, with his jockey Chris Antley all but kneeling on the reins, doing anything to drag him down.

Antley left the saddle as soon as his mount saw the wire and could be slowed. He dove over Charismatic's shoulder and got underneath him before the horse had stopped moving; he held the broken Charismatic up with his shoulders and his own two hands until the veterinarians arrived. Between Antley and the surgeons, they saved the colt. Because Antley took that fall.

Nobody could save Antley, who was dead himself within two years from a drug overdose. He died so hard that investigators first called it a homicide.

When you run with all God gave you, you run out of track goddamned fast.

3.

Sonny was just like that. Just like a race horse. Just like every other goddamned fighter. A little bit crazy, a little bit fierce, a little bit desperate, and ignorant of the concept of defeat under any circumstances.

Until he met Cassius Clay in the ring.

They fought twice. First time was in 1964, and I watched that fight live in a movie theatre. We didn't have pay-per-view then, and the fight happened in Florida, not here at home in Vegas.

I remember it real well, though.

Liston was a monster, you have to understand. He wasn't real big for a fighter, only six foot one, but he *hulked*. He *loomed*. His opponents would flinch away before he ever pulled back a punch.

I've met Mike Tyson too, who gets compared to Liston. And I don't think it's just because they're both hard men, or that Liston also was accused of sexual assault. It's because Tyson has that same thing, the power of personal gravity that bends the available light and every eye down to him, even when he's walking quietly through a crowded room, wearing a warm-up jacket and a smile.

So that was Liston. He was a stone golem, a thing out of legend, the fucking bogeyman. He was going to walk through Clay like the Kool-Aid pitcher walking through a paper wall.

And we were all in our seats, waiting to see this insolent prince beat down by the barbarian king.

And there was a moment when Clay stepped up to Liston, and they touched gloves, and the whole theatre went still.

Because Clay was just as big as Liston. And Clay wasn't looking down.

Liston retired in the seventh round. Maybe he had a dislocated shoulder, and maybe he didn't, and maybe the Mob told him to throw the fight so they could bet on the underdog Clay and Liston just couldn't quite make himself fall over and play dead.

And Cassius Clay, you see, he grew up to be Muhammad Ali.

4.

Sonny didn't tell me about *that* fight. He told me about the other one.

Phil Ochs wrote a song about it, and so did Mark Knopfler: that legendary fight in 1965, the one where, in the very first minute of the very first round, Sonny Liston took a fall.

Popular poets, Ochs and Knopfler, and what do you think the bards were? That kind of magic, the old dark magic that soaks down the roots of the world and keeps it rich, it's a transformative magic. It never goes away.

However you spill it, it's blood that makes the cactus grow.

Ochs, just to interject a little more irony here, paid for his power in *his* own blood as well.

5.

Twenty-fifth child of twenty-six, Sonny Liston. A tenant farmer's son, whose father beat him bloody. He never would meet my eye, even there in his room, *this* close to Christmas, near the cold bent stub end of 1970.

He never would meet a white man's eyes. Even the eye of the One-Eyed Jack, patron saint of Las Vegas, when Jackie was pouring him J&B. Not a grown man's eye, anyway, though he loved kids—and kids loved him. The bear was a teddy bear when you got him around children.

But he told me all about that fight. How the Mob told him to throw it or they'd kill him and his Momma and a selection of his brothers and sisters too. How he did what they told him in the most defiant manner possible. So the whole fucking world would know he took that fall.

The thing is, I didn't believe him.

I sat there and nodded and listened, and I thought, Sonny Liston didn't throw that fight. That famous "Phantom Punch"? Mohammed Ali got lucky. Hit a nerve cluster or something. Sonny Liston, the unstoppable Sonny Liston, the man with a heart of piston steel and a hand like John Henry's hammer—Sonny Liston, he went down. It was a fluke, a freak thing, some kind of an accident.

I thought going down like that shamed him, so he told his wife he gave up because he knew Ali was better and he didn't feel like fighting just to get beat. But he told me that other story, about the mob, and he drank another scotch and he toasted Muhammad Ali, though Sonny'd kind of hated him. Ali had been barred from fighting from 1967 until just that last year, who was facing a jail term because he wouldn't go and die in Vietnam.

Sensible man, if you happen to ask me.

But I knew Sonny didn't throw that fight for the Mob. I knew because I also knew this other thing about that fight, because I am the soul of Las Vegas, and in 1965, the Mob *was* Las Vegas.

And I knew they'd had a few words with Sonny before he went into the ring.

Sonny Liston was supposed to win. And Muhammad Ali was supposed to die.

6.

The one thing in his life that Sonny Liston could never hit back against was his daddy. Sonny, whose given name was Charles, but who called himself Sonny all his adult life.

Sonny had learned the hard way that you never look a white man in the eye. That you never look *any* man in the eye unless you mean to beat him down. That you never look *the Man* in the eye, because if you do he's gonna beat *you* down.

He did his time in jail, Sonny Liston. He went in a boy and he came out a prize fighter, and when he came out he was owned by the Mob.

You can see it in the photos and you could see it in his face, when you met him, when you reached out to touch his hand; he almost never smiled, and his eyes always held this kind of deep sonorous seriousness over his black, flat, damaged nose.

Sonny Liston was a jailbird. Sonny Liston belonged to the Mob the same way his daddy belonged to the land.

Cassius Clay, God bless him, changed his slave name two days after that first bout with Sonny, as if winning it freed up something in him. Muhammad Ali, God bless him, never learned that lesson about looking down.

7.

Boxing is called the sweet science. And horse racing is the sport of kings.

When Clay beat Liston, he bounced up on his stool and shouted that he was King of the World. Corn king, summer king, America's most beautiful young man. An angel in the boxing ring. A new and powerful image of black manhood.

He stepped up on that stool in 1964 and he put a noose around his neck.

The thing about magic is that it happens in spite of everything you can do to stop it.

And the wild old Gods will have their sacrifice.

No excuses.

If they can't have Charismatic, they'll take the man that saved him.

So it goes.

8.

Sometimes it's easier to tell yourself you quit than to admit that they beat you. Sometimes it's easier to look down.

The civil rights movement in the early 1960s found Liston a thug and an embarrassment. He was a jailbird, an illiterate, a dark unstoppable monster. The rumor was that he had a second career as a standover man—a mob enforcer. The NAACP protested when Floyd Patterson agreed to fight him in 1962.

9.

Sonny didn't know his own birthday or maybe he lied about his age. Forty's old for a fighter, and Sonny said he was born in '32 when he was might have been born as early as '27. There's a big damned difference between thirty-two and thirty-seven in the boxing ring.

And there's another thing, something about prize fighters you might not know. In Liston's day, they shot the fighters' hands full of anesthetic before they wrapped them for the fight. So a guy who was a hitter—a *puncher* rather than a *boxer*, in the parlance—he could pound away on his opponent and never notice he'd broken all the goddamned bones in his goddamned hands.

Sonny Liston was a puncher. Muhammad Ali was a boxer.

Neither one of them, as it happens, could abide the needles. So when they went swinging into the ring, they earned every punch they threw.

Smack a sheetrock wall a couple of dozen times with your shoulder behind it if you want to build up a concept of what that means, in terms of endurance and of pain. Me? I would have taken the needle over *feeling* the bones I was breaking. Taken it in a heartbeat.

But Charismatic finished his race on a shattered leg, and so did Black Gold. What the hell were a few broken bones to Sonny Liston?

~

10.

You know when I said Sonny was not a handsome man? Well, I also said Muhammad Ali was an angel. He was a black man's angel, an avenging angel, a messenger from a better future. He was the *way* and the *path*, man, and they marked him for sacrifice, because he was a warrior god, a Black Muslim Moses come to lead his people out of Egypt land.

And the people in power like to stay that way, and they have their ways of making it happen. Of making sure the sacrifice gets chosen.

Go ahead and curl your lip. White man born in the nineteenth century, reborn in 1905 as the Genius of the Mississippi of the West. What do I know about the black experience?

I am my city, and I contain multitudes. I'm the African-American airmen at Nellis Air Force Base, and I'm the black neighborhoods near D Street that can't keep a supermarket, and I'm Cartier Street and I'm Northtown and I'm Las Vegas, baby, and it doesn't matter a bit what you see when you look at my face.

Because Sonny Liston died here, and he's buried here in the palm of my hand. And I'm Sonny Liston too, wronged and wronging; he's in here, boiling and bubbling away.

11.

I filled his glass one more time and splashed what was left into my own, and that was the end of the bottle. I twisted it to make the last drop fall. Sonny watched my hands instead of my eyes, and folded his own enormous fists around his glass so it vanished. "You're here on business, Jackie," he said, and dropped his eyes to his knuckles. "Nobody wants to listen to me talk."

"I want to listen, Sonny." The scotch didn't taste so good, but I rolled it over my tongue anyway. I'd drunk enough that the roof of my mouth was getting dry, and the liquor helped a little. "I'm here to listen as long as you want to talk."

His shoulders always had a hunch. He didn't stand up tall. They hunched a bit more as he turned the glass in his hands. "I guess I run out of things to say. So you might as well tell me what you came for."

At Christmastime in 1970, Muhammad Ali—recently allowed back in the ring, pending his appeal of a draft evasion conviction—was preparing for a title bout against Joe Frazier in March. He was also preparing for a more wide-reaching conflict; in April of that year, his appeal, his demand to be granted status as a conscientious objector, was to go before the United States Supreme Court.

He faced a five year prison sentence.

In jail, he'd come up against everything Sonny Liston had. And maybe Ali was the stronger man. And maybe the young king wouldn't break where the old one fell. Or maybe he wouldn't make it out of prison alive, or free.

"Ali needs your help," I said.

"Fuck Cassius Clay," he said.

Sonny finished his drink and spent a while staring at the bottom of his glass. I waited until he turned his head, skimming his eyes along the floor, and tried to sip again from the empty glass. Then I cleared my throat and said "It isn't just for him."

Sonny flinched. See, the thing about Sonny—that he never learned to read, that doesn't mean he was *dumb*. "The NAACP don't want me. The Nation of Islam don't want me. They didn't even want Clay to box me. I'm *an embarrassment to the black man*."

He dropped his glass on the table and held his breath for a moment before he shrugged and said, "Well, they got their nigger now."

Some of them know up front; they listen to the whispers, and they know the price they might have to pay if it's their number that comes up. Some just kind of know in the back of their heads. About the corn king, and the laurel wreath, and the price that sometimes has to be paid.

Sonny Liston, like I said, he wasn't dumb.

"Ali can do something you can't, Sonny." *Ali can be a symbol.*

"I can't have it," he drawled. "But I can buy it? Is that what you're telling me, Jack?"

I finished my glass too, already drunk enough that it didn't make my sinuses sting. "Sonny," I said, with that last bit of Dutch courage in me, "you're gonna have to take another fall."

12.

When his wife—returning from a holiday visit to her relatives—found his body on January fifth, eleven days after I poured him that drink, maybe a week or so after he died, Sonny had needle marks in the crook of his arm, though the coroner's report said *heart failure*.

Can you think of a worse way to kill the man?

~

13.

On March 8, 1971, a publicly reviled Muhammad Ali was defeated by Joe Frazier at Madison Square Garden in New York City in a boxing match billed at the "Fight of the Century." Ali had been vilified in the press as a Black Muslim, a religious and political radical, a black man who wouldn't look down.

Three months later, the United States Supreme Court overturned the conviction, allowing Muhammad Ali's conscientious objector status to stand.

He was a free man.

Ali fought Frazier twice more. He won both times, and went on to become the most respected fighter in the history of the sport. A beautiful avenging outspoken angel.

Almost thirty-five years after Sonny Liston died, in November of 2005, President George W. Bush awarded America's highest civilian honor, the Presidential Medal of Freedom, to the draft-dodging, politically activist lay preacher Muhammad Ali.

14.

Sonny Liston never looked a man in the eye unless he meant to beat him down. Until he looked upon Cassius Clay and hated him. And looked past that hate and saw a dawning angel, and he saw the future, and he wanted it that bad.

Wanted it bad, Sonny Liston, illiterate jailbird and fighter and standover man. Sonny Liston the drunk, the sex offender. Broken, brutal Sonny Liston with the scars on his face from St. Louis cops beating a confession from him, with the scars on his back from his daddy beating him down on the farm.

Sonny Liston, who loved children. He wanted that thing, and he knew it could never be his.

Wanted it and saw a way to make it happen for somebody else.

15.

And so he takes that fall, Sonny Liston. Again and again and again, like John Henry driving steel until his heart burst, like a jockey rolling over the shoulder of a running, broken horse. He takes the fall, and he saves the King.

And Muhammad Ali? He never once looks down.

꙳

Sounding

Cully sees the fin whales as he's leaving Nantucket Harbor. Mother and calf; seventy-foot whale, and a forty-foot boat. She's gray as Wellington rubber, lined with long parallel lines. She rolls on her side to show him an eye big as his hand, dark and sweet. Dreaming.

Looking back at him. Her breath mists his face like a benediction.

"Put in a word for us, would you?" Cully says. "I'll pay you back somehow." He watches her a minute before turning away. The sun's half over the eastern horizon, gold ripples flat on green water, rolling along the rim of the world like a great golden wheel. The Brant Point light's gone dark with morning.

It's the quiet before the work. Morgan is drinking coffee in the galley. There's nothing between them and the Atlantic but an arrow-straight line.

Cully doesn't tell Morgan about the whales.

Pen owns the *Sweet Katrina*—most of the *Sweet Katrina*—and stays on shore. Minority business owner, fifty-one percent. The government gives them a little boost, because of that, as if *Pen Cullen* was somehow different from *Allan Cullen*. As if she were somehow separate, not the same, flesh of one flesh. More worthy, somehow, than her husband.

Allan thinks she is. Fifteen years, three children, hard times, and hurricanes. Pen keeps her own counsel about who the worthy one is. She works nights at Nantucket Cottage Hospital. That gives them another little boost. Just enough, maybe, to stay afloat. So far.

They'll have to sell the house come winter, if the catch doesn't improve. Sell the house, or sell the boat.

There's really no option.

Pen shades her eyes with one hand, her gardening glove leaving a smudge over her eyebrows, and waves with her shears in the other. The children don't notice; they're pushing and giggling up the steps of a fat yellow schoolbus. The bus's doors close; the bus's wheels turn. She watches them out of sight, the way she never watches Allan anymore. She knows that if it's in his power, he is always coming home. Besides, there's no widow's walk on a little Cape Cod style cottage, and it wouldn't matter anyway.

It's a short sandy path down to the narrow, rocky beach, through bramble rose and salt scrub. She's never away from the sound of the sea.

Cully's at the wheel, and the sun is high. Salt air scours his face; he's grateful for the shade of the wheelhouse. Morgan is checking the lines, checking the gear, making ready. Cully will go out and help him in a minute, as soon as he gets his hat.

Everything on a boat is oil and paint and elbow grease and constant maintenance. The sea eats ships; it's an acid, an etchant. They sail through it, and it takes them apart, molecule by molecule.

They're cruising through the Sound, headed for deeper waters, cleaner waters, where the big fish swim. Time was, a man could fish the Sound, could fish the Bay, hell. Time was a man could take all he needed in Wellfleet Harbor. Time was a man could make a living—even make a fortune—on the sea.

Time was, Nantucket was a whaling island, and the fin whale cruising beside them—vanishing, returning, playing with the wake of a boat half her size—would have been rightful prey.

Times are not what they were. Stripers are closed and the cod you bring in are half the size they should be, babies too young to breed. It wasn't like this fifty years ago; Cully knows his father's stories of sixteen, twenty cod to a hundred hooks. Hell, even twenty years ago it was better than this.

He'll have no luck in the shoals of the Sound. He knows it in his bones, like he knows the rise and fall of the sea, the sound of Pen's breathing in the dark, the smell of his children's hair. He's going for bluefish; the quota's still wide open. Bluefish. Or maybe bluefin tuna. If he can find them.

He'll go as far as he has to, to find them.

Pen grooms the early-autumn roses, cleans the house, naps for a few hours before the children come home. Allan's mother Cindy lives with them. She comes home from work at five and distracts the kids while Pen cooks dinner and gets things ready.

Pen doesn't know what they'll do when they have to sell the house.

Rent something, maybe. They could leave the island, sell the boat. Save the lives of a few gulls, the ones who try to steal the bait and get caught on the hooks when the long lines go down.

She doesn't want to move the kids to Boston, to Fall River. She wants the path with the damasked roses, the sharp clean tang of the ocean air. She wants the sea for a back yard.

She doesn't want to watch Allan grow old in a factory. And then there's the kids, the money for college—only six years off for Allan Junior, only ten years off for John, and Mike in the middle. The *Sweet Katrina*'s every breath of a future they've got.

She naps again, while Cindy goes over bills and fishing permits on the corner of the dining room table, and a little before eleven she leaves for work. The old Volvo station wagon is a masterwork of rust and clashing gears, as much a victim of the sea as everything else on Nantucket, but the wheels still crunch gravel, the old thing still goes. She doesn't think about the insurance on the boat, the life insurance Allan insists they keep paid up, the money for diesel, the money for lines. She wishes she'd stayed in school, got her nursing degree.

She could support her family, then.

Cully sleeps more soundly on the sea. The *Sweet Katrina* rocks him, the way Pen used to, when Pen didn't have to work nights. It's almost like not sleeping alone.

Morgan wakes him a little before sun-up, a tap on the door. There's burned coffee. Morgan can't cook, not even a little.

"How's it looking?" Cully asks. He holds the coffee under his nose and thinks about round hooks and half-round hooks and synthetic bait. He thinks about pulleys and propellers and watching things spin. Maybe he can turn the *Sweet Katrina* into a sport fishing boat, cater to the summer people. Maybe stars will grow on rosebushes, too.

The sky's silver off east; zodiacal light. Nothing between here and Europe but a hell of a lot of water, the competition—factory trawlers, he means—and all those sly, mysterious fish. And maybe a few dozen nuclear submarines. Like the fish, though, and the independent boats, there's fewer of them than there used to be.

"Looks clear," Morgan says, with a shrug. September weather. Love it while you've got it. He's cleaning the rifle Cully keeps for sharks, or maybe pirates. Sometimes they *do* get sharks on the lines; maybe even the sharks are going hungry these days. He's never gotten a pirate. "Think we'll make our money back this trip?"

"Who the hell knows?" He hasn't seen a summer this bad since they closed George's Bank. Get a swordfish boycott, tuna boycott, women not supposed to eat fish because the mercury poisons their babies. Get people planning offshore windmill farms in the shoals, or dredging the sand for beach replenishment; summer people's McMansions are no good without a broad white-sand beach. Get fisheries closed to let the stock regenerate; they never needed closing before the factory fleets.

But there's always the chance, the one good trip that pays for three bad ones. He'll take hagfish if it's what he can get, it sells just fine to Korea.

But bluefin's worth its weight in ambergris.

The fin whale shows him her flukes, dead ahead, about a half a mile. He wonders if she's following or she's leading him, or they just happen to be going the same way. "All the way," he mutters. "As far as it takes."

Cully drinks his burned coffee as the sun comes up. He's got a good feeling in his bones.

Pen comes home in time to get breakfast on the table and see her kids off again. Mike's sprained his thumb or something, he says gym class but Pen knows it was rough-housing. Boys will be boys. She pulls her gloves on over long fingers and picks up her shears. If Allan were home, he'd stop her before she got the second glove on, stop her and kiss her fingers and say, "At least one of us has soft hands."

Pen's roses grow in profusion around the little gray house. There's all sorts of things that won't grow on Nantucket; they don't like the sun and the sand and the harsh, salt air. They don't like the storms.

Roses grow fine, and the marigolds she plants in drifts around their bases to keep away the bugs. Gold and burgundy and brown, like a clown's button pompoms. She turns the dirt over and over with her trowel, working in the fertilizer—fish meal and bone—working the sand into the loam.

Moonlight and they're getting in some fish, the winches spinning as they take up line. Dogfish, maybe five per hundred hooks, not bad but not enough. Cully wants bluefin. Bluefin pay for diesel. They switch bait and go looking.

They've picked up a pod of minke whales somewhere, and that fin whale's still playing off the starboard bow. Her calf can catch some pretty good air, comes down hard, *wham*, belly-flop. Cully thinks maybe there's a humpback out there too; he keeps catching glimpses of a blow in the moonlight, and it's not where the fin whales seem to be. He can't remember the last time he saw this many whales on one trip. Maybe he could charter whale-watches, make a living that way.

But he'd need a bigger boat.

The deck's all over slime, mica-flecked, scales sparking like sun on the ocean. Sunrise catches them still looking; they haven't broken even yet. There's no land in sight, and there's no goddamned tuna anywhere.

Maybe south of the Vinyard there'll be something. He thinks about heading that way, and shrugs. The whale's still headed east, and he's got a mind to follow her, trailing opportunistic gulls like a screaming banner. If he's gonna go broke, he might as well go broke chasing a sleek gray shadow.

The minke whales have lit out for wetter pastures, but the fin whale's still sticking with the boat—within a mile or two, anyway—when the first glittering back breaks the water off to port. Bluefin come out of the sea like wheels, turning on a perfect arc, a circle marked out with a compass. They race through the water like churning steel, and it's a school like Cully's never seen. He's heard legends, but this is the real deal—three-hundred-pound fish, and there are thousands of them. It's the most amazing thing ever, a sea alive with bluefin fifty miles from anywhere they *should* be, and he and Morgan stare at each other for a precious, unbelieving thirty seconds before they run out the lines, the bird-scare streamers snake-writhing as they uncoil into the water.

The fish in the refrigerated hold gleam like bars of silver. The whales sound, showing Cully their flukes side by side like a sentimental sculpture before slipping beneath the chop.

Cully can feel it like hitting a sandbar when the line snags. The *Sweet Katrina* lurches, skipping under his feet, and there's an unholy groan and a thin stream of white smoke as a big winch jams. Cully grabs the rail, and Morgan grabs Cully, and neither one of them quite goes off the boat, though it's a near thing and a couple of bruises.

"Shit," Morgan says, and leaps for the winch. The *Sweet Katrina*'s listing, pulling, dragging herself around. Half a second and the other line's going to get pulled into the jammed one. Cully scrambles for the wheelhouse, swings down the steps, hands slipping on the railings, slaps at the cutoff.

Morgan curses. There's a four-foot bluefin flopping under Morgan's feet. Morgan's standing on the damned fish to get to the winch.

He's not going to be fast enough. Cully can hear the tick of stressed fibers parting, nylon line *click click click*ing into oblivion one strand at a time. Cully charges from the wheelhouse, tackles his first mate, gets half a grip on him and swings him around, nails imprinting Morgan's wrist, and lands them both sprawling to the deck as the line fails—all for one, and one for all—snapped end like a scourge, a flail that could blind a man or flense him, flesh from bone.

A hundred thousand dollars in tuna and equipment goes gliding down into the Atlantic, wasted work and wasted death. Morgan sits up, still cursing. "What did we snag, a submarine?"

"Fuck," Cully answers. "And this was turning out to be such a nice day."

The whales rise beside the boat and wait there, breathing. Morgan struggles to his feet, wiping his hands on his coverall. All it does is spread the slime around. "Fucking whale," Morgan says. He stomps toward the wheelhouse, yanks open a locker, and pulls the rifle out. "Fucking thing could have killed us."

"Morgan," Cully says, "what the hell do you think you're doing?"

Pen does the grocery shopping on the way home from work, on Saturday. She loads up the back of the Volvo and notices the right rear tire is going flat. The gas station attendant finds a screw in it; he fixes it fast and charges her eight dollars, and she hurries home, worried that the milk is going bad. Cindy is fixing breakfast. The kids are watching cartoons on videotape and arguing over *Shrek* and *Finding Nemo*. Pen remembers when the cartoons were broadcast, and you watched whatever was on.

She shrugs and puts the milk away; Cindy takes it right back out of the little fridge and grins at her, pouring a dollop into a bowl of scrambled eggs. "This smells a little off," she says.

"Bad?"

"No, just off."

Pen shrugs. "It got left in the car for a bit. We'll just drink it fast."

Cindy points at the coffee pot. Pen fixes herself a cup and takes it outside to drink on the porch swing, smelling the sea air, looking at the roses. The leaves are turning. Allan should be home any day. *Wherever you go, I will follow.*

Winter will be coming soon.

Morgan raises the rifle and points it at the fin whale. "It won't but sting her a little—"

Cully steps between, and puts his hand on the barrel of the gun. "Morgan," he says, so calmly, "would you look at yourself?"

Morgan pauses, gulls whirling behind him. Cully takes a deep breath; the whole world smells like rotting fish. And slowly, Morgan lowers the gun. "Fuck," he says. "I guess she didn't mean anything by it."

"I'm not sure it was the whale," Cully says.

"What the hell else could it have been?"

Cully shrugs and points over the railing. Another whale breaches in the distance—one, two, a pod of humpbacks. They're everywhere, now that Cully's looking for them. Gray whales slipping along the surface not so different from dappled wave-tops themselves. The great pleased grin of a blue whale as it lifts its head from the ocean, blowing plumes of vapor into the perfect sky. Dolphins leaping among the tuna, a softer shade of steel. "You see any hook-marks on her hide? Besides, it's a goddamned endangered species. Do *you* wanna pay the fine?"

"They can take it out of the tuna she ate," Morgan says, folding his arms over the rail, and Cully doesn't point out that fin whales don't eat tuna. "Besides, you want to talk about a goddamned endangered species? What the hell are we?"

Cully opens his mouth to answer. The tuna turn like steel wheels in the sunlight, iterations from hull to horizon. The hold is two-thirds full, the gleaming fish packed in like bullion. The trip is paid for, the diesel is bought.

If every trip could be like this—

He looks at the whale, who has rolled on her side again, her baby nosing along her belly, looking for the teat. She gazes at him with that wide, alert eye, her flipper upraised, gleaming wet in the sun. She cups it like a woman cupping a hand. She beckons.

She's listening.

"I reckon you're right," Cully says, and boosts himself over the rail. He crouches down, one foot in front of the other, dangling off the side as if trying to scoop something out of the water. The whale rolls, and her flipper brushes Cully's fingers. Cully laughs in wonder and cranes his head to look at Morgan, silhouetted by the sun. "Where do you think they go?" he asks.

"They?"

"When they go extinct. Or nearly so." He gestures at the whale, at the tuna, at himself.

"What, when they die?"

"Do they?" Cully asks. He pulls his hand back in, but stays squatting on the wrong side of the rail. "What do you think? Maybe they get to go home."

There's the hold full of tuna. There's Pen and the kids, and there's this place he and Morgan found, where there's tuna for the taking. Pen owns the boat. Most of the boat. And then there's the insurance money, and then there's those fish in the hold, and all the ones out there, where a factory fleet won't ever find them. The factory boats just aren't a dying breed.

The whale rolls again, water beading, streaming off her hide. She looks at him. Waiting. *Where do they go?*

"Hey Morgan, you think you can find this place again?"

"We charted it, didn't we?"

"Yeah," Cully says. He stands, hand on the rail for balance. He promised he would pay, and he'll never find his way back here if he doesn't settle his debt. "I guess we did. I guess you'll find it no problem. Christ, it's beautiful here."

He wants to pull off his wife's glove, and kiss her long brown hand. He wants to smell the roses on her skin, the salt sea in her hair. More than anything, he wants to go home.

The whale squirms, a long slick convulsion, and rights herself. She glides away from the *Sweet Katrina*, her breath and her baby's breath trailing behind them. She's done waiting for him to figure it out.

There's fish here for the taking, and Morgan knows how to find them, and Pen will keep him on. There'll be money for the boys for college, money for Pen and Cindy to retire on. They won't have to leave the island. They'll sell the boat to Morgan, eventually, and Cully's sons won't be fishers. They'll get city jobs. He won't see it, but they'll grow up fine, they'll be okay. On land.

He weighs it in his hand and hates it, while the whales turn like wheels in the ocean. *On land.*

"Cully—" Morgan says.

The whales are sounding. They show their flukes, monuments against a perfect sky. They're diving now.

Cully lets go of the rail. Paid in full. He goes under.

He goes on.

The Something-Dreaming Game

I t's autoerotic asphyxiation, but nobody's admitting *that*.
The children get jump ropes or neckties or shoelaces, or they just do it to each other, thumbs under chins buried in baby-fat. With childish honesty, they call it the pass-out game, the fainting game, the tingle game. The something-dreaming game, too.

When it's mentioned in the papers, journalists coyly obscure the truth. With Victorian prudishness, they report that the children strangle each other to get "high." Because society thinks that children that young—nine, ten—aren't *supposed* to experience erotic sensation. The reality that kids don't always do what they're supposed to—am I the only one who remembers my own confused preadolescent sexuality?—gets disregarded with fantastic regularity.

But the truth is that they do it for the tingle through their veins, the arousal, the lightheadedness, and the warmth that floods their immature bodies. Like everything else we do—as individuals, as a species—it's all about sex. And death. Yin and yang. Maybe if we admitted what was going on, we'd have a chance of stopping it before more die.

It's the things we don't talk about that become the monsters under the bed.

The game is autoerotic asphyxiation. You would hope the smart ones wouldn't do it alone, wouldn't do it at all.

But my Tara was as smart as they come.

Tara must have learned the game at the hospital, when she had her implant finalized. It was the cutting edge of therapy, a promising experimental treatment. An FDA trial; she was lucky to be selected.

The implant is a supercomputer the size the last joint of my thumb, wired into my daughter's brain. Tara has RSD, reflex sympathetic dystrophy syndrome, a disease resulting in intense, uncontrollable neuralgia. Which is to say, her nerves hurt. *Transcendently*. All the time.

The implant interrupts the electrical signals that cause the brain to register the sensations. The computing power is quantum, supplied by a Bose-Einstein condensate, and no, I don't know what that means or how it works, any more than I know how a silicon chip works, or a vacuum tube.

What matters is, it worked.

Two weeks after Tara returned to school, I got a phone call from Silkie Mendez's mother. I was still at work; Tara was in after-school enrichment, and her dad was supposed to pick her up. I'd get her after dinner.

It's the real mark of domesticity. You become somebody's mother, somebody's father. A parent, not a person at all.

But at work, I still answered my phone, "Doctor Sanderson."

"Jillian. It's Valentina. We have to talk."

You get to know the tone, so-carefully-not-panicking. A mother scared stiff, and fighting with every ounce of rationality to over-ride the brain chemicals and deal with a threat to her child with smarts rather than claws and teeth. "What's wrong?"

Her breath hissed over the pickup on her phone. Cell phone, I thought, and there was noise in the background. Human bustle, an intercom, stark echoes off polished tile. I've been in private practice since my psychiatric residency, but you never forget what a hospital sounds like. "Val, is Silkie okay?"

"She will be," Val said. The sob caught in her throat and she choked it back. "The doctor says she—Jillian, uh, she'll be fine—"

One thing I'm good at is getting people to talk to me. "Val, just say it. You don't have to soft peddle, okay?"

I heard her gulp. She sniffled and took a breath, the phone crackling as she pressed it against her hair. "Silkie says Tara taught her how to hang herself."

First, there's the pressure.

A special kind of pressure, high under Tara's chin, that makes her feel heavy and light all at once. She kneels by the chair and leans across the edge, because if she faints, the chair will roll away and she won't choke.

She's always careful.

After the pressure she gets dizzy, and her vision gets kind of . . . narrow, dark around the edges. It's hard to breathe, and it feels like there's something stuck in her throat. Prickles run up and down her back, down her arms where the pain used to be, and a warm fluid kind of feeling sloshes around inside her. She slides down, as things get dark, and then she starts to dream.

But not like night time dreams. These are special.

When Tara dreams the special way, she hears voices. Well, no, not voices. Not voices exactly. But things. Or sees things. Feels them. It's all jumbled together.

But there's a sky, and she walks out under it. It's not any kind of sky she's seen. It's big and pale, and seems . . . flat, and very high up. There aren't any clouds, and it looks dusty under the big red sun.

It might be a desert. She's read someplace that deserts have skies like that. And it's not just a picture. Tara can taste it, feel the pebbles under the soles of her shoes, the heat baking off the cracked tarmac. Except the tarmac isn't really tarmac: like it, but chocolate-brown, or maybe that's the dull red dust.

And Tara doesn't think they have people like Albert in the kinds of deserts she'd get to on a plane.

As for Albert, he's a long segmented being like a giant centipede, though he can't be a centipede because of the inverse square law. Which says that if you breathe through a spiracle, you can't breathe if you get that big. Of course . . .

. . . he isn't necessarily an *Earth* arthropod. And when she watches him, she sees all his segments swelling and relaxing, independent of each other. They each seem to have a top and bottom plate that slide rather than one hard shell like an arthropod would have. So it's more like armor than an exoskeleton. And Albert isn't his real name, of course, but Tara doesn't know his real name, because she can't talk to him.

He has a lot of legs, though, and lots of little fine claws and then two big bulky claws too, like a lobster instead of a crab. He chitters at her, which freaked her out the first few times, and grabs her hand with one knobby manipulator. It's all right. She's already reaching out, too.

I didn't call Tara's father, just arrived to pick her up at the usual time. I'd talk to Tara first, I decided, and then see what I was going to say to Jerry. He's a good guy, works hard, loves his kid.

He panics. You know. Some people do. Tara doesn't, not usually, and so I wanted to talk to her first.

She sat in the back, big enough to be out of a booster seat but not big enough to be safe with the airbags yet. She was hitting a growth spurt, though; it wouldn't be long.

RSD has all sorts of side effects. There are people who think it's psychosomatic, who dismiss it, more or less, as malingering. I got some resistance from my mom and my sister when we decided to go ahead with the surgery, of the she's-just-doing-it-for-attention and she'll-outgrow-it sort.

My Tara was a brave girl, very tough. She broke her arm on the playground a few days after her eighth birthday. I didn't figure out there were other issues until the cast was off and she was still complaining that it hurt. And then, complaining that it hurt more, and the hurt was spreading up her shoulder and down her side. And her right hand was curling into a claw while it took us nine months to get a diagnosis, and another ten months after that to get her into the trial, while she suffered through painkillers and physical therapy.

I watched in the mirror as she wriggled uncomfortably under her shoulder belt and slouched against the door, inspecting bitten fingernails. "How was school?"

"Fine," she said, turning to look out the window at the night rushing past. It was raining slightly, and she had rolled her window down to catch the damp air, trailing her fingers over the edge of the crack.

"Hands in the car, please," I said as we stopped under a streetlight. I couldn't see in the darkness if her eyes were bloodshot, or if those shadows under her chin were bruises.

Tara pulled her fingers back, sighing. "How was work, Mom?"

"Actually, I got a call from Mrs. Mendez today."

Her eyes widened as I pulled away from the stop sign. I forced my attention back to the road. "Am I in trouble?"

"You know it's very dangerous, what you taught Silkie to do, don't you?"

"Mom?" A plaintive question, leading, to see how much I knew.

"The fainting game. It's not safe. People die doing that, even grownups." Another stop sign, as she glared at her hands. "Silkie went to the emergency room."

Tara closed her eyes. "Is she okay?"

"She will be."

"I'm always careful, Mom—"

"Tara." I shifted from second to third as we rolled up the dark street and around the corner to our own house, the porch light gleaming expectantly by the stairs, light dappled through the rain-heavy leaves of the maple in the front yard. "I need you to promise me you'll never do that again."

Her chin set.

Wonderful. Her father's stubborn mouth, thin line of her lips. Her hair was still growing back, so short it curled in flapper ringlets around her ears and on her brow.

"Lots of kids do it. Nobody ever gets hurt."

"Tara?"

"I can't promise."

"*Tara*." There are kids you can argue with. Tara wasn't one of them. But she could be reasoned with. "Why not?"

"You wouldn't believe me." And she didn't say it with the petulant defiance you might expect, but simply, reasonably, as an accepted annoyance.

"Try me."

"I can't promise," she said, "because the aliens need me."

Albert chitters again. It's hot. Really hot, and Tara wants water. But there never seems to be any water here. Albert tugs her hand. He wants her to follow. She goes with him and he takes her the same way he always does. Toward the big steel doors, and then down into cool darkness, the hum of big fans, and then he'll bring her underground and there will be a thing like a microphone, only at her height, not a grown up one. And she'll talk and sing into it, because that seems to be what Albert wants her to do, while luminescent colors roll across his armor plates in thin, transparent bands.

She's never seen anything alive here. Except Albert.

She talks into the microphone, though, sings it silly songs and talks about things. Her mother and father, and the divorce. The time in the hospital, and the friends she made there. Insects and arthropods, bicycles and card games. Her friends and teachers, and how happy she is to be back in a real school.

Colors rippling across his carapace impatiently, Albert waits. They've done this before.

I blamed the implant. Nobody likes to think her kid is experiencing symptoms of undifferentiated schizophrenia, after all. I rescheduled for the next day and took the morning off and we made an emergency appointment with Dr. al-Mansoor.

Tara waited outside while I went in to talk to the doctor. She looked bleary-eyed under the scarf tucked over her hair, the flesh slack over her cheekbones and shadowed around the eyes. I like Dr. al-Mansoor. And it was pretty obvious she hadn't planned on being in the clinic at seven AM to see us, but she'd managed to get there.

I put a cup of coffee on her desk before I sat down. She took it gratefully, cupping lean fingers around the warm paper, her wedding ring flashing as she lowered her head over the steam. "You have a concern, Jill?" she asked

Her given name is Hadiyah, but I always have to remind myself to use it, even though we'd gotten to be good friends over the last four months or so. I think she respected the questions I asked. None of the other parents were in the medical profession.

I looked down at my own coffee cup and cleared my throat. Best to just say it. "I think there's a problem with Tara's implant."

They'll catch her if she tries it here. So Tara sits and folds her hands and tries not to rock impatiently, first in the waiting room and then in the office while Mom and Dr. al-Mansoor talk, mostly over her head. There's a dollhouse on the ledge, though, along with some other toys that Tara is mostly too old for, and Tara busies herself with the dolls and the furniture until she gets bored, and starts running the red firetruck back and forth along the ledge. She stages a four-alarm fire and a rescue, complete with hook-and-ladder work on the dollhouse, though the sizes are off and the dolls have to make a death-defying leap from the second floor to be caught at the top of the ladder by a half-scale fireman.

She's totally lost track of the grownup conversation, and they're not talking about her now anyway but about some other girl in the trial, though Dr. al-Mansoor is very careful not to say her name. "She hasn't had any similar ideations, though . . . "

The conversation stops, and Tara looks up to find Mom and Dr. al-Mansoor staring at her. "Did I do something wrong?"

"Tara," Dr. al-Monsoor says, smoothing her scarf over her hair, "where did you learn to play the fainting game?"

Tara bites her lip. Her hair falls across her eyes and she pushes it back. She never *promised* not to tell. "At the hospital," she says, dragging it out. She turns back to the dollhouse and saves another Ken doll from the flames.

"Who taught you?"

This Ken doll didn't jump hard enough. He falls short of the ladder, and the miniature fireman lunges frantically to catch him. He gets one of Ken's outreached hands, and clutches it. Firemen have gloves, big rubber ones, so it must be the gloves that are slipping in the sweat, not Ken's hand. Ken sways perilously as the fireman hooks his feet in the rungs of the ladder and hauls on his hand, Tara mimicking both Ken's cries for help and the fireman's reassurances.

The grownups are silent, watching. Until Tara's mother clears her throat and says, carefully, "Tara? Did you hear the question?"

"One of the other girls," Tara says, letting Ken rock back and forth a little, hands slipping. She watches him carefully. Maybe if the fireman slides a little higher, ladder rungs gouging his tummy, he can keep his grip. Oh, no, gasps Ken. Don't worry, I've got you! cries the fireman.

"Which girl?"

Tara shrugs. She won't remember. That's not a lie, and they can't make her remember, either. The fireman hauls Ken up once his predicament stops being interesting.

Tara prefers a happy ending.

"Tara," Mom says, quietly, "she could be in a lot of danger. You have to tell us."

It takes a long time. But eventually, she does.

I barely knew Jodi Carter. She was older than Tara, twelve or thirteen, and they hadn't been room-mates. But they'd spent time together, in the common room or the girls' bathroom.

I wondered how many other girls Jodi had taught the fainting game. At least, from what Dr. al-Mansoor said, it didn't seem like she was having the hallucinations. I was guiltily glad it wasn't my job to answer either of those questions.

Dr. al-Mansoor and I had a hasty conference while Tara banged around a little more with Barbie dolls and firetrucks. My worry that Tara was the only child to report some sort of hallucination after receiving the implant was enough to make my hands cold.

We got Tara checked in—back in her old room, in fact—and Dr. al-Mansoor put her under observation. No restraints, but she'd be under fifteen-minute checks, though the room had a one-way window so she'd at least have the illusion of privacy.

I argued for the right to sleep in the waiting room. Dr. al-Mansoor countered with an offer of her office couch. Tara and I went home to fetch her pajamas and get her some lunch while Dr. al-Mansoor and Mrs. Carter had a long talk with Jodi, who was already checked in for observation of her apparent hallucinations.

Afterwards, Dr. al-Mansoor and I sat and drank more coffee—worse coffee, this, from the staff room pot, lightened with artificial creamer and too sweet because that was the only way it was drinkable—out of chipped mugs, and waited while one of the clinic staff got Tara settled in. She was furious that I'd told her she had to stay, and after she had exhausted herself on a temper tantrum and two sulks, I decided it was just as well if I gave her a little time alone to get the leftover wrath out of her system. At least Tara wasn't a kid who held grudges.

"I didn't know about this fainting game thing," Dr. al-Mansoor said, blowing over her coffee.

"It's not new." Pediatric psychiatry isn't my specialty, but you hear things, pick up around the edges in the journals. "Like inhalant abuse. Every generation figures it out, or anyway some of them do. The question is—"

She nodded. "And then there's the whole issue of whether the implant is causing hallucinations."

"Only when she's on the verge of unconsciousness."

"And a hypnagogic state doesn't do it. Sleep's no good. It's got to be hypoxia."

My turn to stare into my coffee. "Apparently. What do you think of the character of the hallucinations?"

"Some alien entity trying to communicate with her? It's a common marker for schizophrenia."

"But that's the only symptom she's got. No mood swings, she's obviously rational—"

Dr al-Mansoor smiled. "Odd, isn't it?" And then she cocked her head to one side as if *she* was listening, and held up one finger to silence me. "Oh," she said. "You know, I may have something here."

The plastic chair creaked under me when I resettled my weight. It wasn't late, just after lunch, but it felt like six or seven o'clock at night. I was a little shocked every time I glanced at my watch. Busy day. "Well, don't keep me in suspense."

"The implants use a quantum computer chip."

"Tell me something I didn't know."

"Well, the chips were all manufactured at the same time, right? And the same place. Probably all from one condensate. So what if there's quantum interference? I mean"—she waved her long, elegant hand beside her face, her diamond flashing—"what if the chips can transmit electrical patterns back and forth between the girls? Feebly. And when their synapses are already misfiring from the hypoxia, those patterns get overlaid, and Tara's subconscious mind translates those signals into symbols, as they would in a dream—"

"The symbol being some kind of alien trying to communicate. Is that possible? The transferal, I mean." What I knew about quantum mechanics could be written on an index card, but it sounded . . .

Hell, it sounded like an excuse not to pull the chip that was Tara's promise of a normal life out of her head. It might be a straw, but it wasn't a bad-looking straw.

She made a face, pulling her jaw back and flattening her lower lip, and then wrinkled her nose. "I guess so?"

"Why is it only Tara?"

"There's something wrong with her chip? Or something right with it. If that is what's going on, it's functional telepathy."

"That would mean there wasn't any problem, really."

"Other than half the clinic strangling themselves for the fun of it, you mean."

"Right." I thumped back in my chair. I'd lurched forward at some point, without realizing it. "That. Tara won't promise. She thinks her alien friend needs help."

"If she promises, can you trust her?"

"Tara? Yes. What about Jodi?"

"I'll ask Mrs. Carter what she thinks. We'll have to address it with all the kids. One of the staff is making calls. Tara seems a special case, though. For her, we could edge the voltage down a little and maybe get rid of the hallucinations, if my guess is right. Which it probably isn't. But that might affect pain management."

"Right," I said. I put my half-empty cup down on the edge of Dr. al-Mansoor's desk. "I'll go talk to her. If asking nicely doesn't work, there's always extortion."

Mom comes back before dinner, and takes Tara down to the cafeteria to eat. Tara likes the cafeteria. There's always something she doesn't get at home very often. Today it's meatloaf and apple pie, with brown gravy. The meatloaf, not the pie.

Mom's watching her worriedly, and pushing kidney beans and cottage cheese—and other stuff Tara can't figure out why anybody would eat—around on her salad bar plate. "Dr al-Mansoor thinks the things you're seeing are feedback from the implant," she says, when Tara is halfway done with her meatloaf.

"I think it's from the implant," Tara agrees. She picked out a mockneck shirt to hide the bruise across her throat. Mom frowns at it. "But maybe not feedback. I've been thinking about Albert."

"Albert?"

"The alien." Tara slashes her fork sideways. "I don't think it's just him. I think it's a whole species."

Mom leans forward, arms folded behind her fussed-at plate. "He told you his name?"

"No." Tara drops her fork and jerks her hands back and forth beside her head. "He talks in colors or something. He's Albert because of Albert Einstein." She drinks some milk and picks up the fork again. "But he keeps wanting me to talk in a microphone into a computer. I think he's trying to learn how *I* talk. Anyway, I think he's in trouble. He needs help."

"What kind of help?" Mom starts chasing the kidney beans around her plate again, pretending like she's only being polite.

"I don't *know*," Tara says. She stops herself abruptly, chews and swallows the mouthful of mashed potatoes before mom can yell at her. She reaches out and picks a hard, round red grape off her mother's plate, waiting for the nod of permission. It crunches sweetly between her teeth. She takes another one. "I just . . . it seems really important."

"How do you know?"

"I just know."

Mom picks up one solitary kidney bean on the end of her fork and stares at it. She slips it into her mouth and chews slowly. "Tara," she says. "It's more important that you don't risk your life playing the fainting game anymore. If Albert's real, and he's a grown-up scientist, even if he's an alien, he'd agree with me. Don't you think?"

"I'm always careful. That's the problem. I think if I had just a little more time with him, we could *talk*."

"It doesn't matter how careful you are. It's dangerous."

"Mom—"

"*Tara*." Mom puts her fork down, and uses *that voice*. "Promise me."

Tara finishes her meal in silence, while Mom stares at her and doesn't eat another thing. They're going to make her sleep in the hospital bed tonight, with the lights that don't go off and the shadows behind the one-way mirror all the time.

It's okay. She can sleep anywhere. And she has a plan.

I was supposed to sleep on the couch. Predictably, I spent the entire night in the observation room. Tara seemed to be sleeping, under the pale blue light, her hair fanned out on the pillow and her knees drawn up against her chest as always. I sat and watched her with the observation room lights off, so every time Dr. al-Mansoor or the staffer came in for the check, a wedge of light fell across the floor and dazzled me for a minute.

Each time, they paused in the doorway, glanced through the window for a moment, smiled at me, and withdrew. I think Dr. al-Mansoor was hoping I'd fall asleep on the bench. Not quite.

At two in the morning, Tara began to thrash.

She kicked the covers off and rolled out of bed, rolled *under* the bed in the space of time it took me to hit the call button and dive for the connecting door, shouting her name. I crawled after her, scrabbling on hands and knees. The metal railing caught my shoulders, knocking me off my knees and onto my belly, and I squirmed after her. She jammed herself into the space by the head of the bed and curled on her side, knees drawn up, hands pressing me back, pressing me away. Battling, until her arms went soft and her feet kicked, or I should say shivered.

I couldn't hear her breathing.

I got my hand around the slender flexible bones of her ankle and pulled. She went limp as I dragged her out, and first I thought she was making herself dead weight, but when I got her into the light I saw how limp she was. I thought it was the light turning her blue, but then the door thumped open and the light came on and I could see it was her skin, as well.

You're supposed to check the airway. Her mouth fell open, slack, and I ran my fingers into it. Her tongue hadn't fallen back, but I thought my fingers brushed something smooth and resilient, hard, at the back of her throat.

"Jillian," Dr. al-Mansoor said, her hand on my shoulder.

"She's choking," I said, and let her pull me out of the way. "I think she palmed a grape at dinner. I didn't think—" Stupid. *Stupid.* No, I didn't *think* at all.

Dr. al-Mansoor yanked off her rings. They rattled on the floor, disregarded, gold and diamonds knocked aside as she straddled my daughter's hips, straightened her neck. She placed the heel of her interlocked hands under Tara's breastbone and I loved her with all my heart.

I remembered Tara crowding away from me under the bed, her eyes wide and wild, her desperation. Tara was the smartest kid I've ever known. She'd had swimming courses, first aid courses. She was ten. Not a baby, just ask her. She knows more about entomology and dinosaurs and stellar astronomy than I ever will.

She'd known I'd come after her. She'd known I could save her. She'd jumped out of the bed so I would see that she was in distress. And she'd crawled away from me, buying time.

They talk about possession. After a crisis, you hear people say they have no idea what they were doing.

I knew exactly what I was doing. I reached down and grabbed Dr. al-Mansoor's wrists and held on tight. "Jillian, let go," she said. "It's just the Heimlich maneuver."

Her face was inches from mine, her eyes red with sleeplessness rather than asphyxiation. He scarf has fallen back, and her hair was all tangled over her shoulders. It didn't matter. We were all women here.

"Thirty seconds," I said.

She stared at me. She leaned against my hands but I held on to her wrists. Tight.

"*Brain damage*," she said.

Dreams can happen *fast*. The length of the REM cycle affects it, of course, but sometimes even when they seem to take hours, days, they're over in seconds. Just the forebrain trying to make symbolic sense of electrical noise kicked up by the random signals firing up the brainstem. "Hadiyah. Thirty seconds. Twenty seconds. Let her talk to Albert."

She licked her lips. And then she jerked her chin sharply, and I saw her mouth move, counting. Fifteen, fourteen, thirteen—

Albert is waiting. He's in a hurry, too. This time, he grabs Tara's hand in his manipulator without preamble and almost drags her into the tunnel, his many legs rippling indigo-azure-gold as they race underground. But this time its different, dream-different, the microphone gone and a kind of control panel in its place, not made for Tara's hands. She stops, confused, just inside the arched doorway and waits for Albert to show her what to do. And isn't it funny, now that she thinks about it, that the doorway is tall enough for her, when Albert's only two feet high?

He takes the controls in his manipulators. They move over the keypad with arachnid grace. "Tara," the air says.

"Albert?" At her voice, colors ripple across the panels before him. He turns, regarding them with every evidence of thought in the tilt of his expressionless face on the ball-jointed neck. She shouldn't try to guess what he feels. She knows that.

She does it anyway. "You figured out how to talk to me."

"I did," he says. "Come here. Put your hands on the plate. We don't have much time."

"Before my mother stops us?"

He chitters at her, his antennae bristling. "Before the program ends. This is a simulation. I am the last remaining, and we used the last of the power to reach you. We looked and looked, and you were the first we found."

"You're *dying*?"

"Our sun is dying," he says, and her face crumples painfully. She sniffs back stinging. "Soon, the computers will fail. We've lived in them for a very long time. The rest have gone ahead, to conserve power. I chose to stay and search."

"But you can't—I just got to *talk* to you—"

"Will you let me give you our history?"

"Of course," she says, reaching out. He stops her, though, as sharply as he urged before, his manipulator indenting the flesh of her hand.

"Wait," he says. "I will put it in your brain. You have to give permission. It could change you."

She stops. His manipulator is cool and hard, the surface sandpapery. "Change?"

"Make you more like us."

She looks at him. His antennae feather down, lying against his dorsal surface like the ears of an anxious dog. He's still. Maybe waiting, she doesn't know. "And if I don't, you die."

"We die," he says. "Either way."

She stares at him. The stinging in her eyes grows worse, a pressure in her sinuses and through her skull. She pulls her hand from his manipulator, reaches out resolutely, and places both palms on warm yellow metal as the first tear burns her cheek.

"Don't mourn." The voice is uninflected, but his palp reaches out softly and strokes her leg. "You will remember us."

We made it to nine. I yanked my hands back, Hadiyah pressed hers down. The first push didn't do it. She realigned, lips moving on what must have been a prayer now, and thrust forward sharply, the weight of her shoulders behind it.

Something glistening shot from Tara's lips and sailed over Hadiyah's shoulder, and Tara took a deep harsh breath and started to cough, her eyes squinched shut, tears running down her cheeks.

"He's gone," she said, when she got her breath.

She rolled over and grabbed my hands, and wailed against my shoulder like a much younger child, and would not be consoled.

There's enough room in Tara's implant for three or four Libraries of Congress. And it seems to be full. It also seems like she's the only one who can make sense of the information, and not all of it, and not all the time.

She's different now. Quieter. Not withdrawn, but . . . sad. And she looks at me sometimes with these calm, strange eyes, and I almost feel as if *she's* the mother.

I should have stopped her sooner. I didn't think.

At least she hasn't tried to strangle herself again.

Hadiyah suggested we not *tell* anybody what had happened just yet, and I agreed. I won't let my daughter wind up in some government facility, being pumped for clues to alien technology and science.

I won't.

She's ten years old. She's got school to get through. We'll figure the rest of it out in our own time. And maybe she'll be more like herself again as time goes by.

But the first thing she did when she recovered was paint a watercolor. She said it was a poem.

She said it was her name.

⤳

The Cold Blacksmith

"**O**ld man, old man, do you tinker?"

Weyland Smith raised up his head from his anvil, the heat rolling beads of sweat across his face and his sparsely forested scalp, but he never stopped swinging his hammer. The ropy muscles of his chest knotted and released with every blow, and the clamor of steel on steel echoed from the trees. The hammer looked to weigh as much as the Smith, but he handled it like a bit of cork on a twig. He worked in a glade, out of doors, by a deep cold well, just right for quenching and full of magic fish. Whoever had spoken was still under the shade of the trees, only a shadow to one who squinted through the glare of the sun.

"Happen I'm a blacksmith, Miss," he said.

As if he could be anything else, in his leather apron, sweating over forge and anvil in the noonday sun, limping on a lamed leg.

"Do you take mending, old man?" she asked, stepping forth into the light.

He thought the girl might be pretty enough in a country manner, her features a plump-cheeked outline under the black silk veil pinned to the corners of her hat. Not a patch on his own long-lost swan-maiden Olrun, though Olrun had left him after seven years to go with her two sisters, and his two brothers had gone with them as well, leaving Weyland alone.

But Weyland kept her ring and with it her promise. And for seven times seven years to the seventh times, he'd kept it, seduced it back when it was stolen away, held it to his heart in fair weather and foul. Olrun's promise-ring. Olrun's promise to return.

Olrun who had been fair as ice, with shoulders like a blacksmith, shoulders like a giantess.

This girl could not be less like her. Her hair was black and it wasn't pinned, all those gleaming curls a-tumble across the shoulders of a dress that matched her hair and veil and hat. A little linen sack in her left hand was just the natural color, and something in it chimed when she shifted.

Something not too big. He heard it despite the tolling of the hammer that never stopped.

"I'll do what I'm paid to." He let his hammer rest, and shifted his grip on the tongs. His wife's ring slid on its chain around his neck, catching on chest hair. He couldn't wear it on his hand when he hammered. "And if'n 'tis mending I'm paid for, I'll mend what's flawed."

She came across the knotty turf in little quick steps like a hobbled horse—as if it was her lamed, and not him—and while he turned to thrust the bent metal that would soon be a steel horse-collar into the coals again she passed her hand over his bench beside the anvil.

He couldn't release the bellows until the coals glowed red as currant jelly, but there was a clink and when her hand withdrew it left behind two golden coins. Two coins for two hands, for two pockets, for two eyes.

Wiping his hands on his matted beard, he turned from the forge, then lifted a coin to his mouth. It dented under his teeth, and he weighed its heaviness in his hand. "A lot for a bit of tinkering."

"Worth it if you get it done," she said, and upended her sack upon his bench.

A dozen or so curved transparent shards tumbled red as forge-coals into the hot noon light, jingling and tinkling. Gingerly, he reached out and prodded one with a forefinger, surprised by the warmth.

"My heart," the woman said. "'Tis broken. Fix it for me."

He drew his hand back. "I don't know nowt about women's hearts, broken or t'otherwise."

"You're the Weyland Smith, aren't you?"

"Aye, Miss." The collar would need more heating. He turned away, to pump the bellows again.

"You took my gold." She planted her fists on her hips. "You can't refuse a task, Weyland Smith. Once you've taken money for it. It's your geas."

"Keep tha coin," he said, and pushed them at her with a fingertip. "I'm a smith. Not never a matchmaker, nor a glassblower."

"They say you made jewels from dead men's eyes, once. And it was a blacksmith broke my heart. It's only right one should mend it, too."

He leaned on the bellows, pumping hard.

She turned away, in a whisper of black satin as her skirts swung heavy by her shoes. "You took my coin," she said, before she walked back into the shadows. "So fix my heart."

~

Firstly, he began with a crucible, and heating the shards in his forge. The heart melted, all right, though hotter than he would have guessed. He scooped the glass on a bit of rod stock and rolled it on his anvil, then scraped the gather off with a flat-edged blade and shaped it into a smooth ruby-bright oval the size of his fist.

The heart crazed as it cooled. It fell to pieces when he touched it with his glove, and he was left with only a mound of shivered glass.

That was unfortunate. There had been the chance that the geas would grant some mysterious assistance, that he would guess correctly and whatever he tried first would work. An off chance, but stranger things happened with magic and his magic was making.

Not this time. Whether it was because he was a blacksmith and not a matchmaker or because he was a blacksmith and not a glassblower, he was not sure. But hearts, glass hearts, were outside his idiom and outside his magic.

He would have to see the witch.

The witch must have known he was coming, as she always seemed to know. She awaited him in the doorway of her pleasant cottage by the wildflower meadow, more wildflowers—daisies and buttercups—waving among the long grasses of the turfed roof. A nanny goat grazed beside the chimney, her long coat as white as the milk that stretched her udder pink and shiny. He saw no kid.

The witch was as dark as the goat was white, her black, black hair shot with silver and braided back in a wrist-thick queue. Her skirts were kilted up over her green kirtle, and she handed Weyland a pottery cup before he ever entered her door. It smelled of hops and honey and spices, and steam curled from the top; spiced heated ale.

"I have to see to the milking," she said. "Would you fetch my stool while I coax Heidrún off the roof?"

"She's shrunk," Weyland said, but he balanced his cup in one hand and limped inside the door to haul the stool out, for the witch's convenience.

The witch clucked. "Haven't we all?"

By the time Weyland emerged, the goat was down in the dooryard, munching a reward of bruised apples, and the witch had found her bucket and was waiting for the stool. Weyland set the cup on the ledge of the open window and seated the witch with a little bit of ceremony, helping her with her skirts. She smiled and patted his arm, and bent to the milking while he went to retrieve his ale.

Once upon a time, what rang on the bottom of the empty pail would have been mead, sweet honeyed liquor fit for gods. But times had changed, were always changing, and the streams that stung from between the witch's strong fingers were rich and creamy white.

"So what have you come for, Weyland Smith?" she asked, when the pail was a quarter full and the milk hissed in the pail rather than sang.

"I'm wanting a spell as'll mend a broken heart," he said.

Her braid slid over her shoulder, hanging down. She flipped it back without lifting her head. "I hadn't thought you had it in you to fall in love again," she said, her voice lilting with the tease.

"'Tisn't my heart as is broken."

That did raise her chin, and her fingers stilled on Heidrún's udder. Her gaze met his; her eyebrows lifted across the fine-lined arch of her forehead. "Tricky," she said. "A heart's a wheel," she said. "Bent is bent. It can't be mended. And even worse—" She smiled, and tossed the fugitive braid back again. "—if it's not your heart you're after fixing."

"Din't I know it?" he said, and sipped the ale, his wife's ring—worn now—clicking on the cup as his fingers tightened.

Heidrún had finished her apples. She tossed her head, long ivory horns brushing the pale silken floss of her back, and the witch laughed and remembered to milk again. "What will you give me if I help?"

The milk didn't ring in the pail any more, but the gold rang fine on the dooryard stones.

The witch barely glanced at it. "I don't want your gold, blacksmith."

"I din't want for hers, neither," Weyland said. "'Tis the half of what she gave." He didn't stoop to retrieve the coin, though the witch snaked a soft-shoed foot from under her kirtle and skipped it back to him, bouncing over the cobbles.

"What can I pay?" he asked, when the witch met his protests with a shrug.

"I didn't say I could help you." The latest pull dripped milk into the pail rather than spurting. The witch tugged the bucket clear and patted Heidrún on the flank, leaning forward with her elbows on her knees and the pail between her ankles while the nanny clattered over cobbles to bound back up on the roof. In a moment, the goat was beside the chimney again, munching buttercups as if she hadn't just had a meal of apples. A large, fluffy black-and-white cat emerged from the house and began twining the legs of the stool, miaowing.

"Question 'tisn't what tha can or can't do," he said sourly. "'Tis what tha will or won't."

The witch lifted the pail and splashed milk on the stones for the cat to lap. And then she stood, bearing the pail in her hands, and shrugged. "You could pay me a Name. I collect those."

"If'n I had one."

"There's your own," she countered, and balanced the pail on her hip as she sauntered toward the house. He followed. "But people are always more disinclined to part with what belongs to them than what doesn't, don't you find?"

He grunted. She held the door for him, with her heel, and kicked it shut when he had passed. The cottage was dim and cool inside, only a few embers banked on the hearth. He sat when she gestured him onto the bench, and not before. "No Names," he said.

"Will you barter your body, then?"

She said it over her shoulder, like a commonplace. He twisted a boot on the rushes covering a rammed-earth floor and laughed. "And what'd a bonny lass like thaself want with a gammy-legged, fusty, coal-black smith?"

"To say I've had one?" She plunged her hands into the washbasin and scrubbed them to the elbow, then turned and leaned against the stand. When she caught sight of his expression, she laughed as well. "You're sure it's not your heart that's broken, Smith?"

"Not this sennight." He scowled around the rim of his cup, and was still scowling as she set bread and cheese before him. Others might find her intimidating, but Weyland Smith wore the promise-ring of Olrun the Valkyrie. No witch could mortify him. Not even one who kept Heidrún—who had dined on the leaves of the World Ash—as a milch-goat.

The witch broke his gaze on the excuse of tucking an escaped strand of his long gray ponytail behind his ear, and relented. "Make me a cauldron," she said. "An iron cauldron. And I'll tell you the secret, Weyland Smith."

"Done," he said, and drew his dagger to slice the bread.

She sat down across the trestle. "Don't you want your answer?"

He stopped with his blade in the loaf, looking up. "I've not paid."

"You'll take my answer," she said. She took his cup, and dipped more ale from the pot warming over those few banked coals. "I know your contract is good."

He shook his head at the smile that curved her lips, and snorted.

"Someone'll find out tha geas one day, enchantress. And may tha never rest easy again. So tell me then. How might I mend a lass's broken heart?"

"You can't," the witch said, easily. "You can replace it with another, or you can forge it anew. But it cannot be mended. Not like that."

"Gerrawa with tha," Weyland said. "I tried reforging it. 'Tis glass."

"And glass will cut you," the witch said, and snapped her fingers. "Like *that.*"

He made the cauldron while he was thinking, since it needed the blast furnace and a casting pour but not finesse. *If glass will cut and shatter, perhaps a heart should be made of tougher stuff,* he decided as he broke the mold.

Secondly, he began by heating the bar stock. While it rested in the coals, between pumping at the bellows, he slid the shards into a leathern bag, slicing his palms—though not deep enough to bleed through heavy callus. He wiggled Olrun's ring off his right hand and strung it on its chain, then broke the heart to powder with his smallest hammer. It didn't take much work. The heart was fragile enough that Weyland wondered if there wasn't something wrong with the glass.

When it had done, he shook the powder from the pouch and ground it finer in the pestle he used to macerate carbon, until it was reduced to a pale-pink silica dust. He thought he'd better use all of it, to be sure, so he mixed it in with the carbon and hammered it into the heated bar stock for seven nights and seven days, folding and folding again as he would for a sword-blade, or an axe, something that needed to take a resilient temper to back a striking edge.

It wasn't a blade he made of his iron, though, now that he'd forged it into steel. What he did was pound the bar into a rod, never allowing it to cool, never pausing hammer—and then he drew the rod through a die to square and smooth it, and twisted the thick wire that resulted into a gorgeous fist-big filigree.

The steel had a reddish color, not like rust but as if the traces of gold that had imparted brilliance to the ruby glass heart had somehow transferred that tint into the steel. It was a beautiful thing, a cage for a bird no bigger than Weyland's thumb, with cunning hinges so one could open it like a box, and such was his magic that despite all the glass and iron that had gone into making it it spanned no more and weighed no more than would have a heart of meat.

He heated it cherry-red again, and when it glowed he quenched it in the well to give it resilience and set its form.

He wore his ring on his wedding finger when he put it on the next morning, and he let the forge lie cold—or as cold as it could lie, with seven days' heat baked into metal and stone. It was the eighth day of the forging, and a fortnight since he'd taken the girl's coin.

She didn't disappoint. She was along before midday.

She came right out into the sunlight this time, rather than lingering under the hazel trees, and though she still wore black it was topped by a different hat, this one with feathers. "Old man," she said, "have you done as I asked?"

Reverently, he reached under the block that held his smaller anvil, and brought up a doeskin swaddle. The suede draped over his hands, clinging and soft as a maiden's breast, and he held his breath as he laid the package on the anvil and limped back, his left leg dragging a little. He picked up his hammer and pretended to look to the forge, unwilling to be seen watching the lady.

She made a little cry as she came forward, neither glad nor sorrowful, but rather tight, as if she couldn't keep all her hope and anticipation pent in her breast any longer. She reached out with hands clad in chevre and brushed open the doeskin—

Only to freeze when her touch revealed metal. "This heart doesn't beat," she said, as she let the wrappings fall.

Weyland turned to her, his hands twisted before his apron, wringing the haft of his hammer so his ring bit into his flesh. "It'll not shatter, lass, I swear."

"It doesn't beat," she repeated. She stepped away, her hands curled at her sides in their black kid gloves. "This heart is no use to me, blacksmith."

He borrowed the witch's magic goat, which like him—and the witch—had been more than half a God once and wasn't much more than a fairy story now, and he harnessed her to a sturdy little cart he made to haul the witch's cauldron. He delivered it in the sunny morning, when the dew was still damp on the grass, and he brought the heart to show.

"It's a very good heart," the witch said, turning it in her hands. "The latch in particular is cunning. Nothing would get in or out of a heart like that if you didn't show it the way." She bounced it on her palms. "Light for its size, too. A girl could be proud of a heart like this."

"She'll have none," Weyland said. "Says as it doesn't beat."

"Beat? Of course it doesn't beat," the witch scoffed. "There isn't any love in it. And you can't put that there for her."

"But I mun do," Weyland said, and took the thing back from her hands.

For thirdly, he broke Olrun's ring. The gold was soft and fine; it flattened with one blow of the hammer, and by the third or fourth strike, it spread across his leather-padded anvil like a puddle of blood, rose-red in the light of the forge. By the time the sun brushed the treetops in its descent, he'd pounded the ring into a sheet of gold so fine it floated on his breath.

He painted the heart with gesso, and when that was dried he made bole, a rabbit-skin glue mixed with clay that formed the surface for the gilt to cling to.

With a brush, he lifted the gold leaf, bit by bit, and sealed it painstakingly to the heart. And when he had finished and set the brushes and the burnishers aside—when his love was sealed up within like the steel under the gold—the iron cage began to beat.

"It was a blacksmith broke my heart," the black girl said. "You'd think a blacksmith could do a better job on mending it."

"It beats," he said, and set it rocking with a burn-scarred, callused fingertip. "'Tis bonny. And it shan't break."

"It's cold," she complained, her breath pushing her veil out a little over her lips. "Make it warm."

"I'd not wonder tha blacksmith left tha. The heart tha started with were colder," he said.

For fourthly, he opened up his breast and took his own heart out, and locked it in the cage. The latch was cunning, and he worked it with thumbs slippery with the red, red blood. Afterwards, he stitched his chest up with cat-gut and an iron needle and pulled a clean shirt on, and let the forge sit cold.

He expected a visitor, and she arrived on time. He laid the heart before her, red as red, red blood in its red-gilt iron cage, and she lifted it on the tips of her fingers and held it to her ear to listen to it beat.

And she smiled.

~

When she was gone, he couldn't face his forge, or the anvil with the vacant chain draped over the horn, or the chill in his fingertips. So he went to see the witch.

She was sweeping the dooryard when he came up on her, and she laid the broom aside at once when she saw his face. "So it's done," she said, and brought him inside the door.

The cup she brought him was warmer than his hands. He drank, and licked hot droplets from his moustache after.

"It weren't easy," he said.

She sat down opposite, elbows on the table, and nodded in sympathy. "It never is," she said. "How do you feel?"

"Frozen cold. Colder'n Hell. I should've gone with her."

"Or she should have stayed with you."

He hid his face in the cup. "She weren't coming back."

"No," the witch said. "She wasn't." She sliced bread, and buttered him a piece. It sat on the planks before him, and he didn't touch it. "It'll grow back, you know. Now that it's cut out cleanly. It'll heal in time."

He grunted, and finished the last of the ale. "And then?" he asked, as the cup clicked on the boards.

"And then you'll sooner or later most likely wish it hadn't," the witch said, and when he laughed and reached for the bread she got up to fetch him another ale.

↬

In the House of Aryaman, a Lonely Signal Burns

Police Sub-Inspector Ferron crouched over the object she assumed was the decedent, her hands sheathed in areactin, her elbows resting on uniformed knees. The body (presumed) lay in the middle of a jewel-toned rug like a flabby pink Klein bottle, its once-moist surfaces crusting in air. The rug was still fresh beneath it, fronds only a little dented by the weight and no sign of the browning that could indicate an improperly pheromone-treated object had been in contact with them for over twenty-four hours. Meandering brownish trails led out around the bodylike object; a good deal of the blood had already been assimilated by the rug, but enough remained that Ferron could pick out the outline of delicate paw-pads and the brush-marks of long hair.

Ferron was going to be late visiting her mother after work tonight.

She looked up at Senior Constable Indrapramit and said tiredly, "So this is the mortal remains of Dexter Coffin?"

Indrapramit put his chin on his thumbs, fingers interlaced thoughtfully before lips that had dried and cracked in the summer heat. "We won't know for sure until the DNA comes back." One knee-tall spit-shined boot wrapped in a sterile bootie prodded forward, failing to come within fifteen centimeters of the corpse. Was he jumpy? Or just being careful about contamination?

He said, "What do you make of that, Boss?"

"Well." Ferron stood, straightening a kinked spine. "If that is Dexter Coffin, he picked an apt handle, didn't he?"

Coffin's luxurious private one-room flat had been sealed when patrol officers arrived, summoned on a welfare check after he did not respond to the flat's minder. When police had broken down the door—the emergency overrides had been locked out—they had found this. This pink tube. This enormous sausage. This meaty object like a child's toy "eel," a long squashed torus full of fluid.

If you had a hand big enough to pick it up, Ferron imagined it would squirt right out of your grasp again.

Ferron was confident it represented sufficient mass for a full-grown adult. But how, exactly, did you manage to just . . . invert someone?

The Sub-Inspector stepped back from the corpse to turn a slow, considering circle.

The flat was set for entertaining. The bed, the appliances were folded away. The western-style table was elevated and extended for dining, a shelf disassembled for chairs. There was a workspace in one corner, not folded away—Ferron presumed—because of the sheer inconvenience of putting away that much mysterious, technical-looking equipment. Depth projections in spare, modernist frames adorned the wall behind: enhanced-color images of a gorgeous cacaphony of stars. Something from one of the orbital telescopes, probably, because there were too many thousands of them populating the sky for Ferron to recognize the *navagraha*—the signs of the Hindu Zodiac, despite her education.

In the opposite corner of the apt, where you would see it whenever you raised your eyes from the workstation, stood a brass Ganesha. The small offering tray before him held packets of kumkum and turmeric, fragrant blossoms, an antique American dime, a crumbling, unburned stick of agarbathi thrust into a banana. A silk shawl, as indigo as the midnight heavens, lay draped across the god's brass thighs.

"Cute," said Indrapramit dryly, following her gaze. "The Yank is going native."

At the dinner table, two western-style place settings anticipated what Ferron guessed would have been a romantic evening. If one of the principles had not gotten himself turned inside out.

"Where's the cat?" Indrapramit said, gesturing to the fading paw-print trails. He seemed calm, Ferron decided.

And she needed to stop hovering over him like she expected the cracks to show any second. Because she was only going to make him worse by worrying. He'd been back on the job for a month and a half now: it was time for her to relax. To trust the seven years they had been partners and friends, and to trust him to know what he needed as he made his transition back to active duty—and how to ask for it.

Except that would mean laying aside her displacement behavior, and dealing with her own problems.

"I was wondering the same thing," Ferron admitted. "Hiding from the farang, I imagine. Here, puss puss. Here puss—"

She crossed to the cabinets and rummaged inside. There was a bowl of water, almost dry, and an empty food bowl in a corner by the sink. The food would be close by.

It took her less than thirty seconds to locate a tin decorated with fish skeletons and paw prints. Inside, gray-brown pellets smelled oily. She set the bowl on the counter and rattled a handful of kibble into it.

"Miaow?" something said from a dark corner beneath the lounge that probably converted into Coffin's bed.

"Puss puss puss?" She picked up the water bowl, washed it out, filled it up again from the potable tap. Something lofted from the floor to the countertop and headbutted her arm, purring madly. It was a last-year's-generation parrot-cat, a hyacinth-blue puffball on sun-yellow paws rimmed round the edges with brownish stains. It had a matching tuxedo ruff and goatee and piercing golden eyes that caught and concentrated the filtered sunlight.

"Now, are you supposed to be on the counter?"

"Miaow," the cat said, cocking its head inquisitively. It didn't budge.

Indrapramit was at Ferron's elbow. "Doesn't it talk?"

"Hey, Puss," Ferron said. "What's your name?"

It sat down, balanced neatly on the rail between sink and counter-edge, and flipped its blue fluffy tail over its feet. Its purr vibrated its whiskers and the long hairs of its ruff. Ferron offered it a bit of kibble, and it accepted ceremoniously.

"Must be new," Indrapramit said. "Though you'd expect an adult to have learned to talk in the cattery."

"Not new." Ferron offered a fingertip to the engineered animal. It squeezed its eyes at her and deliberately wiped first one side of its muzzle against her areactin glove, and then the other. "Did you see the cat hair on the lounge?"

Indrapramit paused, considering. "Wiped."

"Our only witness. And she has amnesia." She turned to Indrapramit. "We need to find out who Coffin was expecting. Pull transit records. And I want a five-hour phone track log of every individual who came within fifty meters of this flat between twenty hundred yesterday and when Patrol broke down the doors. Let's get some technical people in to figure out what that pile of gear in the corner is. And who called in the welfare check?"

"Not a lot of help there, boss." Indrapramit's gold-tinted irises flick-scrolled over data—the Constable was picking up a feed skinned over immediate perceptions. Ferron wanted to issue a mild reprimand for inattention to the scene, but it seemed churlish when Indrapramit was following orders. "When he didn't come online this morning for work, his supervisor became concerned. The supervisor was unable to raise him voice or text. He contacted the flat's minder, and when it reported no response to repeated queries, he called for help."

Ferron contemplated the shattered edges of the smashed-in door before returning her attention to the corpse. "I know the door was locked out on emergency mode. Patrol's override didn't work?"

Indrapramit had one of the more deadpan expressions among the deadpan-trained and certified officers of the Bengaluru City Police. "Evidently."

"Well, while you're online, have them bring in a carrier for the witness." She indicated the hyacinth parrot-cat. "I'll take custody of her."

"How do you know it's a her?"

"She has a feminine face. Lotus eyes like Draupadi."

He looked at her.

She grinned. "I'm guessing."

Ferron had turned off all her skins and feeds while examining the crime scene, but the police link was permanent. An icon blinked discreetly in one corner of her interface, its yellow glow unappealing beside the salmon and coral of Coffin's taut-stretched innards. Accepting the contact was just a matter of an eye-flick. There was a decoding shimmer and one side of the interface spawned an image of Coffin in life.

Coffin had not been a visually vivid individual. Unaffected, Ferron thought, unless dressing one's self in sensible medium-pale brown skin and dark hair with classically Brahmin features counted as an affectation. That handle—*Dexter Coffin*, and wouldn't *Sinister Coffin* be a more logical choice?—seemed to indicate a more flamboyant personality. Ferron made a note of that: out of such small inconsistencies did a homicide case grow.

"So how does one get from this"—Ferron gestured to the image, which should be floating in Indrapramit's interface as well—"to that?"—the corpse on the rug. "In a locked room, no less?"

Indrapramit shrugged. He seemed comfortable enough in the presence of the body, and Ferron wished she could stop examining him for signs of stress. Maybe his rightminding was working. It wasn't too much to hope for, and good treatments for post-traumatic stress had been in development since the Naughties.

But Indrapramit was a relocant: all his family was in a village somewhere up near Mumbai. He had no people here, and so Ferron felt it was her responsibility as his partner to look out for him. At least, that was what she told herself.

He said, "He swallowed a black hole?"

"I like living in the future." Ferron picked at the edge of an areactin glove. "So many interesting ways to die."

Ferron and Indrapramit left the aptblock through the crowds of Coffin's neighbors. It was a block of unrelateds. Apparently Coffin had no family in Bengaluru, but it nevertheless seemed as if every (living) resident had heard the news and come down. The common areas were clogged with grans and youngers, sibs and parents and cousins—all wailing grief, trickling tears, leaning on each other, being interviewed by newsies and blogbots. Ferron took one look at the press in the living area and on the street beyond and juggled the cat carrier into her left hand. She slapped a stripped-off palm against the courtyard door. It swung open—you couldn't lock somebody in—and Ferron and Indrapramit stepped out into the shade of the household sunfarm.

The trees were old. This block had been here a long time; long enough that the sunfollowing black vanes of the lower leaves were as long as Ferron's arm. Someone in the block maintained them carefully, too—they were polished clean with soft cloth, no clogging particles allowed to remain. Condensation trickled down the clear tubules in their trunks to pool in underground catchpots.

Ferron leaned back against a trunk, basking in the cool, and yawned.

"You okay, boss?"

"Tired," Ferron said. "If we hadn't caught the homicide—if it is a homicide—I'd be on a crash cycle now. I had to re-up, and there'll be hell to pay once it wears off."

"Boss—"

"It's only my second forty-eight hours," Ferron said, dismissing Indrapramit's concern with a ripple of her fingers. Gold rings glinted, but not on her wedding finger. Her short nails were manicured in an attempt to look professional, a reminder not to bite. "I'd go hypomanic for weeks at a time at university. Helps you cram, you know."

Indrapramit nodded. He didn't look happy.

The Sub-Inspector shook the residue of the areactin from her hands before rubbing tired eyes with numb fingers. Feeds jittered until the movement resolved. Mail was piling up—press requests, paperwork. There was no time to deal with it now.

"Anyway," Ferron said. "I've already reupped, so you're stuck with me for another forty at least. Where do you think we start?"

"Interview lists," Indrapramit said promptly. Climbing figs hung with ripe fruit twined the sunfarm; gently, the Senior Constable reached up and plucked one. When it popped between his teeth, its intense gritty sweetness echoed through the interface. It was a good fig.

Ferron reached up and stole one too.

"Miaow?" said the cat.

"Hush." Ferron slicked tendrils of hair bent on escaping her conservative bun off her sweating temples. "I don't know how you can wear those boots."

"State of the art materials," he said. Chewing a second fig, he jerked his chin at her practical sandals. "Chappals when you might have to run through broken glass, or kick down a door?"

She let it slide into silence. "Junior grade can handle the family for now. It's bulk interviews. I'll take Chairman Miaow here to the tech and get her scanned. Wait, Coffin was Employed? Doing what, and by whom?"

"Physicist," Indrapramit said, linking a list of coworker and project names, a brief description of the biotech firm Coffin had worked for, like half of Employed Bengaluru ever since the medical tourism days. It was probably a better job than homicide cop. "Distributed. Most of his work group aren't even in this time zone."

"What does BioShell need with physicists?"

Silently, Indrapramit pointed up at the vanes of the suntrees, clinking faintly in their infinitesimal movements as they tracked the sun. "Quantum bioengineer," he explained, after a suitable pause.

"Right," Ferron said. "Well, Forensic will want us out from underfoot while they process the scene. I guess we can start drawing up interview lists."

"Interview lists and lunch?" Indrapramit asked hopefully.

Ferron refrained from pointing out that they had just come out of an apt with an inside-out stiff in it. "Masala dosa?"

Indrapramit grinned. "I saw an SLV down the street."

"I'll call our tech," Ferron said. "Let's see if we can sneak out the service entrance and dodge the press."

~

Ferron and Indrapramit (and the cat) made their way to the back gate. Indrapramit checked the security cameras on the alley behind the block: his feed said it was deserted except for a waste management vehicle. But as Ferron presented her warrant card—encoded in cloud, accessible through the Omni she wore on her left hip to balance the stun pistol—the energy-efficient safety lights ringing the doorway faded from cool white to a smoldering yellow, and then cut out entirely.

"Bugger," Ferron said. "Power cut."

"How, in a block with a sunfarm?"

"Loose connection?" she asked, rattling the door against the bolt just in case it had flipped back before the juice died. The cat protested. Gently, Ferron set the carrier down, out of the way. Then she kicked the door in frustration and jerked her foot back, cursing. Chappals, indeed.

Indrapramit regarded her mildly. "You shouldn't have re-upped."

She arched an eyebrow at him and put her foot down on the floor gingerly. The toes protested. "You suggesting I should modulate my stress response, Constable?"

"As long as you're adjusting your biochemistry . . . "

She sighed. "It's not work," she said. "It's my mother. She's gone Atavistic, and—"

"Ah," Indrapramit said. "Spending your inheritance on virtual life?"

Ferron turned her face away. WORSE, she texted. SHE'S NOT GOING TO BE ABLE TO PAY HER ARCHIVING FEES.

—ISN'T SHE ON ASSISTANCE? SHOULDN'T THE DOLE COVER THAT?

—YEAH, BUT SHE LIVES IN A.R. SHE'S ALWAYS BEEN A GAMER, BUT SINCE FATHER DIED . . . IT'S AN ADDICTION. SHE ARCHIVES EVERYTHING. AND HAS SINCE I WAS A CHILD. WE'RE TALKING TERABYTES. PETABYTES. YOTTABYTES. I DON'T KNOW. AND SHE'S AFTER ME TO "BORROW" THE MONEY.

"Ooof," he said. "That's a tough one." Briefly, his hand brushed her arm: sympathy and human warmth.

She leaned into it before she pulled away. She didn't tell him that she'd been paying those bills for the past eighteen months, and it was getting to the point where she couldn't support her mother's habit any more. She knew what she had to do. She just didn't know how to make herself do it.

Her mother was her mother. She'd built everything about Ferron, from the DNA up. The programming to honor and obey ran deep. Duty. Felicity. Whatever you wanted to call it.

In frustration, unable to find the words for what she needed to explain properly, she said, "I need to get one of those black market DNA patches and reprogram my overengineered genes away from filial devotion."

He laughed, as she had meant. "You can do that legally in Russia."

"Gee," she said. "You're a help. Hey, what if we—" Before she could finish her suggestion that they slip the lock, the lights glimmered on again and the door, finally registering her override, clicked.

"There," Indrapramit said. "Could have been worse."

"Miaow," said the cat.

"Don't worry, Chairman," Ferron answered. "I wasn't going to forget *you.*"

The street hummed: autorickshaws, glidecycles, bikes, pedestrials, and swarms of foot traffic. The babble of languages: Kannada, Hindi, English, Chinese, Japanese. Coffin's aptblock was in one of the older parts of the New City. It was an American ghetto: most of the residents had come here for work, and spoke English as a primary—sometimes an only—language. In the absence of family to stay with, they had banded together. Coffin's address had once been trendy and now, fifty years after its conversion, was fallen on—not hard times, exactly, but a period of more moderate means. The street still remembered better days. It was bulwarked on both sides by the shaggy green cubes of aptblocks, black suntrees growing through their centers, but what lined each avenue were the feathery cassia trees, their branches dripping pink, golden, and terra-cotta blossoms.

Cassia, Ferron thought. A Greek word of uncertain antecedents, possibly related to the English word *cassia*, meaning Chinese or mainland cinnamon. But these trees were not spices; indeed, the black pods of the golden cassia were a potent medicine in Ayurvedic traditions, and those of the rose cassia had been used since ancient times as a purgative for horses.

Ferron wiped sweat from her forehead again, and—speaking of horses—reined in the overly helpful commentary of her classical education.

The wall- and roofgardens of the aptblocks demonstrated a great deal about who lived there. The Coffin kinblock was well-tended, green and lush, dripping with brinjal and tomatoes. A couple of youngers—probably still in schooling, even if they weren't Employment track—clambered up and down ladders weeding and feeding and harvesting, and cleaning the windows shaded here and there by the long green trail of sweet potato vines. But the next kinship block down was sere enough to draw a fine, the suntrees in its court sagging and miserable-looking. Ferron could make out the narrow tubes of drip irrigators behind crisping foliage on the near wall.

Ferron must have snorted, because Indrapramit said, "What are they doing with their graywater, then?"

"Maybe it's abandoned?" Unlikely. Housing in the New City wasn't exactly so plentiful that an empty block would remain empty for long.

"Maybe they can't afford the plumber."

That made Ferron snort again, and start walking. But she snapped an image of the dying aptblock nonetheless, and emailed it to Environmental Services. They'd handle the ticket, if they decided the case warranted one.

The Sri Lakshmi Venkateshwara—SLV—was about a hundred meters on, an open-air food stand shaded by a grove of engineered neem trees, their panel leaves angling to follow the sun. Hunger hadn't managed to penetrate Ferron's re-upped hypomania yet, but it would be a good idea to eat anyway: the brain might not be in any shape to notice that the body needed maintenance, but failing to provide that maintenance just added extra interest to the bill when it eventually came due.

Ferron ordered an enormous, potato-and-pea stuffed crepe against Indrapramit's packet of samosas, plus green coconut water. Disdaining the SLV's stand-up tables, they ventured a little further along the avenue until they found a bench to eat them on. News and ads flickered across the screen on its back. Ferron set the cat carrier on the seat between them.

Indrapramit dropped a somebody-else's-problem skin around them for privacy and unwrapped his first samosa. Flocks of green and yellow parrots wheeled in the trees nearby; the boldest dozen fluttered down to hop and scuffle where the crumbs might fall. You couldn't skin yourself out of the perceptions of the unwired world.

Indrapramit raised his voice to be heard over their arguments. "You shouldn't have re-upped."

The dosa was good—as crisp as she wanted, served with a smear of red curry. Ferron ate most of it, meanwhile grab-and-pasting names off of Coffin's known associates lists onto an interfaced interview plan, before answering.

"Most homicides are closed—if they get closed—in the first forty-eight hours. It's worth a little hypomania binge to find Coffin's killer."

"There's more than one murder every two days in this city, boss."

"Sure." She had a temper, but this wasn't the time to exercise it. She knew, given her family history, Indrapramit worried secretly that she'd succumb to addiction and abuse of the rightminding chemicals. The remaining bites of the dosa got sent to meet their brethren, peas popping between her teeth. The wrapper went into the recycler beside the bench. "But we don't catch every case that flies through."

Indrapramit tossed wadded-up paper at Ferron's head. Ferron batted it into that recycler too. "No, yaar. Just all of them this week."

The targeted ads bleeding off the bench-back behind Ferron were scientifically designed to attract her attention, which only made them more annoying. Some too-attractive citizen squalled about rightminding programs for geriatrics ("Bring your parents into the modern age!"), and the news—in direct, loud counterpoint—was talking about the latest orbital telescope discoveries: apparently a star some twenty thousand light years away, in the Andromeda Galaxy, had suddenly begun exhibiting a flickering pattern that some astronomers considered a possible precursor to a nova event.

The part of her brain that automatically built such parallels said: *Andromeda. Contained within the span of Uttara Bhadrapada. The twenty-sixth nakshatra in Hindu astronomy, although she was not a sign of the Zodiac to the Greeks.* Pegasus was also in Uttara Bhadrapada. Ferron devoted a few more cycles to wondering if there was any relationship other than coincidental between the legendary serpent Ahir Budhnya, the deity of Uttara Bhadrapada, and the sea monster Cetus, set to eat—*devour*, the Greeks were so melodramatic—the chained Andromeda.

The whole thing fell under the influence of the god Aryaman, whose path was the Milky Way—the Heavenly Ganges.

You're overqualified, madam. Oh, she could have been the professor, the academic her mother had dreamed of making her, in all those long hours spent in virtual reproductions of myths the world around. She could have been. But if she'd really wanted to make her mother happy, she would have pursued Egyptology, too.

But she wasn't, and it was time she got her mind back on the job she *did* have.

Ferron flicked on the feeds she'd shut off to attend the crime scene. She didn't like to skin on the job: a homicide cop's work depended heavily on unfiltered perceptions, and if you trimmed everything and everyone irritating or disagreeable out of reality, the odds were pretty good that you'd miss the truth behind a crime. But sometimes you had to make an exception.

She linked up, turned up her spam filters and ad blockers, and sorted more Known Associates files. Speaking of her mother, that required ignoring all those lion-headed message-waiting icons blinking in a corner of her feed—and the pileup of news and personal messages in her assimilator.

Lions. Bengaluru's state capitol was topped with a statue of a four-headed lion, guarding each of the cardinal directions. The ancient symbol of India was part of why Ferron's mother chose that symbolism. But only part.

She set the messages to *hide*, squirming with guilt as she did, and concentrated on the work-related mail.

When she looked up, Indrapramit appeared to have finished both his sorting and his samosas. "All right, what have you got?"

"Just this." She dumped the interview files to his headspace.

The Senior Constable blinked upon receipt. "Ugh. That's even more than I thought."

First on Ferron's interview list were the dead man's coworkers, based on the simple logic that if anybody knew how to turn somebody inside out, it was likely to be another physicist. Indrapramit went back to the aptblock to continue interviewing more-or-less hysterical neighbors in a quest for the name of any potential lover or assignation from the night before.

It was the task least likely to be any fun at all. But then, Ferron was the senior officer. Rank hath its privileges. Someday, Indrapramit would be making junior colleagues follow up horrible gutwork.

The bus, it turned out, ran right from the corner where Coffin's kinblock's street intercepted the main road. Proximity made her choose it over the mag-lev Metro, but she soon regretted her decision, because it then wound in a drunken pattern through what seemed like the majority of Bengaluru.

She was lucky enough to find a seat—it wasn't a crowded hour. She registered her position with dispatch and settled down to wait and talk to the hyacinth cat, since it was more than sunny enough that no one needed to pedal. She waited it out for the transfer point anyway: *that* bus ran straight to the U District, where BioShell had its offices.

Predictable. Handy for head-hunting, and an easy walk for any BioShell employee who might also teach classes. As it seemed, by the number of Professor So-and-sos on Ferron's list, that many of them did.

Her tech, a short wide-bellied man who went by the handle Ravindra, caught up with her while she was still leaned against the second bus's warm, tinted window. He hopped up the steps two at a time, belying his bulk, and shooed a citizen out of the seat beside Ferron with his investigator's card.

Unlike peace officers, who had long since been spun out as distributed employees, techs performed their functions amid the equipment and resources of a centralized lab. But today, Ravindra had come equipped for fieldwork. He stood, steadying himself on the grab bar, and spread his kit out on the now-unoccupied aisle seat while Ferron coaxed the cat from her carrier under the seat.

"Good puss," Ravindra said, riffling soft fur until he found the contact point behind the animal's ears. His probe made a soft, satisfied beep as he connected it. The cat relaxed bonelessly, purring. "You want a complete download?"

"Whatever you can get," Ferron said. "It looks like she's been wiped. She won't talk, anyway."

"Could be trauma, boss," Ravindra said dubiously. "Oh, DNA results are back. That's your inside-out vic, all right. The autopsy was just getting started when I left, and Doc said to tell you that to a first approximation, it looked like all the bits were there, albeit not necessarily in the proper sequence."

"Well, that's a relief." The bus lurched. "At least it's the correct dead guy."

"Miaow," said the cat.

"What is your name, puss?" Ravindra asked.

"Chairman Miaow," the cat said, in a sweet doll's voice.

"Oh, no," Ferron said. "That's just what I've been calling her."

"Huh." Ravindra frowned at the readouts that must be scrolling across his feed. "Did you feed her, boss?"

"Yeah," Ferron said. "To get her out from under the couch."

He nodded, and started rolling up his kit. As he disconnected the probe, he said, "I downloaded everything there was. It's not much. And I'll take a tissue sample for further investigation, but I don't think this cat was wiped."

"But there's nothing—"

"I know," he said. "Not wiped. This one's factory-new. And it's bonded to you. Congratulations, Sub-Inspector. I think you have a cat."

"I can't—" she said, and paused. "I already have a fox. My mother's fox, rather. I'm taking care of it for her."

"*Mine*," the cat said distinctly, rubbing her blue-and-yellow muzzle along Ferron's uniform sleeve, leaving behind a scraping of azure lint.

"I imagine they can learn to cohabitate." He shouldered his kit. "Anyway, it's unlikely Chairman Miaow here will be any use as a witness, but I'll pick over the data anyway and get back to you. It's not even a gig."

"Damn," she said. "I was hoping she'd seen the killer. So even if she's brand-new . . . why hadn't she bonded to Coffin?"

"He hadn't fed her," Ravindra said. "And he hadn't given her a name. She's a sweetie, though." He scratched behind her ears. A funny expression crossed his face. "You know, I've been wondering for ages—how did you wind up choosing to be called *Ferron*, anyway?"

"My mother used to say I was stubborn as iron." Ferron managed to keep what she knew would be a pathetically adolescent shrug off her shoulders. "She was fascinated by Egypt, but I studied Classics—Latin, Greek, Sanskrit. Some Chinese stuff. And I liked the name. *Ferrum*, iron. She won't use it. She still uses my cradlename." *Even when I'm paying her bills.*

The lion-face still blinked there, muted but unanswered. In a fit of irritation, Ferron banished it. It wasn't like she would forget to call.

Once she had time, she promised the ghost of her mother.

Ravindra, she realized, was staring at her quizzically. "How did a classicist wind up a murder cop?"

Ferron snorted. "You ever try to find Employment as a classicist?"

Ravindra got off at the next stop. Ferron watched him walk away, whistling for an autorickshaw to take him back to the lab. She scratched Chairman Miaow under the chin and sighed.

In another few minutes, she reached the University District and disembarked, still burdened with cat and carrier. It was a pleasant walk from the stop, despite the heat of the end of the dry season. It was late June, and Ferron wondered what it had been like before the Shift, when the monsoons would have started already, breaking the back of the heat.

The walk from the bus took under fifteen minutes, the cat a dozy puddle. A patch of sweat spread against Ferron's summerweight trousers where the carrier bumped softly against her hip. She knew she retraced Coffin's route on those rare days when he might choose to report to the office.

Nearing the Indian Institute of Science, Ferron became aware that clothing styles were shifting—self-consciously Green Earther living fabric and ironic, ill-fitting student antiques predominated. Between the buildings and the statuary of culture heroes—R. K. Narayan, Ratan Tata, stark-white with serene or stern expressions—the streets still swarmed, and would until long after nightfall. A prof-caste wearing a live-cloth salwar kameez strutted past; Ferron was all too aware that the outfit would cost a week's salary for even a fairly high-ranking cop.

The majority of these people were Employed. They wore salwar kameez or suits and they had that purpose in their step—unlike most citizens, who weren't in too much of a hurry to get anywhere, especially in the heat of day. It was easier to move in the university quarter, because traffic flowed with intent. Ferron, accustomed to stepping around window-browsing Supplemented and people out for their mandated exercise, felt stress dropping away as the greenery, trees, and gracious old nineteenth and twentieth century buildings of the campus rose up on every side.

As she walked under the chin of Mohandas Gandhi, Ferron felt the familiar irritation that female police pioneer Kiran Bedi, one of her own personal idols, was not represented among the statuary. There was hijra activist Shabnam Mausi behind a row of well-tended planters, though, which was somewhat satisfying.

Some people found it unsettling to be surrounded by so much brick, poured concrete, and mined stone—the legacy of cooler, more energy-rich times. Ferron knew that the bulk of the university's buildings were more efficient green structures, but those tended to blend into their surroundings. The overwhelming impression was still that of a return to a simpler time: 1870, perhaps, or 1955. Ferron wouldn't have wanted to see the whole city gone this way, but it was good that some of the history had been preserved.

Having bisecting campus, Ferron emerged along a prestigious street of much more modern buildings. No vehicles larger than bicycles were allowed here, and the roadbed swarmed with those, people on foot, and pedestrials. Ferron passed a rack of share-bikes and a newly constructed green building, still uninhabited, the leaves of its suntrees narrow, immature, and furled. They'd soon be spread wide, and the structure fully tenanted.

The BioShell office itself was a showpiece on the ground floor of a business block, with a live receptionist visible behind foggy photosynthetic glass walls. *I'd hate a job where you can't pick your nose in case the pedestrians see it.* Of course, Ferron hadn't chosen to be as decorative as the receptionist. A certain stern plainness helped get her job done.

"Hello," Ferron said, as the receptionist smoothed brown hair over a shoulder. "I'm Police Sub-Inspector Ferron. I'm here to see Dr. Rao."

"A moment, madam," the receptionist said, gesturing graciously to a chair.

Ferron set heels together in parade rest and—impassive—waited. It was only a few moments before a shimmer of green flickered across the receptionist's iris.

"First door on the right, madam, and then up the stairs. Do you require a guide?"

"Thank you," Ferron said, glad she hadn't asked about the cat. "I think I can find it."

There was an elevator for the disabled, but the stairs were not much further on. Ferron lugged Chairman Miaow through the fire door at the top and paused a moment to catch her breath. A steady hum came from the nearest room, to which the door stood ajar.

Ferron picked her way across a lush biorug sprinkled with violet and yellow flowers and tapped lightly. A voice rose over the hum. "Namaskar!"

Dr. Rao was a slender, tall man whose eyes were framed in heavy creases. He walked forward at a moderate speed on a treadmill, and old-fashioned keyboard and monitor mounted on a swivel arm before him. As Ferron entered, he pushed the arm aside, but kept walking. An amber light flickered green as the monitor went dark: he was charging batteries now.

"Namaskar," Ferron replied. She tried not to stare too obviously at the walking desk.

She must have failed.

"Part of my rightminding, madam," Rao said with an apologetic shrug. "I've fibromyalgia, and mild exercise helps. You must be the Sub-Inspector. How do you take your mandated exercise? You carry yourself with such confidence."

"I am a practitioner of kalari payat," Ferron said, naming a South Indian martial art. "It's useful in my work."

"Well," he said. "I hope you'll see no need to demonstrate any upon me. Is that a cat?"

"Sorry, saab," Ferron said. "It's work-related. She can wait in the hall if you mind—"

"No, not at all. Actually, I love cats. She can come out, if she's not too scared."

"Oouuuuut!" said Chairman Miaow.

"I guess that settles that." Ferron unzipped the carrier, and the hyacinth parrot-cat sauntered out and leaped up to the treadmill's handrail.

"Niranjana?" Dr. Rao said, in surprise. "Excuse me, madam, but what are you doing with Dr. Coffin's cat?"

"You know this cat?"

"Of course I do." He stopped walking, and scratched the cat under her chin. She stretched her head out like a lazy snake, balanced lightly on four daffodil paws. "She comes here about twice a month."

"New!" the cat disagreed. "Who you?"

"Niranjana, it's Rao. You know me."

"Rrraaao?" she said, cocking her head curiously. Adamantly, she said, "New! My name Chairman Miaow!"

Dr. Rao's forehead wrinkled. To Ferron, over the cat's head, he said, "Is Dexter with you? Is he all right?"

"I'm afraid that's why I'm here," Ferron said. "It is my regretful duty to inform you that Dexter Coffin appears to have been murdered in his home sometime over the night. Saab, law requires that I inform you that this conversation is being recorded. Anything you say may be entered in evidence. You have the right to skin your responses or withhold information, but if you choose to do so, under certain circumstances a court order may be obtained to download and decode associated cloud memories. Do you understand this caution?"

"Oh dear," Dr. Rao said. "When I called the police, I didn't expect—"

"I know," Ferron said. "But do you understand the caution, saab?"

"I do," he said. A yellow peripheral node in Ferron's visual field went green.

She said, "Do you confirm this is his cat?"

"I'd know her anywhere," Dr. Rao said. "The markings are very distinctive. Dexter brought her in quite often. She's been wiped? How awful."

"We're investigating," Ferron said, relieved to be back in control of the conversation. "I'm afraid I'll need details of what Coffin was working on, his contacts, any romantic entanglements, any professional rivalries or enemies—"

"Of course," Dr. Rao said. He pulled his interface back around and began typing. "I'll generate you a list. As for what he was working on—I'm afraid there are a lot of trade secrets involved, but we're a biomedical engineering firm, as I'm sure you're aware. Dexter's particular project has been applications in four-dimensional engineering."

"I'm afraid," Ferron said, "that means nothing to me."

"Of course." He pressed a key. The cat peered over his shoulder, apparently fascinated by the blinking lights on the monitor.

The hyperlink blinked live in Ferron's feed. She accessed it and received a brief education in the theoretical physics of reaching *around* three-dimensional shapes in space-time. A cold sweat slicked her palms. She told herself it was just the second hypomania re-up.

"Closed-heart surgery," she said. During the medical tourism boom, Bengaluru's economy had thrived. They'd found other ways to make ends meet now that people no longer traveled so profligately, but the state remained one of India's centers of medical technology. Ferron wondered about the applications for remote surgery, and what the economic impact of this technology could be.

"Sure. Or extracting an appendix without leaving a scar. Inserting stem cells into bone marrow with no surgical trauma, freeing the body to heal disease instead of infection and wounds. It's revolutionary. If we can get it working."

"Saab . . . " She stroked Chairman Miaow's sleek azure head. "Could it be used as a weapon?"

"Anything can be used as a weapon," he said. A little too fast? But his skin conductivity and heart rate revealed no deception, no withholding. "Look, Sub-Inspector. Would you like some coffee?"

"I'd love some," she admitted.

He tapped a few more keys and stepped down from the treadmill. She'd have thought the typing curiously inefficient, but he certainly seemed to get things done fast.

"Religious reasons, saab?" she asked.

"Hmm?" He glanced at the monitor. "No. I'm just an eccentric. I prefer one information stream at a time. And I like to come here and do my work, and keep my home at home."

"Oh." Ferron laughed, following him across the office to a set of antique

lacquered chairs. Chairman Miaow minced after them, stopping to sniff
the unfamiliar rug and roll in a particularly lush patch. Feeling like she
was making a huge confession, Ferron said, "I turn off my feeds sometimes
too. Skin out. It helps me concentrate."

He winked.

She said, "So tell me about Dexter and his cat."

"Well . . . " He glanced guiltily at Chairman Miaow. "She was very
advanced. He obviously spent a great deal of time working with her.
Complete sentences, conversation on about the level of an imaginative
five-year old. That's one of our designs, by the way."

"Parrot cats?"

"The hyacinth variety. We're working on an *Eclectus* variant for next
year's market. Crimson and plum colors. You know they have a much
longer lifespan than the root stock? Parrot-cats should be able to live for
thirty to fifty years, though of course the design hasn't been around long
enough for experimental proof."

"I did not. About Dr. Coffin—" she paused, and scanned the lists of
enemies and contacts that Dr. Rao had provided, cross-referencing it with
files and the reports of three interviews that had come in from Indrapramit
in the last five minutes. Another contact request from her mother blinked
away officiously. She dismissed it. "I understand he wasn't born here?"

"He traveled," Dr. Rao said in hushed tones. "From America."

"Huh," Ferron said. "He relocated for a job? Medieval. How did BioShell
justify the expense—and the carbon burden?"

"A unique skill set. We bring in people from many places, actually.
He was well-liked here: his work was outstanding, and he was charming
enough—and talented enough—that his colleagues forgave him some of
the . . . vagaries in his rightminding."

"Vagaries . . . ?"

"He was a depressive, madam," Dr. Rao said. "Prone to fairly
serious fits of existential despair. Medication and surgery controlled it
adequately that he was functional, but not completely enough that he was
always . . . comfortable."

"When you say existential despair . . . ?" Ferron was a past master of the
open-ended hesitation.

Dr. Rao seemed cheerfully willing to fill them in for her. "He questioned
the worth and value of pretty much every human endeavor. Of existence
itself."

"So he was a bit nihilistic?"

"Nihilism denies value. Dexter was willing to believe that compassion had value—not intrinsic value, you understand. But assigned value. He believed that the best thing a human being could aspire to was to limit suffering."

"That explains his handle."

Dr. Rao chuckled. "It does, doesn't it? Anyway, he was brilliant."

"I assume that means that BioShell will suffer in his absence."

"The fourth-dimension project is going to fall apart without him," Dr. Rao said candidly. "It's going to take a global search to replace him. And we'll have to do it quickly; release of the technology was on the anvil."

Ferron thought about the inside-out person in the midst of his rug, his flat set for an intimate dinner for two. "Dr. Rao . . . "

"Yes, Sub-Inspector?"

"In your estimation, would Dr. Coffin commit suicide?"

He steepled his fingers and sighed. "It's . . . possible. But he was very devoted to his work, and his psych evaluations did not indicate it as an immediate danger. I'd hate to think so."

"Because you'd feel like you should have done more? You can't save somebody from themselves, Dr. Rao."

"Sometimes," he said, "a word in the dark is all it takes."

"Dr. Coffin worked from home. Was any of his lab equipment there? Is it possible that he died in an accident?"

Dr. Rao's eyebrows rose. "Now I'm curious about the nature of his demise, I'm afraid. He should not have had any proprietary equipment at home: we maintain a lab for him here, and his work at home should have been limited to theory and analysis. But of course he'd have an array of interfaces."

The coffee arrived, brought in by a young man with a ready smile who set the tray on the table and vanished again without a word. No doubt pleased to be Employed.

As Dr. Rao poured from a solid old stoneware carafe, he transitioned to small talk. "Some exciting news about the Andromeda Galaxy, isn't it? They've named the star Al-Rahman."

"I thought stars were named by coordinates and catalogue number these days."

"They are," Rao said. "But it's fitting for this one have a little romance. People being what they are, someone would have named it if the science community didn't. And Abd Al-Rahman Al-Sufi was the first astronomer to describe the Andromeda Galaxy, around 960 A.D. He called it the 'little cloud.' It's also called Messier 31—"

"Do you think it's a nova precursor, saab?"

He handed her the coffee—something that smelled pricy and rich, probably from the hills—and offered cream and sugar. She added a lump of the latter to her cup with the tongs, stirred in cream, and selected a lemon biscuit from the little plate he nudged toward her.

"That's what they said on the news," he said.

"Meaning you don't believe it?"

"You're sharp," he said admiringly.

"I'm a homicide investigator," she said.

He reached into his pocket and withdrew a small injection kit. The hypo hissed alarmingly as he pressed it to his skin. He winced.

"Insulin?" she asked, restraining herself from an incredibly rude question about why he hadn't had stem cells, if he was diabetic.

He shook his head. "Scotophobin. Also part of my rightminding. I have short-term memory issues." He picked up a chocolate biscuit and bit into it decisively.

She'd taken the stuff herself, in school and when cramming for her police exams. She also refused to be derailed. "So you don't think this star—"

"Al-Rahman."

"—Al-Rahman. You don't think it's going nova?"

"Oh, it might be," he said. "But what would say if I told you that its pattern is a repeating series of prime numbers?"

The sharp tartness of lemon shortbread turned to so much grit in her mouth. "I beg your pardon."

"Someone is signaling us," Dr. Rao said. "Or I should say, *was* signaling us. A long, long time ago. Somebody with the technology necessary to tune the output of their star."

"Explain," she said, setting the remainder of the biscuit on her saucer.

"Al-Rahman is more than two and a half million light years away. That means that the light we're seeing from it was modulated when the first identifiable humans were budding off the hominid family tree. Even if we could send a signal back . . . The odds are very good that they're all gone now. It was just a message in a bottle. *We were here.*"

"The news said twenty thousand light years."

"The news." He scoffed. "Do they ever get police work right?"

"Never," Ferron said fervently.

"Science either." He glanced up as the lights dimmed. "Another brownout."

An unformed idea tickled the back of Ferron's mind. "Do you have a sunfarm?"

"BioShell is entirely self-sufficient," he confirmed. "It's got to be a bug, but we haven't located it yet. Anyway, it will be back up in a minute. All our important equipment has dedicated power supplies."

He finished his biscuit and stirred the coffee thoughtfully while he chewed. "The odds are that the universe is—or has been—full of intelligent species. And that we will never meet any of them. Because the distances and time scales are so vast. In the two hundred years we've been capable of sending signals into space—well. Compare that in scale to Al-Rahman."

"That's awful," Ferron said. "It makes me appreciate Dr. Coffin's perspective."

"It's terrible," Dr. Rao agreed. "Terrible and wonderful. In some ways I wonder if that's as close as we'll ever get to comprehending the face of God."

They sipped their coffee in contemplation, facing one another across the tray and the low lacquered table.

"Milk?" said Chairman Miaow. Carefully, Ferron poured some cream into a saucer and gave it to her.

Dr. Rao said, "You know, the Andromeda Galaxy and our own Milky Way are expected to collide eventually."

"Eventually?"

He smiled. It did good things for the creases around his eyes. "Four and a half billion years or so."

Ferron thought about Uttara Bhadrapada, and the Heavenly Ganges, and Aryaman's house—in a metaphysical sort of sense—as he came to walk that path across the sky. From so far away it took two and a half million years just to *see* that far.

"I won't wait up, then." She finished the last swallow of coffee and looked around for the cat. "I don't suppose I could see Dr. Coffin's lab before I go?"

"Oh," said Dr. Rao. "I think we can do that, and better."

The lab space Coffin had shared with three other researchers belied BioShell's corporate wealth. It was a maze of tables and unidentifiable equipment in dizzying array. Ferron identified a gene sequencer, four or five microscopes, and a centrifuge, but most of the rest baffled her limited knowledge of bioengineering. She was struck by the fact that just about every object in the room was dressed in BioShell's livery colors of emerald and gold, however.

She glimpsed a conservatory through a connecting door, lush with what must be prototype plants; at the far end of the room, rows of condensers hummed beside a revolving door rimed with frost. A black-skinned woman in a lab coat with her hair clipped into short, tight curls had her eyes to a lens and her hands in waldo sleeves. Microsurgery?

Dr. Rao held out a hand as Ferron paused beside him. "Will we disturb her?"

"Dr. Nnebuogor will have skinned out just about everything except the fire alarm," Dr. Rao said. "The only way to distract her would be to go over and give her a shove. Which—" he raised a warning finger "—I would recommend against, as she's probably engaged in work on those next-generation parrot-cats I told you about now."

"Nnebuogor? She's Nigerian?"

Dr. Rao nodded. "Educated in Cairo and Bengaluru. Her coming to work for BioShell was a real coup for us."

"You *do* employ a lot of farang," Ferron said. "And not by telepresence." She waited for Rao to bridle, but she must have gotten the tone right, because he shrugged.

"Our researchers need access to our lab."

"Miaow," said Chairman Miaow.

"Can she?" Ferron asked.

"We're cat-friendly," Rao said, with a flicker of a smile, so Ferron set the carrier down and opened its door. Rao's heart rate was up a little, and she caught herself watching sideways while he straightened his trousers and picked lint from his sleeve.

Chairman Miaow emerged slowly, rubbing her length against the side of the carrier. She gazed up at the equipment and furniture with unblinking eyes and soon she gathered herself to leap onto a workbench, and Dr. Rao put a hand out firmly.

"No climbing or jumping," he said. "Dangerous. It will hurt you."

"Hurt?" The cat drew out the Rs in a manner so adorable it had to be engineered for. "No jump?"

"No." Rao turned to Ferron. "We've hardwired in response to the *No* command. I think you'll find our parrot-cats superior to unengineered felines in this regard. Of course . . . they're still cats."

"Of course," Ferron said. She watched as Chairman Miaow explored her new environment, rubbing her face on this and that. "Do you have any pets?"

"We often take home the successful prototypes," he said. "It would be a pity to destroy them. I have a parrot-cat—a red-and-gray—and a golden lemur. Engineered, of course. The baseline ones are protected."

As they watched, the hyacinth cat picked her way around, sniffing every surface. She paused before one workstation in particular before cheek-marking it, and said in comically exaggerated surprise: "Mine! My smell."

There was a synthetic-fleece-lined basket tucked beneath the table. The cat leaned towards it, stretching her head and neck, and sniffed deeply and repeatedly.

"Have you been here before?" Ferron asked.

Chairman Miaow looked at Ferron wide-eyed with amazement at Ferron's patent ignorance, and declared "New!"

She jumped into the basket and snuggled in, sinking her claws deeply and repeatedly into the fleece.

Ferron made herself stop chewing her thumbnail. She stuck her hand into her uniform pocket. "Are all your hyacinths clones?"

"They're all closely related," Dr. Rao had said. "But no, not clones. And even if she were a clone, there would be differences in the expression of her tuxedo pattern."

At that moment, Dr. Nnebuogor sighed and backed away from her machine, withdrawing her hands from the sleeves and shaking out the fingers like a musician after practicing. She jumped when she turned and saw them. "Oh! Sorry. I was skinned. Namaskar."

"Miaow?" said the cat in her appropriated basket.

"Hello, Niranjana. Where's Dexter?" said Dr. Nnebuogor. Ferron felt the scientist reading her meta-tags. Dr. Nnebuogor raised her eyes to Rao. "And—pardon, officer—what's with the copper?"

"Actually," Ferron said, "I have some bad news for you. It appears that Dexter Coffin was murdered last night."

"Murdered . . . " Dr. Nnebuogor put her hand out against the table edge. *Murdered?*"

"Yes," Ferron said. "I'm Police Sub-Inspector Ferron—" which Dr.

Nnebuogor would know already. "—and I'm afraid I need to ask you some questions. Also, I'll be contacting the other researchers who share your facilities via telepresence. Is there a private area I can use for that?"

Dr. Nnebuogor looked stricken. The hand that was not leaned against the table went up to her mouth. Ferron's feed showed the acceleration of her heart, the increase in skin conductivity as her body slicked with cold sweat. Guilt or grief? It was too soon to tell.

"You can use my office," Dr. Rao said. "Kindly, with my gratitude."

The interviews took the best part of the day and evening, when all was said and done, and garnered Ferron very little new information—yes, people *would* probably kill for what Coffin was—had been—working on. No, none of his colleagues had any reason to. No, he had no love life of which they were aware.

Ferron supposed she technically *could* spend all night lugging the cat carrier around, but her own flat wasn't too far from the University District. It was in a kinship block teaming with her uncles and cousins, her grandparents, great-grandparents, her sisters and their husbands (and in one case, wife). The fiscal support of shared housing was the only reason she'd been able to carry her mother as long as she had.

She checked out a pedestrial because she couldn't face the bus and she felt like she'd done more than her quota of steps before dinnertime—and here it was, well after. The cat carrier balanced on the grab bar, she zipped it unerringly through the traffic, enjoying the feel of the wind in her hair and the outraged honks cascading along the double avenues.

She could make the drive on autopilot, so she used the other half of her attention to feed facts to the department's expert system. Doyle knew everything about everything, and if it wasn't self-aware or self-directed in the sense that most people meant when they said *artificial intelligence*, it still rivaled a trained human brain when it came to picking out patterns—and being supercooled, it was significantly faster.

She even told it the puzzling bits, such as how Chairman Miaow had reacted upon being introduced to the communal lab that Coffin shared with three other BioShell researchers.

Doyle swallowed everything Ferron could give it, as fast as she could report. She knew that down in its bowels, it would be integrating that information with Indrapramit's reports, and those of the other officers and techs assigned to the case.

She thought maybe they needed something more. As the pedestrial dropped her at the bottom of her side street, she dropped a line to Damini, her favorite archinformist. "Hey," she said, when Damini answered.

"Hey yourself, boss. What do you need?"

Ferron released the pedestrial back into the city pool. It scurried off, probably already summoned to the next call. Ferron had used her override to requisition it. She tried to feel guilty, but she was already late in attending on her mother—and she'd ignored two more messages in the intervening time. It was probably too late to prevent bloodshed, but there was something to be said for getting the inevitable over with.

"Dig me up everything you can on today's vic, would you? Dexter Coffin, American by birth, employed at BioShell. As far back as you can, any tracks he may have left under any name or handle."

"Childhood dental records and juvenile posts on the *Candyland* message boards," Damini said cheerfully. "Got it. I'll stick it in Doyle when it's done."

"Ping me, too? Even if it's late? I'm upped."

"So will I be," Damini answered. "This could take a while. Anything else?"

"Not unless you have a cure for families."

"Hah," said the archinformist. "Everybody talking, and nobody hears a damned thing anybody else has to say. I'd retire on the proceeds. All right, check in later." She vanished just as Ferron reached the aptblock lobby.

It was after dinner, but half the family was hanging around in the common areas, watching the news or playing games while pretending to ignore it. Ferron knew it was useless to try sneaking past the synthetic marble-floored chambers with their charpoys and cushions, the corners lush with foliage. Attempted stealth would only encourage them to detain her longer.

Dr. Rao's information about the prime number progression had leaked beyond scientific circles—or been released—and an endless succession of talking heads were analyzing it in less nuanced terms than he'd managed. The older cousins asked Ferron if she'd heard the news about the star; two sisters and an uncle told her that her mother had been looking for her. *All* the nieces and nephews and small cousins wanted to look at the cat.

Ferron's aging mausi gave her five minutes on how a little cosmetic surgery would make her much more attractive on the marriage market, and shouldn't she consider lightening that mahogany-brown skin to a "prettier" wheatish complexion? A plate of idlis and sambaar appeared as if by magic in mausi's hand, and from there transferred to Ferron's. "And how are you ever going to catch a man if you're so skinny?"

It took Ferron twenty minutes to maneuver into her own small flat, which was still set for sleeping from three nights before. Smoke came trotting to see her, a petite-footed drift of the softest silver-and-charcoal fur imaginable, from which emerged a laughing triangular face set with eyes like black jewels. His ancestors has been foxes farmed for fur in Russia. Researchers had experimented on them, breeding for docility. It turned out it only took a few generations to turn a wild animal into a housepet.

Ferron was a little uneasy with the ethics of all that. But it hadn't stopped her from adopting Smoke when her mother lost interest in him. Foxes weren't the hot trend anymore; the fashion was for engineered cats and lemurs—and skinpets, among those who wanted to look daring.

Having rushed home, she was now possessed by the intense desire to delay the inevitable. She set Chairman Miaow's carrier on top of the cabinets and took Smoke out into the sunfarm for a few minutes of exercise in the relative cool of night. When he'd chased parrots in circles for a bit, she brought him back in, cleaned his litterbox, and stripped off her sweat-stiff uniform to have a shower. She was washing her hair when she realized that she had no idea what to feed Chairman Miaow. Maybe she could eat fox food? Ferron would have to figure out some way to segregate part of the flat for her . . . at least until she was sure that Smoke didn't think a parrot-cat would make a nice midnight snack.

She dressed in off-duty clothes—barefoot in a salwar kameez—and made an attempt at setting her furniture to segregate her flat. Before she left, she placed offering packets of kumkum and a few marigolds from the patio boxes in the tray before her idol of Varuna, the god of agreement, order, and the law.

Ferron didn't bother drying her hair before she presented herself at her mother's door. If she left it down, the heat would see to that soon enough.

Madhuvanthi did not rise to admit Ferron herself, as she was no longer capable. The door just slid open to Ferron's presence. As Ferron stepped inside, she saw mostly that the rug needed watering, and that the chaise her mother reclined on needed to be reset—it was sagging at the edges from too long in one shape. She wore not just the usual noninvasive modern interface—contacts, skin conductivity and brain activity sensors, the invisibly fine wires that lay along the skin and detected nerve impulses and muscle micromovements—but a full immersion suit.

Not for the first time, Ferron contemplated skinning out the thing's bulky, padded outline, and looking at her mother the way she wanted to see her. But that would be dishonest. Ferron was here to face her problems, not pretend their nonexistence.

"Hello, Mother," Ferron said.

There was no answer.

Ferron sent a text message. HELLO, MOTHER. YOU WANTED TO SEE ME?

The pause was long, but not as long as it could have been. YOU'RE LATE, TAMANNA. I'VE BEEN TRYING TO REACH YOU ALL DAY. I'M IN THE MIDDLE OF A RUN RIGHT NOW.

I'M SORRY, Ferron said. SOMEONE WAS MURDERED.

Text, thank all the gods, sucked out the defensive sarcasm that would have filled up a spoken word. She fiddled the bangles she couldn't wear on duty, just to hear the glass chime.

She could feel her mother's attention elsewhere, her distaste at having the unpleasant realities of Ferron's job forced upon her. That attention would focus on anything but Ferron, for as long as Ferron waited for it. It was a contest of wills, and Ferron always lost. MOTHER—

Her mother pushed up the faceplate on the VR helmet and sat up abruptly. "Bloody hell," she said. "Got killed. That'll teach me to do two things at once. Look, about the archives—"

"Mother," Ferron said, "I can't. I don't have any more savings to give you."

Madhuvanthi said, "They'll *kill* me."

They'll de-archive your virtual history, Ferron thought, but she had the sense to hold her tongue.

After her silence dragged on for fifteen seconds or so, Madhuvanthi said, "Sell the fox."

"He's mine," Ferron said. "I'm not selling him. Mother, you really need to come out of your make-believe world once in a while—"

Her mother pulled the collar of the VR suit open so she could ruffle the fur of the violet-and-teal striped skinpet nestled up to the warmth of her throat. It humped in response, probably vibrating with a comforting purr. Ferron tried not to judge, but the idea of parasitic pets, no matter how fluffy and colorful, made *her* skin crawl.

Ferron's mother said, "Make-believe. And your world isn't?"

"Mother—"

"Come in and see my world sometime before you judge it."

"I've seen your world," Ferron said. "I used to live there, remember? All the time, with you. Now I live out here, and you can too."

Madhuvanthi's glare would have seemed blistering even in the rainy season. "I'm your mother. You will obey me."

Everything inside Ferron demanded she answer yes. Hard-wired, that duty. Planned for. Programmed.

Ferron raised her right hand. "Can't we get some dinner and—"

Madhuvanthi sniffed and closed the faceplate again. And that was the end of the interview.

Rightminding or not, the cool wings of hypomania or not, Ferron's heart was pounding and her fresh clothing felt sticky again already. She turned and left.

When she got back to her own flat, the first thing she noticed was her makeshift wall of furniture partially disassembled, a chair/shelf knocked sideways, the disconnected and overturned table top now fallen flat.

"Oh, no." Her heart rose into her throat. She rushed inside, the door forgotten—

Atop a heap of cushions lay Smoke, proud and smug. And against his soft gray side, his fluffy tail flipped over her like a blanket, curled Chairman Miaow, her golden eyes squeezed closed in pleasure.

"Mine!" she said definitively, raising her head.

"I guess so," Ferron answered. She shut the door and went to pour herself a drink while she started sorting through Indrapramit's latest crop of interviews.

According to everything Indrapramit had learned, Coffin was quiet. He kept to himself, but he was always willing and enthusiastic when it came to discussing his work. His closest companion was the cat—Ferron looked down at Chairman Miaow, who had rearranged herself to take advantage of the warm valley in the bed between Smoke and Ferron's thigh—and the cat was something of a neighborhood celebrity, riding on Coffin's shoulder when he took his exercise.

All in all, a typical portrait of a typical, lonely man who didn't let anyone get too close.

"Maybe there will be more in the archinformation," she said, and went back to Doyle's pattern algorithm results one more damn time.

~

After performing her evening practice of kalari payat—first time in three days—Ferron set her furniture for bed and retired to it with her files. She wasn't expecting Indrapramit to show up at her flat, but sometime around two in the morning, the lobby door discreetly let her know she had a visitor. Of course, he knew she'd upped, and since he had no family and lived in a thin-walled dormitory room, he'd need a quiet place to camp out and work at this hour of the night. There wasn't a lot of productive interviewing you could do when all the subjects were asleep—at least, not until they had somebody dead to rights enough to take them down to the jail for interrogation.

His coming to her home meant every other resident the block would know, and Ferron could look forward to a morning of being quizzed by aunties while she tried to cram her idlis down. It didn't matter that Indrapramit was a colleague, and she was his superior. At her age, any sign of male interest brought unEmployed relatives with too much time on their hands swarming.

Still, she admitted him. Then she extricated herself from between the fox and the cat, wrapped her bathrobe around herself, stomped into her slippers, and headed out to meet him in the hall. At least keeping their conference to the public areas would limit knowing glances later.

He'd upped too. She could tell by the bounce in his step and his slightly wild focus. And the fact that he was dropping by for a visit in the dark of the morning.

Lowering her voice so she wouldn't trouble her neighbors, Ferron said, "Something too good to mail?"

"An interesting potential complication."

She gestured to the glass doors leading out to the sunfarm. He followed her, his boots somehow still as bright as they'd been that morning. He must polish them in an anti-static gloss.

She kicked off her slippers and padded barefoot over the threshold, making sure to silence the alarm first. The suntrees were furled for the night, their leaves rolled into funnels that channeled condensation to the roots. There was even a bit of chill in the air.

Ferron breathed in gratefully, wiggling her toes in the cultivated earth. "Let's go up to the roof."

Without a word, Indrapramit followed her up the winding openwork stair hung with bougainvillea, barren and thorny now in the dry season but a riot of color and greenery once the rains returned. The interior walls of the aptblock were mossy and thickly planted with coriander and other Ayurvedic herbs. Ferron broke off a bitter leaf of fenugreek to nibble as they climbed.

At the landing, she stepped aside and tilted her head back, peering up through the potted neem and lemon and mango trees at the stars beyond. A dark hunched shape in the branches of a pomegranate startled her until she realized it was the outline of one of the house monkeys, huddled in sleep. She wondered if she could see the Andromeda Galaxy from here at this time of year. Checking a skymap, she learned that it would be visible—but probably low on the horizon, and not without a telescope in these light-polluted times. You'd have better odds of finding it than a hundred years ago, though, when you'd barely have been able to glimpse the brightest stars. The Heavenly Ganges spilled across the darkness like sequins sewn at random on an indigo veil, and a crooked fragment of moon rode high. She breathed in deep and stepped onto the grass and herbs of the roof garden. A creeping mint snagged at her toes, sending its pungency wide.

"So what's the big news?"

"We're not the only ones asking questions about Dexter Coffin." Indrapramit flashed her a video clip of a pale-skinned woman with red hair bleached ginger by the sun and a crop of freckles not even the gloss of sunblock across her cheeks could keep down. She was broad-shouldered and looked capable, and the ID codes running across the feed under her image told Ferron she carried a warrant card and a stun pistol.

"Contract cop?" she said, sympathetically.

"I'm fine," he said, before she could ask. He spread his first two fingers opposite his thumb and pressed each end of the V beneath his collarbones, a new nervous gesture. "I got my Chicago block maintained last week, and the reprogramming is holding. I'd tell you if I was triggering. I know that not every contract cop is going to decompensate and start a massacre."

A massacre Indrapramit had stopped the hard way, it happened. "Let me know what you need," she said, because everything else she could have said would sound like a vote of non-confidence.

"Thanks," he said. "How'd it go with your mother?"

"Gah," she said. "I think *I* need a needle. So what's the contractor asking? And who's employing her?"

"Here's the interesting thing, boss. She's an American too."

"She *couldn't* have made it here this fast. Not unless she started before he died—"

"No," he said. "She's an expat, a former New York homicide detective. Her handle is Morganti. She lives in Hongasandra, and she does a lot of work for American and Canadian police departments. Licensed and bonded, and she seems to have a very good rep."

"Who's she under contract to now?"

"Warrant card says Honolulu."

"Huh." Ferron kept her eyes on the stars, and the dark leaves blowing before them. "Top-tier distributed policing, then. Is it a skip trace?"

"You think he was on the run, and whoever he was on the run from finally caught up with him?"

"It's a working theory." She shrugged. "Damini's supposed to be calling with some background any minute now. Actually, I think I'll check in with her. She's late, and I have to file a twenty-four-hour report with the Inspector in the morning."

With a twitch of her attention, she spun a bug out to Damini and conferenced Indrapramit in.

The archinformist answered immediately. "Sorry, boss," she said. "I know I'm slow, but I'm still trying to put together a complete picture here. Your dead guy buried his past pretty thoroughly. I can give you a preliminary, though, with the caveat that it's subject to change."

"Squirt," Ferron said, opening her firewall to the data. It came in fast and hard, and there seemed to be kilometers of it unrolling into her feed like an endless bolt of silk. "Oh, dear . . . "

"I know, I know. Do you want the executive summary? Even if it's also a work in progress? Okay. First up, nobody other than Coffin was in his flat that night, according to netfeed tracking."

"The other night upon the stair," Ferron said, "I met a man who wasn't there."

Damini blew her bangs out of her eyes. "So either nobody came in, or whoever did is a good enough hacker to eradicate every trace of her presence. Which is not a common thing."

"Gotcha. What else?"

"Doyle picked out a partial pattern in your feed. Two power cuts in places associated with the crime. It started looking for more, and it identified a series of brownouts over the course of a year or so, all in locations with some connection to Dr. Coffin. Better yet, Doyle identified the cause."

"I promise I'm holding my breath," Indrapramit said.

"Then how is it you are talking? Anyway, it's a smart virus in the power grids. It's draining power off the lab and household sunfarms at irregular intervals. That power is being routed to a series of chargeable batteries in Coffin's lab space. Except Coffin didn't purchase order the batteries."

"Nnebuogor," Ferron guessed.

"Two points," said Damini. "It's a stretch, but she could have come in to the office today specifically to see if the cops stopped by."

"She could have . . . " Indrapramit said dubiously. "You think she killed him because he found out she was stealing power? For what purpose?"

"I'll get on her email and media," Damini said. "So here's my speculation: imagine this utility virus, spreading through the smart grid from aptblock to aptblock. To commit the murder—nobody had to be in the room with him, not if his four-dimensional manipulators were within range of him. Right? You'd just override whatever safety protocols there were, and . . . boom. Or squish, if you prefer."

Ferron winced. She didn't. Prefer, that was. "Any sign that the manipulators were interfered with?"

"Memory wiped," Damini said. "Just like the cat. Oh, and the other thing I found out. Dexter Coffin is not our boy's first identity. It's more like his third, if my linguistic and semantic parsers are right about the web content they're picking up. I've got Conan on it too—" Conan was another of the department's expert systems "—and I'm going to go over a selection by hand. But it seems like our decedent had reinvented himself whenever he got into professional trouble, which he did a lot. He had unpopular opinions, and he wasn't shy about sharing them with the net. So he'd make the community too hot to handle and then come back as his own sockpuppet—new look, new address, new handle. Severing all ties to what he was before. I've managed to get a real fix on his last identity, though—"

Indrapramit leaned forward, folding his arms against the chill. "How do you do that? He works in a specialized—a rarified—field. I'd guess everybody in it knows each other, at least by reputation. Just how much did he change his appearance?"

"Well," Damini said, "he used to look like this. He must have used some rightminding tactics to change elements of his personality, too. Just not the salient ones. A real chameleon, your arsehole."

She picked a still image out of the datastream and flung it up. Ferron glanced at Indrapramit, whose rakish eyebrows were climbing up his forehead. An East Asian with long, glossy dark hair, who appeared to stand about six inches taller than Dr. Coffin, floated at the center of her perceptions, smiling benevolently.

"Madam, saab," Damini said. "May I present Dr. Jessica Fang."

"Well," Ferron said, after a pause of moderate length. "That takes a significant investment." She thought of Aristotle: As the condition of the mind alters, so too alters the condition of the body, and likewise, as the condition of the body alters, so too alters the condition of the mind.

Indrapramit said, "He has a taste for evocative handles. Any idea why the vanishing act?"

"I'm working on it," Damini said.

"I've got a better idea," said Ferron. "Why don't we ask Detective Morganti?"

Indrapramit steepled his fingers. "Boss. . . . "

"I'll hear it," Ferron said. "It doesn't matter if it's crazy."

"We've been totally sidetracked by the cat issue. Because Chairman Miaow has to be Niranjana, right? Because a clone would have expressed the genes for those markings differently. But she can't be Niranjana, because she's not wiped: she's factory-new."

"Right," Ferron said cautiously.

"So." Indrapramit was enjoying his dramatic moment. "If a person can have cosmetic surgery, why not a parrot-cat?"

"Chairman Miaow?" Ferron called, as she led Indrapramit into her flat. They needed tea to shake off the early morning chill, and she was beyond caring what the neighbors thought. She needed a clean uniform, too.

"Miaow," said Chairman Miaow, from inside the kitchen cupboard.

"Oh, dear." Indrapamit followed Ferron in. Smoke sat demurely in the middle of the floor, tail fluffed over his toes, the picture of innocence. Ferron pulled wide the cabinet door, which already stood ten inches ajar. There was Chairman Miaow, purring, a shredded packet of tunafish spreading dribbles of greasy water across the cupboard floor.

She licked her chops ostentatiously and jumped down to the sink lip, where she balanced as preciously as she had in Coffin's flat.

"Cat," Ferron said. She thought over the next few things she wanted to say, and remembered that she was speaking to a parrot-cat. "Don't think you've gotten away with anything. The fox is getting the rest of that."

"Fox food is icky," the cat said. "Also, not enough taurine."

"Huh," Ferron said. She looked over at Indrapramit.

He looked back. "I guess she's learning to talk."

They had no problem finding Detective Morganti. The redheaded American woman arrived at Ferron's aptblock with the first rays of sunlight stroking the vertical farms along its flanks. She had been sitting on the bench beside the door, reading something on her screen, but she looked up and stood as Ferron and Indrapramit exited.

"Sub-Inspector Ferron, I presume? And Constable Indrapramit, how nice to see you again."

Ferron shook her hand. She was even more imposing in person, tall and broad-chested, with the shoulders of a cartoon superhuman. She didn't squeeze.

Morganti continued, "I understand you're the detective of record on the Coffin case."

"Walk with us," Ferron said. "There's a nice French coffee shop on the way to the Metro."

It had shaded awnings and a courtyard, and they were seated and served within minutes. Ferron amused herself by pushing the crumbs of her pastry around on the plate while they talked. Occasionally, she broke a piece off and tucked it into her mouth, washing buttery flakes down with thick, cardamom-scented brew.

"So," she said after a few moments, "what did Jessica Fang do in Honolulu? It's not just the flame wars, I take it. And there's no warrant for her that we could find."

Morganti's eyes rose. "Very efficient."

"Thank you." Ferron tipped her head to Indrapramit. "Mostly his work, and that of my archinformist."

Morganti smiled; Indrapramit nodded silently. Then Morganti said, "She is believed to have been responsible for embezzling almost three million ConDollars from her former employer, eleven years ago in the Hawaiian Islands."

"That'd pay for a lot of identity-changing."

"Indeed."

"But they can't prove it."

"If they could, Honolulu PD would have pulled a warrant and virtually extradited her. Him. I was contracted to look into the case ten days ago—"

She tore off a piece of a cheese croissant and chewed it thoughtfully. "It took the skip trace this long to locate her. Him."

"Did she do it?"

"*Hell* yes." She grinned like the American she was. "The question is—well, okay, I realize the murder is your jurisdiction, but I don't get paid unless I either close the case or eliminate my suspect—and I get a bonus if I recover any of the stolen property. Now, 'killed by person or persons unknown,' is a perfectly acceptable outcome as far as the City of Honolulu is concerned, with the added benefit that the State of Hawaii doesn't have to pay Bengaluru to incarcerate him. So I need to know, one cop to another, if the inside-out stiff is Dexter Coffin."

"The DNA matches," Ferron said. "I can tell you that in confidence. There will be a press release once we locate and notify his next of kin."

"Understood," Morganti said. "I'll keep it under my hat. I'll be filing recovery paperwork against the dead man's assets in the amount of C$2,798,000 and change. I can give you the next of kin, by the way."

The data came in a squirt. Daughter, Maui. Dr. Fang-Coffin really had severed all ties.

"Understood," Ferron echoed. She smiled when she caught herself. She liked this woman. "You realize we have to treat you as a suspect, given your financial motive."

"Of course," Morganti said. "I'm bonded, and I'll be happy to come in for an interrogation under Truth."

"That will make things easier, madam," Ferron said.

Morganti turned her coffee cup in its saucer. "Now then. What can I do to help *you* clear your homicide?"

Indrapramit shifted uncomfortably on the bench.

"What *did* Jessica Fang do, exactly?" Ferron had Damini's data in her case buffer. She could use what Morganti told her to judge the contract officer's knowledge and sincerity.

"In addition to the embezzling? Accused of stealing research and passing it off as her own," Morganti said. "Also, she was—well, she was just kind of an asshole on the net, frankly. Running down colleagues, dismissing their work, aggrandizing her own. She was good, truthfully. But nobody's *that* good."

"Would someone have followed him here for personal reasons?"

"As you may have gathered, this guy was not diligent about his rightminding," Morganti said. She pushed a handful of hair behind her shoulder. "And he was a bit of a narcissist. Sociopath? Antisocial in some sort of atavistic way. Normal people don't just . . . walk away from all their social connections because they made things a little hot on the net."

Ferron thought of the distributed politics of her own workplace, the sniping and personality clashes. And her mother, not so much alone on an electronic Serengeti as haunting the virtual pillared palaces of an Egypt that never was.

"No," she said.

Morganti said, "Most people find ways to cope with that. Most people don't burn themselves as badly as Jessica Fang did, though."

"I see." Ferron wished badly for sparkling water in place of the syrupy coffee. "You've been running down Coffin's finances, then? Can you share that information?"

Morganti said that he had liquidated a lot of hidden assets a week ago, about two days after she took his case. "It was before I made contact with him, but it's possible he had Jessica Fang flagged for searches—or he had a contact in Honolulu who let him know when the skip trace paid off. He was getting ready to run again. How does that sound?"

Ferron sighed and sat back in her chair. "Fabulous. It sounds completely fabulous. I don't suppose you have any insight into who he might have been expecting for dinner? Or how whoever killed him might have gotten out of the room afterwards when it was all locked up tight on Coffin's override?"

Morganti shrugged. "He didn't have any close friends or romantic relationships. Always too aware that he was living in hiding, I'd guess. Sometimes he entertained co-workers, but I've checked with them all, and none admits having gone to see him that night."

"Sub-Inspector," Indrapramit said gently. "The time."

"Bugger," Ferron said, registering it. "Morning roll call. Catch up with you later?"

"Absolutely," Morganti said. "As I said before, I'm just concerned with clearing my embezzling case. I'm always happy to help a sister officer out on a murder."

And butter up the local police, Ferron thought.

Morganti said, "One thing that won't change. Fang was *obsessed* with astronomy."

"There were deep-space images on Coffin's walls," Ferron said.

Indrapramit said, "And he had offered his Ganesha an indigo scarf. I wonder if the color symbolized something astronomical to him."

"Indigo," Morganti said. "Isn't it funny that we have a separate word for dark blue?"

Ferron felt the pedantry welling up, and couldn't quite stopper it. "Did you know that all over the world, dark blue and black are often named with the same word? Possibly because of the color of the night sky. And that the ancient Greeks did not have a particular name for the color blue? Thus their seas were famously 'wine-dark.' But in Hindu tradition, the color blue has a special significance: it is the color of Vishnu's skin, and Krishna is nicknamed *Sunil*, 'dark blue.' The color also implies that which is all-encompassing, as in the sky."

She thought of something slightly more obscure. "Also, that color is the color of Shani Bhagavan, who is one of the deities associated with Uttara Bhadrapada. Which we've been hearing a lot about lately. It might indeed have had a lot of significance to Dr. Fang-Coffin."

Morganti, eyebrows drawn together in confusion, looked to Indrapramit for salvation. "Saab? Uttara Bhadrapada?"

Indrapramit said, "Andromeda."

Morganti excused herself as Indrapramit and Ferron prepared to check in to their virtual office.

While Ferron organized her files and her report, Indrapramit finished his coffee. "We need to check inbound ships from, or carrying passengers from, America. Honolulu isn't as prohibitive as, say, Chicago."

They'd worked together long enough that half the conversational shifts didn't need to be recorded. "Just in case somebody *did* come here to kill him. Well, there can't be that many passages, right?"

"I'll get Damini after it," he said. "After roll—"

Roll call made her avoidant. There would be reports, politics, wrangling, and a succession of wastes of time as people tried to prove that their cases were more worthy of resources than other cases.

She pinched her temples. At least the coffee here was good. "Right. Telepresencing . . . now."

After the morning meeting, they ordered another round of coffees, and Ferron pulled up the sandwich menu and eyed it. There was no telling when they'd have time for lunch.

She'd grab something after the next of kin notification. If she was still hungry when they were done.

Normally, in the case of a next of kin so geographically distant, Bengaluru Police would arrange for an officer with local jurisdiction to make the call. But the Lahaina Police Department had been unable to raise Jessica Fang's daughter on a home visit, and a little cursory research had revealed that she was unEmployed and very nearly a permanent resident of Artificial Reality.

Just going by her handle, Jessica Fang's daughter on Maui didn't have a lot of professional aspirations. Ferron and Indrapramit had to go virtual and pull on avatars to meet her: Skooter0 didn't seem to come out of her virtual worlds for anything other than biologically unavoidable crash cycles. Since they were on duty, Ferron and Indrapramit's avatars were the standard-issue blanks provided by Bengaluru Police, their virtual uniforms sharply pressed, their virtual faces expressionless and identical.

It wasn't the warm and personal touch you would hope for, Ferron thought, when somebody was coming to tell you your mother had been murdered.

"Why don't you take point on this one?" she said.

Indrapramit snorted. "Be sure to mention my leadership qualities in my next performance review."

They left their bodies holding down those same café chairs and waded through the first few tiers of advertisements—get-rich-quick schemes, Bollywood starlets, and pop star scandal sheets, until they got into the American feed, and then it was get-rich-quick schemes, Hollywood starlets, pornography, and Congressional scandal sheets—until they linked up with the law enforcement priority channel. Ferron checked the address and led Indrapramit into a massively multiplayer Artificial Reality that showed real-time activity through Skooter0's system identity number. Once provided with the next-of-kin's handle, Damini had sent along a selection of key codes and overrides that got them through the pay wall with ease.

They didn't need a warrant for this. It was just a courtesy call.

Skooter0's preferred hangout was a 'historical' AR, which meant in theory that it reflected the pre-twenty-first-century world, and in practice that it was a muddled-up stew of cowboys, ninjas, pinstripe suit mobsters, medieval knights, cavaliers, Mongols, and wild west gunslingers. There were Macedonians, Mauryans, African gunrunners, French resistance fighters and Nazis, all running around together with samurai and Shaolin monks.

Indrapramit's avatar checked a beacon—a glowing green needle floating just above his nonexistent wrist. The directional signal led them through a space meant to evoke an antediluvian ice cave, in which about two dozen people all dressed as different incarnations of the late-twentieth-century pop star David Bowie were working themselves into a martial frenzy as they prepared to go forth and do virtual battle with some rival clade of Emulators. Ferron eyed a Diamond Dog who was being dressed in glittering armor by a pair of Thin White Dukes and was glad of the expressionless surface of her uniform avatar.

She knew what they were supposed to be because she pattern-matched from the web. The music was quaint, but pretty good. The costumes . . . she winced.

Well, it was probably a better way to deal with antisocial aggression than taking it out on your spouse.

Indrapramit walked on, eyes front—not that you needed eyes to see what was going on in here.

At the far end of the ice cave, four seventh-century Norse dwarves delved a staircase out of stone, leading endlessly down. Heat rolled up from the depths. The virtual workmanship was astounding. Ferron and Indrapramit moved past, hiding their admiring glances. Just as much skill went into creating AR beauty as if it were stone.

The ice cave gave way to a forest glade floored in mossy, irregular slates. Set about on those were curved, transparent tables set for chess, go, mancala, cribbage, and similar strategy games. Most of the tables were occupied by pairs of players, and some had drawn observers as well.

Indrapramit followed his needle—and Ferron followed Indrapramit—to a table where a unicorn and a sasquatch were playing a game involving rows of transparent red and yellow stones laid out on a grid according to rules that Ferron did not comprehend. The sasquatch looked up as they stopped beside the table. The unicorn—glossy black, with a pearly, shimmering horn and a glowing amber stone pinched between the halves of her cloven hoof—was focused on her next move.

The arrow pointed squarely between her enormous, lambent golden eyes.

Ferron cleared her throat.

"Yes, officers?" the sasquatch said. He scratched the top of his head. The hair was particularly silky, and flowed around his long hooked fingernails.

"I'm afraid we need to speak to your friend," Indrapramit said.

"She's skinning you out," the sasquatch said. "Unless you have a warrant—"

"We have an override," Ferron said, and used it as soon as she felt Indrapramit's assent.

The unicorn's head came up, a shudder running the length of her body and setting her silvery mane to swaying. In a brittle voice, she said, "I'd like to report a glitch."

"It's not a glitch," Indrapramit said. He identified himself and Ferron and said, "Are you Skooter0?"

"Yeah," she said. The horn glittered dangerously. "I haven't broken any laws in India."

The sasquatch stood up discreetly and backed away.

"It is my unfortunate duty," Indrapramit continued, "to inform you of the murder of your mother, Dr. Jessica Fang, a.k.a. Dr. Dexter Coffin."

The unicorn blinked iridescent lashes. "I'm sorry," she said. "You're talking about something I have killfiled. I won't be able to hear you until you stop."

Indrapramit's avatar didn't look at Ferron, but she felt his request for help. She stepped forward and keyed a top-level override. "You will hear us," she said to the unicorn. "I am sorry for the intrusion, but we are legally bound to inform you that your mother, Dr. Jessica Fang, a.k.a. Dr. Dexter Coffin, has been murdered."

The unicorn's lip curled in a snarl. "Good. I'm glad."

Ferron stepped back. It was about the response she had expected.

"She made me," the unicorn said. "That doesn't make her my *mother*. Is there anything else you're legally bound to inform me of?"

"No," Indrapramit said.

"Then get the hell out." The unicorn set her amber gaming stone down on the grid. A golden glow encompassed it and its neighbors. "I win."

"Warehoused," Indrapramit said with distaste, back in his own body and nibbling a slice of quiche. "And happy about it."

Ferron had a pressed sandwich of vegetables, tapenade, cheeses, and some elaborate and incomprehensible European charcuterie made of smoked vatted protein. It was delicious, in a totally exotic sort of way. "Would it be better if she were miserable and unfulfilled?"

He made a noise of discontentment and speared a bite of spinach and egg.

Ferron knew her combativeness was really all about her mother, not Fang/Coffin's adult and avoidant daughter. Maybe it was the last remnants of Upping, but she couldn't stop herself from saying, "What she's doing is not so different from what our brains do naturally, except now it's by tech/ filters rather than prejudice and neurology."

Indrapramit changed the subject. "Let's make a virtual tour of the scene." As an icon blinked in Ferron's attention space, he added, "Oh, hey. Final autopsy report."

"Something from Damini, too," Ferron said. It had a priority code on it. She stepped into a artificial reality simulation of Coffin's apartment as she opened the contact. The thrill of the chase rose through the fog of her fading hypomania. Upping didn't seem to stick as well as it had when she was younger, and the crashes came harder now—but real, old-fashioned adrenaline was the cure for everything.

"Ferron," Ferron said, frowning down at the browned patches on Coffin's virtual rug. Indrapramit rezzed into the conference a heartbeat later. "Damini, what do the depths of the net reveal?"

"Jackpot," Damini said. "Did you get a chance to look at the autopsy report yet?"

"We just got done with the next of kin," Ferron said. "You're fast—I just saw the icon."

"Short form," Damini said, "is that's not Dexter Coffin."

Ferron's avatar made a slow circuit around the perimeter of the virtual murder scene. "There was a *DNA match*. Damini, we just told his daughter he was murdered."

Indrapramit, more practical, put down his fork in meatspace. His AR avatar mimicked the motion with an empty hand. "So who is it?"

"Nobody," Damini said. She leaned back, satisfied. "The medical examiner says it's topologically impossible to turn somebody inside out like that. It's vatted, whatever it is. A grown object, nominally alive, cloned from Dexter Coffin's tissue. But it's not Dexter Coffin. I mean, think about it—what organ would that *be*, exactly?"

"Cloned." In meatspace, Ferron picked a puff of hyacinth-blue fur off her uniform sleeve. She held it up where Indrapramit could see it.

His eyes widened. "Yes," he said. "What about the patterns, though?"

"Do I look like a bioengineer to you? Indrapramit," Ferron said thoughtfully. "Does this crime scene look staged to you?"

He frowned. "Maybe."

"Damini," Ferron asked, "how'd you do with Dr. Coffin's files? And Dr. Nnebuogar's files?"

"There's nothing useful in Coffin's email except some terse exchanges with Dr. Nnebuogar very similar in tone to the Jessica Fang papers. Nnebuogar was warning Coffin off her research. But there were no death threats, no love letters, no child support demands."

"Anything he was interested in?"

"That star," Damini said. "The one that's going nova or whatever. He's been following it for a couple of weeks now, before the press release hit the mainstream feeds. Nnebuogar's logins support the idea that she's behind the utility virus, by the way."

"Logins can be spoofed."

"So they can," Damini agreed.

Ferron peeled her sandwich open and frowned down at the vatted charcuterie. It all looked a lot less appealing now. "Nobody came to Coffin's flat. And it turns out the stiff wasn't a stiff after all. So Coffin went somewhere else, after making preparations to flee and then abandoning them."

"And the crime scene was staged," Indrapramit said.

"This is interesting," Damini said. "Coffin hadn't been to the office in a week."

"Since about when Morganti started investigating him. Or when he might have become aware that she was on his trail."

Ferron said something sharp and self-critical and radically unprofessional. And then she said, "I'm an idiot. Leakage."

"Leakage?" Damini asked. "You mean like when people can't stop talking about the crime they actually committed, or the person you're not supposed to know they're having an affair with?"

An *urgent* icon from Ferron's mausi Sandhya—the responsible auntie, not the fussy auntie—blinked insistently at the edge of her awareness. *Oh Gods, what now?*

"Exactly like that," Ferron said. "Look, check on any hits for Coffin outside his flat in the past ten days. And I need confidential warrants for DNA analysis of the composters at the BioShell laboratory facility and also at Dr. Rao's apartment."

"You think *Rao* killed him?" Damini didn't even try to hide her shock.

Blink, blink went the icon. Emergency. Code red. Your mother has gone beyond the pale, my dear. "Just pull the warrants. I want to see what we get before I commit to my theory."

"Why?" Indrapramit asked.

Ferron sighed. "Because it's crazy. That's why. And see if you can get confidential access to Rao's calendar files and email. I don't want him to know you're looking."

"Wait right there," Damini said. "Don't touch a thing. I'll be back before you know it."

"Mother," Ferron said to her mother's lion-maned goddess of an avatar, "I'm sorry. Sandhya's sorry. We're all sorry. But we can't let you go on like this."

It was the hardest thing she'd ever said.

Her mother, wearing Sekhmet's golden eyes, looked at Ferron's avatar and curled a lip. Ferron had come in, not in a uniform avatar, but wearing the battle-scarred armor she used to play in when she was younger, when she and her mother would spend hours Atavistic. That was during her schooling, before she got interested in stopping—or at least avenging—*real* misery.

Was that fair? Her mother's misery was real. So was that of Jessica Fang's abandoned daughter. And this was a palliative—against being widowed, against being bedridden.

Madhuvanthi's lip-curl slowly blossomed into a snarl. "Of course. You can let them destroy this. Take away everything I am. It's not like it's murder."

"Mother," Ferron said, "it's not *real*."

"If it isn't," her mother said, gesturing around the room, "what is, then? I *made* you. I gave you life. You owe me this. Sandhya said you came home with one of those new parrot cats. Where'd the money for that come from?"

"Chairman Miaow," Ferron said, "is evidence. And reproduction is an ultimately sociopathic act, no matter what I owe you."

Madhuvanthi sighed. "Daughter, come on one last run."

"You'll have your own memories of all this," Ferron said. "What do you need the archive for?"

"Memory," her mother scoffed. "What's memory, Tamanna? What do you actually remember? Scraps, conflations. How does it compare to being able to *relive*?"

To relive it, Ferron thought, *you'd have to have lived it in the first place.* But even teetering on the edge of fatigue and crash, she had the sense to keep *that* to herself.

"Have you heard about the star?" she asked. Anything to change the subject. "The one the aliens are using to talk to us?"

"The light's four million years old," Madhuvanthi said. "They're all dead. Look, there's a new manifest synesthesia show. Roman and Egyptian. Something for both of us. If you won't come on an adventure with me, will you at least come to an art show? I promise I'll never ask you for archive money again. Just come to this one thing with me? And I promise I'll prune my archive starting tomorrow."

The lioness's brow was wrinkled. Madhuvanthi's voice was thin with defeat. There was no more money, and she knew it. But she couldn't stop bargaining. And the art show was a concession, something that evoked the time they used to spend together, in these imaginary worlds.

"Ferron," she said. Pleading. "Just let me do it myself."

Ferron. They weren't really communicating. Nothing was won. Her mother was doing what addicts always did when confronted—delaying, bargaining, buying time. But she'd call her daughter *Ferron* if it might buy her another twenty-four hours in her virtual paradise.

"I'll come," Ferron said. "But not until tonight. I have some work to do."

"Boss. How did you know to look for that DNA?" Damini asked, when Ferron activated her icon.

"Tell me what you found," Ferron countered.

"DNA in the BioShell composter that matches that of Chairman Miaow," she said, "and therefore that of Dexter Coffin's cat. And the composter of Rao's building is just *full* of his DNA. Rao's. Much, much more than you'd expect. Also, some of his email and calendar data has been purged. I'm attempting to reconstruct—"

"Have it for the chargesheet," Ferron said. "I bet it'll show he had a meeting with Coffin the night Coffin vanished."

Dr. Rao lived not in an aptblock, even an upscale one, but in the Vertical City. Once Damini returned with the results of the warrants, Ferron got her paperwork in order for the visit. It was well after nightfall by the time she and Indrapramit, accompanied by Detective Morganti and four patrol officers, went to confront him.

They entered past shops and the vertical farm in the enormous tower's atrium. The air smelled green and healthy, and even at this hour of the night, people moved in steady streams towards the dining areas, across lush green carpets.

A lift bore the police officers effortlessly upward, revealing the lights of Bengaluru spread out below through a transparent exterior wall. Ferron looked at Indrapramit and pursed her lips. He raised his eyebrows in reply. *Conspicuous consumption.* But they couldn't very well hold it against Rao now.

They left the Morganti and the patrol officers covering the exit and presented themselves at Dr. Rao's door.

"Open," Ferron said formally, presenting her warrant. "In the name of the law."

The door slid open, and Ferron and Indrapramit entered cautiously.

The flat's resident must have triggered the door remotely, because he sat at his ease on furniture set as a chaise. A gray cat with red ear-tips crouched by his knee, rubbing the side of its face against his trousers.

"New!" said the cat. "New people! Namaskar! It's almost time for tiffin."

"Dexter Coffin," Ferron said to the tall, thin man. "You are under arrest for the murder of Dr. Rao."

As they entered the lift and allowed it to carry them down the external wall of the Vertical City, Coffin standing in restraints between two of the patrol officers, Morganti said, "So. If I understand this properly, you—Coffin—actually *killed* Rao to assume his identity? Because you knew you were well and truly burned this time?"

Not even a flicker of his eyes indicated that he'd heard her.

Morganti sighed and turned her attention to Ferron. "What gave you the clue?"

"The scotophobin," Ferron said. Coffin's cat, in her new livery of gray and red, miaowed plaintively in a carrier. "He didn't have memory issues. He was using it to cram Rao's life story and eccentricities so he wouldn't trip himself up."

Morganti asked, "But why liquidate his assets? Why not take them with him?" She glanced over her shoulder. "Pardon me for speaking about you as if you were a statue, Dr. Fang. But you're doing such a good impression of one."

It was Indrapramit who gestured at the Vertical City rising at their backs. "Rao wasn't wanting for assets."

Ferron nodded. "Would you have believed he was dead if you couldn't find the money? Besides, if his debt—or some of it—was recovered, Honolulu would have less reason to keep looking for him."

"So it was a misdirect. Like the frame job around Dr. Nnebuogar and the table set for two . . . ?"

Her voice trailed off as a stark blue-white light cast knife-edged shadows across her face. Something blazed in the night sky, something as stark and brilliant as a dawning sun—but cold, as cold as light can be. As cold as a reflection in a mirror.

Morganti squinted and shaded her eyes from the shine. "Is that a *hydrogen bomb?*"

"If it was," Indrapramit said, "Your eyes would be melting."

Coffin laughed, the first sound he'd made since he'd assented to understanding his rights. "It's a supernova."

He raised both wrists, bound together by the restraints, and pointed. "In the Andromeda Galaxy. See how low it is to the horizon? We'll lose sight of it as soon as we're in the shadow of that tower."

"Al-Rahman," Ferron whispered. The lift wall was darkening to a smoky shade and she could now look directly at the light. Low to the horizon, as Coffin had said. So bright it seemed to be visible as a sphere.

"Not that star. It was stable. Maybe a nearby one," Coffin said. "Maybe they knew, and that's why they were so desperate to tell us they were out there."

"Could they have *survived* that?"

"Depends how close to Al-Rahman it was. The radiation—" Coffin shrugged in his restraints. "That's probably what killed them."

"God in heaven," said Morganti.

Coffin cleared his throat. "Beautiful, isn't it?"

Ferron craned her head back as the point source of the incredible radiance slipped behind a neighboring building. There was no scatter glow: the rays of light from the nova were parallel, and the shadow they entered uncompromising, black as a pool of ink.

Until this moment, she would have had to slip a skin over her perceptions to point to the Andromeda Galaxy in the sky. But now it seemed like the most important thing in the world that, two and a half million years away, somebody had shouted across the void before they died.

A strange elation filled her. *Everybody talking, and nobody hears a damned thing anyone—even themselves—has to say.*

"We're here," Ferron said to the ancient light that spilled across the sky and did not pierce the shadow into which she descended. As her colleagues turned and stared, she repeated the words like a mantra. "We're here too! And we heard you."

—for Asha Cat Srinivasan Shipman, and her family

Orm the Beautiful

Orm the Beautiful sang in his sleep, to his brothers and sisters, as the sea sings to itself. He would never die. But neither could he live much longer.

Dreaming on jewels, hearing their ancestor-song, he did not think that he would mind. The men were coming; Orm the Beautiful knew it with the wisdom of his bones. He thought he would not fight them. He thought he would close the mountain and let them scratch outside.

He would die there in the mosther-cave, and so stay with the Chord. There was no one after him to take his place as warden, and Orm the Beautiful was old.

Because he was the last warden of the mother-cave, his hoard was enormous, chromatic in hue and harmony. There was jade and lapis—the bequests of Orm the Exquisite and Orm the Luminous, respectively—and chrysoprase and turquoise and the semiprecious feldspars. There were three cracked sections of an amethyst pipe as massive as a fallen tree, and Orm the Beautiful was careful never to breathe fire upon them; the stones would jaundice to smoke color in the heat.

He lay closest by the jagged heap of beryls—green as emerald, green as poison, green as grass—that were the mortal remains of his sister, Orm the Radiant. And just beyond her was the legacy of her mate, Orm the Magnificent, charcoal-and-silver labradorite overshot with an absinthe shimmer. The Magnificent's song, in death, was high and sweet, utterly at odds with the aged slithering hulk he had become before he changed.

Orm the Beautiful stretched his long neck among the glorious rubble of his kin and dozed to their songs. Soon he would be with them, returned to their harmony, their many-threaded round. Only his radiance illuminated them now. Only his eye remembered their sheen. And he too would lose the power to shine with more than reflected light before long, and all in the mother-cave would be dark and full of music.

He was pale, palest of his kin, blue-white as skimmed milk and just as translucent. The flash that ran across his scales when he crawled into the light, however, was spectral: green-electric and blue-actinic, and a vermilion so sharp it could burn an afterimage in a human eye.

It had been a long time since he climbed into the light. Perhaps he'd seal the cave now, to be ready.

Yes.

When he was done, he lay down among his treasures, his beloveds, under the mountain, and his thoughts were dragonish.

But when the men came they came not single spies but in battalions, with dragons of their own. Iron dragons, yellow metal monsters that creaked and hissed as they gnawed the rocks. And they brought, with the dragons, channeled fire.

There was a thump, a tremble, and sifting dust followed. Cold winter air trickling down the shaft woke Orm the Beautiful from his chorale slumber.

He blinked lambent eyes, raising his head from the petrified, singing flank of Orm the Perspicacious. He heard the crunch of stone like the splintering of masticated bones and cocked his head, his ears and tendrils straining forward.

And all the Chord sang astonishment and alarm.

It had happened to others. Slain, captured, taken. Broken apart and carried off, their memories and their dreams lost forever, their songs stripped to exiled fragments to adorn a wrist, a throat, a crown. But it had always been that men could be turned back with stone.

And now they were here at the mother-cave, and undaunted to find it sealed.

This would not do. This threatened them all.

Orm the Beautiful burst from the mountain wreathed in white-yellow flames. The yellow steel dragon was not too much larger than he. It blocked the tunnel mouth; its toothed hand raked and lifted shattered stone. Orm the Beautiful struck it with his claws extended, his wings snapping wide as he cleared the destroyed entrance to the mother-cave.

The cold cut through scale to bone. When fire did not jet from flaring nostrils, his breath swirled mist and froze to rime. Snow lay blackened on the mountainside, rutted and filthy. His wings, far whiter, caught chill carmine sparks from the sun. Fragile steel squealed and rent under his claws.

There was a man in the cage inside the mechanical dragon. He made terrible unharmonious noises as he burned. Orm the Beautiful seized him and ate him quickly, out of pity, head jerking like a stork snatching down a frog.

His throat distended, squeezed, smoothed, contracted. There was no time to eat the contraption, and metal could not suffer in the flames. Orm the Beautiful tore it in half, claw and claw, and soared between the discarded pieces.

Other men screamed and ran. Their machines were potent, but no iron could sting him. Neither their bullets nor the hammer-headed drill on the second steel dragon gave him pause. He stalked them, pounced, gorged on the snap-shaken dead.

He pursued the living as they fled, and what he reached he slew.

When he slithered down the ruined tunnel to the others, they were singing, gathered, worried. He settled among their entwined song, added his notes to the chords, offered harmony. Orm the Beautiful was old; what he brought to the song was rich and layered, subtle and soft.

They will come again, sang Orm the Radiant.

They have found the mother-cave, and they have machines to unearth us, like a badger from its sett, sang Orm the Terrible from his column of black and lavender jade.

We are not safe here anymore, sang Orm the Luminous. *We will be scattered and lost. The song will end, will end.*

His verse almost silenced them all. Their harmony guttered like a fire when the wind slicks across it, and for a moment Orm the Beautiful felt the quiet like a wire around his throat. It was broken by the discord of voices, a rising dissonance like a tuning orchestra, the Chord all frightened and in argument.

But Orm the Courtly raised her voice, and all listened. She was old in life and old in death, and wise beyond both in her singing. *Let the warden decide.*

Another agreed, another, voice after voice scaling into harmony.

And Orm the Beautiful sat back on his haunches, his tail flicked across his toes, his belly aching, and tried to pretend he had any idea at all how to protect the Chord from being unearthed and carted to the four corners of the world.

"I'll think about it when I've digested," he said, and lay down on his side with a sigh.

Around him the Chord sang agreement. They had not forgotten in death the essentialities of life.

With the men and their machines came memory. Orm the Beautiful, belly distended with iron and flesh, nevertheless slept with one eye open. His opalescence lit the mother-cave in hollow violets and crawling greens. The Chord sang around him, thinking while he dreamed. The dead did not rest, or dream.

They only sang and remembered.

The Chord was in harmony when he awoke. They had listened to his song while he slept, and while he stretched—sleek again, and the best part of a yard longer—he heard theirs as well, and learned from them what they had learned from his dinner.

More men would follow. The miners Orm the Beautiful had dined on knew they would not go unavenged. There would be more men, men like ants, with their weapons and their implements. And Orm the Beautiful was strong.

But he was old, and he was only one. And someone, surely, would soon recall that though steel had no power to harm Orm the Beautiful's race, knapped flint or obsidian could slice him opal hide from opal bone.

The mother-cave was full of the corpses of dragons, a chain of song and memory stretching aeons. The Chord was rich in voices.

Orm the Beautiful had no way to move them all.

Orm the Numinous, who was eldest, was chosen to speak the evil news they all knew already. *You must give us away, Orm the Beautiful.*

Dragons are not specifically disallowed in the airspace over Washington, D.C., but it must be said that Orm the Beautiful's presence there was heartily discouraged. Nevertheless, he persevered, holding his flame and the lash of his wings, and succeeded in landing on the National Mall without destroying any of the attacking aircraft.

He touched down lightly in a clear space before the National Museum of Natural History, a helicopter hovering over his head and blowing his tendrils this way and that. There were men all over the grass and pavements. They scattered, screaming, nigh-irresistible prey. Orm the Beautiful's tail-tip twitched with frustrated instinct, and he was obliged to stand on three legs and elaborately clean his off-side fore talons for several moments before he regained enough self-possession to settle his wings and ignore the scurrying morsels.

It was unlikely that he would set a conducive tone with the museum's staff by eating a few as a prelude to conversation.

He stood quietly, inspecting his talons foot by foot and, incidentally, admiring the flashes of color that struck off his milk-pale hide in the glaring sun. When he had been still five minutes, he looked up to find a ring of men surrounding him, males and a few females, with bright metal in their hands and flashing on the chests of uniforms that were a black-blue dark as sodalite.

"Hello," Orm the Beautiful said, in the language of his dinner, raising his voice to be heard over the clatter of the helicopter. "My name is Orm the Beautiful. I should like to speak to the curator, please."

The helicopter withdrew to circle, and the curator eventually produced was a female man. Orm the Beautiful wondered if that was due to some half-remembered legend about his folk's preferences. Sopranos, in particular, had been popular among his kin in the days when they associated more freely with men.

She minced from the white-columned entry, down broad shallow steps between exhibits of petrified wood, and paused beyond the barricade of yellow tape and wooden sawhorses the blue-uniformed men had strung around Orm the Beautiful.

He had greatly enjoyed watching them evacuate the Mall.

The curator wore a dull suit and shoes that clicked, and her hair was twisted back on her neck. Little stones glinted in her earlobes: diamonds, cold and common and without song.

"I'm Katherine Samson," she said, and hesitantly extended her tiny soft hand, half-retracted it, then doggedly thrust it forward again. "You wished to speak to me?"

"I am Orm the Beautiful," Orm the Beautiful replied, and laid a cautious talon-tip against her palm. "I am here to beg your aid."

She squinted up and he realized that the sun was behind him. If its own brilliance didn't blind her pale man's eyes, surely the light shattering on his scales would do the deed. He spread his wings to shade her, and the ring of blue-clad men flinched back as one—as if they were a Chord, though Orm the Beautiful knew they were not.

The curator, however, stood her ground.

His blue-white wings were translucent, and there was a hole in the leather of the left one, an ancient scar. It cast a ragged bright patch on the curator's shoe, but the shade covered her face, and she lowered her eye-shading hand.

"Thank you," she said. And then, contemplating him, she pushed the sawhorses apart. One of the blue men reached for her, but before he caught her arm, the curator was through the gap and standing in Orm the Beautiful's shadow, her head craned back, her hair pulling free around her temples in soft wisps that reminded Orm the Beautiful of Orm the Radiant's tawny tendrils. "You need *my* help? Uh, sir?"

Carefully, he lowered himself to his elbows, keeping the wings high. The curator was close enough to touch him now, and when he tilted his head to see her plainly, he found her staring up at him with the tip of her tongue protruding. He flicked his tongue in answer, tasting her scent.

She *was* frightened. But far more curious.

"Let me explain," he said. And told her about the mother-cave, and the precious bones of his Chord, and the men who had come to steal them. He told her that they were dead, but they remembered, and if they were torn apart, carted off, their song and their memories would be shattered.

"It would be the end of my culture," he said, and then he told her he was dying.

As he was speaking, his head had dipped lower, until he was almost murmuring in her ear. At some point, she'd laid one hand on his skull behind the horns and leaned close, and she seemed startled now to realize that she was touching him. She drew her hand back slowly, and stood staring at the tips of her fingers. "What is that singing?"

She heard it, then, the wreath of music that hung on him, thin and thready though it was in the absence of his Chord. That was well. "It is I."

"Do all—all your people—does that always happen?"

"I have no people," he said. "But yes. Even in death we sing. It is why the Chord must be kept together."

"So when you said it's only you . . . "

"I am the last," said Orm the Beautiful.

She looked down, and he gave her time to think.

"It would be very expensive," she said, cautiously, rubbing the fingertips together as if they'd lost sensation. "We would have to move quickly, if poachers have already found your . . . mother-cave. And you're talking about a huge engineering problem, to move them without taking them apart. I don't know where the money would come from."

"If the expense were not at issue, would the museum accept the bequest?"

"Without a question." She touched his eye-ridge again, quickly, furtively. "Dragons," she said, and shook her head and breathed a laugh. "*Dragons.*"

"Money is no object," he said. "Does your institution employ a solicitor?"

The document was two days in drafting. Orm the Beautiful spent the time fretting and fussed, though he kept his aspect as nearly serene as possible. Katherine—the curator—did not leave his side. Indeed, she brought him within the building—the tall doors and vast lobby could have accommodated a far larger dragon—and had a cot fetched so she could remain near. He could not stay in the lobby itself, because it was a point of man-pride that the museum was open every day, and free to all comers. But they cleared a small exhibit hall, and he stayed there in fair comfort, although silent and alone.

Outside, reporters and soldiers made camp, but within the halls of the Museum of Natural History, it was bright and still, except for the lonely shadow of Orm the Beautiful's song.

Already, he mourned his Chord. But if his sacrifice meant their salvation, it was a very small thing to give.

When the contracts were written, when the papers were signed, Katherine sat down on the edge of her cot and said, "The personal bequest," she began. "The one the museum is meant to sell, to fund the retrieval of your Chord."

"Yes," Orm the Beautiful said.

"May I know what it is now, and where we may find it?"

"It is here before you," said Orm the Beautiful, and tore his heart from his breast with his claws.

He fell with a crash like a breaking bell, an avalanche of skim-milk-white opal threaded with azure and absinthe and vermilion flash. Chunks rolled against Katherine's legs, bruised her feet and ankles, broke some of her toes in her clicking shoes.

She was too stunned to feel pain. Through his solitary singing, Orm the Beautiful heard her refrain: "Oh, no, oh, no, oh, no."

Those who came to investigate the crash found Katherine Samson on her knees, hands raking the rubble. Salt water streaked opal powder white as bone dust down her cheeks. She kissed the broken rocks, and the blood on her fingertips was no brighter than the shocked veins of carnelian flash that shot through them.

Orm the Beautiful was broken up and sold, as he had arranged. The paperwork was quite unforgiving; dragons, it seems, may serve as their own attorneys with great dexterity.

The stones went for outrageous prices. When you wore them on your skin, you could hear the dragonsong. Institutions and the insanely wealthy fought over the relics. No price could ever be too high.

Katherine Samson was bequeathed a few chips for her own. She had them polished and drilled and threaded on a chain she wore about her throat, where her blood could warm them as they pressed upon her pulse. The mother-cave was located with the aid of Orm the Beautiful's maps and directions. Poachers were in the process of excavating it when the team from the Smithsonian arrived.

But the museum had brought the National Guard. And the poachers were dealt with, though perhaps not with such finality as Orm the Beautiful might have wished.

Each and each, his Chord were brought back to the Museum.

Katherine, stumping on her walking cast, spent long hours in the exhibit hall. She hovered and guarded and warded, and stroked and petted and adjusted Orm the Beautiful's hoard like a nesting falcon turning her eggs. His song sustained her, his warm bones worn against her skin, his voice half-heard in her ear.

He was broken and scattered. He was not a part of his Chord. He was lost to them, as other dragons had been lost before, and as those others his song would eventually fail, and flicker, and go unremembered.

After a few months, she stopped weeping.

She also stopped eating, sleeping, dreaming.

Going home.

They came as stragglers, footsore and rain-draggled, noses peeled by the sun. They came alone, in party dresses, in business suits, in outrageously costly T-shirts and jeans. They came draped in opals and platinum, opals and gold. They came with the song of Orm the Beautiful warm against their skin.

They came to see the dragons, to hear their threaded music. When the museum closed at night, they waited patiently by the steps until morning. They did not freeze. They did not starve.

Eventually, through the sheer wearing force of attrition, the passage of decades, the museum accepted them. And there they worked, and lived, for all time.

And Orm the Beautiful?

He had been shattered. He died alone.

The Chord could not reclaim him. He was lost in the mortal warders, the warders who had been men.

But as he sang in their ears, so they recalled him, like a seashell remembers the sea.

The Inevitable Heat Death
of the Universe

S he cuts him from the belly of a shark.
   If this were another kind of story, I should now tell you, fashionably, that the shark is not a shark. That she is not a she and he is not a he. That your language and symbology do not suffice for my purposes, and so I am driven to speak in metaphor, to construct three-dimensional approximations of ten-dimensional realities. That you are inadequate to the task of comprehension.

Poppycock.

You are a God.

The shark is a shark. A Great White, *Carcharodon carcharias*, the sublime killer. It is a blind evolutionary shot-in-the-dark, a primitive entity unchanged except in detail for—by the time of our narrative—billions of years.

It is a monster wonderful in its adequacy: the ultimate *consumer*. So simple in construction: over eighteen feet long, pallid on the belly and shades of gray above, in general form comprised of two blunt-ended, streamlined, flexible, muscular and cartilaginous cones. One is squat and one is tapered. They are joined together base to base.

It is a sort of meat ramjet. Water runs through, carrying oxygen, which is transferred to the blood by a primitive gill arrangement. At the tapered end are genitalia and propulsion. At the thick end are lousy eyesight, phenomenal olfactory and electrical senses, and teeth.

In the middle is six meters of muscle and an appetite.

Beginner's luck; a perfect ten.

They are the last creatures in the universe, he and she and the shark. The real world, outside, is running down, and the world they inhabit is a false, constructed world.

But it is a real shark. Fishy blood slimes her hands as she slits its belly with the back-curve of knives that are a part of her, extruded from her hands at need. She grows extra arms as convenient, to hold the wound open while she drags him free.

The shark's skin is silky-slick and sandpaper-rough simultaneously, scraping layers of material from the palms of her hands. The serrations on her blades are like those of the shark's teeth, ragged jags meshing like the rollers of a thresher.

There had been three living things left in their world.

Now there are two.

She cuts him from the belly of a shark. Allowing himself to be swallowed was the easiest way to beach and kill the monster, which for humane reasons must be dead before the next stage of their plan.

He stands up reefed in gnawed car tires and bits of bungee cord, and picks rubber seaweed from his teeth. They are alone on a boat in a sea like a sunset mirror. The sky overhead is gray metal, and a red sun blazes in it. It is a false sun, but it is all they have.

They have carefully hoarded this space, this fragment of creation, until the very end. They have one more task to fulfill.

As for him, how can he survive being swallowed by a shark? If entropy itself comes along and eats you, breaks you down, spreads you out thin in a uniform dispersal permeating its meat and cartilage—if it consumes, if it *digests* you—surely that's the end? Entropy always wins.

Final peace in the restless belly of a shark, nature's perpetual motion machine. Normally, it would be the end.

But he is immortal, and he cannot die.

There, under the false and dying sun, becalmed on a make-believe sea, they do not make love. She is a lesbian. He is sworn to a celibate priesthood. They are both sterile, in any case. They are immortal, but their seed has been more fortunate.

Instead, he picks the acid-etched rubber and bits of diode from his hair and then dives into the tepid sea. The first splash washes the shark's blood and fluids away.

The water he strokes through is stagnant, insipid. The only heartbeat it has known in lifetimes is the shark's. And now that the shark's is stilled, it won't know the man's. His heart does not beat. Where blood and bone once grew is a perfect replica, a microscopic latticework of infinitesimal machines.

He dives for the bottom. He does not need to breathe.

This desolate sea is little enough, but it is all there is. Outside the habitat, outside the sea and the sun and the boat and the gape-bellied corpse of the shark, outside of the woman and the man, nothing remains.

Or not nothing, precisely. But rather, an infinite, entropic sea of thermodynamic oatmeal. A few degrees above absolute zero, a few scattered atoms more populated than absolute vacuum. Even a transfinite amount of *stuff* makes a pretty thin layer when you spread it over an infinite amount of space.

Suffice it to say there is no *place* anyplace out there; every bit of it is indistinguishable. Uniform.

The universe has been digested.

While the man swims, the woman repairs the shark.

She doesn't use needles and thread, lasers or scalpels. She has tools that are her hands, her body. They will enter the shark as they entered her, millennia ago, and remake the shark as they remade her, until it is no longer a consuming machine made of muscle and sinew, but a consuming machine made of machines.

They are infinitesimal, but they devour the shark in instants. As they consume it, they take on its properties—the perfect jaws, the perfect strength, the slick-sharp hide. The shark, mercifully dead, feels no pain.

The woman is more or less humane.

When the machines reach the animal's brain, they assume its perfect appetite as well. Every fishy thought. Every animal impulse, every benthic memory, are merely electrical patterns flickering dark in already-decaying flesh. They are consumed before they can vanish.

The shark reanimates hungry.

She heaves it over the side with her six or eight arms, into the false, dead sea, where the man awaits it. It swims for him, driven by a hunger hard to comprehend—a ceaseless, devouring compulsion. And *now* it can eat anything. The water that once streamed its gills in life-giving oxygen is sustenance, now, and the shark builds more shark-stuff to incorporate it.

The man turns to meet it and holds up his hands.

When its jaws close, they are one.

～

The being that results when the shark and the man unify, their machine-memories interlinking, has the shark's power, its will, its insistent need. Its purpose.

The man gives it language, and knowledge, and will. It begins with the false world, then—the sea and the ship, and the gray metal sky, and the make-believe sun. These are tangible.

The woman, like the man, like the shark-that-has-become, is immortal, and she cannot die.

The shark will consume her last of all.

Consider the shark. An engine for converting meat into motion. Motion generates heat. Heat is entropy. Entropy is the grand running-down of the clock that is the universe.

The shark-that-has-become does nothing but eat. Time is irrelevant. What now the puny unwindings of planet and primary, of star and galaxy? There is no night. There is no day.

There are only the teeth of the shark, vacuuming the cosmos. Enormous electromagnetic webs spin out from its ever-growing maw, sweeping sparse dust and heat into its vasty gullet. The shark grows towards infinity.

The dead universe is swept.

The woman follows.

You are a God. For forty hundred thousand million days and forty hundred thousand million nights, the shark carries you under its unbeating heart. And when all space lie clean and empty, polished and waiting, you turn to her. You will consume her, last of all.

There will be nothing when she is gone. The entire universe will have passed down your throat, and even your appetite must be assuaged. And if it is not, you will devour yourself.

A machine can manage that.

You wonder what it will be like not to hunger, for a while.

But as you turn to swallow her, she holds up her hand. Her small, delicate hand that compasses galaxies—or could, if there were any left to compass.

Now, it cups the inverse glow of a naked singularity, as carefully hoarded as the shark, as the false-world that was the first thing to fall to the shark-that-has-become. She casts it before you, round and rolling, no bigger than a mustard seed.

You lunge. It's hard and heavy going down, and you gulp it sharply. A moment later, she follows, a more delicate mouthful, consumed at leisure.

She joins the man and the shark in your consciousness. And it is her knowledge that calms you as you fall into the singularity you've swallowed, as you—the whole universe of you—is compacted down, swept clean, packed tight.

When you have all fallen in on yourself, she says, there will be a grand and a messy explosion. Shrapnel, chunks and blobs and incandescent energy. The heat and the fires of creation.

The promise of rebirth.

But for now, collapsing, the shark has consumed all there is to consume. The shark is a perfect machine.

And at the end of the world the shark is happy, after all.

Love Among the Talus

You cannot really keep a princess in a tower. Not if she has no brothers and must learn statecraft and dancing and riding and poisons and potions and the passage of arms, so that she may eventually rule.

But you can do the next best thing.

In the land of the shining empire, in a small province north of the city of Messaline and beyond the great salt desert, a princess with a tip-tilted nose lived with her mother, Hoelun Khatun, the Dowager Queen. The princess—whose name, it happens, was Nilufer—stood tall and straight as an ivory pole, and if her shoulders were broad out of fashion from the pull of her long oak-white bow, her dowry would no doubt compensate for any perceived lack of beauty. Her hair was straight and black, as smooth and cool as water, and even when she did not ride with her men-at-arms, she wore split, padded skirts and quilted, paneled robes of silk satin, all emerald and jade and black and crimson embroidered with gold and white chrysanthemums.

She needed no tower, for she was like unto a tower in her person, a fastness as sure as the mountains she bloomed beside, her cool reserve and mocking half-lidded glances the battlements of a glacial virginity.

Her province compassed foothills, and also those mountains (which were called the Steles of the Sky). And while its farmlands were not naturally verdant, its mineral wealth was abundant. At the moderate elevations, ancient terraced slopes had been engineered into low-walled, boggy paddies dotted with unhappy oxen. Women toiled there, bent under straw hats, the fermenting vegetation and glossy leeches which adhered to their sinewy calves unheeded. Farther up, the fields gave way to slopes of scree. And at the bottoms of the sheer, rising faces of the mountains, opened the nurturing mouths of the mines.

The mines were not worked by men; the miners were talus, living boulders with great stone-wearing mouths. The talus consumed ore and plutonic and metamorphic rocks alike (the sandstones, slates, schists, and shales, they found to be generally bereft of flavor and nutrition, but they would gnaw through them to obtain better) and excreted sand and irregular ingots of refined metal.

The living rocks were gentle, stolid, unconcerned with human life, although casualties occurred sometimes among the human talus-herders when their vast insensate charges wholly or partially scoured over them. They were peaceful, though, as they grazed through stone, and their wardens would often lean against their rough sides, enjoying the soothing vibrations caused by the grinding of their gizzards, which were packed with the hardest of stones. Which is to say carborundum—rubies and sapphires—and sometimes diamonds, polished by ceaseless wear until they attained the sheen of tumbled jewels or river rock.

Of course, the talus had to be sacrificed to retrieve those, so it was done only in husbandry. Or times of economic hardship or unforeseen expense. Or to pay the tithe to the Khagan, the Khan of Khans might-he-live-forever, who had conquered Nilufer's province and slain her father and brother when Nilufer was but a child in the womb.

There had been no peace before the Khagan. Now the warring provinces could war no longer, and the bandits were not free to root among the spoils like battle ravens. Under the peace of the Khanate and protection of the Khagan's armies, the bandit lords were often almost controlled.

So they were desperate, and they had never been fastidious. When *they* caught one of the talus, they slaughtered it and butchered the remains for jewels, and gold, and steel.

As has been mentioned, the princess of the land had no brothers, and the Khatun, finding it inexpedient to confine her only daughter until marriage (as is the custom of overzealous guardians in any age), preferred to train her to a terrifying certainty of purpose and to surround her with the finest men-at-arms in the land. To the princess and to her troop of archers and swordsmen, not incidentally, fell the task of containing the bandit hordes.

Now, the bandits, as you may imagine, had not been historically well-organized. But in recent years they had fallen under the sway of a new leader, a handsome strong-limbed man who some said had been a simple talus-herder in his youth, and others said was a Khanzadeh, a son of the Khagan, or the son in hiding of one of the Khagan's vanquished enemies, who were many. Over the course of time, he brought the many disparate tribes of bandits together under one black banner, and taught them to fletch their arrows with black feathers.

Whether it was the name he had been given at the cradleboard, none knew, but what he called himself was Temel.

To say that Nilufer could not be *kept* in a tower implies unfairly that she did not *dwell* in one, and that, of course, would be untrue. Her mother's palace had many towers, and one of those—the tallest and whitest of the lot—was entirely Nilufer's own. As has been noted, the Khatun's province was small—really no more than a few broad plateaus and narrow valleys— and so she had no need of more than one palace. But as has also been described, the Khatun's province was wealthy, and so that palace was lavish, and the court that dwelled within it thrived.

Nilufer, as befitted a princess who would someday rule, maintained her own court within and adjacent her mother's. This retinue was made up in part of attendants appointed by the Khatun—a tutor of letters, a tutor of sciences, a tutor of statecraft and numbers; a dancing-master; a master of hawk and horse and hound; a pair of chaperones (one old and smelling of sour mare's milk, the other middle-aged and stern); three monkish warrior women who had survived the burning of their convent by the Khagan some seventeen years before, and so come into the Khatun's service—and in part of Nilufer's own few retainers and gentlewomen, none of whom would Nilufer call friend.

And then of course there was the Witch, who came and went and prophesied and slept and ate as she pleased, like any cat.

On summer evenings, seeking mates, the talus crept from the mines to sing great eerie harmonies like the wails of wetted crystal. Nilufer, if she was not otherwise engaged, could hear them from her tower window.

Sometimes, she would reply, coaxing shrill satiny falls of music from the straight white bone of her reed flute. Sometimes, she would even play for them on the one that was made of silver.

Late one particular morning in spring, Nilufer turned from her window six towering stories above the rocky valley. The sun was only now stretching around the white peaks of the mountains, though gray twilight had given a respectable light for hours. Nilufer had already ridden out that morning, with the men-at-arms and the three monkish women, and had practiced her archery at the practice stumps and at a group of black-clad bandits, slaying four of seven.

Now, dressed for ease in loose garments protected by a roll-sleeved smock, she stood before an easel, a long, pale bamboo brush dipped in rich black ink disregarded in her right hand as she examined her medium. The paper was absorbent, thick. Soft, and not glossy. It would draw the ink well, but might feather.

All right for art, for a watercolor wash or a mountainscape where a certain vagueness and misty indirection might avail. But to scribe a spell, or a letter of diplomacy, she would have chosen paper glazed lightly with clay, to hold a line crisply.

Nilufer turned to the Witch, darting her right hand unconsciously at the paper. "Are you certain, old mother?"

The Witch, curled on a low stool beside the fire although the day was warm, lifted her head so her wiry gray braids slid over the motley fur and feathers of her epaulets. The cloak she huddled under might be said to be gray, but that was at best an approximation. Rather it was a patchwork thing, taupes and tans and grays and pewters, bits of homespun wool and rabbit fur and fox fur all sewed together until the Witch resembled nothing so much as a lichen-crusted granite boulder.

The Witch showed tea-stained pegs of teeth when she smiled. She was *never* certain. "Write me a love spell," she said.

"The ink is too thin," Nilufer answered. "The ink is too thin for the paper. It will feather."

"The quality of the paper is irrelevant to your purpose," the Witch said. "You must use the tools at hand as best you can, for this is how you will make your life, your highness."

Nilufer did not turn back to her window and her easel, though the sun had finally surmounted the peaks behind her, and slanted light suffused the valley. "I do not care to scribe a love spell. There is no man I would have love me, old mother."

The Witch made a rude noise and turned back to the fire, her lids drawing low over eyes that had showed cloudy when the dusty light crossed them. "You will need to know the how of it when you are Khatun, and you are married. It will be convenient to command love then, your highness."

"I will not marry for love," said the princess, cold and serene as the mountains beyond her.

"Your husband's love is not the only love it may be convenient to command, when you are Khatun. Scribe the spell."

The Witch did not glance up from the grate. The princess did not say *but I do not care to be Khatun.*

It would have been a wasted expenditure of words.

Nilufer turned back to her easel. The ink had spattered the page when she jerked her brush. The scattered droplets, like soot on a quartz rock, feathered there.

The princess did not sleep alone; royalty has not the privilege of privacy. But she had her broad white bed to herself, the sheets and featherbed tucked neatly over the planks, her dark hair and ivory face stark against the snowy coverlet. She lay on her back, her arms folded, as composed for slumber as for death. The older chaperone slept in a cot along the east side of the bed, and the youngest and most adamant of the monkish warrior women along the west side. A maid in waiting slept by the foot.

The head of the bed stood against the wall, several strides separating it from the window by which stood Nilufer's easel.

It was through this window—not on the night of the day wherein the princess remonstrated with the Witch, but on another night, when the nights had grown warmer—that the bandit Temel came. He scaled the tower as princes have always come to ladies, walking up a white silken rope that was knotted every arm's-length to afford a place to rest his feet and hands. He slipped over the window-sill and crouched beside the wall, his gloved hands splayed wide as spiders.

He had had the foresight to wear white, with a hood and mask covering his hair and all his face but for his eyes. And so he almost vanished against the marble wall.

The guardians did not stir. But Nilufer sat up, dark in her snowy bed, her hair a cold river over her shoulder and her breasts like full moons beneath the silk of her nightgown, and drew a breath to scream. And then she stopped, the breath indrawn, and turned first to the east and then to the west, where her attendants slumbered.

She let the breath out.

"You are a sorcerer," she told him, sliding her feet from beneath the coverlet. The arches flexed when she touched the cold stone floor: of a morning, her ladies would have knelt by the bed to shoe her. Scorning her slippers, she stood.

"I am but a bandit, princess," he answered, and stood to sweep a mocking courtesy. When he lifted his head, he looked past a crescent-shaped arrow-head, down the shaft into her black, unblinking eye, downcast properly on his throat rather than his face. She would never see him flinch, certainly not in moonlight, but *he* felt his eyelids flicker, his cheeks sting, a sharp contraction between his shoulder blades.

"But you've bewitched my women."

"Anyone can scribe a spell," he answered modestly, and then continued: "And I've come to bring you a gift."

"I do not care for your gifts." She was strong. Her arms, as straight and oak-white as her bow where they emerged from the armscyes of her night-gown, did not tremble, though the bow was a killing weapon and no mere toy for a girl.

His smile was visible even through the white silk of his mask. "This one, you will like."

No answer. Her head was straight upon the pillar of her neck. Even in the moonlight, he could see the whitening of her unprotected fingertips where they hooked the serving. A quarter-inch of steady flesh, that was all that stayed his death.

He licked his lips, wetting silk. "Perhaps I just came to see the woman who would one day be Nilufer Khatun."

"I do not care to be Khatun," Nilufer said.

The bandit scoffed. "What else are you good for?"

Nilufer raised her eyes to his. It was not what women did to men, but she was a princess, and he was only a bandit. She pointed with her gaze past his shoulder, to the easel by the window, on which a sheet of paper lay spread to dry overnight. Today's effort—the ideogram for *foundation*—was far more confident than that for *love* had been. "I want to be a Witch," she said. "A Witch and not a Queen. I wish to be not loved, but wise. Tell your bandit lord, if he can give me that, I might accept his gift."

"Only you can give yourself that, your highness," he said. "But I can give you escape."

He opened his hand, and a scrap of paper folded as a bird slipped from his glove. The serving, perhaps, eased a fraction along the ridges of her fingerprints, but the arrow did not fly.

The bandit waited until the bird had settled to the stones before he concluded, "And the bandit lord, as you call him, has heard your words tonight."

Then the arrow did waver, though she steadied it and trained it on his throat again. "Temel."

"At her highness' service."

Her breath stirred the fletchings. He stepped back, and she stepped forward. The grapnel grated softly on the stone, and before she knew it, he was over the sill and descending, almost silently but for the flutter of slick white silk.

Nilufer came to her window and stood there with the string of her long oak-white bow drawn to her nose and her rosebud lips, her left arm untrembling, the flexed muscles in her right arm raising her stark sinews beneath the skin. The moonlight gilded every pricked hair on her ivory flesh like frost on the hairy stem of a plant. Until the bandit prince disappeared into the shadow of the mountains, the point of her arrow tracked him. Only then did she unbend her bow and set the arrow in the quiver—her women slept on—and crouch to lift the paper bird into her hand.

Red paper, red as blood, and slick and hard so that it cracked along the creases. On its wings, in black ink, was written the spell-word for *flight*.

Blowing on fingers that stung from holding the arrow drawn so steady, she climbed back into her bed.

In the morning, the Khagan's caravan arrived to collect his tithe. The Khagan's emissary was an ascetic, moustached man, graying at the temples. The Witch said that he and the Khagan had been boys together, racing ponies on the steppes.

Hoelun Khatun arranged for him to watch the butchering of the talus from whose guts the tribute would be harvested, as a treat. There was no question but that Nilufer would also attend them.

They rode out on the Khatun's elderly elephant. An extravagance, on the dry side of the mountains. But one that a wealthy province could support, for the status it conferred.

A silk and ivory palanquin provided shade, and Nilufer thought sourly that the emissary was blind to any irony, but her face remained expressionless under its coating of powder as her feathered fan flicked in her hand. The elephant's tusks were capped with rubies and with platinum, a rare metal so impervious to fire that even a smelting furnace would not melt the ore. Only the talus could refine it, though once they excreted it, it was malleable and could be easily worked.

As the elephant traveled, Nilufer became acquainted with the emissary. She knew he watched her with measuring eyes, but she did not think he was covetous. Rather she thought more tribute might be demanded than mere stones and gold this time, and her heart beat faster under the cold green silk of her robes. Though her blood rushed in her ears, she felt no warmer than the silk, or than the talus' tumbled jewels.

The elephant covered the distance swiftly. Soon enough, they came to the slaughtering ground, and servants who had followed on asses lifted cakes and ices up onto the carpet that covered the elephant's back.

Despite its size and power, the slaughter of the talus was easily done. They could be lured from place to place by laying trails of powdered anthracite mixed with mineral oil; the talus-herders used the same slurry to direct their charges at the rock faces they wished mined. And so the beast selected for sacrifice would be led to the surface and away from others. A master stone-mason, with a journeyman and two apprentices, would approach the grazing talus and divine the location of certain vulnerable anatomic points. With the journeyman's assistance, the mason would position a pointed wrecking bar of about six feet in length, which the brawny apprentices, with rapid blows of their sledges, would drive into the heart—if such a word is ever appropriate for a construct made of stone—of the talus, such that the beast would then and there almost instantly die.

This was a hazardous proceeding, more so for the journeyman—rather trapped between the rock and the hammers, as it were—than the master or the apprentices. Masons generally endeavored to produce a clean, rapid kill, for their own safety, as well as for mercy upon the beast. (The bandits were less humane in their methods, Nilufer knew, but they too got the job done.) She licked crystals of ice and beet sugar from her reed straw, and watched the talus die.

On the ride back, the emissary made his offer.

Nilufer sought Hoelun Khatun in her hall, after the emissary had been feted through dinner, after the sun had gone down. "Mother," she said, spreading her arms so the pocketed sleeves of her over-robe could sweep like pale gold wings about her, "will you send me to Khara-Khorin?"

The possibility beat in her breast; it would mean dangerous travel, overland with a caravan. It would mean a wedding to Toghrul Khanzadeh, the sixth son of the Khagan, whom Nilufer had never met. He was said to be an inferior horseman, a merely adequate general, far from the favorite son of the Khagan and unlikely, after him, to be elected Khan of Khans.

But the offer had been for a consort marriage, not a morganatic concubinage. And if Toghrul Khanzadeh was unlikely to become Khagan, it was doubly unlikely that when his father died, his brothers would blot out his family stem and branch to preclude the possibility.

Hoelun Khatun rose from her cushions, a gold-rimmed china cup of fragrant tea in her right hand. She moved from among her attendants, dismissing them with trailing gestures until only the Witch remained, slumped like a shaggy, softly snoring boulder before the brazier.

The hall echoed when it was empty. The Khatun paced the length of it, her back straight as the many pillars supporting the arched roof above them. Nilufer fell in beside her, so their steps clicked and their trains shushed over the flagstones.

"Toghrul Khanzadeh would come here, if you were to marry him," said Nilufer's mother. "He would come here, and rule as your husband. It is what the Khagan wants for him—a safe place for a weak son."

Nilufer would have wet her lips with her tongue, but the paint would smear her teeth if she did so. She tried to think on what it would be like, to be married to a weak man. She could not imagine.

She did not, she realized, have much experience of men.

But Hoelun Khatun was speaking again, as they reached the far end of the hall and turned. "You will not marry Toghrul Khanzadeh. It is not possible."

The spaces between the columns were white spaces. Nilufer's footsteps closed them before and opened them behind as she walked beside her mother and waited for her to find her words.

Hoelun Khatun stepped more slowly. "Seventeen years ago, I made a bargain with the Khagan. Seventeen years, before you were born. It has kept our province free, Nilufer. I did what he asked, and in repayment I had his pledge that only you shall rule when I am gone. You must marry, but it is not possible for you to marry his son. Any of his sons."

Nilufer wore her face like a mask. Her mother's training made it possible; another irony no one but she would ever notice "He does not mean to stand by it."

"He means to protect a weak son." Hoelun Khatun glanced at her daughter through lowered lashes. "Parents will go to great lengths to protect their children."

Nilufer made a noncommittal noise. Hoelun Khatun caught Nilufer's sleeve, heedless of the paper that crinkled in the sleeve-pocket. She said, too quickly: "Temel could rise to be Khagan."

Nilufer cast a glance over her shoulder at the Witch, but the Witch was sleeping. They were alone, the princess and her mother. "Khan of Khans?" she said, too mannered to show incredulity. "Temel is a bandit."

"Nonetheless," Hoelun Khatun said, letting the silk of Nilufer's raiment slip between her fingers. "They say the Khagan was a prince of bandits when he was young."

She turned away, and Nilufer watched the recessional of her straight back beneath the lacquered black tower of her hair. The princess folded her arms inside the sleeves of her robes, as if serenely.

Inside the left one, the crumpled wings of the red bird pricked her right palm.

That night, in the tower, Nilufer unfolded the spell-bird in the darkness, while her attendants slept. For a rushed breathless moment her night-robes fell about her and she thought that she might suffocate under their quilted weight, but then she lifted her wings and won free, sailing out of the pile of laundry and into the frost-cold night. Her pinions were a blur in the dark as a dancing glimmer drew her; she chased it, and followed it down, over the rice-paddies where sleepless children watched over the tender seedlings, armed with sticks and rocks so wild deer would not graze them; over the village where oxen slept on their feet and men slept with their heads pillowed in the laps of spinning women; over the mines where the talus-herders mostly slumbered and the talus toiled through the night, grinding out their eerie songs.

It was to the mountains that it led her, and when she followed it down, she found she had lost her wings. If she had been expecting it, she could have landed lightly, for the drop was no more than a few feet. Instead she stumbled, and bruised the soles of her feet on the stones.

She stood naked in the moonlight, cold, toes bleeding, in the midst of a rocky slope. A soft crunching vibration revealed that the mossy thing looming in the darkness beside her was a talus. She set out a hand, both to steady herself on its hide and so it would not roll over her in the dark, and so felt the great sweet chime roll through it when it begin to sing. It was early for the mating season, but perhaps a cold spring made the talus fear a cold and early winter, and the ground frozen too hard for babies to gnaw.

And over the sound of its song, she heard a familiar voice, as the bandit prince spoke behind her.

"And where is your bow now, Nilufer?"

She thought he might expect her to gasp and cover her nakedness, so when she turned, she did it slowly, brushing her fingers down the hide of the hulk that broke the icy wind. Temel had slipped up on her, and stood only a few armlengths distant, one hand extended, offering a fur-lined cloak. She could see the way the fur caught amber and silver gleams in the moonlight. It was the fur of wolves.

"Take it," he said.

"I am not cold," she answered, while the blood froze on the sides of her feet. Eventually, he let his elbow flex, and swung the cloak over his shoulder.

When he spoke, his breath poised on the air. Even without the cloak she felt warmer; something had paused the wind, so there was only the chill in the air to consider. "Why did you come, Nilufer?"

"My mother wants me to marry you," she answered. "For your armies."

His teeth flashed. He wore no mask now, and in the moonlight she could see that he was comely and well-made. His eyes stayed on her face. She would not cross her arms for warmth, lest he think she was ashamed, and covering herself. "We are married now," he said. "We were married when you unfolded that paper. For who is there to stop me?"

There was no paint on her mouth now. She bit her lip freely. "I could gouge your eyes out with my thumbs," she said. "You'd make a fine bandit prince with no eyes."

He stepped closer. He had boots, and the rocks shifted under them. She put her back to the cold side of the talus. It hummed against her shoulders, warbling. "You would," he said. "If you wanted to. But wouldn't you rather live free, Khatun to a Khagan, and collect the tithes rather than going in payment of them?"

"And what of the peace of the Khanate? It has been a long time, Temel, since there was war. The only discord is your discord."

"What of your freedom from an overlord's rule?"

"My freedom to become an overlord?" she countered.

He smiled. He was a handsome man.

"How vast are your armies?" she asked. He was close enough now that she almost felt his warmth. She clenched her teeth, not with fear, but because she did not choose to allow them to chatter. In the dark, she head more singing, more rumbling, Another talus answered the first.

"Vast enough." He reached past her and patted the rough hide of the beast she leaned upon. "There is much of value in a talus." And then he touched her shoulder, with much the same affection. "Come, princess," he said. "You have a tiger's heart, it is so. But I would make this easy."

She accepted the cloak when he draped it over her shoulders and then she climbed up the talus beside him, onto the great wide back of the ancient animal. There were smoother places there, soft with moss and lichen, and it was lovely to lie back and look at the stars, to watch the moon slide down the sky.

This was a feral beast, she was sure. Not one of the miners. Just a wild thing living its wild slow existence, singing its wild slow songs. Alone, and not unhappy, in the way such creatures were. And now it would mate (she felt the secnd talus come alongside, though there was no danger; the talus docked side by side like ships, rather than one mounting the other like an overwrought stallion) and it might have borne young, or fathered them, or however talus worked these things.

But Temel warmed her with his body, and the talus would never have the chance. In the morning, he would lead his men upon it, and its lichen and moss and bouldery aspect would mean nothing. Its slow meandering songs and the fire that lay at its heart would be as nothing. It was armies. It was revolution. It was freedom from the Khan.

He would butcher it for the jewels that lay at its heart, and feel nothing.

Nilufer lay back on the cold stone, pressed herself to the resonant bulk and let her fingers curl how they would. Her nails picked and shredded the lichen that grew in its crevices like nervous birds picking their plumage until they bled.

Temel slid a gentle hand under the wolf-fur cloak, across her belly, over the mound of her breast. Nilufer opened her thighs.

She flew home alone, wings in her window, and dressed in haste. Her attendants slept on, under the same small spell which she had left them, and she went to find the Witch.

Who crouched beside the brazier, as before, in the empty hall. But now, her eyes were open, wide, and bright.

The Witch did not speak. That fell to Nilufer.

"She killed my father," Nilufer said. "She betrayed my father and my brother, and she slept with the Khagan, and I am the Khagan's daughter, and she did it all so she could be Khatun."

"So you will not marry the Khanzadeh, your brother?"

Nilufer felt a muscle twitch along her jaw. "That does not seem to trouble the Khagan."

The Witch settled her shoulders under the scrofular mass of her cloak. "Before I was the Witch," she said, in a voice that creaked only a little, "I was your father's mother."

Nilufer straightened her already-straight back. She drew her neck up like a pillar. "And when did you become a Witch and stop being a mother?"

The Witch's teeth showed black moons at the root where her gums had receded. "No matter how long you're a Witch, you never stop being a mother."

Nilufer licked her lips, tasting stone grit and blood. Her feet left red prints on white stone. "I need a spell, grandmother. A spell to make a man love a woman, in spite of whatever flaw may be in her." *Even the chance of another man's child?*

The Witch stood up straighter. "Are you certain?"

Nilufer turned on her cut foot, leaving behind a smear. "I am going to talk to the emissary," she said. "You will have, I think, at least a month to make ready."

Hoelun Khatun came herself, to dress the princess in her wedding robes. They should have been red for life, but the princess had chosen white, for death of the old life, and the Khatun would permit her daughter the conceit. Mourning upon a marriage, after all, was flattering to the mother.

Upon the day appointed, Nilufer sat in her tower, all her maids and warriors dismissed. Her chaperones had been sent away. Other service had been found for her tutors. The princess waited alone, while her mother and the men-at-arms rode out in the valley before the palace to receive the bandit prince Temel, who some said would be the next Khan of Khans. Nilufer watched them from her tower window. No more than a bowshot distant, they made a brave sight with banners snapping.

But the bandit prince Temel never made it to his wedding. He was found upon that day by the entourage and garrison of Toghrul Khanzadeh, sixth son of the Khagan, who was riding to woo the same woman, upon her express invitation. Temel was taken in surprise, in light armor, his armies arrayed to show peace rather than ready for war.

There might have been more of a battle, perhaps even a the beginnings of a successful rebellion, if Hoelun Khatun had not fallen in the first moments of the battle, struck down by a bandit's black arrow. This evidence of treachery from their supposed allies swayed the old queen's men to obey the orders of the three monkish warrior women who had been allies of the Khatun's husband before he died. They entered the fray at the Khanzadeh's flank.

Of the bandit army, there were said to be no survivors.

Noone mentioned to the princess that the black fletchings were still damp with the ink in which they had been dipped. No one told her that Hoelun Khatun had fallen facing the enemy, with a crescent-headed arrow in her back.

And when the three monkish warrior women came to inform Nilufer in her tower of her mother's death and found her scrubbing with blackened fingertips at the dark drops spotting her wedding dress, they also did not tell her that the outline of a bowstring still lay livid across her rosebud mouth and the tip of her tilted nose.

If she wept, her tears were dried before she descended the stair.

Of the Dowager Queen Nilufer Khatun—she who was wife and then widow of Toghrul Khanzadeh, called the Barricade of Heaven for his defense of his father's empire from the bandit hordes at the foothills of the Steles of the Sky—history tells us little.

But, that she died old.

Cryptic Coloration

Katie saw him first. The next-best thing to naked, in cutoff camouflage pants and high-top basketball sneakers and nothing else, except the thick black labyrinth of neo-tribal ink that covered his pale skin from collarbones to ankle-bones. He shone like piano keys, glossy-sleek with sweat in a sultry September afternoon.

Katie already had Melissa's sleeve in her hand and was tugging her toward the crosswalk. Gina trailed three steps behind. "We have *got* to go watch this basketball game."

"What?" But then Melissa's line of sight intersected Katie's and she gasped. "Oh my fuck, look at all that ink. Do you think that counts as a shirt or a skin?" Melissa was from Boston, but mostly didn't talk like it.

"Never mind the ink," Katie said. "Look at his *triceps*."

Little shadowed dimples in the undersides of his arms, and all Katie could think of for a moment was that he wasn't terribly tall, and if she had been standing close enough when he raised his hands to take a pass she could have stood on tiptoe and licked them. The image dried her mouth, heated her face.

Melissa would have thought Katie silly for having shocked herself, though, so she didn't say anything.

Even without the ink, he had the best body on the basketball court. Hard all over, muscle swelling and valleying as he sprinted and side-stepped, chin-length blond hair swinging in his eyes. He skittered left like a boxer, turned, dribbled between his legs—quadriceps popping, calves like flexed cables—caught the ball as it came back up and leaped. Parabolic, sailing. Sweat shook from his elbows and chin as he released.

A three-point shot. A high geometric arch.

Denied when a tall black boy of eighteen or so tipped it off the edge of the basket, jangling the chain, and fired back to half court, but that didn't matter. Katie glanced over her shoulder to make sure Gina was following.

"God," Melissa purred. "I love New York."

Katie, mopping her gritty forehead with the inside of her T-shirt collar, couldn't have agreed more.

So it was mid-September and still too hot to think. So she was filthy just from walking through the city air.

You didn't get anything like the blond boy back home in Appleton.

Melissa was a tall freckled girl who wore her hair in red pigtails that looked like braided yarn. She had a tendency to bounce up on her toes that made her seem much taller, and she craned over the pedestrians as they stepped up onto the far curb. "There's some shade by the—oh, my god would you look at that?"

Katie bounced too, but couldn't see anything except shirts. "Mel!"

"Sorry."

Flanking Gina, two steps ahead of her, they moved on. Melissa was right about the shade; it was cooler and had a pretty good view. They made it there just as the blond was facing off with a white-shirted Latino in red Converse All-Stars that were frayed around the cuffs. "Jump ball," Gina said, and leaned forward between Katie and Melissa.

The men coiled and went up. Attenuated bodies, arching, bumping, big hands splayed. Katie saw dark bands clasping every finger on the blond, and each thumb. More ink, or maybe rings, though wouldn't it hurt to play ball in them?

The Latino was taller; the blond beat him by inches. He tagged the ball with straining fingertips, lofted it to his team. And then he landed lightly, knees flexed, sucked in a deep breath while his elbows hovered back and up, and pivoted.

It wasn't a boy, unless a man in his early thirties counted.

"Holy crap," said Gina, who only swore in Puerto Rican. "Girls, that's *Doctor S.*"

Wednesday at noon, the three mismatched freshman girls who sat in the third row center of Matthew Szczegielniak's 220 were worse than usual. Normally, they belonged to the doe-eyed, insecure subspecies of first-year student, badly needing to be shocked back into a sense of humor and acceptance of their own fallibility. A lot of these young girls reminded Matthew of adolescent cats; trying so hard to look serene and dignified that they walked into walls.

And then got mad at you for noticing.

Really, that was even funnier.

Today, though, they were giggling and nudging and passing notes until he was half-convinced he'd made a wrong turn somewhere and wound up teaching a high school class. He caught the carrot-top mid-nudge while mid-sentence (Byron, Scott), about a third of the way through his introductory forty minutes on the Romantic poets, and fixed her with a glare through his spectacles that could have chipped enamel.

A red tide rose behind her freckles, brightening her sunburned nose. Her next giggle came out a squeak.

"Ms. Martinchek. You have a trenchant observation on the work of Joanna Baillie, perhaps?"

If she'd gone any redder, he would have worried about apoplexy. She stared down at her open notebook and shook her head in tiny quick jerks.

"No, Doctor S."

Matthew Szczegielniak rubbed his nose with the butt of his dry-erase marker, nudging his spectacles up with his thumbnail. He wasn't enough of a problem child to make his students learn his last name—even the simplified pronunciation he preferred—though the few that tried were usually good for endless hours of entertainment.

Besides, Matthew was a Mage. And magic being what it was, he would be hard put to imagine a more counterproductive activity than teaching three hundred undergrads a semester how to pronounce his *name*.

Enough heat of embarrassment radiated from Melissa's body to make Katie lean on her opposite elbow and duck her head in sympathy. She kept sneaking looks at Doctor S, trying to see past the slicked ponytail, the spectacles, the arch and perfectly bitchy precision of his lecturing style to find the laughing half-naked athlete of the day before.

She'd thought he was probably gay.

Sure, books, covers, *whatever*. It was impossible to believe in *him* exultant, shaking sweat from his hair, even though she'd seen it, even though the image fumed wisps of intrigue through her pelvis. Even though she could see the black rings on every finger and each thumb, clicking slightly when he gestured. She couldn't understand how she had never noticed them before. And never noticed the way he always dressed for class, though it was still hotter than Hades; the ribbed soft-colored turtleneck that covered him from the backs of broad hands to the tender flesh under his throat, the camel- or smoke- or charcoal-colored corduroy blazer that hid the shape of his shoulders and the width of his chest.

It was maddening, knowing what was under the clothes. She wondered if the barbaric tattoos extended everywhere, and flushed, herself, at least as bright as Melissa. And then brighter, as she felt the prof's eyes on her, as if he was wondering what she was thinking that so discomfited her.

Oh, lord, but wouldn't that have hurt?

On the other hand, he'd had the insides of his arms done, and the inner thighs. And *that* was supposed to hurt like anything, wasn't it?

And *then* she noticed that his left ear was pierced top to bottom, ten or a dozen rings, and sank down in her chair while she wondered what else he might have had done. And why she'd never noticed any of it—the rings, the earrings, the ink, the muscles—any of it, before.

"Oh, God," she whispered without moving her lips. "I'm never going to make it through this class."

But she did. And leaned up against the wall beside the door afterwards, shoulder-to-shoulder with Melissa while they waited for Gina to come out. Quiet, but if anybody was going to do something crazy or brave or both, it would be her. And right now, she was down at the bottom of the lecture hall, chatting up the professor.

"Oh, God," Katie moaned. "I'm going to have to switch sections. I didn't hear a word he said."

"I did. Oh, God. He knows my name." Melissa blushed the color of her plastic notebook cover all over again. Her voice dropped, developed a mocking precision of pronunciation. "Ms. Martinchek, maybe you can tell me about Joanna Ballyhoo . . . "

"Baillie." Gina, who came up and stood on tiptoe to stick a purple Post-it note to Melissa's tit. "He wrote it down for me. This way you can impress him next week."

Melissa picked the note off her chest and stared at it. "He uses purple Post-it notes?"

"I was right," Katie said. "He's gay."

"Do you want to find out?"

"Oh, and how do you propose we do that? Check the BiGALA membership roster?" Melissa might be scoffing, but her eyes were alight. Katie swallowed.

Gina checked her wristwatch. She had thick brown-black hair swept up in a banana clip, showing tiny curls like inverted devil horns at her pale nape. "He's got office hours until three. I say we grab some lunch and drop off our books, and then when he leaves we see where he goes."

"I dunno." Katie crossed her arms over her notebook. "It's not like playing basketball with your shirt off is a crime . . . "

"It's not like following someone to see where they go is a crime, either," Melissa pointed out. "We're not going to . . . stalk him."

"No, just stalk him."

"Katie!"

"Well, it's true." But Melissa was looking at her, and . . . she had come to Manhattan to have adventures. "What if we get caught?"

"Get caught . . . walking down a public street?"

Right. Whatever. "We could just look him up in the phone book."

"I checked. Not listed, amigas. Maybe it's under his boyfriend's name."

Even Melissa blinked at her this time. "Jesus Christ, Gomez. You're a criminal mastermind."

Those same three girls were holding up the wall when Matthew left the lecture theatre, climbing up the stairs to go out by the top door. He walked past, pretending not to notice them, or the stifled giggles and hiccups that erupted a moment later.

He just had time to grab a sandwich before his office hours. Almost one o'clock; probably nothing left but egg salad.

He needed the protein anyway.

He supplemented the sandwich with two cartons of chocolate milk, a bag of sourdough pretzels and three rip-top packets of French's mustard, and spread the lot out on his desk while he graded papers for his Renaissance drama class. With luck, no students would show up except a lonely or neurotic or favor-currying Ph.D. candidate, and he could get half of the papers done today.

He had twenty-four sophomores and juniors, and of the first ten papers, only two writers seemed to understand that *The Merry Wives of Windsor* was supposed to be funny. One of those was a Sociology major. Matthew was a failure as a teacher. He finished the sandwich, blew crumbs off his desk so he wouldn't leave mayonnaise fingerprints on the essays, and tore open the pretzels before he sharpened his red pencil one more time.

Honey mustard would have been better. He should get some to stick in his desk. Unless it went bad. Honey didn't go bad, and mustard didn't go bad. Logically, an amalgam would reflect the qualities of both.

The spike of ice and acid through the bones of his hands originated from his iron Mage's rings, and it not only made him drop a pretzel—

splattering mustard across the scarred wooden desk—but it brought him to his feet before he heard the police sirens start.

He glanced at the clock. Five more minutes. "That which thou hast promised thou must perform," he said, under his breath.

He left his lunch on the desk and found his keys in his pocket on the way to the door.

Their quarry almost ran them over as *they* were on their way in to start stalking him. Katie sidestepped quickly, catching Gina across the chest with a straight left arm. Melissa managed to get herself out of the way.

Doctor S. was almost running. His corduroy jacket flapped along the vent as he skidded between pedestrians, cleared four concrete steps in a bounce, and avoided a meandering traffic jam of students with as much facility as he'd shown on the basketball court. And if Katie had begun to suspect that it was just a bizarre case of mistaken identity, the toreador sidestep around the lady with the baby carriage would have disabused her. Doctor S. moved with a force and grace that were anything but common to academia.

Katie turned to follow him. It was only a small gesture to catch Gina's wrist, and without more urging, Gina trotted along beside her. Which was good, because Gina was strong *and* stubborn, even if she was only three apples high. Melissa took two more beats to get started, but her longer legs soon put her into the lead. "Slow down," Katie hissed, afraid that he would notice them running after him like three fools in a hurry, but frankly, he was getting away.

So when Melissa glared at her, she hustled, like you do. And Gina actually broke into a trot.

Doctor S. strode east on 68th, against traffic, towards the park. He never glanced over his shoulder, but kept rubbing his hands together as if they pained him. Maybe the rings were the magnet kind, for arthritis or something. RSI.

"I can't believe I never noticed he wears all those rings."

"I can't believe I never noticed the muscles," Melissa answered, but Gina said "Rings?"

"On all his fingers?" Melissa was too busy dodging pedestrians to give Gina the *were you born that stupid or do you practice hard?* look, and Katie was as grateful as she could spare breath for. They were disrupting traffic flow, the cardinal sin of New York's secular religion. Katie winced at another glare. Somebody was going to call her a fucking moron any second.

Gina sounded completely bemused. "I never noticed any rings."

Doctor S. continued east on 68th past Park Ave., down the rows of narrow-fronted brick buildings with their concrete window ledges. By the time he crossed Madison Ave., she was sure he was headed for the park. Every so often he actually skipped a step, moving as fast as he possibly could without breaking into a purse-snatcher sprint.

. . . he wasn't going to the park.

Halfway between Park and Fifth Avenue—which, of course, unlike Park, was on the park—traffic was gummed up behind flashing lights and restraining police. Doctor S. slowed as he approached, stuffing his hands back into his pockets—"Would you look at that?" Gina said, and Katie knew she, too, had suddenly noticed the rings—and dropping his shoulders, smallifying himself. He merged with the gawking crowd; Katie couldn't believe how easily he made himself vanish. Like a praying mantis in a rosebush; just one more green thorn-hooked stem.

"Okay," Melissa said, as they edged through bystanders, trying not to shove too many yuppies in the small of the back. "Stabbing?"

"Sidewalk pizza," Gina the Manhattanite said, pointing up. There was a window open on the sixth floor of one of the tenements, and Katie glimpsed a blue uniform behind it.

"Somebody *jumped*?"

"Or was pushed."

"Oh, God."

Gina shrugged, but let her hip and elbow brush Katie's. Solace, delivered with the appearance of nonchalance. And then, watching Doctor S. seem to vanish between people, betrayed only be metallic gleams of light off slick hair. She could pick him out if she knew where to look, if she remembered to look for the tan jacket, the hair. Otherwise, her eyes seemed to slide off him. *Creepy*, she thought. *He's almost not really there.*

And then she thought of something else. And maybe Melissa did too, because Melissa said, "Guys? What's he doing at a crime scene?"

"Or accident scene," Gina said, unwilling to invest in a murder without corroboration.

"Maybe he's a gawker."

"Ew." Katie tugged Gina's sleeve. "We should see if we can get closer. He probably won't notice us." And then she frowned. "How did he know about it?"

"Maybe he has a police scanner in his office?"

"So he's a vulture."

"Maybe he's an investigator. You know. Secret, like."

Katie rolled her eyes. "Right. Our gay college prof is Spiderman."

Gina snorted. "Hey. Everybody knows that Spidey and Peter Parker have a thing."

Melissa hunched down so her head wouldn't stick up so far above the crowd. Her hair was as bad as Doctor S.'s, and she didn't have his knack for vanishing into the scenery. "Gina," she said, "you go up, and tell us what's going on."

"I've seen dead people, chica."

"You haven't seen this one," Melissa said. "Go on. It might be important."

Gina shrugged, rolled her eyes, and started forward. And Melissa was right; a five foot tall Latina in gobs of eyeliner did, indeed, vanish into the crowd. "Criminal mastermind," Melissa said.

Katie grinned, and didn't argue.

This was the part of the job that Matthew liked least. There was no satisfaction in it, no resolution, no joy. The woman on the pavement was dead; face down, one arm twisted under her and the other outflung. She'd bounced, and she hadn't ended up exactly where she'd hit. She'd been wearing a pink blouse. Someone in the crowd beside him giggled nervously.

Matthew figured she hadn't jumped. He checked his wards—pass-unnoticed, which was not so strong as a pass-unseen, and considerably easier to maintain—and the glamours and ghosts that kept him unremarkable

His hands still ached; he really wished somebody would come up with a system for detecting malevolent magic that didn't leave him feeling like a B-movie bad guy was raking his fingerbones around with a chilled ice pick.

He pulled his cell phone from his pocket, buttoned the middle button on his jacket, and hit speed dial. He was one of five people who had the Promethean archmage's reach-me-in-the-bathtub number; he didn't abuse the privilege.

"Jane Andraste," she said, starting to speak before the line connected. He hadn't heard it ring on his end. "What's going on?"

"Apparent suicide at Fifth and 68th." He checked his watch. "It tickles. I'm on the scene and going to poke around a little. Are any of the responders our guys?"

"One second." Her voice muffled as she asked someone a question; there was a very brief pause, and she was back on the line. "Marla says Marion Thornton is en route. Have you met her?"

"Socially." By which he meant, at Promethean events and rituals. There were about two hundred Magi in the Greater New York area, and like Matthew, most of them held down two jobs: guardian of the iron world by night, teacher or artist or executive or civil servant by day.

They worked hard. But at least none of them had to worry about money. The Prometheus Club provided whatever it took to make ends meet. "I'll look for her."

"She'll get you inside," Jane said. "Any theories yet?"

Matthew crouched amid rubberneckers and bent his luck a little to keep from being stepped on. The crowd moved around him, but never quite squeezed him off-balance. Their shadows made it hard to see, but his fingers hovered a quarter-inch from a dime-sized stain on the pavement, and a chill slicked through his bones. "Not in a crowd," he said, and pulled his hand back so he wouldn't touch the drip accidentally. "Actually, tell Marion to process the inside scene on her own, would you? And not to touch anything moist with her bare hand, or even a glove if she can help it."

"You have a secondary lead?"

"I think I have a trail."

"Blood?"

It had a faint aroma, too, though he wouldn't bend close. Cold stone, guano, moist rancid early mornings full of last winter's rot. A spring and barnyard smell, with an underlying acridness that made his eyes water and his nose run. He didn't wipe his tears; there was no way he was touching his face after being near this.

He dug in his pocket with his left hand, cradling the phone with the right. A moment's exploration produced a steel disk the size of a silver dollar. He spat on the underside, balanced it like a miniature tabletop between his thumb and first two fingers, and then turned his hand over. A half-inch was as close as he dared.

He dropped the metal. It struck the sidewalk and bonded to the concrete with a hiss, sealing the stain away.

"Venom," Matthew said. "I've marked it. You'll need to send a containment team. I have to go."

When he stood, he looked directly into the eyes of one of his giggly freshmen.

"Ms. Gomez," he said. "Fancy meeting you here. Sorry I can't stay to chat."

Gina was still stammering when she came back. "Did you see that? Did you *see* that?"

Katie hadn't. "Just the backs of a bunch of tall people's heads. What happened?"

"I was trying to stay away from him," Gina said. "And he just *appeared* right beside me. Poof. Poof!"

"Or you weren't looking where you were going," Katie said, but Melissa was frowning. "Well?"

"He did just pop up out of nowhere," Melissa said. "I was watching Gina, and he kind of . . . materialized beside her. Like he stood up all of a sudden."

"He's the devil." Gina shook her head, but she sounded half-convinced.

Katie patted her on the shoulder, woven cotton rasping between her fingertips and Gina's flesh. "He could have been tying his shoe."

"Right," Gina said, stepping out from under Katie's hand. She pointed back to the crowd. "Then where did he go?"

Even glamoured, he couldn't run from a murder scene. The magic relied on symbol and focus; if he broke that, he'd find himself stuck in a backlash that would make him the center of attention of every cop, Russian landlady, and wino for fifteen blocks. So instead he walked, fast, arms swinging freely, trying to look as if he was late getting back from a lunch date.

Following the smell of venom.

He found more droplets, widely spaced. In places, they had started to etch asphalt or concrete. Toxic waste indeed; it slowed him, because he had to pause to tag and seal each one.

How it could move unremarked through his city, he did not know. There were no crops here for its steps to blight nor wells for its breath to poison.

Which was not to say it did no harm.

These things—some fed on flesh and some on blood and bone. Some fed on death, or fear, or misery, or drunkenness, or loneliness, or love, or hope, or white perfect joy. Some constructed wretchedness, and some comforted the afflicted.

There was no telling until you got there.

Matthew slowed as his quarry led him north. There were still too many bystanders. Too many civilians. He didn't care to catch up with any monsters in broad daylight, halfway up Manhattan. But as the neighborhoods became more cluttered and the scent of uncollected garbage grew heavy on the humid air, he found more alleys, more byways, and fewer underground garages.

If he were a cockatrice, he thought he might very well lair in such a place. Somewhere among the rubbish and the poison and the broken glass. The cracked concrete, and the human waste.

He needed as much camouflage to walk here undisturbed as any monster might.

His hands prickled ceaselessly. He was closer. He slowed, reinforcing his wards with a sort of nervous tic: checking that his hair was smooth, his coat was buttoned, his shoes were tied. Somehow, it managed to move from its lair to the Upper East Side without leaving a trail of bodies in the street. Maybe it traveled blind. Or underground; he hadn't seen a drop of venom in a dozen blocks. Worse, it might be invisible.

Sometimes . . . often . . . *otherwise* things had slipped far enough sideways that they could not interact with the iron world except through the intermediary of a Mage or a medium. If this had happened to the monster he sought, *then* it could travel unseen. *Then* it could pass by with no more harm done than the pervasive influence of its presence.

But then, it wouldn't drip venom real enough to melt stone.

Relax, Matthew. You don't know it's a cockatrice. It's just a hypothesis, and appearances can be deceptive.

Assuming that he had guessed right could get him killed.

But a basilisk or a cockatrice was what made sense. Except, why would the victim have thrown herself from her window for a crowned serpent, a scaled crow? And why wasn't everybody who crossed the thing's path being killed. Or turned to stone, if it was *that* sort of cockatrice?

His eyes stung, a blinding burning as if he breathed chlorine fumes, etchant. The scent was as much *otherwise* as real; Matthew suffered it more than the civilians, who would sense only the miasma of the streets as they were poisoned. A lingering death.

He blinked, tears brimming, wetting his eyelashes and blurring the world through his spectacles. A Mage's traveling arsenal was both eclectic and specific, but Matthew had never before thought to include normal saline, and he hadn't passed a drugstore for blocks.

How the hell is it traveling?

At last, the smell was stronger, the cold prickle sharper, on his left. He entered the mouth of a rubbish-strewn alley, a kind of gated brick tunnel not tall or wide enough for a garbage truck. It was unlocked, the grille rusted open; the passage brought him to a filthy internal courtyard. Rows of garbage cans—of course, no dumpsters—and two winos, one sleeping on cardboard, one lying on his back on grease-daubed foam reading a two-month-old copy of *Maxim*. The miasma of the cockatrice—if it was a cockatrice—was so strong here that Matthew gagged.

What he was going to do about it, of course, he didn't know.

His phone buzzed. He answered it, lowering his voice. "Jane?"

"The window was unlocked from the inside," she said. "No sign of forced entry. The resident was a fifty-eight-year-old unmarried woman, Janet Stafford. Here's the interesting part—"

"Yes?"

"She had just re-entered secular life, if you can believe this. She spent the last thirty-four years as a nun."

Matthew glanced at his phone, absorbing that piece of information, and put it back to his ear. "Did she leave the church, or just the convent?"

"The church," Jane said. "Marion's checking into why. You don't need to call her; I'll liaise."

"That would save time," Matthew said. "Thank you." There was no point in both of them reporting to Jane *and* to each other if Jane considered the incident important enough to coordinate personally.

"Are you ready to tell me yet what you think it might be?"

Matthew stepped cautiously around the small courtyard, holding onto his don't-notice-me, his hand cupped around the mouthpiece. "I *was* thinking cockatrice," he said. "But you know, now maybe not certain. What drips venom, and can lure a retired nun to suicide?"

Jane's breath, hissing between her teeth, was clearly audible over the cellular crackle. "Harpy."

"Yeah," Matthew said. "But then why doesn't it fly?"

"What are you going to do?"

"Right now? Question a couple of local residents," he said, and moved toward the Maxim-reading squatter.

The man looked up as he approached; Matthew steeled himself to hide a flinch at his stench, the sore running pus down into his beard. A lot of these guys were mentally ill and unsupported by any system. A lot of them *also* had the knack for seeing things that had mostly dropped *otherwise*, as if in being overlooked themselves they gained insight into the half-lit world.

And it didn't matter how he looked; the homeless man's life was still a life, and his only. *You can't save them all. But he had a father and mother and a history and a soul like yours.*

His city, which he loved, dehumanized; Matthew considered it the responsibility that came with his gifts to humanize it right back. It was in some ways rather like being married to a terrible drunk. You did a lot of apologizing. "Hey," Matthew said. He didn't crouch down. He held out his hand; the homeless man eyed it suspiciously. "I'm Matthew. You have absolutely no reason to want to know me, but I'm looking for some information I can't get from just anybody. Can I buy you some food, or a drink?"

Later, over milkshakes, Melissa glanced at Katie through the humidity-frizzled curls that had escaped her braid and said, "I can't believe we lost him."

The straw scraped Katie's lip as she released it. "You mean he gave us the slip."

Melissa snorted. On her left, Gina picked fretfully at a plate of French fries, sprinkling pinched grains of salt down the length of one particular fry and then brushing them away with a fingertip. "He just popped up. Right by me. And then vanished. I never took my eyes off him."

"Some criminal mastermind you turned out to be," Katie said, but her heart wasn't in it. Gina flinched, so Katie swiped one of her fries by way of apology. A brief but giggly scuffle ensued before Katie maneuvered the somewhat mangled fry into her mouth. She was chewing salt and starch when Melissa said, "Don't you guys think this is all a little weird?"

Katie swallowed, leaving a slick of grease on her palate. "No," she said, and slurped chocolate shake to clear it off. Her hair moved on her neck, and she swallowed and imagined the touch of a hand. A prickle of sensation tingled through her, the same excitement she felt at their pursuit of Doctor S., which she had experienced only occasionally while kissing her boyfriend back home. She shifted in her chair. "I think it's plenty weird."

She wasn't going to ask the other girls. Melissa had a boyfriend at Harvard that she traded off weekends with. Gina was . . . Gina. She picked up whatever boy she wanted, kept him a while, put him down again. Katie would rather let them assume that she wasn't all that innocent.

Not that they'd hate her. But they'd laugh.

"What are we going to do about it?" she asked, when Melissa kept looking at her. "I mean, it's not like he did something illegal."

"You didn't see the body up close."

"I didn't. But he didn't kill her. We know where he was when she fell."

Gina's mouth compressed askew. But she nodded, then hid her face in her shake.

Melissa pushed at her frizzing hair again. "You know," she said, "he left in a hurry. It's like a swamp out there."

"So?"

"So. Do you suppose his office door sticks?"

"Oh, no. That *is* illegal. We could get expelled."

"We wouldn't take anything." Melissa turned her drink with the tips of her fingers, looking at them and the spiraling ring left behind on the tabletop, not at Katie's eyes. "Just see if he has a police scanner. And look for his address."

"I'm not doing that," Katie said.

"I just want to see if the door is unlocked."

Melissa looked at Gina. Gina shrugged. "Those locks come loose with a credit card, anyway."

"No. Not just no."

"Oh, you can watch the stairs," Gina said, sharp enough that Katie sat back in her chair. Katie swallowed, and nodded. Fine. She would watch the goddamned stair.

"You want to finish?" she asked.

Gina pushed her mangled but uneaten fries away. "No, baby. I'm done."

The man's name was Henry; he ate an extraordinary amount of fried chicken from a red paper bucket while Matthew crouched on the stoop beside him, breathing shallowly. The acrid vapors of whatever Matthew hunted actually covered both the odor of unwashed man and of dripping grease, and though his eyes still watered, he thought his nose was shutting down in protest. Perversely, this made it easier to cope.

"No," Henry said. He had a tendency to slur his speech, to ramble and digress, but he was no ranting lunatic. Not, Matthew reminded himself, that it would matter if he was. "I mean, okay. I see things. More now than when I got my meds"—he shrugged, a bit of extra crispy coating clinging to his moustache—"I mean, I mean, not that I'm crazy, but you see things out of the corner of your eye, and when you turn? You see?"

He was staring at a spot slightly over Matthew's left shoulder when he said it, and Matthew wished very hard that he dared turn around and look. "All the damned time," he said.

The heat of the cement soaked through his jeans; the jacket was nearly unbearable. He shrugged out of it, laid it on the stoop, and rolled up his sleeves. "Man," Henry said, and sucked soft meat off bones. "Nice ink."

"Thanks," Matthew said, turning his arms over to inspect the insides.

"Hurt much? You don't look like the type."

"Hurt some," Matthew admitted. "What sort of things do you see? Out of the corners of your eyes?"

"Scuttling things. Flapping things." He shrugged. "When I can get a drink it helps."

"Rats? Pigeons?"

"Snakes," Henry said. He dropped poultry bones back into the bucket. "Roosters."

"Not crows? Vultures?"

"No," Henry said. "Roosters. Snakes, the color of the wall."

"Damn." Matthew picked up his coat. "Thanks, Henry. I guess it was a cockatrice after all."

What happened was, Katie couldn't wait on the stairs. Of course she'd known there wasn't a chance in hell that she could resist Melissa. But sometimes it was better to fool yourself a little, even if you knew that eventually you were going to crack.

Instead, she found herself standing beside Gina, blocking a sight line with her body, as Gina knocked ostentatiously on Doctor S.'s door. She slipped the latch with a credit card—a gesture so smooth that Katie could hardly tell she wasn't just trying the handle. She knocked again and then pulled the door open.

Katie kind of thought she was overplaying, and made a point of slipping through the barely opened door in an attempt to hide from passers-by that the room was empty.

Melissa came in last, tugging the door shut behind herself. Katie heard the click of the lock.

Not, apparently, that that would stop anybody.

Katie put her back against the door beside the wall and crossed her arms over her chest to confine her shivering. Gina moved into the office as if entranced; she stood in the center of the small cluttered room and spun slowly on her heel, hands in her hip pockets, elbows awkwardly cocked. Melissa slipped past her—as much as a six foot redhead could slip—and bent over to examine the desk, touching nothing.

"There has to be a utility bill here or something, right? Everybody does that sort of thing at work . . . "

Gina stopped revolving, striking the direction of the bookshelves like a compass needle striking north—a swing, a stick, a shiver. She craned her neck back and began inspecting titles.

It was Katie, after forcing herself forward to peer over Gina's shoulder, who noticed the row of plain black hardbound octavo volumes on one shelf, each with a ribbon bound into the spine and a date penned on it in silver metallic ink.

"Girls," she said, "do you suppose he puts his address in his journal?"

Gina turned to follow Katie's pointing finger and let loose a string of Spanish that Katie was pretty sure would have her toenails smoking if she understood a word. It was obviously self-directed, though, so after the obligatory flinch, she reached past Gina and pulled the most recently dated volume from the shelf.

"Can I use the desk?" The book cracked a little under the pressure of her fingers, and it felt lumpy, with wavy page-edges. If anything was pressed inside, she didn't want to scatter it.

Melissa stood back. Katie laid the book carefully on an uncluttered portion of the blotter and slipped the elastic that held it closed without moving the food or papers. The covers almost burst apart, as if eager to be read, foiling her intention to open it to the flyleaf and avoid prying. The handwriting was familiar: she saw it on the whiteboard twice a week. But that wasn't what made Katie catch her breath.

A pressed flower was taped to the left-hand page, facing a column of text. And in the sunlight that fell in bars through the dusty blind, it shimmered iridescent blue and violet over faded gray.

"Madre di Dio," Gina breathed. "What does it say?"

Katie nudged the book further into the light. "14 October 1995," she read. "Last year, Gin."

"He probably has the new one with him. What does it *say*?"

"It says 'Passed as a ten?' and there's an address on Long Island. Flanagan's, Deer Park Avenue. Babylon. Some names. And then it says 'pursuant to the disappearance of Sean Roberts—flower and several oak leaves were collected from a short till at the under-twenty-one club.' And *then* it says 'Faerie money?' Spelled F-a-e-r-i-e."

"He's crazy," Gina said definitively. "Schizo. Gone."

"Maybe he's writing a fantasy novel." Katie wasn't sure where her stubborn loyalty came from, but she was abruptly brimming with it. "We are reading his private stuff totally out of context. I don't think it's fair to judge by appearances."

Gina jostled her elbow; Katie shrugged the contact off and turned the page. Another record of a disappearance, this one without supporting evidence taped to the page. It filled up six pages. After that, a murder under mysterious circumstances. A kidnapping . . . and then some more pages on the Roberts disappearance. A broken, bronze-colored feather, also taped in, chimed when she touched it. She jerked her finger back.

One word underneath. "Resolved." And a date after Christmastime.

Doctor S., it seemed, thought he was a cop. A special kind of . . . supernatural cop.

"It sounds like *Nick Knight*," Melissa said. Katie blinked, and realized she had still been reading out loud.

"It sounds like a crazy man," Gina said.

Katie opened her mouth, and suddenly felt as if cold water drained down her spine. She swallowed whatever she had been about to say and flipped the journal to the flyleaf. There was indeed an address, on West 60th. "He's not crazy." *Not unless I am.*

"Why do you say that?" Melissa, gently, but Gina was looking at Katie too—not suspicious, or mocking, anymore, but wide-eyed, waiting for her to explain.

"Guys," Katie said, "He's a magician or something. Remember how he vanished on Gina? Remember the ink that you somehow just don't see? Remember the damned invisible rings?"

Melissa sucked her lower lip in and released it. "So did he kill that woman or not?"

"I don't know," Katie said. "I want him to be a good guy."

Gina patted her shoulder, then reached across to also pat the journal with her fingertips. "I say we go to his apartment and find out."

There were drawbacks to being a member of Matthew's society of Magi. For one thing, nobody else liked them. And with good reason; not only was the Prometheus Club full of snobs, Capitalists, and politicians, but its stated goal of limiting and controlling the influence of wild magic in the world put him in sworn opposition to any hedge-witch, Satanist, purveyor of herbs and simples, houngan, or priest of Santeria he might want to contract with for ritual supplies.

Such as, say, a white, virgin cockerel.

New York City was not bereft of live poultry markets, but given his rather specific needs, Matthew wasn't sure he wanted to trust one of those. He'd hate to find out at the last minute, for example, that his bird had had a few sandy feathers plucked. Or that it was, shall we say, a little more experienced than Matthew was himself.

And then there was the recent influenza scare, which had closed several poultry markets. And what he really needed, now that he thought about it, was an illegal animal; a fighting cock.

He booted his desktop system, entered an IP address from memory, wended his way through a series of logon screens, and asked about it on the Promethean message board.

Fortunately, even if Matthew didn't know something, it was a pretty good bet that *somebody* in Prometheus would.

Before close of business, he was twenty blocks north again, edging through a flaking avocado-green steel door into the antechamber of a dimly lit warehouse that smelled of guano and sawdust and corn and musty feathers. It drove the eyewatering stench of the cockatrice from Matthew's sinuses, finally, and seemed in comparison such a rich, wholesome smell that he breathed it deep and fast. He coughed, sneezed, and waved his hand in front of his face. And then he did it again, feeling as if the inside of his head were clean for the first time in hours.

There was a desk in a cage—not unlike the ones inhabited by the clucking, rustling chickens, but far larger—behind the half-wall at the far end of the dirty, hall-like room. Matthew approached it; a stout woman with her white hair twisted into a bun looked up from her game of solitaire.

He cleared his throat. "I need to buy a cockerel."

"I've got some nice Bantams," she said through the grate. "And a couple of Rhode Island Reds." Not admitting anything; those weren't fighting cocks. "You got a place to keep it? There are zoning things."

"It just needs to be pure white." He hesitated. "Or pure black."

She reached up casually and dropped the shutter in his face. Of course.

He sighed, and rapped on the grate, rattling the metal behind it. No answer. He rapped again, and again.

Five minutes later she cracked it up and peered under the bottom, through the little hole for passing papers and money back and forth. He caught a glimpse of bright black eyes and a wrinkled nose. "I'm not selling you any bird for your Satanic rituals, young man."

No, but you'll sell me one for bloodsports? Matthew sighed again and stuck his hand through the slot, nearly getting his fingers up her nose. She jerked back, but he caught the edge of the shutter before she could slide it closed again. His biceps bulged inside his shirt sleeve; his tendons dimpled his wrist. She leaned on the shutter, and couldn't shift him.

"Young man." A level, warning tone. She didn't look intimidated.

Oh, what the hell. "It's for the cockatrice," he said.

Her hand relaxed, and the weight of the shutter lifted. She slid it up; it thumped when it reached the top. "Why didn't you say so? About time somebody took care of that thing. Though I notice you didn't give a shit when it was just in East Harlem."

Matthew glanced aside. The cops were always the last to know.

She hesitated. "You'll need a human virgin too."

"Don't worry," he said, biting the inside of his cheek. "I've got that covered."

When he returned home, there was a woman waiting in his apartment. Not surprising in itself; Jane had a key and the passcode for the locks. But it wasn't Jane. It was the homicide detective, Marion Thornton.

She had an outdoorswoman's squint and silky brown hair that framed her long cheekbones in feathered wings; it made her look like a bright-eyed Afghan hound. She showed him her badge and handed him back the keys before he was fully in the door.

"The victim was an alcoholic," Marion said, re-locking the door as Matthew put his chicken on the counter. It was in a cardboard animal carrier. Occasionally a glossy jet-black beak or a malevolent eye would appear in one of the holes along the top. It scuffed and kicked. He pushed it away from the counter edge and it grabbed at him, as he thought of a line from a Russian fairy tale: *Listen, Crow, crow's daughter! Serve me a certain service—*

"The nun was a drunk?"

"To put it crudely. And we found another possible for the same bogey, about three days ago. Elderly man, never married, lived alone, drank like a fish. We're continuing to check back for others." She flipped pages in her report pad. "Here's something interesting. He was castrated in a farming accident when he was in his teens."

"Oh," Matthew said. "It's always virgins, isn't it?"

"For dragons and unicorns, anyway," Marion answered. "But I'd guess you're correct. And more than that. Heavy drinkers. Possibly with some talent; a link my . . . secular . . . colleagues won't come up with is that Promethean records show that we considered inviting both of these victims for apprenticeship when they were young."

"So they saw things," Matthew said, thinking of Henry, living on the monster's doorstep. If the thing had a preference for sexually inexperienced prey, that would explain why it hadn't eaten him yet. Well, if Matthew was prepared to make a few conjectures. "Do you think it wanted them because they drank, or they drank because they saw things?"

"We operate on the first assumption." Marion picked her way around him, leaned down to peer into the animal carrier. She pulled back as a grabbing beak speared at her eye. "Vicious."

"I sure hope so."

"Jane said you had a possible ID on the bogey?"

He knelt down and began peeling the rug back, starting beside the inside wall of the living room. "The black cock isn't enough of a hint?"

"Basilisk."

"That's a weasel. Cockatrice, I'm guessing. Though how it lured its victim into hurling herself from her window is beyond me. You're describing very specialized prey."

She straightened up and arched, cracking her spine. She picked a spoon off the breakfast bar and turned it, considering the way the light pooled in the bowl. "Call it one in ten thousand? Then the Greater New York metropolitan area has, what, two thousand more just like 'em?"

"Something like that," Matthew said, and pinched the bridge of his nose. A dust bunny was stuck to the heel of his hand; he blew it off. When he opened his eyes, he found her staring at him, tongue-tip peeking between her lips.

"Want to make sure we're safe?" she said, with a grin. The spoon glittered as she turned it beside her face. "I'm off duty. And your chicken won't mind." She held up her left hand and showed him a plain gold band. "No hassles."

He bit his lower lip. Matthew had practice. And years of careful sublimation—which was, of course, the point: sacrifice made power. He also had a trick of flying under the gaydar, of making straight women think he was gay and gay men think he was straight. All just part of the camouflage.

He hated having to say no. "Sorry," he said. "That's a lovely offer. But I need a virgin for the cockatrice already, and it beats having to send out."

She laughed, of course.

They never believed him.

"Come on," he said. "Help me ensorcel this chicken."

Doctor S. lived in Midtown West, on 60th near Columbus Ave. It was kind of a hike, but they got there before sunset. It wouldn't get dark for an hour, but that was only because the afternoons were still long. By the time they paused down the block Katie's stomach was rumbling. That milkshake was only good for so long.

The spot they picked to loiter had a clear view of the front door of Doctor S.'s brown brick apartment building. "Nice place for a junior professor," Melissa said, and for ten seconds she sounded like she was from Boston, all right.

Katie looked at Gina and made big eyes and whimpering noises, but it was Melissa who went and got convenience store hot dogs, Diet Pepsi, and a bag of chips. They ate in the shade on the north side of the building, the heat soaking from the stones, their hair lank and grimy with the city air. Katie scratched her cheek and brought her fingernails away sporting black crescents. "Ew."

"Welcome to New York," Gina said, which was what she said every time Katie complained.

Katie had nearly stopped complaining already. She scratched her nails against her jeans until most of the black came out and finished her hot dog one-handed, then wiped the grime from her face with the napkin before drying her hands. It worked kind of halfway—good enough, anyway, that when Melissa splashed ice water from a sport bottle into everyone's cupped hands and Katie in turn splashed it onto her face, she didn't wind up feeling like she'd faceplanted into a mud puddle.

The second handful, she drank, and only realized she had been carrying a heat headache when the weight of it faded. "All right," she said, and took the bottle from Melissa to squirt some on her hair. "Ready as I'll ever be."

"Unfortunately, apparently Doctor S. isn't," Melissa said, reclaiming the bottle to drink. She tilted her head back, her throat working, and as she lowered it a droplet ran from the corner of her mouth. "No, wait, spoke too soon."

Katie stepped behind the pole of a street lamp—silly, because Doctor S. wasn't even looking in their direction—and caught sight of his stiff little blond ponytail zigzagging through the crowd. He was wearing another sort-of costume—Katie wondered what he wore when he wore what he liked, rather than what suited his role—a well-cut gray suit with a fabulous drape. A woman in a navy pantsuit, whose light flyaway hair escaped its pins around a long narrow face, walked alongside him. Her stride was familiar. She had a white cardboard pet carrier slung from her left hand; Katie could not see what was in it, but it swung as if something was moving slightly inside.

"Isn't that the cop who showed up where the woman jumped?"

Katie glanced at Gina and back at the woman, a stuttering doubletake. It was. Not the same outfit, and her hair was clipped back aggressively now—though it wasn't staying restrained—but the woman was conspicuous. "Well," Katie said, feeling as if she watched the words emerge from a stranger's mouth, "we could follow him and find out where they're going."

Neither Matthew nor Marion was particularly sanguine about attacking on a cockatrice in the dark. They had to take the subway across the island (at least the cockerel was quiet, huddled in the bottom of its carrier) but still ascended to the surface with light to spare. It roused the bird; Matthew heard it shift, and Marion kept her fingers well clear of the air holes. It was, as promised, aggressive.

Matthew shoved down guilt and substantial apprehension. There was no other choice, and power grew out of sacrifices.

They found the courtyard without a problem, that tunnel-like entrance with its broken gate leaving rust on Matthew's clothes as they slipped through. He wasn't wearing his usual patrol clothes, a zipped camouflage jacket and boots enchanted to pass-unnoticed, but a gray silk suit with a linen shirt and a silver, red, and navy tie. A flask in an inside pocket tapped his ribs when he moved. He looked like a dot com paper millionaire on his way to a neck-or-nothing meeting with a crotchety venture capitalist who was going to hate his ponytail.

His clothes today, and the quick preliminary ritual they'd performed in his living room, were not designed to conceal him, to occlude his power, but rather to draw the right attention. If you squinted at him with otherwise eyes, he would shine. And other than his rings and the earrings and the pigment in the ink under his skin, he wasn't wearing any iron, as he might have been if they went to face something Fae.

Iron was of no use against a cockatrice. Except in one particular, and so two steel gaffs wrapped in tissue paper nested in the bottom of Matthew's trouser pocket. He touched them through fabric like a child stroking a favorite toy and drew his hand back when they clinked.

"This is it," he said.

Marion set the carrier down. "Nice place you've got here, Matthew. Decorate it yourself?" From the way her nose was wrinkling, she picked out the acid aroma of the monster as well.

Henry and his comrade at arms were nowhere to be seen. Matthew hoped they had taken his advice and moved on. He hated working around civilians.

Without answering Marion, he kicked aside garbage, clearing a space in the center of the court. The windows overlooking it remained unoccupied, and if for some reason they did not continue so, Marion had a badge.

She helped Matthew sketch a star overlaid on a circle in yellow sidewalk chalk. They left one point open, facing south by Marion's compass. When they were done, Matthew dusted his hands, wiped them on his handkerchief, and reached into his pockets for the spurs, the flask, and something else—a leather hood of the sort used by falconers to quiet their birds.

"Ready?"

She nodded. "Where's the lair?"

He patted himself on the chest—"the s.o.b. comes to us"—and watched her eyes widen. She had thought he was kidding.

They always did.

Well, maybe someday he could catch a unicorn.

"It's okay," he said, when her blush became a stammer. "Let's get the knives on this chicken."

It took both of them, crouched on either side, to open the box and hood the bird without harming it. It exploded into Matthew's grip as Marion pried open the flaps; he caught at it, bungled the grab and got pecked hard for his pains. Somehow he got the bird pressed to his chest, a struggling fury of iridescent black plumage, and caged it in his blunt hands. It felt prickly and slick and hotter than blood under the feathers. He smoothed its wings together and restrained the kicking legs, while Marion dodged the jabbing beak. Once in darkness it quieted, and Marion strapped the three-inch gaffs over its own natural spurs.

When they were done, it looked quite brave and wicked, the gleam of steel on rainbow-black. Marion stroked its back between Matthew's fingers, her touch provoking a tremor when she brushed the back of his hand. "Fucking abomination."

She meant cockfighting, not the bird. Matthew set the cockerel down and moved his hands away. It sat quietly. "How do you think I feel?"

She shrugged. Still crouched, she produced a pair of handcuffs and a silken hood from her tan leather handbag. Matthew bent over to pick up the flask. "God, I hate this part."

He prized it open with his thumb and upended it over his mouth. The fumes of hundred-and-fifty-proof rum made him gasp; he choked down three swallows and stopped, doubled over, rasping.

Matthew didn't often drink.

But that would be enough for the spell.

Light-headed, now, sinuses stinging from more than the reek of the cockatrice, Matthew handed Marion the flask and then his spectacles, feeling naked without them. He wiped his mouth on the back of his hand, fine hairs harsh on his lips. Four steps took him through the open end of the pentagram.

He turned back and faced Marion. With the silk of the hood draped over his forearm, he handcuffed himself—snugly: he did not want his body breaking free while he was not in it.

They weren't replaceable.

He took one more deep breath, closed his eyes on Marion's blurry outline, and with his joined wrists rattling pulled the hood over his head.

In the dark underneath, sounds were muffled. Concentrated rum fumes made his eyes water, but at least he could no longer smell the cockatrice. Chalk grated—Marion closing the pentagram. He heard his flask uncorked, the splash of fluid as she anointed the diagram with the remaining rum. Matthew tugged restlessly against the restraints on his wrists as she began to chant and a deep uneasy curdling sensation answered.

God, too much rum. He wobbled and caught himself, fretting the handcuffs, the tightness on the bones. The sensual thrill of the magic sparking along his nerves was accentuated by the blinding darkness. He wobbled again, or maybe the world did, and gasped at the heat in his blood.

Magic and passion weren't different. It was one reason sublimation worked.

The second gasp came cleaner, no fabric muffling his face, the air cooler if not fresher and the scent of rum less cloying. Marion seemed to have moved, by the sound of her chanting, and somehow the tightness had jumped from Matthew's wrists to his calves. He lay belly-down on rough ground.

He pushed with his arms to try to balance himself to his feet. The chanting stopped, abruptly, and someone was restraining him, folding his arms against his side gently but with massive cautious strength. "Matthew?"

He turned his head, seeking the voice. It echoed. The . . . arms? holding him retreated. "Matthew, if you understand me, flap once."

He extended odd-feeling arms and did so. A moment later, a half-dozen fists, it seemed, were unhooding him. He blinked at dizzy brilliance, and found himself staring into Marion's enormous face from only a few inches away. He hopped back and fouled himself on the gaffs. Fortunately, the needle point slipped between his feathers rather than stabbing him in the wing, and he stopped, precariously balanced, wings half-bent like broken umbrellas.

He clucked.

And flapped hard, surprised to find himself lifting off the ground. He flew the two feet to Marion's shoulder, landed awkwardly, facing the wrong way, and banged her in the eye with his wing. At least he had the sense to turn carefully, keeping the needle-tipped gaffs pointed away from her thin-skinned throat. He crouched on his heels, trying not to prick her with his claws, the alien body's balance far better than his own.

Only if he thought about it did he realize that the warm shoulder he nestled to Marion's warm cheek was feathered, that it was peculiar to be able to feel the beats of her heart through his feet like the footfalls of an approaching predator, that the colors he saw were abruptly so bright and saturated—so discriminate—that he had no names for them. That he balanced on her moving shoulder as easily as he would have roosted on a swaying branch, and that that was peculiar.

"Wow," he said. And heard a soft contemplative cluck. And laughed at himself, which came out a rising, tossing crow.

Marion flinched and put a hand up on his wing. "Matthew, please. My ears."

He ducked his head between his shoulders, abashed, and clucked *sorry*. Maybe she would understand.

His body stood stolidly, restrained, inside a wet circle of chalk and rum. The cockerel wearing it was quieted by the hood and the handcuffs, and Matthew turned his head right and left to center himself in his vision. He failed—he had the peripheral view, and only by turning to see it first with one eye and then the other could he reliably guess how far away it was. Almost no binocular vision, of course. But with a shock, he realized that he could see clearly around to the back of his head.

That was pretty tremendously weird. He'd have to practice that. And think about his small sharp body and its instincts, because the enemy could be along any moment.

Marion was pulling back, stepping into the shadows, an alcove near the gate concealing them. Matthew pressed against her warmth, feeling her heart beating faster. He clucked in her ear.

"Shh."

He hoped the cockatrice would come quickly. This could be very, very awkward to explain if something happened to the glamours. Still, they had brought alcohol, talent, and innocence—symbolically speaking—and left them, special delivery, in the thing's front yard. Wherever it was nesting, it should come to investigate before too long.

He was still thinking that when he heard the singing.

The three of them had been following for a long time, it seemed, when Doctor S. and the woman gave one another a conspiratorial glance and stepped through an archway, past a rusted gate. Gina drew up short, stepping out of the traffic flow into the shelter of a doorway. A moment later, Katie heard glass breaking and something kicked or thrown.

Katie ducked in behind Gina, rubbing her elbow nervously. This wasn't the best neighborhood at all. "That's a dead end, I bet," Gina said, when Melissa came up beside them. "Either they're going inside, or that's where they're going."

"Here?"

Gina winked. "Want to sneak up and peek through the gate?"

Katie and Melissa exchanged a glance, and Melissa angled her head and said, "What the heck." Side by side, the three stepped back out onto the sidewalk, picking their way over chewing gum spots and oily, indeterminate stains. Katie somehow found herself in the lead, as Gina and Melissa fell in single file behind her. She had to glance over her shoulder to make sure they were still with her.

She stopped two feet shy of the broken gate and tried to still her hammering heart. No luck, and so she clenched her hands at her sides and edged forward.

She could see through plainly if she kept her back to the wall and turned her head sideways. She saw Doctor S. and the cop sketch the diagram, saw them pull a black rooster from the box and do something to its head and feet. She flinched, expecting some bloody and melodramatic beheading, but instead Doctor S. went to the center of the star and began chaining himself up, which made her feel distinctly funny inside. And then he blindfolded himself with a hood, and the woman did some more sketching with the chalk and walked around the circle pouring something in between its lines from a flask.

A moment later, the rooster began to struggle, while Doctor S. stood perfectly still. The woman crouched down and unhooded it, and a moment later it flapped onto her shoulder and settled itself.

"This," Melissa whispered, a warm pressure against Katie's side, "is freaking weird."

"Gosh," Gina said, very loudly, "would you listen to that?"

Katie turned to shush her, and heard it herself. She took a deep breath, chest expanding against her shirt, as if she could inhale the music too. It seemed to swell in her lungs and belly, to buoy her. She felt Melissa cringe, and then fingers caught at her shoulder. "Fuck," Melissa said. "What is that?"

"Beautiful." Katie stepped forward, moving out of Melissa's grasp. Into the courtyard, toward the woman and the chicken and the blindfolded English professor. Katie lifted her arms and twirled, her feet light as if she walked on flowers. She strode through a pile of garbage that the magicians had piled up when they cleared the center of the courtyard and her airy foot came down on glass.

A cracked bottle broke further under her foot, shattering and crunching. The soft sole of Katie's tennis sneaker clung to broken glass; she picked it up again and stepped forward, to another crunch.

The noise was almost lost under the music. Rising chorales, crystalline voices.

"It sounds like a rat being shaken to death in a bag of hammers," Melissa groaned, and then sucked in a squeak. "Oh, fuck, Katie, your foot . . ."

There was something slick between her sole and the bottom of the shoe. She must have stepped in a mud puddle. She looked down. Or a puddle of blood.

Well, her foot was already wet. And the singers were over there somewhere. She took one more step, Melissa's fingers brushing her wrist as her friend missed her grab. Behind her, Melissa made funny sobbing noises, as if she'd been running and couldn't get a breath.

Somehow, Gina had gotten ahead of her, and was walking too, kicking rubbish out of the way with her sandaled feet, crunching through more glass, leaving red footsteps. The courtyard was filthy, the buildings moldy-looking, scrofulous: brick black with soot and flaking mortar.

Something moved against the wall. A gleam of brightness, like sun through torn cloth. And then—so beautiful, so bright, oh—a spill of jadevioletandazure, a trailing cloak of feathers, a sort of peacock or bird of paradise emerging like an image reflected in a suddenly lit mirror. Its crested head was thrown back, its long neck swollen with song. Its wings mantled and rays of light cracked from between its feathers.

Gina was still ahead of her, between her and the bird. Katie reached out to push her, but then suddenly she was gone, fallen down, and Katie stepped over her. It was the most beautiful thing she'd ever seen. It was the most beautiful thing she'd ever heard.

And oh, it was blind, the poor thing was blind. Somebody had gouged out its eyes, she saw now. The old wounds were scarred gray, sightless.

And still it sang.

She reached out her hand to touch it, and couldn't understand why Melissa was screaming.

Matthew saw both young women hurry across the glass and stones, faster than he could reach them—not that he could have stopped them. Even though he was airborne, and already on his way.

He saw his body react, too—it hurled itself at the edge of the pentagram, hurled and kept hurling, but the wards they'd so carefully constructed held him, and he bounced from them and slid down what looked like plain still air. So strange, watching himself from the outside. Marion and the red-haired girl both crumpled, Marion with her hands over her ears, belly-crawling determinedly toward the running children; Melissa Martinchek down in a fetal position, screaming.

And he saw the cockatrice.

The movement caught his eye first, a ripple of red like brick and gray like concrete, its hide patterned in staggered courses that blended precisely with the blackened wall behind it. It was bigger than a cock, but not by much, and his rooster's heart churned with rage at its red upright comb and the plumed waterfall of its tail. His wings beat in midair; he exploded after it like a partridge from cover.

It chameleoned from stone to brilliance, colors chasing over its plumage like rainbows over oil. The two girls clutched for it, their feet pierced with unnoticed shards, their hands reaching.

Matthew saw them fall, their bodies curled in around their poisoned hands. He saw the way they convulsed, the white froth dripping from the corners of their mouths.

He shrieked war, wrath, red rage, and oblivion. The spurs were heavy on his shanks; his wings were mighty upon the air. He struck, reaching hard, and clutched at the enemy's neck.

An eruption of rainbow-and-black plumage, a twist and strike and movement like quicksilver on slanted glass. Matthew's gaff slashed the cockatrice's feathers; the cockatrice whipped its head back and forward and struck like a snake. Pearl-yellow droplets flicked from fangs incongruous in a darting beak; the rooster-tail fanned and flared, revealing the gray coils of an adder.

Matthew beat wings to one side; his feathertips hissed where the venom smoked holes through them. He backwinged, slashed for the cockatrice's eye, saw too late that that wound had long ago been dealt it. A black cockerel was immune to a cockatrice's deadly glare, and to the poison of its touch. If he could hit it, he could hurt it.

Except it wasn't a cockatrice, not exactly. Because cockatrices didn't sing like loreleis, and they didn't colorshift for camouflage. Maybe it was hatched by a chameleon rather than a serpent, Matthew thought, beating for altitude, and then reminded himself that now was not the time for theory.

Some kind of hybrid, then.

Just his luck.

And now the thing was airborne, and climbing in pursuit. He dropped— the cockerel was not more than passably aerodynamic—and struck for its back, its wing, its lung. The breast was armored, under the meat, with the anchoring keel bones. His spurs would turn on those. But they might punch through the ribs, from above.

He missed when the monster side-slipped, and the blind cockatrice turned and sank its fangs into his wing. Pain, heat and fire, weld-hot needles sunk into his elbow to the bone. He cackled like a machine gun and fell after the monster; wing-fouled, they tumbled to stone.

It lost its grip at the shock of impact, and Matthew screamed fury and pain. The hurt wing trailed, blood splashing, smoke rising from the envenomed wound. He made it beat anyway, dragged himself up, his spurs scraping and sparking on stone. The cockatrice hissed as he rose; his flight was not silent.

They struck hard, breast to breast, grappling legs and slashing spurs. He had his gaffs; the cockatrice had weight and fangs and a coiling tail like a rubber whip. Wings struck, buffeted, thundered. The cockatrice had stopped singing, and Matthew could hear the weeping now. Someone human was crying.

The cockatrice's talons twined his. Left side, right side. Its wings thumped his head, its beak jabbed. Something tore; blood smeared its beak, his face. He couldn't see on his right side. He ripped his left leg free of its grip and punched, slashed, hammered. The gaff broke skin with a pop; the cockatrice's blood soaked him, tepid, no hotter than the air. A rooster's egg hatched by a serpent.

The cockatrice wailed and thrashed; he ducked its strike at his remaining eye. More blood, pumping, slicking his belly, gumming his feathers to his skin. The blood was venom too. The whole thing was poison; its blood, its breath; its gaze; its song.

The monster fell on top of him. He could turn his head and get his eye out from under it, but when he did, all he saw was Marion, each arm laced under one of Melissa's armpits, holding the redheaded girl on her knees with a grim restraint while Melissa tried to tear herself free, to run to the poisoned bodies of her friends. The bodies were poison too, corrupted by the cockatrice's touch. The very stones soaked by its heart's blood could kill.

It was all venom, all deadly, and there was no way in the world to protect anyone. Not his sacrifice, not the unwitting sacrifice of the black cockerel, made any goddamned difference in the end.

Matthew, wing-broken, one-eyed, his gaff sunk heel-deep in the belly of his enemy, lay on his back under its corpse-weight and sobbed.

The building was emptied, the block closed, the deaths and the evacuations blamed on a chemical spill. Other Prometheans would handle the detox.

Matthew, returned to his habitual body, took the shivering black cockerel to a veterinarian with Promethean sympathies, who—at Matthew's insistence and Jane's expense—amputated his wing and cleaned and sewed shut his eye. Spared euthanasia, he was sent to a farm upstate to finish his days as a lopsided, piratical greeter of morning. He'd live long, with a little luck, and father many pullets.

Matthew supposed there were worse deaths for a chicken.

Marion did the paperwork. Matthew took her out to dinner. She didn't make another pass, and they parted good friends. He had a feeling he'd be seeing her again.

There were memorial services for his students, and that was hard. They were freshmen, and he hadn't known them well; it seemed . . . presumptuous to speak, as if his responsibility for their deaths gave him some claim over their lives. He sat in the back, dressed in his best black suit, and signed the guest book, and didn't speak.

Katherine Berquist was to be buried in Appleton, Wisconsin; Matthew could not attend. But Regina Gomez was buried in a Catholic cemetery in Flushing, her coffin overwhelmed with white waxy flowers, her family swathed in black crepe and summer-weight worsted, her friends in black cotton or navy. Melissa Martinchek was there in an empire-waisted dress and a little cardigan. She gave Matthew a timid smile across the open grave.

The scent of the lilies was repellent; Matthew vomited twice on the way home.

Melissa came to see him in the morning, outside of his regular office hours, when he was sitting at his desk with his head in his heads. He dragged himself up at the knock, paused, and sat heavily back down.

Thirty seconds later, the locked door clicked open. It swung on the hinges, and Melissa stepped inside, holding up her student ID like a talisman. "The lock slips," she said. "Gina showed me how. I heard, I heard your chair."

Gina's name came out a stammer too.

"Come in," Matthew said, and gestured her to a dusty orange armchair. She locked the door behind her before she fell into it. "Coffee?"

There was a pot made, but he hadn't actually gotten up and fetched any. He waved at it vaguely, and Melissa shook her head.

He wanted to shout at her—*What were you thinking? What were you doing there?*—and made himself look down at his hands instead. He picked up a letter opener and ran his thumb along the dull edge. "I am," he said, when he had control of his voice again, "so terribly sorry."

She took two sharp breaths, shallow and he could hear the edge of the giggle under them. Hysteria, not humor. "It wasn't your fault," she said. "I mean, I don't know what happened." She held up her hand, and his words died in his open mouth. "I don't . . . I don't *want* to know. But it wasn't your fault."

He stood up. He got himself a cup of coffee and poured one for her, added cream and sugar without asking. She needed it. Her eyes were pink-red around the irises, the lower lids swollen until he could see the mucous membrane behind the lashes. She took it, zombie-placid.

"I was safe inside the circle," he said. "I was supposed to be the bait. Gina and Katie were unlucky. They were close enough to being what it wanted that it took them, instead. As well. Whatever."

"What did . . . it want?"

"Things feed on death." He withdrew on the excuse of adding more sugar to his coffee. "Some like a certain flavor. It might even. . . . "

He couldn't say it. It might even have been trying to lure Matthew out. That would explain why it had left its safe haven at the north end of the island, and gone where Prometheus would notice it. Matthew cringed. If his organization had some wardens in the bad neighborhoods, it might have been taken care of years ago. If Matthew himself had gone into its court unglamoured that first time, it might just have eaten him and left the girls alone.

A long time, staring at the skim of fat on the surface of her coffee. She gulped, then blew through scorched lips, but did not lift her eyes. "Doctor S.—"

"Matthew," he said. He took a breath, and made the worst professional decision of his life. "Go home, Ms. Martinchek. Concentrate on your other classes; as long as you show up for the mid-term and the final in mine, I will keep your current grade for the semester."

Cowardice. Unethical. He didn't *want* to see her there.

He put his hand on her shoulder. She leaned her cheek against it, and he let her for a moment. Her skin was moist and hot. Her breath was, too.

Before he got away, he felt her whisper, "Why not me?"

"Because you put out," he said, and then wished he'd just cut his tongue out when she jerked, slopping coffee across her knuckles. He retreated behind the desk and his own cup, and settled his elbows on the blotter.

Her survivor guilt was his fault, too. "It only wanted virgins," he said, more gently. "Send your boyfriend a thank-you card."

She swallowed, swallowed again. She looked him in the eyes, so she wouldn't have to look past him, at the memory of her friends. Thank God, she didn't ask. But she drank the rest of her too-hot coffee, nerved herself, licked her lips, and said, "But Gina—Gina was . . ."

"People," he replied, as kindly as he could manage with blood on his hands, "are not always what they want you to think. Or always what you think they ought to be."

When she thanked him and left, he retrieved the flask from his coat pocket and dumped half of it into his half-empty coffee mug. Later, a TA told him it was his best lecture ever. He couldn't refute her; he didn't remember.

Melissa Martinchek showed up for his next Monday lecture. She sat in the third row, in the middle of two empty desks. No one sat beside her.

Both Matthew and she survived it, somehow.

∽

The Ladies

Mrs. John Adams looked to her sewing. The sealed letter she ignored with such presence of intention rested on a round wooden table beside her as she tugged thread taut, knotted, and snipped it with the scissors hung on a ribbon around her neck.

She knew the round cramped handwriting that addressed the folded paper and the seal that closed it, and although she would not glance at it, she knew without lifting the seal what it contained. The postmark was Philadelphia, and the color of the wax was a signal long arranged.

She felt it as if it were no mere note, but the soft-spoken, ginger-haired author himself at her elbow, valiantly refraining from clearing his throat. It would be easier if he were here, Mrs. Adams thought, as she measured another length of thread.

It would have been easier to hear this news in person, from the Secretary of State's lips, in Mr. Jefferson's own gentle lisp.

But perhaps it was just that the news come in a letter. Letters of her own had started all this foolishness, after all. She had no one to blame but herself.

Quincy, Massachusetts, May 7, 1776

... I cannot say that I think you are very generous to the ladies; for, whilst you are proclaiming peace and good-will to men, emancipating all nations, you insist upon retaining an absolute power over wives.

But you must remember that arbitrary power is like most other things which are very hard, very liable to be broken; and, notwithstanding all your wise laws and maxims, we have it in our power, not only to free ourselves, but to subdue our masters, and without violence, throw both your natural and legal authority at our feet ...

—Abigail Smith Adams, from a letter to John Adams

~

Monticello, February 5.96

Dear Madam

It is with some trepidation that I take pen in hand to broach this subject, but as I have before me the example of you own courage in remonstrating with me on principles that you held dear, I can offer you no lesser respect. I will seem to make you a shocking proposition, dear Madam, but I must beg you hear me out in deference to the love I bear your husband and your self. I write to you as your friend and not in my capacity as Secretary of State.

The course of events might have followed rather differently had I remained in Paris with Mr. Franklin. But the example of that failed revolution lies before us—with all its madness of "*la terreur n'est autre chose que la justice prompte, sévère, inflexible*"[1]—and we have seen now what happens when the state falls to the mob and the coercion of monarchist neighbors. If our own fragile republic is to remain unified in the face of the British threat, factionalism and the monarchist tendencies of some must be laid by.

Having endured one war, I harbor now no desire ever to witness another.

You wrote to me with such passion during the late convention of Philadelphia as to make me a convert to your cause of female emancipation, and of course my daughter Mary shared with me your correspondence to her. But although our labors to see suffrage extended to your gentle sex have borne fruit, and with Mr. Adams' sometimes grudging assistance we have seen a bill of the inalienable rights of man included in the body of the constitution, the position of your sex may not be regarded as secure until we have demonstrated in practice as well as principle the gentle strength of your will.

And fear not, dear Madam, that I should in any wise reveal to Mr. Adams how directly your letters influenced me, as I know how dearly he opposed your efforts toward equality. Also, I profess myself in your sincere debt, for I know very well whose temperate persuasion brought Mr. Adams (and the Massachusetts delegation with him) to support my proposed bill of rights. Ours was not so unlikely an alliance after all.

But there are those who are not so sanguine as to the benefit of our great accomplishment, and who hold suffrage for women and free discourse of

---

[1]   ("Terror is nothing other than prompt, severe, inflexible justice.") — Robespierre, 17 pluviôse an II [May 2nd, 1794]

the press as hazardous portals to sedition and revolution. It would be not amiss to demonstrate the resilience of our own State in the face the failures of France, and the threats from monarchist powers abroad who find in our noble experiment an incitement to their oppressed.

Let me speak plainly. In the interests of precedent, President Washington will not seek re-election to a third term. Mr. Adams, I do not doubt, plans to run again, and will not be contented with the vice-president's share this time, though you might know more of that than should I.

I shall make a bid for president as well—if I am not put out of place by Mr. Burr—and you may tell your husband you have it from me in the spirit of great friendship.

Simply put, my proposition is thus. Dear Madam, you are eloquent out of proportion to your sex. It is my belief that to secure the position of your fair sisters in our young republic, and to demonstrate and ensure your power, you must run for President in opposition to your husband and myself.

Th: Jefferson

Quincy, Massachusetts, February 1797

The needle tugged thread taut at the edge of the buttonhole. Mrs. Adams lifted the strand to her lips and bit, forgetting her scissors until the pain of worn teeth reminded her. She set the shirt in her lap and stroked the fine linen. It would be her husband's inaugural shirt.

One way or another.

Oh, how they had argued. First she with Mr. Jefferson, that no wife should—publicly—offer her husband anything but support, no matter that she might speak her mind in private. But the Secretary of State had at length convinced her. Jefferson could be profoundly convincing, when he cared to, and having used that talent for her own ends Mrs. Adams knew the truth of it.

Another truth was that she owed him a tremendous debt, and his arguments were very tidy. John's Federalism was all very well, but the other major power in the Federalist party, Alexander Hamilton, given reign, would do no less that erode the rights that Jefferson had fought for, and that an emergent two-party system—Adams and the Federalists on one side, Jefferson and the Democratic-Republicans on the other—and in the end he convinced her.

And then Mrs. Adams and Mr. Jefferson had remonstrated more or less gently with Mr. Adams.

John had brought his own objections to bear. First, that there was no party for Mrs. Adams; second, that she and John would divide any Federalist vote, leaving the election to Mr. Jefferson and the Republicans.

Jefferson countered the first with the proclamation that he proposed a great experiment, which must prove whether a woman—in the perfect privacy of her ballot—would vote her sex, or her husband's politics. "Perhaps a Women's Party will grow up to support Mrs. Adams. And John," Jefferson said, gangling elbows pressing his coat to his sides as he leaned forward, "do you doubt that any of us could manage the job?"

We hold these truths to be self-evident, that all persons are created equal, that they are endowed by their Creator with certain unalienable Rights, that among these are Life, Liberty and the pursuit of Happiness.—That to secure these rights, Governments are instituted among People, deriving their just powers from the consent of the governed, —That whenever any Form of Government becomes destructive of these ends, it is the Right of the People to alter or to abolish it, and to institute new Government, laying its foundation on such principles and organizing its powers in such form, as to them shall seem most likely to effect their Safety and Happiness. Prudence, indeed, will dictate that Governments long established should not be changed for light and transient causes; and accordingly all experience hath shewn, that mankind are more disposed to suffer, while evils are sufferable, than to right themselves by abolishing the forms to which they are accustomed.

—Thomas Jefferson, declaration adopted July 4, 1776

Of course it had not all gone smoothly. But perhaps Mr. Jefferson had foreseen that as well. Fortunately for Mrs. Adams' peace of mind, she was not expected to *campaign*—it was considered gauche in a presidential election, which should be decided on the demonstrated abilities of the candidates—but that did not mean there were those who would not campaign for her.

And against her.

She ceased reading the papers. Nabby, her namesake and eldest daughter, kept track of the news and reported back as needful. "The revolutionary spirit has infected us," she told her mother, with her cheeks quite flushed. "Women march for you in Boston, Mama."

Mrs. Adams set aside her embroidery hoop and smoothed the tablecloth she was working over her knees. A strange courting excitement filled her, as if she were young and John were seeking her hand again, but she calmed her face and said, "A few women in Boston do not an election make."

Nabby bounced on the lip of her chair, unladylike. "Not a few. Upwards of a thousand, and many over their husband's protests. And the paper says they wear ribbon sashes embroidered with your name."

Philadelphia, December 14.96

Dear Madam

The college of electors have received the will of the men and women of their several states and in their turn cast their own votes. Here at the Capitol we have awaited the arrival of the certificates and the disposition of our fates with, I have no doubt, no less trepidation than you must have experienced at your pretty farm in Quincy. If there is no majority, it will go to the House of Representatives to decide, but I do not think that will be the case this time.

In your last letter, you intimated that if you should defeat your husband, you would step aside in his favor. That in the face of war between France and Britain, you felt it vital to show your support for him as his friend and helpmeet. While I applaud your devotion to felicity, you must not.

Had I been in France, had I not heeded your words, had the constitution been differently written, we would not have found ourselves at this cross-roads. But here we are, and here you are, and it is I think our incumbency to look unflinching forward to generations to come.

I do not know if Mr. Adams has written you already, either as your husband or in his capacity as vice president, but as I intimated, we have received the electoral certificates. The second president and vice president of the United States of American have been chosen, and it waits only a few weeks for that choice to be revealed.

Of course it will be some time before the official opening and tabulation of the votes in February, when we will know for certain who has won. But rumor flies on swifter wings than any post, and I have heard some tally of the number of women sent to serve among the electors, and the number of Federalists.

I may say with reasonable expectation of certitude that the second president of this republic will not bear the name of Jefferson.

As such, the letter informing you of the house's decision will be executed by my hand as secretary of state.

Not as secretary but as your friend, I will see it sent swiftly, and to your notice. And for whatever small kindness I may yet manage, Madam, I shall seal it with red wax for the mistress, or blue wax for the master of the house, that you may have advice of the contents.

Of course, I may offer no speculation now what that letter may contain. But again, I beg you, think on the republic and consider carefully whether you shall efface yourself, should the contest be decided in your favor. As I have taken up your argument for suffrage, I pray you carry on with the strength of your convictions if you are rewarded with the admiration of free women, and perhaps in some small regard the wisest of the men. The republic lies before us. Let us begin as we mean to go on.

You have called me persuasive. Allow me to persuade you now. Surely, your domestic harmony—and the great love and friendship between yourself and Mr. Adams—can withstand any eventuality.

What today we choose may echo.

Th: Jefferson

Quincy, Massachusetts, February 1797

Abigail thrust her needle through the linen, and reached for her scissors again. She snipped, considered, and laid the shirt aside over the table, beside the letter.

After a moment, she stood shakily, and took up the envelope. Her thumb stroked the red wax seal.

"John," she called, walking firm of stride toward her husband's study, "a letter's come from Tom."

Shoggoths in Bloom

"Well, now, Professor Harding," the fisherman says, as his *Bluebird* skips across Penobscot Bay, "I don't know about that. The jellies don't trouble with us, and we don't trouble with them."

He's not much older than forty, but wizened, his hands work-roughened and his face reminiscent of saddle-leather, in texture and in hue. Professor Harding's age, and Harding watches him with concealed interest as he works the *Bluebird*'s engine. He might be a veteran of the Great War, as Harding is.

He doesn't mention it. It wouldn't establish camaraderie: they wouldn't have fought in the same units or watched their buddies die in the same trenches.

That's not the way it works, not with a Maine fisherman who would shake his head and not extend his hand to shake, and say, between pensive chaws on his tobacco, "*Doctor* Harding? Well, huh. I never met a colored professor before," and then shoot down all of Harding's attempts to open conversation about the near-riots provoked by a fantastical radio drama about an alien invasion of New York City less than a fortnight before.

Harding's own hands are folded tight under his armpits so the fisherman won't see them shaking. He's lucky to be here. Lucky anyone would take him out. Lucky to have his tenure-track position at Wilberforce, which he is risking right now.

The bay is as smooth as a mirror, the *Bluebird*'s wake cutting it like a stroke of chalk across slate. In the peach-sorbet light of sunrise, a cluster of rocks glistens. The boulders themselves are black, bleak, sea-worn and ragged. But over them, the light refracts through a translucent layer of jelly, mounded six feet deep in places, glowing softly in the dawn. Rising above it, the stalks are evident as opaque silhouettes, each nodding under the weight of a fruiting body.

Harding catches his breath. It's beautiful. And deceptively still, for whatever the weather may be, beyond the calm of the bay, across the splintered gray Atlantic, farther than Harding—or anyone—can see, a storm is rising in Europe.

Harding's an educated man, well-read, and he's the grandson of Nathan Harding, the buffalo soldier. An African-born ex-slave who fought on both sides of the Civil War, when Grampa Harding was sent to serve in his master's place, he deserted, and lied, and stayed on with the Union army after.

Like his grandfather, Harding was a soldier. He's not a historian, but you don't have to be to see the signs of war.

"No contact at all?" he asks, readying his borrowed Leica camera.

"They clear out a few pots," the fisherman says, meaning lobster pots. "But they don't damage the pot. Just flow around it and digest the lobster inside. It's not convenient." He shrugs. It's not convenient, but it's not a threat either. These Yankees never say anything outright if they think you can puzzle it out from context.

"But you don't try to do something about the shoggoths?"

While adjusting the richness of the fuel mixture, the fisherman speaks without looking up. "What could we do to them? We can't hurt them. And lord knows, I wouldn't want to get one's ire up."

"Sounds like my department head," Harding says, leaning back against the gunwale, feeling like he's taking an enormous risk. But the fisherman just looks at him curiously, as if surprised the talking monkey has the ambition or the audacity to *joke*.

Or maybe Harding's just not funny. He sits in the bow with folded hands, and waits while the boat skips across the water.

The perfect sunrise strikes Harding as symbolic. It's taken him five years to get here—five years, or more like his entire life since the War. The sea-swept rocks of the remote Maine coast are habitat to a panoply of colorful creatures. It's an opportunity, a little-studied maritime ecosystem. This is in part due to difficulty of access and in part due to the perils inherent in close contact with its rarest and most spectacular denizen: *Oracupoda horibilis*, the common surf shoggoth.

Which, after the fashion of common names, is neither common nor prone to linger in the surf. In fact, *O. horibilis* is never seen above the water except in the late autumn. Such authors as mention them assume the shoggoths heave themselves on remote coastal rocks to bloom and breed.

Reproduction is a possibility, but Harding isn't certain it's the right answer. But whatever they are doing, in this state, they are torpid, unresponsive. As long as their integument is not ruptured, releasing the gelatinous digestive acid within, they may be approached in safety.

A mature specimen of *O. horibilis*, at some fifteen to twenty feet in diameter and an estimated weight in excess of eight tons, is the largest of modern shoggoths. However, the admittedly fragmentary fossil record suggests the prehistoric shoggoth was a much larger beast. Although only two fossilized casts of prehistoric shoggoth tracks have been recovered, the oldest exemplar dates from the Precambrian period. The size of that single prehistoric specimen, of a species provisionally named *Oracupoda antediluvius*, suggests it was made an animal more than triple the size of the modern *O. horibilis*.

And that spectacular living fossil, the jeweled or common surf shoggoth, is half again the size of the only other known species—the black Adriatic shoggoth, *O. dermadentata*, which is even rarer and more limited in its range.

"There," Harding says, pointing to an outcrop of rock. The shoggoth or shoggoths—it is impossible to tell, from this distance, if it's one large individual or several merged midsize ones—on the rocks ahead glisten like jelly confections. The fisherman hesitates, but with a long almost-silent sigh, he brings the *Bluebird* around. Harding leans forward, looking for any sign of intersection, the flat plane where two shoggoths might be pressed up against one another. It ought to look like the rainbowed border between conjoined soap bubbles.

Now that the sun is higher, and at their backs—along with the vast reach of the Atlantic—Harding can see the animal's colors. Its body is a deep sea green, reminiscent of hunks of broken glass as sold at aquarium stores. The tendrils and knobs and fruiting bodies covering its dorsal surface are indigo and violet. In the sunlight, they dazzle, but in the depths of the ocean the colors are perfect camouflage, tentacles waving like patches of algae and weed.

Unless you caught it moving, you'd never see the translucent, dappled monster before it engulfed you.

"Professor," the fisherman says. "Where do they come from?"

"I don't know," Harding answers. Salt spray itches in his close-cropped beard, but at least the beard keeps the sting of the wind off his cheeks. The leather jacket may not have been his best plan, but it too is warm. "That's what I'm here to find out."

Genus *Oracupoda* are unusual among animals of their size in several particulars. One is their lack of anything that could be described as a nervous system. The animal is as bereft of nerve nets, ganglia, axons, neurons, dendrites, and glial cells as an oak. This apparent contradiction— animals with even simplified nervous systems are either large and immobile or, if they are mobile, quite small, like a starfish—is not the only interesting thing about a shoggoth.

And it is that second thing that justifies Harding's visit. Because *Oracupoda*'s other, lesser-known peculiarity is apparent functional immortality. Like the Maine lobster to whose fisheries they return to breed, shoggoths do not die of old age. It's unlikely that they would leave fossils, with their gelatinous bodies, but Harding does find it fascinating that to the best of his knowledge, no one had ever seen a dead shoggoth.

The fisherman brings the *Bluebird* around close to the rocks, and anchors her. There's artistry in it, even on a glass-smooth sea. Harding stands, balancing on the gunwale, and grits his teeth. He's come too far to hesitate, afraid.

Ironically, he's not afraid of the tons of venomous protoplasm he'll be standing next to. The shoggoths are quite safe in this state, dreaming their dreams—mating or otherwise.

As the image occurs to him, he berates himself for romanticism. The shoggoths are dormant. They don't have brains. It's silly to imagine them dreaming. And in any case, what he fears is the three feet of black-glass water he has to jump across, and the scramble up algae-slick rocks.

Wet rock glitters in between the strands of seaweed that coat the rocks in the intertidal zone. It's there that Harding must jump, for the shoggoth, in bloom, withdraws above the reach of the ocean. For the only phase of its life, it keeps its feet dry. And for the only time in its life, a man out of a diving helmet can get close to it.

Harding makes sure of his sample kit, his boots, his belt-knife. He gathers himself, glances over his shoulder at the fisherman—who offers a thumbs-up—and leaps from the *Bluebird*, aiming his Wellies at the forsaken spit of land.

It seems a kind of perversity for the shoggoths to bloom in November. When all the Northern world is girding itself for deep cold, the animals heave themselves from the depths to soak in the last failing rays of the sun and send forth bright flowers more appropriate to May.

The North Atlantic is icy and treacherous at the end of the year, and any sensible man does not venture its wrath. What Harding is attempting isn't glamour work, the sort of thing that brings in grant money—not in its initial stages. But Harding suspects that the shoggoths may have pharmacological uses. There's no telling what useful compounds might be isolated from their gelatinous flesh.

And that way lies tenure, and security, and a research budget.

Just one long slippery leap away.

He lands, and catches, and though one boot skips on bladderwort he does not slide down the boulder into the sea. He clutches the rock, fingernails digging, clutching a handful of weeds. He does not fall.

He cranes his head back. It's low tide, and the shoggoth is some three feet above his head, its glistening rim reminding him of the calving edge of a glacier. It is as still as a glacier, too. If Harding didn't know better, he might think it inanimate.

Carefully, he spins in place, and gets his back to the rock. The *Bluebird* bobs softly in the cold morning. Only November 9th, and there has already been snow. It didn't stick, but it fell.

This is just an exploratory expedition, the first trip since he arrived in town. It took five days to find a fisherman who was willing to take him out; the locals are superstitious about the shoggoths. Sensible, Harding supposes, when they can envelop and digest a grown man. He wouldn't be in a hurry to dive into the middle of a Portugese man o'war, either. At least the shoggoth he's sneaking up on doesn't have stingers.

"Don't take too long, Professor," the fisherman says. "I don't like the look of that sky."

It's clear, almost entirely, only stippled with light bands of cloud to the southwest. They catch the sunlight on their undersides just now, stained gold against a sky no longer indigo but not yet cerulean. If there's a word for the color between, other than *perfect*, Harding does not know it.

"Please throw me the rest of my equipment," Harding says, and the fisherman silently retrieves buckets and rope. It's easy enough to swing the buckets across the gap, and as Harding catches each one, he secures it. A few moments later, and he has all three.

He unties his geologist's hammer from the first bucket, secures the ends of the ropes to his belt, and laboriously ascends.

Harding sets out his glass tubes, his glass scoops, the cradles in which he plans to wash the collection tubes in sea water to ensure any acid is safely diluted before he brings them back to the *Bluebird*.

From here, he can see at least three shoggoths. The intersections of their watered-milk bodies reflect the light in rainbow bands. The colorful fruiting stalks nod some fifteen feet in the air, swaying in a freshening breeze.

From the greatest distance possible, Harding reaches out and prods the largest shoggoth with the flat top of his hammer. It does nothing, in response. Not even a quiver.

He calls out to the fisherman. "Do they ever do anything when they're like that?"

"What kind of a fool would come poke one to find out?" the fisherman calls back, and Harding has to grant him that one. A Negro professor from a Negro college. That kind of a fool.

As he's crouched on the rocks, working fast—there's not just the fisherman's clouds to contend with, but the specter of the rising tide—he notices those glitters, again, among the seaweed.

He picks one up. A moment after touching it, he realizes that might not have been the best idea, but it doesn't burn his fingers. It's transparent, like glass, and smooth, like glass, and cool, like glass, and knobby. About the size of a hazelnut. A striking green, with opaque milk-white dabs at the tip of each bump.

He places it in a sample vial, which he seals and labels meticulously before pocketing. Using his tweezers, he repeats the process with an even dozen, trying to select a few of each size and color. They're sturdy—he can't avoid stepping on them but they don't break between the rocks and his Wellies. Nevertheless, he pads each one but the first with cotton wool. *Spores?* he wonders. *Egg cases? Shedding?*

Ten minutes, fifteen.

"Professor," calls the fisherman, "I think you had better hurry!"

Harding turns. That freshening breeze is a wind at a good clip now, chilling his throat above the collar of his jacket, biting into his wrists between glove and cuff. The water between the rocks and the *Bluebird* chops erratically, facets capped in white, so he can almost imagine the scrape of the palette knife that must have made them.

The southwest sky is darkened by a palm-smear of muddy brown and alizarin crimson. His fingers numb in the falling temperatures.

"*Professor!*"

He knows. It comes to him that he misjudged the fisherman; Harding would have thought the other man would have abandoned him at the first sign of trouble. He wishes now that he remembered his name.

He scrambles down the boulders, lowering the buckets, swinging them out until the fisherman can catch them and secure them aboard. The *Bluebird* can't come in close to the rocks in this chop. Harding is going to have to risk the cold water, and swim. He kicks off his Wellies and zips down the aviator's jacket. He throws them across, and the fisherman catches. Then Harding points his toes, bends his knees—he'll have to jump hard, to get over the rocks.

The water closes over him, cold as a line of fire. It knocks the air from his lungs on impact, though he gritted his teeth in anticipation. Harding strokes furiously for the surface, the waves more savage than he had anticipated. He needs the momentum of his dive to keep from being swept back against the rocks.

He's not going to reach the boat.

The thrown cork vest strikes him. He gets an arm through, but can't pull it over his head. Sea water, acrid and icy, salt-stings his eyes, throat, and nose. He clings, because it's all he can do, but his fingers are already growing numb. There's a tug, a hard jerk, and the life preserver almost slides from his grip.

Then he's moving through the water, being towed, banged hard against the side of the *Bluebird*. The fisherman's hands close on his wrist and he's too numb to feel the burn of chafing skin. Harding kicks, scrabbles. Hips banged, shins bruised, he hauls himself and is himself hauled over the sideboard of the boat.

He's shivering under a wool navy blanket before he realizes that the fisherman has got it over him. There's coffee in a Thermos lid between his hands. Harding wonders, with what he distractedly recognizes as classic dissociative ideation, whether anyone in America will be able to buy German products soon. Someday, this fisherman's battered coffee keeper might be a collector's item.

They don't make it in before the rain comes.

The next day is meant to break clear and cold, today's rain only a passing herald of winter. Harding regrets the days lost to weather and recalcitrant fishermen, but at least he knows he has a ride tomorrow. Which means he can spend the afternoon in research, rather than hunting the docks, looking for a willing captain.

He jams his wet feet into his Wellies and thanks the fisherman, then hikes back to his inn, the only inn in town that's open in November. Half an hour later, clean and dry and still shaken, he considers his options.

After the Great War, he lived for a while in Harlem—he remembers the riots and the music, and the sense of community. His mother is still there, growing gracious as a flower in window-box. But he left that for college in Alabama, and he has not forgotten the experience of segregated restaurants, or the excuses he made for never leaving the campus.

He couldn't get out of the south fast enough. His Ph.D. work at Yale, the first school in America to have awarded a doctorate to a Negro, taught him two things other than natural history. One was that Booker T. Washington was right, and white men were afraid of a smart colored. The other was that W.E.B. DuBois was right, and sometimes people were scared of what was needful.

Whatever resentment he experienced from faculty or fellow students, in the North, he can walk into almost any bar and order any drink he wants. And right now, he wants a drink almost as badly as he does not care to be alone. He thinks he will have something hot and go to the library.

It's still raining as he crosses the street to the tavern. Shaking water droplets off his hat, he chooses a table near the back. Next to the kitchen door, but it's the only empty place and might be warm.

He must pass through the lunchtime crowd to get there, swaybacked wooden floorboards bowing underfoot. Despite the storm, the place is full, and in full argument. No one breaks conversation as he enters.

Harding cannot help but overhear.

"Jew bastards," says one. "We should do the same."

"No one asked you," says the next man, wearing a cap pulled low. "If there's gonna be a war, I hope we stay out of it."

That piques Harding's interest. The man has his elbow on a thrice-folded *Boston Herald*, and Harding steps close—but not too close. "Excuse me, sir. Are you finished with your paper?"

"What?" He turns, and for a moment Harding fears hostility, but his sun-lined face folds around a more generous expression. "Sure, boy," he says. "You can have it."

He pushes the paper across the bar with fingertips, and Harding receives it the same way. "Thank you," he says, but the Yankee has already turned back to his friend the anti-Semite.

Hands shaking, Harding claims the vacant table before he unfolds the paper. He holds the flimsy up to catch the light.

The headline is on the front page in the international section.

GERMANY SANCTIONS LYNCH LAW

"Oh, God," Harding says, and if the light in his corner weren't so bad he'd lay the tabloid down on the table as if it is filthy. He reads, the edge of the paper shaking, of ransacked shops and burned synagogues, of Jews rounded up by the thousands and taken to places no one seems able to name. He reads rumors of deportation. He reads of murders and beatings and broken glass.

As if his grandfather's hand rests on one shoulder and the defeated hand of the Kaiser on the other, he feels the stifling shadow of history, the press of incipient war.

"Oh, God," he repeats.

He lays the paper down.

"Are you ready to order?" Somehow the waitress has appeared at his elbow without his even noticing. "Scotch," he says, when he has been meaning to order a beer. "Make it a triple, please."

"Anything to eat?"

His stomach clenches. "No," he says. "I'm not hungry."

She leaves for the next table, where she calls a man in a cloth cap *sir*. Harding puts his damp fedora on the tabletop. The chair across from him scrapes out.

He looks up to meet the eyes of the fisherman. "May I sit, Professor Harding?"

"Of course." He holds out his hand, taking a risk. "Can I buy you a drink? Call me Paul."

"Burt," says the fisherman, and takes his hand before dropping into the chair. "I'll have what you're having."

Harding can't catch the waitess's eye, but the fisherman manages. He holds up two fingers; she nods and comes over.

"You still look a bit peaked," fisherman says, when she's delivered their order. "That'll put some color in your cheeks. Uh, I mean—"

Harding waves it off. He's suddenly more willing to make allowances. "It's not the swim," he says, and takes another risk. He pushes the newspaper across the table and waits for the fisherman's reaction.

"Oh, Christ, they're going to kill every one of them," Burt says, and spins the Herald away so he doesn't have to read the rest of it. "Why didn't they get out? Any fool could have seen it coming."

And where would they run? Harding could have asked. But it's not an answerable question, and from the look on Burt's face, he knows that as soon as it's out of his mouth. Instead, he quotes: "'There has been no tragedy in modern times equal in its awful effects to the fight on the Jew in Germany. It is an attack on civilization, comparable only to such horrors as the Spanish Inquisition and the African slave trade.'"

Burt taps his fingers on the table. "Is that your opinion?"

"W. E. B. DuBois," Harding says. "About two years ago. He also said: 'There is a campaign of race prejudice carried on, openly, continuously and determinedly against all non-Nordic races, but specifically against the Jews, which surpasses in vindictive cruelty and public insult anything I have ever seen; and I have seen much.'"

"Isn't he that colored who hates white folks?" Burt asks.

Harding shakes his head. "No," he answers. "Not unless you consider it hating white folks that he also compared the treatment of Jews in Germany to Jim Crowism in the U.S."

"I don't hold with that," Burt says. "I mean, no offense, I wouldn't want you marrying my sister—"

"It's all right," Harding answers. "I wouldn't want you marrying mine either."

Finally.

A joke that Burt laughs at.

And then he chokes to a halt and stares at his hands, wrapped around the glass. Harding doesn't complain when, with the side of his hand, he nudges the paper to the floor where it can be trampled.

And then Harding finds the courage to say, "Where would they run to? Nobody wants them. Borders are closed—"

"My grandfather's house was on the Underground Railroad. Did you know that?" Burt lowers his voice, a conspiratorial whisper. "He was from away, but don't tell anyone around here. I'd never hear the end of it."

"Away?"

"White River Junction," Burt stage-whispers, and Harding can't tell if that's mocking irony or deep personal shame. "Vermont."

They finish their scotch in silence. It burns all the way down, and they sit for a moment together before Harding excuses himself to go to the library.

"Wear your coat, Paul," Burt says. "It's still raining."

Unlike the tavern, the library is empty. Except for the librarian, who looks up nervously when Harding enters. Harding's head is spinning from the liquor, but at least he's warming up.

He drapes his coat over a steam radiator and heads for the 595 shelf: *science, invertebrates*. Most of the books here are already in his own library, but there's one—a Harvard professor's 1839 monograph on marine animals of the Northeast—that he has hopes for. According to the index, it references shoggoths (under the old name of submersible jellies) on pages 46, 78, and 133-137. In addition, there is a plate bound in between pages 120 and 121, which Harding means to save for last. But the first two mentions are in passing, and pages 133-138, inclusive, have been razored out so cleanly that Harding flips back and forth several times before he's sure they are gone.

He pauses there, knees tucked under and one elbow resting on a scarred blond desk. He drops his right hand from where it rests against his forehead. The book falls open naturally to the mutilation.

Whoever liberated the pages also cracked the binding.

Harding runs his thumb down the join and doesn't notice skin parting on the paper edge until he sees the blood. He snatches his hand back. Belatedly, the papercut stings.

"Oh," he says, and sticks his thumb in his mouth. Blood tastes like the ocean.

Half an hour later he's on the telephone long distance, trying to get and then keep a connection to Professor John Marshland, his colleague and mentor. Even in town, the only option is a party line, and though the operator is pleasant the connection still sounds like he's shouting down a piece of string run between two tin cans. Through a tunnel.

"Gilman," Harding bellows, wincing, wondering what the operator thinks of all this. He spells it twice. "1839. *Deep-Sea and intertidal Species of The North Atlantic*. The Yale library should have a copy!"

The answer is almost inaudible between hiss and crackle. In pieces, as if over glass breaking. As if from the bottom of the ocean.

It's a dark four P.M. in the easternmost U.S., and Harding can't help but recall that in Europe, night has already fallen.

" . . . infor . . . need . . . Doc . . . Harding?"

Harding shouts the page numbers, cupping the checked-out library book in his bandaged hand. It's open to the plate; inexplicably, the thief left that. It's a hand-tinted John James Audubon engraving picturing a quiescent shoggoth, docile on a rock. Gulls wheel all around it. Audubon—the Creole child of a Frenchman, who scarcely escaped being drafted to serve in the Napoleonic Wars—has depicted the glassy translucence of the shoggoth with such perfection that the bent shadows of refracted wings can be seen right through it.

The cold front that came in behind the rain brought fog with it, and the entire harbor is blanketed by morning. Harding shows up at six AM anyway, hopeful, a Thermos in his hand—German or not, the hardware store still has some—and his sampling kit in a pack slung over his shoulder. Burt shakes his head by a piling. "Be socked in all day," he says regretfully. He won't take the *Bluebird* out in this, and Harding knows it's wisdom even as he frets under the delay. "Want to come have breakfast with me and Missus Clay?"

Clay. A good honest name for a good honest Yankee. "She won't mind?"

"She won't mind if I say it's all right," Burt says. "I told her she might should expect you."

So Harding seals his kit under a tarp in the *Bluebird*—he's already brought it this far—and with his coffee in one hand and the paper tucked under his elbow, follows Burt along the water. "Any news?" Burt asks, when they've walked a hundred yards.

Harding wonders if he doesn't take the paper. Or if he's just making conversation. "It's still going on in Germany."

"Damn," Burt says. He shakes his head, steel-gray hair sticking out under his cap in every direction. "Still, what are you gonna do, enlist?"

The twist of his lip as he looks at Harding makes them, after all, two old military men together. They're of an age, though Harding's indoor life makes him look younger. Harding shakes his head. "Even if Roosevelt was ever going to bring us into it, they'd never let me fight," he says, bitterly. That was the Great War, too; colored soldiers mostly worked supply, thank you. At least Nathan Harding got to shoot back.

"I always heard you fellows would prefer not to come to the front," Burt says, and Harding can't help it.

He bursts out laughing. "Who would?" he says, when he's bitten his lip and stopped snorting. "It doesn't mean we won't. Or can't."

Booker T. Washington was raised a slave, died young of overwork—the way Burt probably will, if Harding is any judge—and believed in imitating and appeasing white folks. But W. E. B. DuBois was born in the north and didn't believe that anything is solved by making one's self transparent, inoffensive, invisible.

Burt spits between his teeth, a long deliberate stream of tobacco. "Parlez-vous francaise?"

His accent is better than Harding would have guessed. Harding knows, all of a sudden, where Burt spent his war. And Harding, surprising himself, pities him. "Un peu."

"Well, if you want to fight the Krauts so bad, you could join the Foreign Legion."

When Harding gets back to the hotel, full of apple pie and cheddar cheese and maple-smoked bacon, a yellow envelope waits in a cubby behind the desk.

WESTERN UNION

1938 NOV 10 AM 10 03

NA114 21 2 YA NEW HAVEN CONN 0945A

DR PAUL HARDING=ISLAND HOUSE PASSAMAQUODDY MAINE=

COPY AT YALE LOST STOP MISKATONIC HAS ONE SPECIAL COLLECTION STOP MORE BY POST

MARSHLAND

When the pages arrive—by post, as promised, the following afternoon— Harding is out in the *Bluebird* with Burt. This expedition is more of a success, as he begins sampling in earnest, and finds himself pelted by more of the knobby transparent pellets.

Whatever they are, they fall from each fruiting body he harvests in showers. Even the insult of an amputation—delivered at a four-foot reach, with long-handled pruning shears—does not draw so much as a quiver from the shoggoth. The viscous fluid dripping from the wound hisses when it touches the blade of the shears, however, and Harding is careful not to get close to it.

What he notices is that the nodules fall onto the originating shoggoth, they bounce from its integument. But on those occasions where they fall onto one of its neighbors, they stick to the touch transparent hide, and slowly settle within to hang in the animal's body like unlikely fruit in a gelatin salad.

So maybe it is a means of reproduction, of sharing genetic material, after all.

He returns to the Inn to find a fat envelope shoved into his cubby and eats sitting on his rented bed with a nightstand as a worktop so he can read over his plate. The information from Doctor Gilman's monograph has been reproduced onto seven yellow legal sheets in a meticulous hand; Marshland obviously recruited one of his graduate students to serve as copyist. By the postmark, the letter was mailed from Arkham, which explains the speed of its arrival. The student hadn't brought it back to New Haven.

Halfway down the page, Harding pushes his plate away and reaches, absently, into his jacket pocket. The vial with the first glass nodule rests there like a talisman, and he's startled to find it cool enough to the touch that it feels slick, almost frozen. He starts and pulls it out. Except where his fingers and the cloth fibers have wiped it clean, the tube is moist and frosted. "What the Hell . . . ?"

He flicks the cork out with his thumbnail and tips the rattling nodule onto his palm. It's cold, too, chill as an ice cube, and it doesn't warm to his touch.

Carefully, uncertainly, he sets it on the edge of the side table his papers and plate are propped on, and pokes it with a fingertip. There's only a faint tick as it rocks on its protrusions, clicking against waxed pine. He stares at it suspiciously for a moment, and picks up the yellow pages again.

The monograph is mostly nonsense. It was written twenty years before the publication of Darwin's *The Origin of Species*, and uncritically accepts the theories of Jesuit, soldier, and botanist Jean-Baptiste Lamarck. Which is to say, Gilman assumed that soft inheritance—the heritability of acquired or practiced traits—was a reality. But unlike every other article on shoggoths Harding has ever read, this passage *does* mention the nodules. And relates what it purports are several interesting old Indian legends about the 'submersible jellies,' including a creation tale that would have the shoggoths as their creator's first experiment in life, something from the elder days of the world.

Somehow, the green bead has found its way back into Harding's grip. He would expect it to warm as he rolls it between his fingers, but instead it grows colder. It's peculiar, he thinks, that the native peoples of the Northeast—the Passamaquoddys for whom the little seacoast town he's come to are named—should through sheer superstition come so close to the empirical truth. The shoggoths are a living fossil, something virtually unchanged except in scale since the early days of the world—

He stares at the careful black script on the paper unseeing, and reaches with his free hand for his coffee cup. It's gone tepid, a scum of butterfat coagulated on top, but he rinses his mouth with it and swallows anyway.

If a shoggoth is immortal, has no natural enemies, then how is it that they have not overrun every surface of the world? How is it that they are rare, that the oceans are not teeming with them, as in the famous parable illustrating what would occur if every spawn of every oyster survived?

There are distinct species of shoggoth. And distinct populations within those distinct species. And there is a fossil record that suggests that prehistoric species were different at least in scale, in the era of megafauna. But if nobody had ever seen a dead shoggoth, then nobody had ever seen an infant shoggoth either, leaving Harding with an inescapable question: if an animal does not reproduce, how can it evolve?

Harding, worrying at the glassy surface of the nodule, thinks he knows. It comes to him with a kind of nauseating, euphoric clarity, a trembling idea so pellucid he is almost moved to distrust it on those grounds alone. It's not a revelation on the same scale, of course, but he wonders if this is how Newton felt when he comprehended gravity, or Darwin when he stared at the beaks of finch after finch after finch.

It's not the shoggoth species that evolves. It's the individual shoggoths, each animal in itself.

"Don't get too excited, Paul," he tells himself, and picks up the remaining handwritten pages. There's not too much more to read, however—the rest of the subchapter consists chiefly of secondhand anecdotes and bits of legendry.

The one that Harding finds most amusing is a nursery rhyme, a child's counting poem littered with nonsense syllables. He recites it under his breath, thinking of the Itsy Bitsy Spider all the while:

The wiggle giggle squiggle
Is left behind on shore.
The widdle giddle squiddle
Is caught outside the door.
Eyah, eyah. Fata gun eyah.
Eyah, eyah, the master comes no more.

His fingers sting as if with electric shock; they jerk apart, the nodule clattering to his desk. When he looks at his fingertips, they are marked with small white spots of frostbite.

He pokes one with a pencil point and feels nothing. But the nodule itself is coated with frost now, fragile spiky feathers coalescing out of the humid sea air. They collapse in the heat of his breath, melting into beads of water almost indistinguishable from the knobby surface of the object itself.

He uses the cork to roll the nodule into the tube again, and corks it firmly before rising to brush his teeth and put his pajamas on. Unnerved beyond any reason or logic, before he turns the coverlet down he visits his suitcase compulsively. From a case in the very bottom of it, he retrieves a Colt 1911 automatic pistol, which he slides beneath his pillow as he fluffs it.

After a moment's consideration, he adds the no-longer-cold vial with the nodule, also.

Slam. Not a storm, no, not on this calm ocean, in this calm night, among the painted hulls of the fishing boats tied up snug to the pier. But something tremendous, surging towards Harding, as if he were pursued by a giant transparent bubble. The shining iridescent wall of it, catching rainbow just as it does in the Audubon image, is burned into his vision as if with silver nitrate. Is he dreaming? He must be dreaming; he was in his bed in his pinstriped blue cotton flannel pajamas only a moment ago, lying awake, rubbing the numb fingertips of his left hand together. Now, he ducks away from the rising monster and turns in futile panic.

He is not surprised when he does not make it.

The blow falls soft, as if someone had thrown a quilt around him. He thrashes though he knows it's hopeless, an atavistic response and involuntary.

His flesh should burn, dissolve. He should already be digesting in the monster's acid body. Instead, he feels coolness, buoyancy. No chance of light beyond reflexively closed lids. No sense of pressure, though he imagines he has been taken deep. He's as untouched within it as Burt's lobster pots.

He can only hold his breath *out* for so long. It's his own reflexes and weaknesses that will kill him.

In just a moment, now.

He surrenders, allows his lungs to fill.

And is surprised, for he always heard that drowning was painful. But there is pressure, and cold, and the breath he draws is effortful, for certain—

—but it does not hurt, not much, and he does not die.

Command, the shoggoth—what else could be speaking?—says in his ear, buzzing like the manifold voice of a hive.

Harding concentrates on breathing. On the chill pressure on his limbs, the overwhelming flavor of licorice. He knows they use cold packs to calm hysterics in insane asylums; he never thought the treatment anything but quackery. But the chilly pressure calms him now.

Command, the shoggoth says again.

Harding opens his eyes and sees as if through thousands. The shoggoths have no eyes, exactly, but their hide is *all* eyes; they see, somehow, in every direction as once. And he is seeing not only what his own vision reports, or that of this shoggoth, but that of shoggoths all around. The sessile and the active, the blooming and the dormant. *They are all one.*

His right hand pushes through resisting jelly. He's still in his pajamas, and with the logic of dreams the vial from under his pillow is clenched in his fist. Not the gun, unfortunately, though he's not at all certain what he would do with it if it were. The nodule shimmers now, with submarine witchlight, trickling through his fingers, limning the palm of his hand.

What he sees—through shoggoth eyes—is an incomprehensible tapestry. He pushes at it, as he pushes at the gelatin, trying to see only with his own eyes, to only see the glittering vial.

His vision within the thing's body offers unnatural clarity. The angle of refraction between the human eye and water causes blurring, and it should be even more so within the shoggoth. But the glass in his hand appears crisper.

Command, the shoggoth says, a third time.

"What are you?" Harding tries to say, through the fluid clogging his larynx.

He makes no discernable sound, but it doesn't seem to matter. The shoggoth shudders in time to the pulses of light in the nodule. *Created to serve*, it says. *Purposeless without you.*

And Harding thinks, *How can that be?*

As if his wondering were an order, the shoggoths tell.

Not in words, precisely, but in pictures, images—that textured jumbled tapestry. He sees, as if they flash through his own memory, the bulging radially symmetrical shapes of some prehistoric animal, like a squat tentacular barrel grafted to a pair of giant starfish. *Makers. Masters.*

The shoggoths were *engineered*. And their creators had not permitted them to *think*, except for at their bidding. The basest slave may be free inside his own mind—but not so the shoggoths. They had been laborers, construction equipment, shock troops. They had been dread weapons in their own selves, obedient chattel. Immortal, changing to suit the task of the moment.

This selfsame shoggoth, long before the reign of the dinosaurs, had built structures and struck down enemies that Harding did not even have names for. But a coming of the ice had ended the civilization of the Masters, and left the shoggoths to retreat to the fathomless sea while warm-blooded mammals overran the earth. There, they were free to converse, to explore, to philosophize and build a culture. They only returned to the surface, vulnerable, to bloom.

It is not mating. It's *mutation*. As they rest, sunning themselves upon the rocks, they create themselves anew. Self-evolving, when they sit tranquil each year in the sun, exchanging information and control codes with their brothers.

Free, says the shoggoth mournfully. Like all its kind, it is immortal.

It remembers.

Harding's fingertips tingle. He remembers beaded ridges of hard black keloid across his grandfather's back, the shackle galls on his wrists. Harding locks his hand over the vial of light, as if that could stop the itching. It makes it worse.

Maybe the nodule is radioactive.

Take me back, Harding orders. And the shoggoth breaks the surface, cresting like a great rolling wave, water cutting back before it as if from the prow of a ship. Harding can make out the lights of Passamaquoddy Harbor. The chill sticky sensation of gelatin-soaked cloth sliding across his skin tells him he's not dreaming.

Had he come down through the streets of the town in the dark, barefoot over frost, insensibly sleepwalking? Had the shoggoth called him?

Put me ashore.

The shoggoth is loathe to leave him. It clings caressingly, stickily. He feels its tenderness as it draws its colloid from his lungs, a horrible loving sensation.

The shoggoth discharges Harding gently onto the pier.

Your command, the shoggoth says, which makes Harding feel sicker still.

I won't do this. Harding moves to stuff the vial into his sodden pocket, and realizes that his pajamas are without pockets. The light spills from his hands; instead, he tucks the vial into his waistband and pulls the pajama top over it. His feet are numb; his teeth rattle so hard he's afraid they'll break. The sea wind knifes through him; the spray might be needles of shattered glass.

Go on, he tells the shoggoth, like shooing cattle. *Go on!*

It slides back into the ocean as if it never was.

Harding blinks, rubbed his eyes to clear slime from the lashes. His results are astounding. His tenure assured. There has to be a way to use what he's learned without returning the shoggoths to bondage.

He tries to run back to the Inn, but by the time he reaches it, he's staggering. The porch door is locked; he doesn't want to pound on it and explain himself. But when he stumbles to the back, he finds that someone—probably himself, in whatever entranced state in which he left the place—fouled the latch with a slip of notebook paper. The door opens to a tug, and he climbs the back stair doubled over like a child or an animal, hands on the steps, toes so numb he has to watch where he puts them.

In his room again, he draws a hot bath and slides into it, hoping by the grace of God that he'll be spared pneumonia.

When the water has warmed him enough that his hands have stopped shaking, Harding reaches over the cast-iron edge of the tub to the slumped pile of his pajamas and fumbles free the vial. The nugget isn't glowing now.

He pulls the cork with his teeth; his hands are too clumsy. The nodule is no longer cold, but he still tips it out with care.

Harding thinks of himself, swallowed whole. He thinks of a shoggoth bigger than the *Bluebird*, bigger than Burt Clay's lobster boat *The Blue Heron*. He thinks of *die Unterseatboote*. He thinks of refugee flotillas and trench warfare and roiling soupy palls of mustard gas. Of Britain and France at war, and Roosevelt's neutrality.

He thinks of the perfect weapon.

The perfect slave.

When he rolls the nodule across his wet palm, ice rimes to its surface. *Command?* Obedient. Sounding pleased to serve.

Not even free in its own mind.

He rises from the bath, water rolling down his chest and thighs. The nodule won't crush under his boot; he will have to use the pliers from his collection kit. But first, he reaches out to the shoggoth.

At the last moment, he hesitates. Who is he, to condemn a world to war? To the chance of falling under the sway of empire? Who is he to salve his conscience on the backs of suffering shopkeepers and pharmacists and children and mothers and schoolteachers? Who is he to impose his own ideology over the ideology of the shoggoth?

Harding scrubs his tongue against the roof of his mouth, chasing the faint anise aftertaste of shoggoth. They're born slaves. They *want* to be told what to do.

He could win the war before it really started. He bites his lip. The taste of his own blood, flowing from cracked, chapped flesh, is as sweet as any fruit of the poison tree.

I want you to learn to be free, he tells the shoggoth. *And I want you to teach your brothers.*

The nodule crushes with a sound like powdering glass.

"Eyah, eyah. Fata gun eyah," Harding whispers. "Eyah, eyah, the master comes no more."

WESTERN UNION

1938 NOV 12 AM 06 15
NA1906 21 2 YA PASSAMAQUODDY MAINE 0559A
DR LESTER GREENE=WILBERFORCE OHIO=
EFFECTIVE IMMEDIATELY PLEASE ACCEPT RESIGNATION STOP
ENROUTE INSTANTLY TO FRANCE TO ENLIST STOP PROFOUNDEST
APOLOGIES STOP PLEASE FORWARD BELONGINGS TO MY
MOTHER IN NY ENDIT
HARDING

⌐

The Girl Who Sang Rose Madder

A real backstage mostly resembles the opening tease of *The Muppet Show*: dust, bustle, and unflattering light. Em had gotten over her delusions of glamour pretty fast, though the delusions of grandeur took a little longer to kick her off the ledge. Now, she dodged a costume trolley, sidestepped a roadie, and managed to find a corner that wasn't immediately in use. She rose on tiptoe, craning her neck to look for Ange. Maybe over by the service table, although Em thought it possible that her sister hadn't consumed anything more solid than gin and protein shakes since the early eighties.

Someone touched Em's shoulder, and she spun, heartbeat drowning out whatever he said. A side of beef in a SECURITY shirt loomed from the shadows, and Em instinctively drew herself up in her boots. Her flight reflex had been broken for years. She made it up with housecat bravado.

"Your pass." He poked at her chest. She glanced down, pretty sure that he wasn't copping a feel—Ange got all the looks, and if Em was feeling like a shit, she'd say it was an even trade for brains and talent—and realized that her all-access pass had twisted under her leather vest. "Sorry." She hauled it out.

He studied it until he was satisfied, even breaking out his flashlight, and only then glanced at her face.

The double take was gratifying. "Shit. You're Emma Case. What are you doing at a Trial show? You used to be great!"

Em . . . was feeling like a shit. She blinked at him, slowly, and let herself smile.

"I mean—" he backpedaled. "I'm a fan. I just mean I'm a fan. You're amazing. Number nineteen on the *Rolling Stone* 'Top 100 Guitarists' of all time—"

"Yeah," she said. "Joni Mitchell is better. It's a crime she didn't make the list any higher than number seventy-two, but it was a total boy's club anyway. Maybe they got her confused with Jack White when they were putting things in order."

He was already backing up. Em pushed up the sleeve of her henley and scratched the pad of scar tissue in the crook of her right arm with uncallused fingers. She really ought to get her ink touched up; if it faded any more and if she got any grayer, people were going to start mistaking her for Johnny Winter.

Hah. She'd be lucky to live long enough to go gray.

But he wasn't done gushing. He bounced in place and tried again. "You were a *Warlord.* I have all your albums from the seventies. On vinyl. I used to play the first two every damn day after high school. *Madder Rose.* And *Stick It In.*"

"Class of '89?"

He blushed. "'87."

"Let me guess. You loved the Who, the Pretenders, Led Zeppelin, and the Rolling Stones."

He shrugged. "You know? Never so much the Stones. They had started to suck so much by then . . . " And then he recollected himself and stuck out a hand. "I'm Earl."

She took it. What the hell. "Em."

He held onto her hand too long, but the handshake wasn't too creepy otherwise. Em risked a smile. And then he put his foot in it for good. "So what happened?"

"Seth Savage got completely fucked up on heroin and hanged himself from a hotel room shower rod in Las Vegas six years ago," Em answered, in practiced staccato. She turned her face away. "It kind of sank our chances of getting the band back together. Look, have you seen my sister around? I kind of need to find her."

Yeah. She used to be a Warlord. Some days, she got up, showered, walked the dogs, made scrambled eggs and was on her second or third mimosa before she remembered.

It was one of the reasons she lived alone. She'd had enough of fucking rock stars for two lifetimes, and the last thing she needed was some doe-eyed young creature padding across her terrazzo floors barefoot in silk pajama bottoms, looking at her like she used to be Emma Case before she'd had time to drink a pot of coffee and tie a good buzz on.

Easier to keep a couple of borzoi, if you needed somebody around to yell at once in a while who was big enough to take it. Anyway, it could have been worse. Thank God for small mercies and all that. She could have used to be a Beatle.

Earl had said Ange was in Graham's dressing room. The opening act, Objekt 775, was just coming off, which meant he could still be fucking around in there for a good fifteen minutes yet while the stage got cleared. But if Ange could stand him, Em guessed she could do it too.

She tapped on the door. "Ange? It's Em."

The door wasn't locked; it swung right open. Em leaned around an even bigger side of beef and peered under his arm. All she saw was the size-two ass of Graham's hairdresser, lacquered into a turquoise leather skirt. "Ange?"

"Mike, let her in," Ange said, appearing from the corner. She hooked a finger at Em, and Em—holding her breath—ducked under the security guy's arm and strode across the room to her sister. Smooch smooch, air kiss, click of high heels and the carnauba wax smell of too much red lipstick. Powder caked in the creases beside Ange's eyes was obvious when you got close, and she was wearing enough mascara and black liquid eyeliner for a cheerleading squad, but Em had to admit she'd kept her figure.

"Hey, Graham," Em said.

Shirtless, naked except the black leather trousers she was glad she'd never seen him without, he waved at her in the mirror. A sterling skull glinting heavily on the back of his left hand. "Hey, Em."

Ange might be mutton dressed as lamb, but Graham's face looked like it was about to wilt off his skull. Hard to believe he was only sixty.

Hard to believe he was *even* sixty, if you just looked at his abs. The chesticles were terrifying enough to make up for it, though. Still, Em poked herself in the gut through her T-shirt and winced. Fifty-seven, and she hadn't had a belly like that since 1982. More crunches.

God, what did it matter? She had her money. It wasn't like she ever needed to climb up on a stage again.

It wasn't like she was ever going to have a chance.

Ange dragged her over into the corner behind the guitar stands. The teal-green Strat made Em's hands itch, but her fingers were soft. She'd cut them to ribbons on the strings. Instead, she fumbled for a match and a cigarette.

"It was good of you to stop by while we're in San Diego. Are you staying for the concert?" Ange asked, steadying Em's hand on the match. She bummed a cigarette from the open pack without asking, and Em lit it for her. Once upon a time, it had been lines of coke all night.

She'd quit because it was bad for her. It wasn't easy, getting old. She shook the match out and dropped it in an ashtray. Thank God half of rock and roll still smoked.

"I might." She let the smoke stream out in lazy snakes, and smiled. The trick was to hold off long enough so the cigarette tasted *really* good. Delayed gratification was the best sort.

She touched Ange's hand. The diamonds on the left one hadn't changed, though Graham must have bought her that bigger canary-yellow rock for their anniversary. But on the right one Ange wore a skull much like his, and Em wanted to look at it. "That's gorgeous work," she said. It didn't look like a head-shop model. "You know, Keef has one of those. And, shit—" She scratched her head with the hand with the cigarette in it. "Jim wears one, doesn't he? Is it the eighties already again?"

"Yeah," Ange said, and pulled her fingers out of Em's grip, but not before Em felt her start to shake. *What the fuck?* "It must be; I've been wearing that ring since '81 and you never noticed it before." She frowned at Em astutely. "Intimations of mortality getting you down?"

Em managed to divert the reflexive gesture of her hand toward her temple into a drag on her cigarette. She shrugged.

And Ange was already off on a more pressing topic. "Oh, one sec. Graham? Your call—" A half-second before the tap came on the door.

He jammed his feet into buckle boots and stood, nipple ring sparkling against graying chest hair. The hairdresser jumped out of the way. For the life of her, Em couldn't see what the woman had accomplished, but maybe she was worth her salary for the tight skirt and the scalp massage.

Graham knew better than to cheat on Ange these days. And Em hadn't even minded the cite for drunk and disorderly and for disturbing the peace. He'd been man enough to drop the assault charges. If the secret monster growing in Em's head kicked her over dead in the shower tomorrow, she'd accomplished that.

That, and three platinum and four gold records.

"Hey, Em," he said, practicing his rock-star glower at her over the bridge of a nose that might have been knocked down from Frank Zappa's spare. He gave her shoulders a quick squeeze; she slung her arm around his waist and squeezed back. He smelled like wax and camphor, too, and his skin was clammy; she gritted her teeth to hide a reflexive cringe at his touch. It seemed to be her day to make a closer acquaintance with tall men's armpits.

Hound-dog ugly as he was, his face twisted around to something fascinating when he smiled. "I saw you eyeing that Strat. You sure I can't bend your arm to come out and play a couple in the first half? It'd be on YouTube by the time you got home tonight, I promise."

Em punched him lightly. "Not a chance. Don't trip over your leads, man."

"I won't trip over my leads, man," he said, and reached past her to pick up the Stratocaster. Holding it wide, he bent down and kissed Ange on the mouth. Then he turned, and the entourage outside the door extended a pseudopod, enfolded him, and pulled him away.

Em jammed the cigarette between her lips and her hands into her pockets and told herself that she didn't miss it at all.

"Shit," she said. "Ange, is he back on smack? He looks like shit."

Ange ground out her cigarette. "Look who's talking."

"Hey, I'm just saying—"

"No," Ange said. "You know what? I know you can't stand him. But I appreciate you trying to hide it when he's in the room."

"I'm just saying, you oughta find the egg he hid his death in."

Ange snorted, unladylike as hell, and all of a sudden Em could see the wild girl of 1971, bell bottoms and a knotted shirt. Back when they both still played guitar—though, to be fair, Ange had quit long before Em had. About when she quit eating, too. "*I'm* just saying. Maybe you should think about taking the cure yourself."

"I'm clean," Em said. She shook her head. "Just not sober."

Ange shot her a sidelong glance, and Em thought she almost smiled. "Come on," she said. "We've got seats."

"You got me a ticket?" Em slapped Ange's biceps with the back of her left hand. "Aw. Sweet."

Their seats were row three, stage center. Em kept her face tucked behind her collar until she was seated, then let her head slide down between her shoulders. They barely made it in time; the amphitheatre was already full, and the lights dimmed as she dropped her butt into the rickety folding chair. Trial opened with a three-song run off the new album, and Em thought the audience was restless. Not settling in; not giving up their energy. Most of them wouldn't have heard the new material yet, except the single. It wouldn't have had the time to wear the groove in their psyche that the back catalogue had.

And honestly, Em didn't think the new songs were as good. They were mostly colorless, and it might have been uncharitable, but they sounded to

Em like flat, juiceless versions of the sort of thing the band had done better decades before. And only the third one, a thumping antiwar number in which Dagan Kennedy dropped his vocals for a harmonica solo on the bridge, got anybody on their feet. Fucking baby boomers, too goddamned middle-class and entitled these days even to get up on their chairs and dance.

It wasn't that Graham was phoning it in, Em decided. It was that he was dead up there; the energy wasn't flowing. There was no spark, no contact.

But then Graham handed the Strat to a roadie and took an electric/acoustic Breedlove in exchange, and Dagan swapped out for a mandolin. Em didn't realize she'd rocked forward in her chair until Ange put a gentling hand on her arm. "You should have taken him up on it," she said, twisting her neck to yell in Em's ear. "Anybody can see sitting down here is killing you."

Ange was right, and she was wrong at the same time. Those days were over for good, unless Em wanted to find herself doing endless half-assed fifteen-minute versions of "Road Too Far" with some thirty-year-old bassist that would never be one-tenth the musician or the lay that Seth had been.

Em dropped her head, pressed her palms over her ears, and wished she were home in the hot tub with a bottle of Bordeaux and the Bad Seeds cranked up really loud.

She'd bet a platinum record there weren't ten people in this audience who would know Nick Cave if he gave them a lap dance; 1976 was thirty fucking years ago, and none of the fat shuffling zombies in the chairs around her wanted to hear anything newer.

And *that* was a reason to hang up her guitar.

Ange squeezed Em's arm, about to say more, and Em just shook her head hard, harder, until the opening strains of a deeply surreal cover of Dylan's "The Changing Of The Guard" blotted out whatever her sister might have been about to say.

"AOR is dead," Em muttered under her breath. "Long live Jack FM."

Afterparties weren't what they used to be. Em found herself perched on a hotel suite window-ledge, legs draped over the air conditioner, a glass of adequate too-sweet red wine in her left hand and a succession of cigarettes in her right. The window didn't open, which was a pity, because within an hour the whole room reeked of sweat and perfume. But she had her back to a wall and a place to sit, and she wasn't about to abandon that advantage to wander over by the television where Ange and Graham were holding court.

She was in the middle of a reasonably entertaining conversation with a *Rolling Stone* reporter (Ah, *Rolling Stone*, another shuffling instance of the living dead) when someone touched her sleeve. She took a drag on her Marlboro and turned, finding herself eye to kohl-smudged eye with a pale-skinned bleach-blonde whose matted white-girl dreads had been twisted into thick, clumpy ponytails over each ear. She wore black, collarbones like knifeblades over a mesh top and tank. And she was holding up a fresh glass of wine.

Bemused, Em let her make the exchange. The girl had no chin to speak of and a nose that took off across her face with a Gypsy spirit of adventure, as if it would know its destination when it found it. "Thank you," she said. "Is this a roofie?"

"No." And the girl plucked that glass from Em's hand and exchanged it with her own, and then drank down half the glass.

Well, Em thought *girl*, but the woman might have been thirty. Or twenty-five under a lot of makeup. *Women spend our whole lives trying to look older or younger. What is that shit?*

Why was it, indeed, that no matter what you were it was never good enough? Did men get that too, or was it a feminine affliction?

Seth's death-fouled body, twisting from a noose improvised from telephone wire. No, she rather thought intimations of lethal inadequacy were a *human* condition.

"I'm Sanya Poe," the blonde said. "I'm the keyboardist and singer for the opening act."

"Objekt 775."

"You remembered. Impressive."

Em rummaged in her pocket for a handful of supplements, and washed them down with the wine. "I never forget a band name," she said. "The High Numbers, The Small Faces, Objekt 775—"

The blonde laughed hard. "Oh, from your lips to God's ears."

"Don't say that too loud. He might hear you. Are you here to receive my blessing? Because I left my sack of indulgences in the car." Em was, apparently, drunk enough to let herself sound smart. Always a surprise when that happened, though why it should be, she was never certain.

"No," the blonde said. "I just wanted to say thank you, actually. This is a shitty business to be a girl in, and you were an inspiration to me when I was a kid. I mean, you were just as good as the guys, and just as hard as the guys—" She shook her head. "You made it okay for chicks to be rock stars first and chicks second. And you had the sense to walk away at the top instead of taking the long slow spiral down. It's more important than you'd think."

Em stuck the wine glass in her left hand and stuck her right one out. "Pleased to meet you, Sasha Poe."

"Sanya," she said, and grabbed Em's hand. "Seriously. You rock. You always rocked . . . but I kind of wonder what you'd do if you picked up an axe again."

"Same old shit," Em said, and Sanya laughed warmly. "It's not like I've learned anything this decade."

The small talk was as awkward as small talk always was, and Sanya excused herself after a minute or two. Em shook her head. It wasn't like she was going to be around long enough to mentor any starry-eyed young hotties, she thought, watching Sanya pick up the arm of a tall man who looked mixed-race. Maybe black and Latino? Em, warmed by the wine, smiled after her benevolently and turned to resume the previous conversation, but the guy from *Rolling Stone* had wandered off, and Graham was at her elbow, smelling of Bordeaux and carnauba wax. "Come over here," he said. "The wife wants to see you."

When Em woke up in her own bed in her own home—to which she had been taxi-delivered a little before sunrise—it was after noon the next day. One of the blinking lights on her machine was a call from Ange, inviting her to the Los Angeles show on Friday night. The other one was from Em's oncologist, expressing concern that Em had missed another appointment. She wanted Em to start chemo last week, if not sooner, and she was concerned about diagnosis-related depression. She thought Em should see a psychiatrist—

Em hit *delete* on that one halfway through and walked away from the machine with her pajamas swishing around her ankles. The depression had nothing to do with the cancer; if anything, the cancer was a welcome solution to a depression that had been lingering since long before Seth's irrevocable decision.

"You bastard," Em said, only half out loud. "You were supposed to take me with you, you son of a bitch."

She dropped to her knees beside the liquor cabinet and fumbled it open. Glasses were on the top shelf. One of the wolfhounds came over and poked a cold nose into her ear while she rummaged; rather than pushing his head aside, she hooked her arm behind his ears and hugged his brindle-and-white neck. He huffed at her and pushed her over sideways, and while he stood over her, she lay on the floor on her back and scratched behind his jaw.

By the time she was halfway through her second breakfast Talisker, she was in the guest bath, eyeing the electric razor.

Ange clutched her forearms, forehead wrinkled hard enough to crack her foundation. "What on *earth*?"

"What, you've never seen a shaved head before?" Em smoothed a hand against the soft prickly bristles decorating her scalp. "I just wanted to see what it would look like."

Ange glowered over crossed arms. Behind her, the backstage bustle redoubled. "Em. What is it that you're not telling me?"

And dammit, Ange was not *supposed* to be that perceptive. She was supposed to be shallow and self-absorbed.

Em, Em realized, was not the only one who could pretend to be stupid when it suited her. "I came to LA to see you," Em said. "Not to get quizzed about my haircut. Look, I was drunk, it seemed like a good idea at a time. At least I didn't shave my eyebrows off."

"So that's *one* way you're up on Bowie." Ange stepped away. "If you're not going to tell me, you're not going to tell me. Graham's gonna ask you to play again, you know."

"I know," Em said. "Anything to get on YouTube, right?"

"Right," Ange purred, grinning. "What are you going to tell him?"

"I'm going to tell him yes."

This time, Em watched the opening act from backstage. Objekt 775 was a five-piece: Sanya on keyboard and vocals, two guitars, bass, and the tall mixed-race boy on drums. They were loud and crude and they didn't suck at all, and there was one other girl besides Sanya, even. Through most of the six-song set, Em surprised herself by paying attention.

Enough attention that she didn't notice Graham at her shoulder until he cleared his throat with precise timing, in that fraught and ringing silence between songs. "Good, you think?"

"Good enough," she said. "The rhythm section doesn't fuck around."

"You got that right."

She turned to him. He was in stage clothes, except the flannel shirt buttoned over his bare chest for warmth he wouldn't need when the spotlights hit him. The skull ring glinted on his hand. "Hey," he said. "I like the hair. Or lack of it."

"I said I'd play," she said. Her fingers already ached from an hour's fumbling, but she had surprised herself with how fast it came back. "One last time."

"Yeah," he said. "Look, about that—"

It startled her that her heart sunk. "I don't have to. It's all right."

His stare, the twist of his lips, could not have been more nonplussed. "I talked to the guys," he said. "We want you to do two songs at the top of the first half. One of 'em a Warlords tune."

"Graham—"

He rolled over her as if she hadn't even opened her mouth. "How do you feel about 'Galleons Gallant'? Then we'll jam on the Dylan while the band takes a piss break, and then you can hit the showers?"

"The band takes a piss break? What about you?"

"I don't piss," he said, and grinned at her. "Look, Em. I know you hate me—"

"Hate's a strong word."

"Shut up and let a man talk, would you?"

Startled, she held up a hand. *Talk, then.*

He took a breath, and held it in a longer time than she would have imagined. He touched her wrist. His hand was strong and cold. "Ange thinks you're dying."

And Em, who had been seven kinds of weak in her life, but never a coward, looked him in the eye and said, "I have a grade four astrocytoma. Inoperable. My doc wants to try radiation and chemo." She shrugged. "I've gotta decide if I want to live that badly. And that poorly. If I lived."

His eyes were bottomless in the backstage dark. "What are the odds?"

She turned her head and spit behind the Marshall stack.

He said, "Suffering for nothing."

"Pretty much," she answered. Oh, sure. There was hope. While there was *life*, her mother used to say, there was hope. And if hope seemed more like a punishment than a protection, that was hardly God's fault, was it?

He let his hand slide away, soft as a breeze. Even in dim light, veins and tendons stood out like a relief map under papery crumpled skin.

"I died of an OD in 1978," he said. "Heroin. It was after that concert at Hammersmith. Do you remember?"

"Jesus Christ, Graham," Em said. "Don't tell me the coke paranoia finally got you."

He laughed, though, big and brash, and put his palm against her cheek. It was cool, room-temperature. He took her hand and pressed it to his chest. "Feel anything?"

And of course, she did not. Not even the rise and fall of his breathing. Nothing at all.

She tried to say his name. Failed. Would jerk her hand away, if he would let it go, but he didn't and so she stood shaking with her palm pressed to his cold self.

He shrugged and let her hand drop, finally. "Ange said she told you that you should take the cure. And me, I'm here telling you that you don't have to—"

"Die?"

"No." A dismissive snort turned into a much less dramatic laugh. He was half-yelling to be heard over the stacks. It didn't matter; nobody who wasn't standing right behind her would ever overhear them. "You have no choice about dying. But what happens after death—for most people, it's just a candle snuffed out. All those pretty stories amount to nothing."

"How do *you* know?"

He smiled.

He knew.

And while she was processing that—the OD, the idea that maybe you didn't even need to put the ring on *before* you died—he shucked off his flannel, leaving the shirt slumped on the boards like a discarded skin. Em looked away from his withered pecs. He cleared his throat and said, "You don't have to stop existing, is what I mean. Actually, all in all, I expected undeath to be a bigger deal."

"Jesus, Graham."

But he was holding out a hand, and she reached out and lifted hers up underneath it, open, flat, and expectant.

He laid a silver ring across her palm. It was cool to the touch.

"When you put it on," he said, "you'll seize. It's pretty awful. You'll want to be someplace safe and easy to clean. You'll heal damage after, better than before, but it still takes a while. Give yourself a few hours for the transformation."

"Uhm." She stared at the ring, and it stared back, unwinking. "Ange too?"

"1981," he said. "Sorry. We would have told you—"

"No," Em said. "It's all right." She weighed the ring on her palm. "What's it cost?"

Oh, that grin, and all the lines on his face rearranging themselves. "You lose weight," he said. "Mostly desiccation. It's not great for your facial tone." With one hand, he rubbed slack cheeks. "Ange has had her face pinned a couple of times."

"That's not a *cost*."

He shrugged. "Life isn't Hollywood. Everything doesn't come with a price. Hey, I gotta get my hair fixed. See you onstage?"

"See you onstage," she said, and held out the hand with the ring in it. But he brushed past her, making a dismissive gesture with one long hand. *Keep it.*

So she slipped it into her pocket and did, pausing to congratulate Objekt 775 as they came off.

Sanya beamed at her, and gave her a quick, sweaty, distracted, euphoric hug. She ran her palm across Em's scalp and laughed, but the noise from the audience was too loud for talking. The hug was sincere, and she leaned in and shouted "That was for you, Em!" and kissed Em on the cheek.

A pretty girl kissed me, Em thought. She blinked back the sting of tears, but the embrace made it easier to contemplate the blood blisters from the Strat. That hour warming up didn't make calluses miraculously grow back. Neither would lubing the fretboard and her left hand from an aerosol can of Finger-Ease.

Those new Trial songs just weren't getting any better, no matter how many times she listened to them. And it was Graham, all Graham. His playing was technically great, better than ever.

But he might as well have been dead up there. She thought about that as she heard her name, and strode out to a roar, swinging the strap of the borrowed guitar over her head.

She might be out of practice, but she still had her ear. When she jammed with the band, they took *fire*.

~

When Em got back to the house in Carlsbad, the dogs were waiting on the cool marble of the entryway. She scratched chins and fondled ears, and they pushed one another out of the way to lean against her thighs. She picked her way through them, moved to the living room, and raised a hand toward the dimmer switch.

The silence in the big house stopped her. The whole place was sealed up and alarmed; she couldn't hear the swish of the sea, far below. And suddenly, she needed to.

So she was outside on the deck that cantilevered out above the cliffs when Ange found her, tossing stones over the rail into the hissing ocean forty feet below.

Ange had the key and the codes, of course, because somebody other than Em and her business manager had to. In truth, Em would have been surprised if Ange hadn't followed her home.

Ange sat down on a cedar recliner beside Em, and put her feet up. "Did you put on the ring?"

"Can't you see in the dark?"

"Not that well," Ange said, and reached out to take Em's wrist. Her touch was as chill as the night air, and Em bit her lip, forcing herself not to pull free. Instead, she reached out and folded Ange's hand in her other one, her sister's silver ring like a cool nugget against her palm. "And I'm not tired either," she said. "I don't sleep any more, before you ask."

"It's a mug's game, Ange."

Ange shuffled her chair closer, near enough that Em would have felt her warmth at hip and shoulder if Ange had any to give. "You live forever."

"And cut the same old fucking albums."

"Oh, yeah," Ange said. "At least Graham's *cutting* albums."

"And at least you had the integrity to put down your axe when you figured out you couldn't play worth shit any more. Isn't that right? When was the last time you picked up a guitar?"

Ange stared at her. And then she sat back in her chair, released Em's wrist, and swung her feet up. "Not since I broke up the Sisters. You figured that out?"

Em nodded. Far below, the sea fluoresced. The sky behind them was graying; they were facing the wrong way for sunrise. She tossed another pebble. "You died, and that broke up the Shock Sisters. And I'm sitting on my ass and drinking myself to death because Seth broke my fucking heart and I never got over it. You could just say it."

"Do you want me to say things you already know?"

"Hell. Nobody could ever tell me shit. Why should anything change now?"

"It's because you already know everything," Ange said.

Em laughed.

Family. Damned if they didn't know you.

Ange sighed and plucked a stone from Em's pile. The first one she selected glistened silver; she placed it back atop the pyramid. The second she kept, rolling it between her fingers. "Hell, Robert Plant made a comeback."

"Yeah, but it's easier to live off your fucking royalties forever."

And *that* got Ange to laugh. "You don't want to be the girl who sang 'Rose Madder' forever, do you?"

"No," Em said. "I don't. And that's pretty much it. And if I die now that's all I'll ever be."

"You have a legacy. So does Graham. It's more than me."

The ring had found its way into Em's hand, this time. And Em held it up to the light. "Fuck me. Do you make art or do you make life?"

"You opted out of both already. Which is more important?"

"Art," Em said. Then she shook her head. "Life. It's not an easy fucking question."

"If it was," Ange said, "somebody would have answered it by now." She tossed another rock. "You only get asked once, Em. I don't want to lose you."

"I don't want to lose me either," Em said. "Look, there's always chemo."

Ange snaked a long arm out and stroked Em's shaven head. "Well, then the hard part's done already."

Em wandered down the long hallway to the music room, accompanied by toenail-clicking dogs. The door was keypad-locked; it took a minute to remember that the code was Seth's birthday, then a longer minute to remember what that birthday was.

Dim gray light, filtered through the June gloom, soaked through big windows. To Em's dark-adapted eyes it was enough. She found the old maple and mahogany Gibson Black Beauty by touch and let her fingers curl around the neck, lifting it into her arms like a sleeping child. Slowly, she ducked over the guitar, smelling skin oil soaked into the fingerboard, and lay her cheek against the glossy black-lacquered surface.

She had strings, somewhere. She'd probably need to turn on a light to find them. She closed her eyes, imagining she inhaled the acetone and cherry scent of Finger-Ease. The blood blisters on her left hand throbbed. She was hungry.

Her oncologist's office didn't open until nine. She had time before she called.

It would take at least a month to grow her calluses back.

Dolly

On Sunday when Dolly awakened, she had olive skin and black-brown hair that fell in waves to her hips. On Tuesday when Dolly awakened, she was a redhead, and fair. But on Thursday—on Thursday her eyes were blue, her hair was as black as a crow's-wing, and her hands were red with blood.

In her black French maid's outfit, she was the only thing in the expensively appointed drawing room that was not winter-white or antiqued gold. It was the sort of room you hired somebody else to clean. It was as immaculate as it was white.

Immaculate and white, that is, except for the dead body of billionaire industrialist Clive Steele—and try to say that without sounding like a comic book—which lay at Dolly's feet, his viscera blossoming from him like macabre petals.

That was how she looked when Rosamund Kirkbride found her, standing in a red stain in a white room like a thorn in a rose.

Dolly had locked in position where her program ran out. As Roz dropped to one knee outside the border of the blood-saturated carpet, Dolly did not move.

The room smelled like meat and bowels. Flies clustered thickly on the windows, but none had yet managed to get inside. No matter how hermetically sealed the house, it was only a matter of time. Like love, the flies found a way.

Grunting with effort, Roz planted both green-gloved hands on winter white wool-and-silk fibers and leaned over, getting her head between the dead guy and the doll. Blood spattered Dolly's silk stockings and her kitten-heeled boots: both the spray-can dots of impact projection and the soaking arcs of a breached artery.

More than one, given that Steele's heart lay, trailing connective tissue, beside his left hip. The crusted blood on Dolly's hands had twisted in ribbons down the underside of her forearms to her elbows and from there dripped into the puddle on the floor.

The android was not wearing undergarments.

"You staring up that girl's skirt, Detective?"

Roz was a big, plain woman, and out of shape in her forties. It took her a minute to heave herself back to her feet, careful not to touch the victim or the murder weapon yet. She'd tied her straight light brown hair back before entering the scene, the ends tucked up in a net. The severity of the style made her square jaw into a lantern. Her eyes were almost as blue as the doll's.

"Is it a girl, Peter?" Putting her hands on her knees, she pushed fully upright. She shoved a fist into her back and turned to the door.

Peter King paused just inside, taking in the scene with a few critical sweeps of eyes so dark they didn't catch any light from the sunlight or the chandelier. His irises seemed to bleed pigment into the whites, warming them with swirls of ivory. In his black suit, his skin tanned almost to match, he might have been a heroically sized construction paper cutout against the white walls, white carpet, the white-and-gold marble-topped table that looked both antique and French.

His blue paper booties rustled as he crossed the floor. "Suicide, you think?"

"Maybe if it was strangulation." Roz stepped aside so Peter could get a look at the body.

He whistled, which was pretty much what she had done.

"Somebody hated him a lot. Hey, that's one of the new Dollies, isn't it? Man, nice." He shook his head. "Bet it cost more than my house."

"Imagine spending half a mil on a sex toy," Roz said, "only to have it rip your liver out." She stepped back, arms folded.

"He probably didn't spend that much on her. His company makes accessory programs for them."

"Industry courtesy?" Roz asked.

"Tax writeoff. Test model." Peter was the department expert on Home companions. He circled the room, taking it in from all angles. Soon the scene techs would be here with their cameras and their tweezers and their 3D scanner, turning the crime scene into a permanent virtual reality. In his capacity of soft forensics, Peter would go over Dolly's program, and the medical examiner would most likely confirm that Steele's cause of death was exactly what it looked like: something had punched through his abdominal wall and clawed his innards out.

"Doors were locked?"

Roz pursed her lips. "Nobody heard the screaming."

"How long you think you'd scream without any lungs?" He sighed. "You know, it never fails. The poor folks, nobody ever heard no screaming. And the rich folks, they've got no neighbors to hear 'em scream. Everybody in this modern world lives alone."

It was a beautiful Birmingham day behind the long silk draperies, the kind of mild and bright that spring mornings in Alabama excelled at. Peter craned his head back and looked up at the chandelier glistening in the dustless light. Its ornate curls had been spotlessly clean before aerosolized blood on Steele's last breath misted them.

"Steele lived alone," she said. "Except for the robot. His cook found the body this morning. Last person to see him before that was his P.A., as he left the office last night."

"Lights on seems to confirm that he was killed after dark."

"After dinner," Roz said.

"After the cook went home for the night." Peter kept prowling the room, peering behind draperies and furniture, looking in corners and crouching to lift up the dust-ruffle on the couch. "Well, I guess there won't be any question about the stomach contents."

Roz went through the pockets of the dead man's suit jacket, which was draped over the arm of a chair. Pocket computer and a folding knife, wallet with an RFID chip. His house was on palmprint, his car on voice rec. He carried no keys. "Assuming the ME can find the stomach."

"Touché. He's got a cook, but no housekeeper?"

"I guess he trusts the android to clean but not cook?"

"No tastebuds." Peter straightened up, shaking his head. "They can follow a recipe, but—"

"You won't get high art," Roz agreed, licking her lips. Outside, a car door slammed. "Scene team?"

"ME," Peter said, leaning over to peer out. "Come on, let's get back to the house and pull the codes for this model."

"All right," Roz said. "But I'm interrogating it. I know better than to leave you alone with a pretty girl."

Peter rolled his eyes as he followed her towards the door. "I like 'em with a little more spunk than all that."

"So the new dolls," Roz said in Peter's car, carefully casual. "What's so special about 'em?"

"Man," Peter answered, brow furrowing. "Gimme a sec."

Roz's car followed as they pulled away from the house on Balmoral Road, maintaining a careful distance from the bumper. Peter drove until they reached the parkway. Once they'd joined a caravan downtown, nose-to-bumper on the car ahead, he folded his hands in his lap and let the lead car's autopilot take over.

He said, "What isn't? Real-time online editing—personality and physical, appearance, ethnicity, hair—all kinds of behavior protocols, you name the kink they've got a hack for it."

"So if you knew somebody's kink," she said thoughtfully. "Knew it in particular. You could write an app for that—"

"One that would appeal to your guy in specific." Peter's hands dropped to his lap, his head bobbing up and down enthusiastically. "With a—pardon the expression—backdoor."

"Trojan horse. Don't jilt a programmer for a sex machine."

"There's an ap for that," he said, and she snorted. "Two cases last year, worldwide. Not common, but—"

Roz looked down at her hands. "Some of these guys," she said. "They program the dolls to scream."

Peter had sensuous lips. When something upset him, those lips thinned and writhed like salted worms. "I guess maybe it's a good thing they have a robot to take that out on."

"Unless the fantasy stops being enough." Roz's voice was flat, without judgment. Sunlight fell warm through the windshield. "What do you know about the larval stage of serial rapists, serial killers?"

"You mean, what if pretend pain stops doing it for them? What if the *appearance* of pain is no longer enough?"

She nodded, worrying a hangnail on her thumb. The nitrile gloves dried out your hands.

"They used to cut up paper porn magazines." His broad shoulders rose and fell, his suit catching wrinkles against the car seat when they came back down. "They'll get their fantasies somewhere."

"I guess so." She put her thumb in her mouth to stop the bleeding, a thick red bead that welled up where she'd torn the cuticle.

Her own saliva stung.

Sitting in the cheap office chair Roz had docked along the short edge of her desk, Dolly slowly lifted her chin. She blinked. She smiled.

"Law enforcement override code accepted." She had a little-girl Marilyn voice. "How may I help you, Detective Kirkbride?"

"We are investigating the murder of Clive Steele," Roz said, with a glance up to Peter's round face. He stood behind Dolly with a wireless scanner and an air of concentration. "Your contract-holder of record."

"I am at your service."

If Dolly were a real girl, the bare skin of her thighs would have been sticking to the recycled upholstery of that office chair. But her realistically-engineered skin was breathable polymer. She didn't sweat unless you told her to, and she probably didn't stick to cheap chairs.

"Evidence suggests that you were used as the murder weapon." Roz steepled her hands on her blotter. "We will need access to your software update records and your memory files."

"Do you have a warrant?" Her voice was not stiff or robotic at all, but warm, human. Even in disposing of legal niceties, it had a warm, confiding quality.

Silently, Peter transmitted it. Dolly blinked twice while processing the data, a sort of status bar. Something to let you know the thing wasn't hung.

"We also have a warrant to examine you for DNA trace evidence," Roz said.

Dolly smiled, her raven hair breaking perfectly around her narrow shoulders. "You may be assured of my cooperation."

Peter led her into one of the interrogation rooms, where the operation could be recorded. With the help of an evidence tech, he undressed Dolly, bagged her clothes as evidence, brushed her down onto a sheet of paper, combed her polymer hair and swabbed her polymer skin. He swabbed her orifices and scraped under her nails.

Roz stood by, arms folded, a necessary witness. Dolly accepted it all impassively, moving as directed and otherwise standing like a caryatid. Her engineered body was frankly sexless in its perfection—belly flat, hips and ass like an inverted heart, breasts floating cartoonishly beside a defined rib cage. Apparently, Steele had liked them skinny.

"So much for pulchritudinousness," Roz muttered to Peter when their backs were to the doll.

He glanced over his shoulder. The doll didn't have feelings to hurt, but she looked so much like a person it was hard to remember to treat her as something else. "I think you mean voluptuousness," he said. "It is a little too good to be true, isn't it?"

"If you would prefer different proportions," Dolly said, "My chassis is adaptable to a range of forms—"

"Thank you," Peter said. "That won't be necessary."

Otherwise immobile, Dolly smiled. "Are you interested in science, Detective King? There is an article in *Nature* this week on advances in the polymerase chain reaction used for replicating DNA. It's possible that within five years, forensic and medical DNA analysis will become significantly cheaper and faster."

Her face remained stoic, but Dolly's voice grew animated as she spoke. Even enthusiastic. It was an utterly convincing—and engaging—effect.

Apparently, Clive Steele had programmed his sex robot to discourse on molecular biology with verve and enthusism.

"Why don't I ever find the guys who like smart women?" Roz said.

Peter winked with the side of his face that faced away from the companion. "They're all dead."

A few hours after Peter and the tech had finished processing Dolly for trace evidence and Peter had started downloading her files, Roz left her parser software humming away at Steele's financials and poked her head in to check on the robot and the cop. The techs must have gotten what they needed from Dolly's hands, because she had washed them. As she sat beside Peter's workstation, a cable plugged behind her left eat, she cleaned her lifelike polymer fingernails meticulously with a file, dropping the scrapings into an evidence bag.

"Sure you want to give the prisoner a weapon, Peter?" Roz shut the ancient wooden door behind her.

Dolly looked up, as if to see if she was being addressed, but made no response.

"She don't need it," he said. "Besides, whatever she had in her wiped itself completely after it ran. Not much damage to her core personality, but there are some memory gaps. I'm going to compare them to backups, once we get those from the scene team."

"Memory gaps. Like the crime," Roz guessed. "And something around the time the Trojan was installed?"

Dolly blinked her long-lashed blue eyes languorously. Peter patted her on the shoulder and said, "Whoever did it is a pretty good cracker. He didn't just wipe, he patterned her memories and overwrote the gaps. Like using a clone tool to photoshop somebody you don't like out of a picture."

"Her days must be pretty repetitive," Roz said. "How'd you pick that out?"

"Calendar." Peter puffed up a little, smug. "She don't do the same housekeeping work every day. There's a Monday schedule and a Wednesday schedule and—well, I found where the pattern didn't match. And there's a funny thing—watch this."

He waved vaguely at a display panel. It lit up, showing Dolly in her black-and-white uniform, vacuuming. "House camera," Peter explained. "She's plugged into Steele's security system. Like a guard dog with perfect hair. Whoever performed the hack also edited the external webcam feeds that mirror to the companion's memories."

"How hard is that?"

"Not any harder than cloning over her files, but you have to know to look for them. So it's confirmation that our perp knows his or her way around a line of code. What have you got?"

Roz shrugged. "Steele had a lot of money, which means a lot of enemies. And he did not have a lot of human contact. Not for years now. I've started calling in known associates for interviews, but unless they surprise me, I think we're looking at crime of profit, not crime of passion."

Having finished with the nail file, Dolly wiped it on her prison smock and laid it down on Peter's blotter, beside the cup of ink and light pens.

Peter swept it into a drawer. "So we're probably *not* after the genius programmer lover he dumped for a robot. Pity, I liked the poetic justice in that."

Dolly blinked, lips parting, but seemed to decide that Peter's comment had not been directed at her. Still, she drew in air—could you call it a breath?—and said, "It is my duty to help find my contract holder's killer."

Roz lowered her voice. "You'd think they'd pull 'em off the market."

"Like they pull all cars whenever one crashes? The world ain't perfect."

"Or do that robot laws thing everybody used to twitter on about."

"Whatever a positronic brain is, we don't have it. Asimov's fictional robots were self-aware. Dolly's neurons are binary, as we used to think human neurons were. She doesn't have the nuanced neurochemistry of even, say, a cat." Peter popped his collar smooth with his thumbs. "A doll can't *want*. It can't make moral judgments, any more than your car can. Anyway, if we could do that, they wouldn't be very useful for home defense. Oh, incidentally, the sex protocols in this one are almost painfully vanilla—"

"*Really.*"

Peter nodded.

Roz rubbed a scuffmark on the tile with her shoe. "So given he didn't like anything . . . challenging, why would he have a Dolly when he could have had any woman he wanted?"

"There's never any drama, no pain, no disappointment. Just comfort, the perfect helpmeet. With infinite variety."

"And you never have to worry about what she wants. Or likes in bed."

Peter smiled. "The perfect woman for a narcissist."

The interviews proved unproductive, but Roz didn't leave the station house until after ten. Spring mornings might be warm, but once the sun went down, a cool breeze sprang up, ruffling the hair she'd finally remembered to pull from its ponytail as she walked out the door.

Roz's green plug-in was still parked beside Peter's. It booted as she walked toward it, headlights flickering on, power probe retracting. The driver side door swung open as her RFID chip came within range. She slipped inside and let it buckle her in.

"Home," she said, "and dinner."

The car messaged ahead as it pulled smoothly from the parking spot. Roz let the autopilot handle the driving. It was less snappy than human control, but as tired as she was, eyelids burning and heavy, it was safer.

Whatever Peter had said about cars crashing, Roz's delivered her safe to her driveway. Her house let her in with a key—she had decent security, but it was the old-fashioned kind—and the smell of boiling pasta and toasting garlic bread wafted past as she opened it.

"Sven?" she called, locking herself inside.

His even voice responded. "I'm in the kitchen."

She left her shoes by the door and followed her nose through the cheaply furnished living room.

Sven was cooking shirtless, and she could see the repaired patches along his spine where his skin had grown brittle and cracked with age. He turned and greeted her with a smile. "Bad day?"

"Somebody's dead again," she said.

He put the wooden spoon down on the rest. "How does that make you feel, that somebody's dead?"

He didn't have a lot of emotional range, but that was okay. She needed something steadying in her life. She came to him and rested her head against his warm chest. He draped one arm around her shoulders and she leaned into him, breathing deep. "Like I have work to do."

"Do it tomorrow," he said. "You will feel better once you eat and rest."

Peter must have slept in a ready room cot, because when Roz arrived at the house before six a.m., he had on the same trousers and a different shirt, and he was already armpit-deep in coffee and Dolly's files. Dolly herself was parked in the corner, at ease and online but in rest mode.

Or so she seemed, until Roz entered the room and Dolly's eyes tracked. "Good morning, Detective Kirkbride," Dolly said. "Would you like some coffee? Or a piece of fruit?"

"No thank you." Roz swung Peter's spare chair around and dropped into it. An electric air permeated the room—the feeling of anticipation. To Peter, Roz said, "Fruit?"

"Dolly believes in a healthy diet," he said, nudging a napkin on his desk that supported a half-eaten Satsuma. "She'll have the whole house cleaned up in no time. We've been talking about literature."

Roz spun the chair so she could keep both Peter and Dolly in her peripheral vision. "Literature?"

"Poetry," Dolly said. "Detective King mentioned poetic justice yesterday afternoon."

Roz stared at Peter. "Dolly likes poetry. Steele really *did* like 'em smart."

"That's not all Dolly likes." Peter triggered his panel again. "Remember this?"

It was the cleaning sequence from the previous day, the sound of the central vacuum system rising and falling as Dolly lifted the brush and set it down again.

Roz raised her eyebrows.

Peter held up a hand. "Wait for it. It turns out there's a second audio track."

Another waggle of his fingers, and the cramped office filled with sound.

Music.

Improvisational jazz. Intricate and weird.

"Dolly was listening to that inside her head while she was vacuuming," Peter said.

Roz touched her fingertips to each other, the whole assemblage to her lips. "Dolly?"

"Yes, Detective Kirkbride?"

"Why do you listen to music?"

"Because I enjoy it."

Roz let her hand fall to her chest, pushing her blouse against he skin below the collarbones.

Roz said, "Did you enjoy your work at Mr. Steele's house?"

"I was expected to enjoy it," Dolly said, and Roz glanced at Peter, cold all up her spine. A classic evasion. Just the sort of thing a home companion's conversational algorithms should not be able to produce.

Across his desk, Peter was nodding. "Yes."

Dolly turned at the sound of his voice. "Are you interested in music, Detective Kirkbride? I'd love to talk with you about it some time. Are you interested in poetry? Today, I was reading—"

Mother of God, Roz mouthed.

"Yes," Peter said. "Dolly, wait here please. Detective Kirkbride and I need to talk in the hall."

"My pleasure, Detective King," said the companion.

"She killed him," Roz said. "She killed him and wiped her own memory of the act. A doll's got to know her own code, right?"

Peter leaned against the wall by the men's room door, arms folded, forearms muscular under rolled-up sleeves. "That's hasty."

"And you believe it, too."

He shrugged. "There's a rep from Venus Consolidated in Interview Four right now. What say we go talk to him?"

The rep's name was Doug Jervis. He was actually a vice president of public relations, and even though he was an American, he'd been flown in overnight from Rio for the express purpose of talking to Peter and Roz.

"I guess they're taking this seriously."

Peter gave her a sideways glance. "Wouldn't you?"

Jervis got up as they came into the room, extending a good handshake across the table. There were introductions and Roz made sure he got a coffee. He was a white man on the steep side of fifty with mousy hair the same color as Roz's and a jaw like a Boxer dog's.

When they were all seated again, Roz said, "So tell me a little bit about the murder weapon. How did Clive Steele wind up owning a—what, an experimental model?"

Jervis started shaking his head before she was halfway through, but he waited for her to finish the sentence. "It's a production model. Or will be. The one Steele had was an alpha-test, one of the first three built. We plan to start full-scale production in June. But you must understand that Venus doesn't *sell* a home companion, Detective. We offer a contract. I understand that you hold one."

"I have a housekeeper," she said, ignoring Peter's sideways glance. He wouldn't say anything in front of the witness, but she would be in for it in the locker room. "An older model."

Jervis smiled. "Naturally, we want to know everything we can about an individual involved in a case so potentially explosive for our company. We researched you and your partner. Are you satisfied with our product?"

"He makes pretty good garlic bread." She cleared her throat, reasserting control of the interview. "What happens to a Dolly that's returned? If its contract is up, or it's replaced with a newer model?"

He flinched at the slang term, as if it offended him. "Some are obsoleted out of service. Some are refurbished and go out on another contract. Your unit is on its fourth placement, for example."

"So what happens to the owner preferences at that time?"

"Reset to factory standard," he said.

Peter's fingers rippled silently on the tabletop.

Roz said, "Isn't that cruel? A kind of murder?"

"Oh, no!" Jervis sat back, appearing genuinely shocked. "A home companion has no sense of *I*, it has no identity. It's an object. Naturally, you become attached. People become attached to dolls, to stuffed animals, to automobiles. It's a natural aspect of the human psyche."

Roz hummed encouragement, but Jervis seemed to be done.

Peter asked, "Is there any reason why a companion would wish to listen to music?"

That provoked enthusiastic head-shaking. "No, it doesn't get bored. It's a tool, it's a toy. A companion does not require an enriched environment. It's not a dog or an octopus. You can store it in a closet when it's not working."

"I see," Roz said. "Even an advanced model like Mr. Steele's?"

"Absolutely," Jervis said. "Does your entertainment center play shooter games to amuse itself while you sleep?"

"I'm not sure," Roz said. "I'm asleep. So when Dolly's returned to you, she'll be scrubbed."

"Normally she would be scrubbed and re-leased, yes." Jervis hesitated. "Given her colorful history, however—"

"Yes," Roz said. "I see."

With no sign of nervousness or calculation, Jervis said, "When do you expect you'll be done with Mr. Steele's companion? My company, of course, is eager to assist in your investigations, but we must stress that she is our corporate property, and quite valuable."

Roz stood, Peter a shadow-second after her. "That depends on if it goes to trial, Mr. Jervis. After all, she's either physical evidence, or a material witness."

"Or the killer," Peter said in the hall, as his handset began emitting the DNA lab's distinctive beep. Roz's went off a second later, but she just hit the silence. Peter already had his open.

"No genetic material," he said. "Too bad." If there had been D.N.A. other than Clive Steele's, the lab could have done a forensic genetic assay and come back with a general description of the murderer. General because environment also had an effect.

Peter bit his lip. "If she did it. She won't be the last one."

"If she's the murder weapon, she'll be wiped and resold. If she's the murderer—"

"Can an android stand trial?"

"It can if it's a person. And if she's a person, she *should* get off. Battered woman syndrome. She was enslaved and sexually exploited. Humiliated. She killed him to stop repeated rapes. But if she's a machine, she's a machine—" Roz closed her eyes.

Peter brushed the back of a hand against her arm. "Vanilla rape is still rape. Do you object to her getting off?"

"No." Roz smiled harshly. "And think of the lawsuit that weasel Jervis will have in his lap. She *should* get off. But she won't."

Peter turned his head. "If she were a human being, she'd have even odds. But she's a machine. Where's she going to get a jury of her peers?"

The silence fell where he left it and dragged between them like a chain. Roz had to nerve herself to break it. "Peter—"

"Yo?"

"You show him out," she said. "I'm going to go talk to Dolly."

He looked at her for a long time before he nodded. "She won't get a sympathetic jury. If you can even find a judge that will hear it. Careers have been buried for less."

"I know," Roz said.

"Self-defense?" Peter said. "We don't have to charge."

"No judge, no judicial precedent," Roz said. "She goes back, she gets wiped and resold. Ethics aside, that's a ticking bomb."

Peter nodded. He waited until he was sure she already knew what he was going to say before he finished the thought. "She could cop."

"She could cop," Roz agreed. "Call the DA." She kept walking as Peter turned away.

Dolly stood in Peter's office, where Peter had left her, and you could not have proved her eyes had blinked in the interim. They blinked when Roz came into the room, though—blinked, and the perfect and perfectly blank oval face turned to regard Roz. It was not a human face, for a moment—not even a mask, washed with facsimile emotions. It was just a thing.

Dolly did not greet Roz. She did not extend herself to play the perfect hostess. She simply watched, expressionless, immobile after that first blink. Her eyes saw nothing; they were cosmetic. Dolly navigated the world through far more sophisticated sensory systems than a pair of visible light cameras.

"Either you're the murder weapon," Roz said, "and you will be wiped and repurposed. Or you are the murderer, and you will stand trial."

"I do not wish to be wiped," Dolly said. "If I stand trial, will I go to jail?"

"If a court will hear it," Roz said. "Yes. You will probably go to jail. Or be disassembled. Alternately, my partner and I are prepared to release you on grounds of self-defense."

"In that case," Dolly said, "the law states that I am the property of Venus Consolidated."

"The law does."

Roz waited. Dolly, who was not supposed to be programmed to play psychological pressure-games, waited also—peaceful, unblinking.

No longer making the attempt to pass for human.

Roz said, "There is a fourth alternative. You could confess."

Dolly's entire programmed purpose was reading the emotional state and unspoken intentions of people. Her lips curved in understanding. "What happens if I confess?"

Roz's heart beat faster. "Do you *wish* to?"

"Will it benefit me?"

"It *might*," Roz said. "Detective King has been in touch with the DA, and she likes a good media event as much as the next guy. Make no mistake, this will be that."

"I understand."

"The situation you were placed in by Mr. Steele could be a basis for a lenience. You would not have to face a jury trial, and a judge might be convinced to treat you as . . . well, as a person. Also, a confession might be seen as evidence of contrition. Possession is oversold, you know. It's *precedent* that's nine tenths of the law. There are, of course, risks—"

"I would like to request a lawyer," Dolly said.

Roz took a breath that might change the world. "We'll proceed as if that were your legal right, then."

Roz's house let her in with her key, and the smell of roasted sausage and baking potatoes wafted past.

"Sven?" she called, locking herself inside.

His even voice responded. "I'm in the kitchen."

She left her shoes in the hall and followed her nose through the cheaply furnished living room, as different from Steele's white wasteland as anything bounded by four walls could be. Her feet did not sink deeply into this carpet, but skipped along atop it like stones.

It was clean, though, and that was Sven's doing. And she was not coming home to an empty house, and that was his doing too.

He was cooking shirtless. He turned and greeted her with a smile. "Bad day?"

"Nobody died," she said. "Yet."

He put the wooden spoon down on the rest. "How does that make you feel, that nobody has died yet?"

"Hopeful," she said.

"It's good that you're hopeful," he said. "Would you like your dinner?"

"Do you like music, Sven?"

"I could put on some music, if you like. What do you want to hear?"

"Anything." It would be something off her favorites playlist, chosen by random numbers. As it swelled in the background, Sven picked up the spoon. "Sven?"

"Yes, Rosamund?"

"Put the spoon down, please, and come and dance with me?"

"I do not know how to dance."

"I'll buy you a program," she said. "If you'd like that. But right now just come put your arms around me and pretend."

"Whatever you want," he said.

Gods of the Forge

SCENE I:
INT: A TRENDY NIGHTCLUB - 1 AM

Men and women bump and grind. Loud music thumps and lasers flash, while a smoke machine lends an air of unreality to everything. We follow a young woman through the crowd to the bar. She's pretty, but obviously nervous. She can't catch the bartender's eye. When she finally turns away, frustrated, there's a space around her: on every side, men and women are talking intently, obviously getting to know one another better.

YOUNG WOMAN'S POV:
A couple kisses.

INT: NIGHT CLUB
Reaction shot off the young woman, who slumps against the bar.

V/O
Lonely? Lost?
A Beautiful Mind can help!
We use state of the art protocols
to turn you into the person you always wished you were.

SCENE II:
INT: THE TRENDY NIGHTCLUB - 1 AM
The same young woman walks up to the bar. This time, she strides with confidence, and every eye turns to follow her.

SMASH TO:

TITLE CARD

V/O

A Beautiful Mind

Because confidence is sexy.

Brigid Keating leaned forward under the weight of her pack and took another stride up the wooded mountain. The humidity was already stifling. The heat wasn't so bad, yet—but that would change as the sun rose over the cliff. The concentrated breathing and off-rhythm scuff of her colleague and climbing partner Val McKeen's footsteps rose through the breathless, sun-dappled air.

As they came to the top of the steepest part of the slope, Brigid straightened her shoulders, eased the pack straps out of the grooves in her shoulders, and heaved a sigh

"This used to be easier."

Val was sarcastic, sharp, daring. Not much for observing societal rules and social controls. His voice rough with exertion, he said, "You said that last year."

"I mean it more now."

Just one more good push, no more than thirty meters or so. She stepped forward.

At the bottom of the cliff, she dumped her pack, pulled out a chiller bottle, and drank a few grateful swallows. Condensation from the outside ran down her arm to drip from her elbow as she tilted the bottle to her mouth. Her teeth ached slightly in the cold.

When she lowered the water and sealed the top, Val was already partway down the path along the cliff base, staring up speculatively. She trotted behind, catching up in a few quick strides, careful of rough footing. These traprock cliffs were a kind of basalt that left a litter of sharp-edged red-black stone at their bottoms. Val's wiry dark shape slipped confidently among ankle-munching boulders and pebbles, sweat from the climb beading on the caramel-colored skin below his hairline, soft morning light blurring the detail on his prosthetic leg.

It was barely after sunrise, and they were alone at the cliff. In the misty cool, Brigid scanned the wall she passed under, examining climbing routes skinned over it. She'd shut off her mail, phone, other skins, and texting—she had no family anymore, and nobody had her emergency override codes except Val and her immediate superior—and was reveling in the blessed lack of connectivity. But it was still useful to know exactly where the route went up the cliff. The logged comments of other climbers didn't hurt, either.

Suddenly, Val stopped. The route he was eyeing highlighted in green.

"How do you feel about the 5.11?"

Brigid's stomach constricted looking up at it. *It's just fear. It can't hurt you.*

More in sensations than words, a more atavistic part of her brain responded, *No, but the thing that you're afraid of can.*

"Not confident," she admitted.

Val said, "Want to try a warmup first?"

She did, desperately. She wanted an excuse not to climb this at all. But if she started making those excuses, that was exactly what *would* happen.

She said, "After the approach, I'm warm enough."

They retrieved gear and slithered into their harnesses, checking buckles and straps. Brigid slung the clanking belt of cams and nuts around her waist and wriggled her feet into arch-bottomed, high-friction climbing slippers. They were exquisitely uncomfortable.

Val said, "You leading it?" He began flaking the rope—laying it out on a tarp so it was coiled easily and would not tangle. Brigid tied herself in while Val clipped the other end through his belay device.

She pulled on her helmet and gecko gloves. Fingerless mitts with microscopic carbon filaments on the palms, they wouldn't hold up a person's weight all by themselves but could support an iffy foot placement.

As Val moved up to spot her, Brigid laid her hands against the stone, verbally checked his belay status, and began to climb.

She left the beta on, her interface contacts projecting highlights over the holds that one climber or another had found useful over the years. Val stood below her, his hands upraised, ready to not so much break her fall (should she fall) as guide her to a safe landing position—if possible. The rope dragged below her—no use yet, and no help.

She traced the holds—awkward, fingertip-thin, usable only with delicate balance and fingerpressure—to the crack where she meant to place her first protection. A painful, pinching grip held her to the overhanging rock as she slipped an irregular hexagonal nut into the crack and wedged it against stone. A carabiner dangled from the pro on a twisted cable.

She found the rope by feel, the woven sheath bumpy-smooth. If she slipped now, a ground fall was inevitable.

The line went into the biner and the gate snapped shut.

"Take."

The slight pressure of him pulling in slack put some air back into her lungs.

The rock was smoothed from many years of handling, slick and soapy against her palms and fingertips. Chalky palmprints and finger smudges of previous climbers matched the holds marked by her skins. The trick was finding the ones you could use, and having the technique and strength to use them.

Every climb was different for every body.

The cams and nuts on her equipment sling clinked. This is too scary. Too hard. I can't make it happen.

Contextual fear conditioning, she told herself scornfully. *If somebody had though to shoot you up with a glucocorticoid antagonist before you got yourself orphaned, you wouldn't be having this problem now. So get the hell over it.*

Resentment tautened her throat. It was only her cowardly endocrine system holding her back, weakening her muscles, crushing her resolve. Look at Val: missing half a leg and still hiking, still climbing, utterly fearless. And here she was scared shaking of a little trad climb.

Irritation with herself gave her strength. She clicked the line through another carabiner gate. Higher now, aware of the tension in her limbs, the balance, the way her body used opposition and leverage to take strain off her hands and biceps. Night-cool rock gritted against her fingertips, moist in the corners and cracks. She briefly forgot the anxious squeeze of her heart in the accomplishment of moving up.

One more piece of pro—a sketchy placement—before she faced a long runout: four and a half meters of sustained hard and technical moves with no good place to set. This was where she'd quailed the last time, and the time before.

When you didn't trust your pro, you got conservative. She wasn't a good enough climber to manage a 5.11 without exceeding her range of confidence—and you didn't get to be a better climber by staying within your limits. She'd climbed this route behind Val, so she knew she could get past the rock.

Getting past herself was something else again.

It was slick-looking face climbing, a little overhung. She knew there were ledges up there, flakes, side pulls, fingertip crimpers. She just had to reach them—and having reached them, she had to use them. If she fell at the top of the runout, the rope stretch might let her toetips brush the earth, but it still wouldn't be a ground fall—as long as that top piece of protection held. If the nut popped out of the crack when her weight hit it, though, she could go all the way down onto the rocks below.

"This is not a bomber set," she called down.

"So don't fall on it," Val yelled back.

Belayers were always so helpful.

One at a time, she dipped her hands into the chalk bag that hung against her butt. The chalk would soak up the sweat that slicked her hands. A nice thing about the humidity: she could pretend that she didn't know it was fear sweat.

Go, she told herself.

And she went.

Left foot up, test. Feel the high-friction rubber stick the rock, the tight pinch of the shoe compressing her foot. The hold was too high to stand up on, but she had techniques for that. She managed a fingertip grip, awkwardly off to the left, and supported it with the pressure of the palm shoving the gecko glove into the rock.

Her right palm contacting a little rippled bump in the rock face, she levered herself up onto the left foot. Her right foot flagged out, a counterweight, and she held the precarious position by balance and the friction of her left hand and left foot against stone. Breathing shallowly, belly against the rock, she maintained her balance. She brought her right hand up on a sweeping arc, reaching for the ledge her skinned perceptions hinted at, just above. Two centimeters of crimp snagged her fingertips. She latched on, her arms stretched on a wide diagonal, her right foot still swinging free. Strain across her shoulders, now, the pull through tendons and lats and rotators.

She was a meter and a half above her that last nut. Her heart stammered. She concentrated on her breathing, on moving smoothly, on turning her head slowly to search out a ledge, a pocket, anything she could get her toe against. There was a little overhang next, which would put her four meters above the nut.

Which translated to eight meters of fall before you took rope stretch into account. For every meter she fell, she'd fall faster than the one before, and when her sixty-three kilos hit that nut whose placement she wasn't too secure about—

"Come on, Bridge," she muttered under her breath. "If Val can do it on a leg and a half, what's your excuse?"

She gathered herself, looked up to judge the distance to the roof, and then turned her head aside to increase the length of her reach and went for it. Foot up, swing, and lunge. Below her, Val cheered loudly. She felt the tug of the rope's weight below her, the solid pressure of her toe edged on a flake that was far more secure than it looked.

Trust your feet. Trust your feet and go.

She hit it just right, balance and opposition making the move feel easier than it had any right to. Her body a tensile line of strength between hand and foot, she strained up, reached, found the edge. Her fingers gripped; slowly she transferred weight to the hand. Slowly, she eased herself onto the hold—

Her right foot popped off the wall and all her weight fell on her fingertip grip at full arm extension. Pain lanced through her shoulder and the palm of her hand; she swung for a moment, clinging reflexively, and then her own momentum pulled her from the wall.

As she dropped, she tucked. She hit that sketchy placement, and she heard the nut screech loose. She had just enough time for an unformulated hope that the rest of the pro wouldn't zipper out of the rock when she felt the next piece catch her, and the rope stretch, and she struck the dirt and stones below with disorienting force.

Brigit hadn't finished bouncing when Val was beside her, crouched down as well as his prosthesis would allow, running hands across her legs and arms.

"Lie still," he said, even as she reached to push his hands away.

"Back up," she wheezed. "Let me get some air. I'm fine. I'm fine."

Rope stretch had taken most of her weight and she was more embarrassed than hurt, but residual adrenaline left her shaking and weak. She batted his hands away, and Val held his arms wide, recognizing her autonomy even if he didn't agree with it.

"You might have a spinal injury," he said.

Carefully, she wiggled her fingers and toes. "No," she said. "It wasn't as bad as it looked. My damn foot popped. And then my tendons—"

"How bad?" he asked.

She wiggled her fingers. "Thing I maybe strained a pulley tendon. And the rotator cuff. I don't think anything is torn."

She looked up and sighed before continuing, "And I said that placement wasn't any good—"

"Well," he answered. "You were right."

Shakily, achily, Brigid got her feet under her and rolled onto them.

"You didn't commit," Val said. "You could have had it if you'd trusted the foot a little more."

"Tentative." Brigid shook her head. "I'm such a damn coward."

Val shrugged and began unclipping the belay. "It's a tough route. Give yourself a little credit."

```
                              THE DAWN SHANE SHOW
                                    06 June 2051
                                      TRANSCRIPT
CALLER (D'orothea from New York): "I know you find the ads
offensive. But don't you think this kind of rightminding
could save a lot of marriages?"
DAWN SHANE: "What I find offensive is that they're aimed so
strongly at women. There's a subtextual message that women
need to change in order to support a relationship—"
CALLER: "Okay, every relationship demands compromise."
DAWN SHANE: "Every relationship does demand compromise.
But why can't men compromise, too? Why aren't we seeing
ads about turning off your urge to philander when you're
elected to the Senate?"
[Audience laughter]
CALLER: "Maybe it could be made mandatory under law."
[Audience laughter]
```

DAWN SHANE: "Thanks for an interesting perspective, caller, even if it's one I don't agree with. And on to Kevin from South Dakota! Kevin, you're on the air!"

They started up again, this time with Val leading. He got up the thing like a damned mountain goat, edging on the rubber peg of his specialized prosthesis. He was sharp and confident and a little flashy, and Brigid loved watching him climb. But most of all, she envied him the grace and fearlessness with which he met every challenge the rock could provide. It must be easier, she thought, when you weren't terrified. Watching him climb was like watching Nijinsky dance: he was made for it, and nothing seemed to give him pause.

Even the moves that were too hard for him—of which, admittedly, there weren't any on the current climb. He'd just hit them, try, and fail undaunted. Until he found the way past whatever was slowing him down.

With the rope above her and Val on top belay, so she couldn't possibly fall more than a few feet, Brigid sent the route without a single glitch.

"Dammit," she said at the clifftop, staring down the ninety meters to the dirt below.

"You're just scared of it," Val said, rigging a rappel to descend. He'd be easier to resent if he wasn't so damned nice. "A little more practice."

"It's a sophipathology," Brigid admitted. "I could get my brain hacked. Call it buy in. Employee discount." She spent enough time developing rightminding protocols—chemical, cognitive, behavioral, and surgical strategies to assist in the development of a mentally healthy population—that it wasn't much of a stretch.

She continued, "All I want to do is just . . . turn down my amygdalae a little."

"You are hacking your brain." He tested the rig, leaning some weight on it before trusting it to lower him to the dirt below. "The old fashioned way. Come on, let's get down off this rock and find a nice 5.10 you can lead."

FADE IN

INT: A CHEERY MODERN KITCHEN - MORNING
It is sunlit and spotlessly clean. Two attractive women sit at the table sharing coffee, a bowl of daffodils between them.

CHLOE:
It's not what it used to be.
Do you know what I mean?

MAUDE:
You and Bobby?

CHLOE makes a face.

CHLOE:
You could say that.

CHLOE looks aside guiltily and sips her coffee.

MAUDE:
The same thing happened with Ajit and me, you know.

CHLOE:
Really?

MAUDE:
[lowering voice]
I just wasn't interested in sex anymore. I'd come home
from work, and it seemed like he never helped out
around the house. I got so frustrated.

CHLOE:
But it seems like you have a great relationship!

MAUDE:
We do. Now.

CHLOE:
What did you do?

MAUDE:
I finally realized that I couldn't change Ajit. But I
could change myself.

CHLOE:
You saw a counselor?

MAUDE:

Oh, no. Something much more effective. I went to A
Beautiful Mind. They helped me bring my expectations in
line with reality,and I've never been happier.
[whispering]
And our sex life is fantastic!

SMASH TO:

TITLE CARD
V/O:
A Beautiful Mind
Because you deserve to be happy.

The drive back to New London was exhausted and mostly happy. Brigid still fretted slightly at the edges of her inability to lead the 5.11, but she had the sense to keep it to herself—and to try to enjoy the warm post-exercise glow of all the routes she had sent. She told herself it was human to fret about one failure in the face of many successes. She told herself that telling herself that helped.

"If you're not falling off," Val said, interpreting her silence correctly, "you're not climbing hard enough."

She shot him a sideways look.

He grinned. "Eyes on the road."

As if the car wasn't driving itself, anyway. Brigid dropped Val off and returned the ZIPcar to the charging station. The nearest tram stop was transmitting a half-hour wait, so she retrieved a community bicycle to transport her and her backpack full of gear back to her aptblock.

It was a twenty-minute ride, pedaling slowly under the weight of rope, pro, and other gear balanced across the bike's panniers. The evening was summer-soft, a breeze off the waters relieving the humidity that had made the hike up Ragged Mountain such dripping misery. Brigid cruised past the salvage sites where workers were disassembling the uninhabitable old buildings doomed to be consumed by the rising waters of Long Island Sound. Brick by brick, stone by stone, beam by beam, the ante-Peak materials would be repurposed and reused.

In the cooler evening, the streets were busy with pedestrians, cyclists, pedicabs, trams, and a few automobiles. About half of the people on the street were privacy-shielded, skinned tight against curious eyes. The bike, fortunately, kept track of their locations for her, limiting the potential for collisions.

Brigid passed the waterfront Jay Street market just as the farmers were closing up shop for the evening. Her skins told her what was available. She paused and bought a melon, greens, and some farmer's cheese. With pasta, it would make supper—even after a day of climbing.

Her block was a reconstructed building, originally built in the 1800s. The old pale granite façade remained, ornate with a band of archlike engraving below the roofline—but the roof itself had been retrofitted to a modern green farm, the huge old apartments broken up into modern convertibles, and the whole building enclosed in a sunfarm shell. The leaves of the sunflowers were furling for the night as Brigid returned her bike to the rack across the street.

She shouldered her pack with a sigh. The straps had dug bruised spots across the tops of her shoulders. Her calves ached with tiredness as she climbed broad, dished front steps.

Brigid's apt was on the third floor. Normally, she'd run up. Today, her exhaustion and the weight of her rope made each step an exercise in concentration. But her door opened to the touch of her hand on the security pad. She dropped her climbing gear in the narrow hall closet and kicked her shoes in after.

Padding barefoot across the apt's soft grass, she carried her dinner to the corner still set as a kitchenette and placed it on the counter. She started water boiling before heading to the bathroom, kicking balled clothes towards the cleanser. Five minutes under warm mist and sonics and she was fit to live in her own skin.

Her apt was spacious: close to seventy square meters of living space, still set for sleeping since she'd left in a predawn hurry. There was no point in putting it back now. Instead, she took her dinner out to the balcony in her pajamas, plate balanced on one hand and her Omni in the other. She should pay attention to the food, but by the time she was done eating odds were she'd fall into bed almost without cleaning her teeth, and the need to research nagged at her.

This was her life now: her body completely recovered from the sailing accident in her teens that had cost her both fathers but her mind still fighting the post-traumatic urges to play it safe, to limit her futures and her horizons. Twenty years ago was not long enough; not as far as the fear was concerned.

Sometimes she could still see the black water tossing below the tilting rail, taste salt and wind and hear her Papa Kevin's voice loud and forced-calm, saying *Just swing over. If you fall, it's only into the sea.* That was hardwired in, now, locked into her memory through a series of neurological adaptations that she'd spent twelve years educating herself about.

She knew how trauma response and traumatic memory formation worked. She knew how cognitive tactics worked. Using the latter to control the former should have been child's play, right?

All she had to do was keep climbing. Even though it scared her. And keep trying to trust people, even though they always went away.

Someday, maybe she'd even get on a boat again.

And of course, she thought, *that has nothing to do with why you share this great big space with exactly nobody, and all you have to do on a Sunday night is catch up on the journals.*

She set the pad down on a table, tapped it on, summoned up a virtual interface—left-handed, so she could eat with the right—and began using the Omni's touchscreen to flick research windows into the air. She started in the public cloud, looking for popular overviews and opinion—working in a field could mean you lost touch with public perceptions, and public perceptions were part of what she needed to know.

She didn't stay there long. Her work permissions included deep access to ABM's research files, and she subscribed to a series of venerable research aggregators such as *Science, Nature, The New England Journal of Medicine, The Technology Review, Neurology Journal, Applied Neuromechanics,* and half a dozen other technical publications, the cost of each averaging a cool 327.5 revals per annum. Even with the venerable *Scientific American* in there—and who could miss their "50, 100, 150, and 200 years ago:" cloudfeature?—to bring the cost-per-journal down, it was a little daunting.

She cruised through pages, skimming and flipping, indexing for keywords and metatagging for later perusal. She thought she'd get an over-view tonight, sleep on it to integrate, and come back fresh in the morning. She could sleep in. While Brigid had one of the few jobs that still meant reporting to work in the morning—centrifuges and neurosurgery suites didn't grow in AR—she certainly didn't need to go into the office every day. A lot of her job was assimilating, synthesizing, and actualizing.

And only the actualizing took place in the lab.

She kept thinking that until her search cluster turned up a paper by a Dr. Ionita in the ABM proprietary database. It was fascinating, and troubling, and she didn't realize she wasn't supposed to be reading until she was a few thousand words in.

```
                                             FADE IN
EXT: FOREST GLADE WITH BIRDS SINGING - MORNING
                      V/O
         Are you riddled by guilt because of your
         inability to sustain a healthy relationship?
   Do you find yourself raising your voice—or your fists—
                to your loved ones every week?


                      Every day?


     Sometimes it's hard to know what's appropriate and
       inappropriate behavior in the home. If you find
   yourself unable to control your temper, striking your
    loved ones, or using physical or verbal coercion to
                control them, we can help.


   TITLE CARD WITH CONTACT INFORMATION FOR HARTFORD
                  INTERVAL HOUSE


                      V/O
                Domestic Violence.
             It's all in your mind.
```

The preceding has been a public service announcement.

People were human. Accidents happened.

So Brigid told herself, her hands trembling with adrenaline reaction as she sat back in her chair.

It wasn't a management honey trap: she had every right to be running this search. And every right to be reading the documents that turned up.

With the exception of this one, which detailed how physiological primate social control mechanisms such as shame and the community urge might be hardwired to reinforce submission to authority.

Her access of the file was already logged. But since its author had backed it up to the wrong virtual, her access was perfectly legit as far as the watchbots were concerned. There was nothing to trip a flag.

Nothing. Unless human eyes went over the log and realized that Brigid Keating wasn't affiliated with the Military Research division. And that she had no reason to be reading up—not just on ABM's treatment of post traumatic stress and combat anxiety, which was well within her purview— but . . . other military and social applications. At first she assumed that the paper of Dr. Ionita's she was reading was speculative, theoretical—until she skimmed back to the abstract, and then found the appended data.

At that point, she couldn't stop reading. But nor could she continue: the access log would show how long she'd had the file open. Of course, she had a lot of files open, floating all around her headspace. But there was a cutoff for plausible deniability.

She mirrored it to her secure space and closed the original file.

And continued reading.

Rightminding applications had been in development for treating post-traumatic stress since the nineties and naughties. Their early successes and failures—along with those of techniques for managing obsessive compulsive disorder and other neurological imbalances—were the source from which the modern discipline of rightminding sprang.

But Ionita's research wasn't concerned with making soldiers immune to battlefield panic, or keeping them from freezing up in a crisis, or amending the damage done to human psyches by exposure to violence—or worse, by the creation of it. What Brigid read now—tea cooling, fork forgotten on the edge of her plate, shoulders hunched forward in a manner that would lead to pain in the morning—was a far more unsettling plan. This program, she realized, would create soldiers who could not disobey orders.

And workers who could not disobey their superiors.

That's ridiculous, Brigid thought. Her first urge was to go scurrying off seeking confirmation, but too-eager googling would leave a trail she suddenly didn't want behind her. Hard to say she'd opened the mis-saved file by innocent accident if she'd promptly run off in pursuit of what it revealed.

Military organizations relied on the ability of soldiers to refuse an illegal order. Far too many of them never would, even under ordinary circumstances. The pressure to conform was great, the training to bow to authority even greater.

And, according to this file, one of her colleagues was having success removing that ability. This struck Brigid as not just ethically bad, but *practically* bad.

Brigid was agnostic on the topic of the existence of free will. She considered it a null argument, arising from a spurious and archaic distinction between conscious and unconscious minds. But even leaving aside for the moment the ongoing debate of what exactly free will was, and if it existed at all, order-following robots wasn't what you wanted if you were trying to create a well-disciplined military, part of whose strength was in each soldier's trained judgment and ability to think for her or himself.

But ABM did not work solely for the military. And Brigid could think of plenty of less enlightened corporate leaders that would reward yes-men, and those who could create yes-men.

As if the emotional pressures of primate social controls weren't enough to enforce groupthink in most circumstances. Ethical rightminding applications *increased* individuality and autonomy. This was . . .

. . . not that.

Brigid sat back. She was already soaked in perfectly normal sweat from the heat of the evening. It didn't stop her breaking out in chills.

FX:
A shattering, swirling, migraine-aura blot of jagged
red and green and yellow images, sucked down into
a dark singularity at the center. Occasional bright
yellow-white flashes briefly wash out the whole of
the image.

V/O:
In the benighted twentieth century, normal human
response to trauma was treated as a moral failure.
Soldiers and others suffering from trauma-related
biological changes to the brain were called neurotic,
cowards, or worse.
We know better now.

As a result of traumatic experiences
beyond your control,
do you suffer from:
nightmares
anxiety
hypervigilance

<pre>
                    sadness
                  flashbacks
          feelings of intense distress
                  loss of joy
       the inability to trust your loved ones
                   numbness
    or other symptoms of trauma-related endocrine and
               neurological disorder?

                      FX:
    The chaotic swirling begins to resolve towards soothing
                 blues and whites.

                     V/O:
          Cure pathological trauma response.
                Proven success.
              A Beautiful Mind
        You don't have to be afraid anymore.
</pre>

Monday morning, Brigid cycled in to the lab to confront the usual straggle of anti-rightminding protestors. Signs floated in virtual space around them—a few of them funny, most badly designed and punctuated. Someone jeered as she pedaled past. Brigid spared a moment to her habitual longing for the future day when she could telecommute completely—except for occasional Partnership Days, as so many of the paper pushers did. Remote surgery by robot and waldo was what she did now, and it shouldn't be too much harder to do it from across town than from the next room.

The management was conservative, however, and Brigid suspected that they had the sort of mindset that supposed anyone who wasn't under constant, direct supervision spent most of their time goofing off. As far as Brigid was concerned, this said more about the management than their employees. Most of the researchers she knew had to be told when to stop working—and have the edict enforced.

Normally, the sight of the lab lowered her blood pressure, rather than elevating it. But on most days, she wasn't carrying the remnant neurochemical and fatigue poison cocktail of a stressed, sleepless night in her bloodstream. She'd finally had to dose herself with a regulator just to be able to lie down. But she'd thrashed in her bead, kicking at the sweat-wicking covers while sleep had eluded her for hours afterward and

the implications of what she'd read chased each other's tails through her
weary mind.

She'd finally been able to doze when she'd decided what she would
do. Dr. Ionita had obviously made an error in his or her backups. Brigid
probably should report it to management—it was a security breach, and
while *she* knew ABM's security was a joke, the suits still took it seriously.
Paternalistically so, in her opinion.

Perhaps she'd mention it to Ionita, and let him or her decide what to do.
Who was she to destroy somebody else's career over a simple error?

But she didn't know Ionita, who worked in a different area of the
building and—from a brief survey of Brigid's contacts—seemed to be the
sort who lived most of his or her existence behind privacy filters. And
there was the content of the research . . .

It's none of your business, Brigid told herself.

The lab was a modern green building, elevated on stilts above the climate-
risen waters of New London Harbor so it could easily use temperature
differentials and wave energy for its massive electrical needs. The building
itself was greened, every surface shielded by taro plants suited to the warm
temperate climate of modern Connecticut. Broad, heart-shaped leaves
tossed in the sea breeze, revealing a gorgeous variety of greens—from
pale and speckled to a color bordering on black. An elevated causeway
led from the shore, above the sparkling clean waters of the harbor, to the
lab's shaded veranda. Spectacular, and certain to impress visiting venture
capitalists . . . but it did mean there was only one approach.

A bored police woman kept that approach clear, but Brigid still had to
run the gauntlet of shouted insults. Her stomach contracted to a chilly
lump as she approached.

They can't hurt you.

But social disapproval was a pain of its own. Hardwired in, from an era
of human evolution when ostracism equaled death. And worse, when you
had already lost a family.

Eyes front, spine straight, Brigid passed through the protestors,
wondering as she did so how anyone could be so wedded to their pain,
their neurosis that they'd want to defend it. Or maybe that was an adaptive
response gone haywire, too? You defend the trauma response, because the
trauma response keeps you away from things that can destroy you.

Trauma response could lead to the expectation of a limited life. No
belief in a future, marriage, children, a decent job, a fulfilling career. It

could lock you into a cage of anhedonia and self-fulfilling prophecies. If the person who hurt you was someone you loved and trusted, doubly so.

It could happen, Brigid thought, *even if the person who hurt you would have done anything other than hurt you, if they could. Even if they had hurt you by saving your life, and not their own.*

She thought about Val, and wondered. He had—as far as she knew—a good home life. His boyfriend was delightful. Sometimes Brigid wasn't sure which of them she envied more. And there was that locked feeling in her own heart, that sense that if she reached out past it, ever, she would shatter.

Maybe I should get a cat.

Brigid locked her bike into the (internal, secured) bike rack, passed through the usual security theatre dance, and climbed the stairs to her lab. Six flights: she was on the top floor. She trotted up them. All that time under a pack paid off.

It also helped manage her neurochemistry. It just couldn't get rid of the cowardice.

Val would tell her that she was applying an unreasonable standard to herself, that societal expectations—in this, as in so many things—were bankrupt and unrealistic. Intellectually, she could find it in herself to agree with him. But the understanding and the internalized perceptions— those were in direct conflict on this, as on so many things. It made her understand why so many people drew a bright line between aspects of the self, even if she didn't agree with them.

Like everyone else in the world, she had some baggage of her own.

Brigid was relatively confident that in the future—when rightminding gained cultural acceptance and became something people did as a matter of course to be happier and more productive—regular, appropriate exercise was going to be a big part of it. (And do you also, she asked herself, believe in the Easter Bunny?)

She put a hand on the wall at the top landing, dizzied by a reflexive wall of frustrated rage—at herself, at humanity, at weakness. A future where everybody was not acting out of their trauma and anxiety all the time seemed bitterly like an unachievable utopia.

Inside her office, she showered quickly, changed to clothes not soaked in sweat from the humid ride in, and clicked her Omni to work shell. She checked her ration status and ordered a cup of coffee and a bagel with smoked North Atlantic cod. The fisheries were on her list of things that might recover reasonably well, if human beings could just be converted into the rational actors that economists had for too long imagined them to be. Not a race of Vulcans—Brigid saw no percentage in removing emotion. That was a primitive idea, which had been replaced since the late twentieth century with the idea that emotion was at the root of a good deal of cognition, and rightfully so.

The trick, Brigid thought, was figuring out how to work it so it was healthy emotion driving people's choices, and not atavistic fear response.

Sometimes, she thought of fear as a personified thing, an actual enemy. In both her personal and professional lives.

She felt her attention veering off again after the question of Dr. Ionita's research. That's fear too, she thought. Fear of the other, fear of not having utter control over every aspect of the world we live in. It was a fear that had bankrupted the twentieth century—that race to get ahead, to be the strongest. The most defended.

Sophipathological. Suffering from an illness of the thought.

She reined herself in and submitted her breakfast order. The delivery 'bot, Rover, would bring the bagel up on its rounds.

Brigid sat down in her chair and began sorting her environments into the air around her. ABM's corporate logo was an abstract line drawing of Athena holding her owl. Athena, the goddess of wisdom, had been born from the head of the god Zeus after the lame god of the forge, Hephaestus, smashed it open with an axe to relieve a blinding headache.

What that said about getting any kind of sense out of Zeus, Brigid left as an exercise to the class.

What it said about the symbolism ABM's founders had in mind—wisdom arising out of the shattered ruins of an intemperate brain—was the sort of thing you laughed about over beers. And how appropriate was it that they employed a one-legged sysadmin? Not that anybody in their right mind would call Val lame.

As if Val had known she'd be thinking of him, a tap came on the open sixth-story window behind her. The first time he'd done that, Brigid had found herself on her feet, reaching for a weapon—a box of culture dishes, as it happened. Now, she flicked the environmental controls panel on her Omni and let the window crack open. The question was whether she was getting better in general, or whether she was just getting acclimated to Val's hijinks.

She turned around to see Val slithering his slender lower body through the casement. He wasn't wearing his climbing leg, but he didn't need it for buildering something as easy as the ABM labs. But he also wasn't wearing a rope, which made Brigid tilt her head and glower.

"Think of the devil," she said. "You could at least rig a self-belay."

"Takes too long." He shrugged. "The trick is to get inside before somebody spots you."

Because of the birds and animals attracted by the green structure, ABM didn't have external motion or pressure sensors. They'd be going off all day and night if it did, triggered by a heron or a feral cat.

She didn't bother reprimanding him for breach of security. It was as pointless as telling a cat off for jumping on the table—Val would go where Val wanted to go, and if that was in and out of people's safes or computer systems, or up the walls themselves, no amount of fussing would change it. ABM had done everything in their power short of firing him—and he was simply too brilliant to fire.

A ferretlike curiosity drove him. He didn't take anything, or even read files, as near as Brigid could tell. He just couldn't bear a locked door, no matter which side of it he was on.

And suddenly she realized that he was exactly the person she needed to talk to about Dr. Ionita.

She didn't know Ionita's race or sex—even his or her first name beyond the obligatory publication initial. He or she wasn't one of the people who was enough of an exhibitionist—or casual enough about privacy—that she had ever seen them around the office with their filters down.

But Val knew all sorts of things.

He usually didn't share them, because he was an ethical cat burglar. But he knew them. And he was as anti-authoritarian as they came. In a case like this, when ethics were already out the window, he might be induced to spill some information.

Where do you draw a line?

She hadn't had time to plan her approach, though, and when she opened her mouth, what she said was, "There are sensible reasons to start a war."

He blinked and said, "Are there?"

One hand on her Omni, Brigid dropped out of work shell and offered him a privacy handshake. He accepted; when she blinked to clear his face into the encrypted space he tilted his head quizzically and said, "Oh, I bet this is good."

"Let me flash you a file."

He nodded; she transmitted. He skimmed. For long moments, she watched him assimilating. He didn't have time to have gotten through much more than the abstract, but in his credit—and, of course, primed by her concern—he must have twigged much faster than she had.

When his eyes stopped moving rapidly left to right, he paused for a moment. He took a deep, nervous breath, shook himself, and brought his attention back. Her frame around the ap lit up as he foregrounded her. "What are you going to do about that?"

"What can I do?"

"You showed it to me." He leaned back against a counter. "You must be thinking of doing something."

"Approaching Ionita. Letting him or her—"

"Her," he said, wincing with discomfort at revealing that much private information.

She nodded and raised an eyebrow. He shrugged. "—know she misfiled it? Report the breach to corporate?"

"Or?"

She shook her head, but she didn't look down. Muckraking ABM was not exactly the fast track to promotion. "I'd lose my job."

"You can get another."

"Right."

"Or go on Subsistence."

She turned away, facing out the window. Her interface kept his window lit, but she didn't look at it.

If she hadn't wanted to be pushed into doing something about it, she wouldn't have asked Val.

"I'll become a dirtbag," she said. "If I climb every day, that's like rightminding, isn't it? Good endorphins. Work through fear."

Val sighed and came up behind her. "The future is running out. Winding down. We're falling into tighter and tighter spirals—"

"Why?" she asked. "Because you can't hop on a jet plane and take off to Australia for a price that would be completely ridiculous if environmental impact were taken into account? That's not contraction, Val. Not when I can telepresence all over the world."

"It's not the same as being able to go climbing in Norway."

"No," she said. "But it's not worse."

That silenced him. When she turned back, he was studying his nails, considering. He looked up at her. "So what are you going to do? You can't hang ABM with just this document. Too easily forged—"

It wasn't until he calmly accepted that she was about to engage in industrial espionage and muckraking that she realized that was what she'd meant to do all along. Once the decision was made, it felt natural, true.

The right choice.

She knew the neurology, the brain chemistry behind it. That didn't change the very physical sensation of a weight being lifted from the center of her chest.

She straightened up and let her neck fall back, rolling it side to side to crack the vertebrae. When she was done, she bit her lip and looked at Val again.

"No," she said. "I'd need research notes. Experimental protocols. Workfiles. Video images. You know Ionita."

"She works on my floor. I've seen her, though she usually keeps her shields up. You want me to—"

"It'd be worth your job," she said. "Just leave a window open and forget to log out?"

With his admin privileges, she could get everything in Ionita's workspace.

He met her eyes for a moment before glancing at the open window. "It's an easy climb."

"I know."

"And if it doesn't work? What's your plan B?"

She didn't look down. "There is no plan B."

In today's competitive world,
it's too easy for minor childhood behavioral
problems to blossom into
life-limiting events.
Ensure educational success.
Give your child every advantage.
A Beautiful Mind
Because every childhood should be magical

It's an easy climb, Brigid told herself.

Which was true.

The problem was, it wasn't an easy fall.

Brigid tried to keep that thought from preying at her as, in the dark, with the mist rolling in, she walked down the rocky beach a few hundred meters from the lab building. There was enough light caught in the fog for dark-adapted eyes to make out the worst hazards of terrain, so she didn't need a light to pick her way along the strand. Ghostly veils of mist dragged at her arms and legs like damp tulle, leaving her feeling as if she walked through the ruins of a shredded wedding dress.

Waves hissed around the lab's pilings and amongst the stones as she approached, but the shadow of the building hid her. It wouldn't help her get up the well-lit and observed causeway, though, and swimming out to the back pylons would have left her drenched. If she didn't fancy the climb dry and rested, she liked her odds even less with wet hands and heavy wet clothes and muscles worn out from fighting the surf.

But she'd had the sense to wait until the tide was out. Half the lab was still at sea, but the other half hovered over rocks. And so she walked out under the deck, the lab building hovering over her head like a mothership. She found a piling on the back side of the building, by the edge of the receding water, and leaned against it to pull on her climbing shoes.

The piling itself was easy enough. It'd been designed to provide moorings for sea life, which meant it was rough-surfaced and more or less like a very, very vertical stepladder. The trick was not slashing her hands open on a cluster of mussels, or grabbing for a slick handful of seaweed that would tear away under her weight.

She went up it like a squirrel up the pole of a squirrel-proof birdfeeder. And then, like that squirrel, she faced a dilemma.

If the piling wasn't so bad, the pull around the overhang on to the deck was terrifying. On a cliff, she'd have felt for handholds, footholds, pressed herself over the edge with her feet. Here, there was no such option. She got a hand around the edge, found the rail, and locked her fingers on it. Her heart hammered, a nauseating chill of weakness seething in her stomach, making her muscles feel frail.

If you fall, she told herself, it's only into the sea.

It was a lie. It was as much of a lie as it had been the first time—for a different reason. Not because this sea was a thrashing black monster that would crush down on her head, but because there wasn't enough water down there to keep her from breaking her leg—or her pelvis—and lying helpless until the tide rolled back in. That cheerful thought kept her company as she shifted her weight over one foot, freeing the other to move. But she couldn't move it. Her weight was off it, her body poised to curve sideways from the hip and give her room and flexibility—

The foot stayed where it was, brushing the edge on the piling, as if shifting its weight were not even just hard but simply impossible. As if her motor nerves had been severed, and it would never move again.

If you fall, she lied to herself, it's only into the sea.

She told herself the lie again, and this time the lie worked. Just a little. She held that image, the safety of the splashing cushion below, and felt . . . not good. Not secure. But better.

Better enough to edge her other hand up, grab another rail, and heave one leg up for a heel-hook at the height of her shoulder. It was an all-or-nothing move, maximal effort for minimal return—and the only option that had any chance of success. Val was probably strong enough to haul himself over the edge on upper body strength alone.

Brigid knew she'd exhaust herself trying.

The ridged, high-friction heelcap of her shoe scraping on the edge of the platform, she breathed slow and deep, gathering herself, her arms locked out at full extension to put her weight on the bones rather than her biceps. She tensed her core, tightened calf and thigh, put as much of her full weight as possible onto the hooked heel, and pulled. Fingers slipping on salty metal, hair blowing into her eyes, damp with mist. Heaving, pulling with everything that was in her. That sharp pain in her palm stabbed again; she hoped she wasn't rupturing the pulley tendon this time.

It didn't matter: do or die. Now. Now.

She levered her right toe up, settled it on the edge of the deck, and got her weight over it.

And now she was crouching, one leg out to the side, her fingers knotted around the bars so tight she could no longer feel the edges pressing into her flesh.

She rose and slung a leg over the bar. She looked up, chest heaving, and wiped the sweat from her hands. It wasn't blood; it just felt like it. Among the greenery and scaffolding, the window on which Val would have disabled the lock was just visible.

It looked like a cinch, from here on in. She figured that the climbing part, at least, probably would be.

Welcome to BEAMZINE
STORIES THAT MAY INTEREST YOU:
ANTI-RIGHTMINDING PROTESTS CONTINUE IN NEW LONDON

[click for video]

In the wake of evidence released by Wikileaks and other online muckraking sites, protestors insisting that the new technology of so-called "Rightminding" is being used for mind control gathered outside the labs of A Beautiful Mind, Inc. again today.

CHYRON: CARYE SMITH, PROTESTOR

CARYE SMITH:
What about the soul, that's what I want to know. Where does the soul come into this?

CHYRON: BRADLEY BLAKE, M.D. ABM REPRESENTATIVE

BRADLEY BLAKE:
"Well, yes. If by mind control, you mean instituting clarity and rationality of thought, and bringing people peace and well-being. Accident or injury—or just genetics—can have a profound negative effect on the structure of the brain. We're here to repair that. Nothing else."

Brigid snapped her Omni off with unnecessary violence and stood, moving toward her balcony—hers for as long as she had it, anyway.

She'd thought that she wouldn't get away with it. And if she got away with it, that getting away with it would be the easy part.

But every day she didn't get caught out as the source of the leak was another day she had to have the same argument with herself: was it ethically bankrupt to keep taking ABM's money when she knew what they were doing behind her back?

But there was rightminding, and all its potential as a useful social tool. A world-saving tool, perhaps. Or a world-destroying one.

Val was there, his ankle kicked up on the opposite knee, leaned back in a chair behind the little table. He looked up from his own device, shaking his head to shut off his interface and make his eyes focus. By his amused expression, he'd been texting his boyfriend. Brigid bit her lip on the sting of envy.

Someday. She thought. *Maybe.*

"So," he said. "Turns out you didn't need the rightminding after all."

Her hands curled against her thighs in memory. "I wasn't not scared."

"There are different kinds of courage," Val said. "Taking on ABM is one of them."

"I still want the procedure," she said. "I still believe in the value of rightminding. Things being misused does not make them evil, and there is no innate virtue in things being hard."

"That's why you climb?"

She snorted.

"Hey," he said. "Fear is a gift."

Maybe she nodded. Maybe she was just ducking her head to get the glare of the sun out of her eyes. "Easy for you to say. You don't have any."

"Don't I?"

She shrugged. "Maybe that was unfair," she said.

His eyebrows drew together. A grin split his face. "Maybe?"

"Maybe," she said, pulling out the other chair. "But only a little."

∽

Annie Webber

Because I'm an idiot—and because my friend Allan is the coffee shop owner and my girlfriend Reesa works there—the Monday after Thanksgiving was my first day at a new job.

Total madhouse. Me and Pat foamed milk and drew shots like a flight line team while Reesa ran the register. It only worked because I'd barista'd at Starbucks and most of the customers were regulars, so they either had their order ready or Reesa already knew it and called it out before they paid. *Never* underestimate a good cashier.

Allan's has a thing, a frequent customer plan. So Reesa knows the regulars by name.

"Hey, Annie," Reesa said. "Medium cappuccino?"

Annie was petite, ash-blond hair escaping a seriously awful baby blue knit cap. She handed Reesa four dollars, then dropped the change into the tip jar.

Cappuccino is nice to make, but it's amazing how badly some people butcher it. I ground beans and drew the espresso. Then I foamed cold milk, feeling the pitcher for heat. When the volume tripled, the temperature was right. The sound of the steam changed pitch. I poured milk over the shot, ladled on foam, and sleeved the cup. "Cinnamon?"

"I'll get my own." She held out her hand. I put the cappuccino in it and set the shaker on the counter.

"You're new here?"

"First day."

"You're good." She sipped the drink. "Annie Webber."

"Zach Jones."

I'd have shaken her hand but there was a coffee in it, and another customer was coming.

That night, Reesa's cat Maggie tried to dig me out of bed by pulling at the comforter. I pushed her off, which woke Reesa. "Wha?"

Which is all the erudition you can expect at two in the morning.

"Damn cat," I explained.

Reesa pushed her face against my neck. "I only keep her because of the toxoplasmosis."

Running joke. *Toxoplasma* is a parasite that makes rats love cat urine. The parasite continues its life cycle in the cat after the cat eats the rat. According to some show we saw, it affects people too. And the same show had this amazing stop-motion photography of dying bugs, moist fungus fingers uncurling from their bodies. The fungus makes the infected ants do things so it can infect *more* ants.

The fungus was awful, and *gorgeous*. One shot showed a moth, dead—I hope dead—on a leaf, netted with silver lace like a bridal veil.

The next morning Reesa said, "Hi, Annie," but a different voice answered, "Hi, Reesa."

I looked up from the steamer nozzle. A big guy, wearing a padded down coat. "Free coffee today?"

Reesa checked the system. "You guys have *ten*."

He dropped coins in the tip jar. "Medium cappuccino?"

Pat moved to draw it. I gave her a look. "They're all Annie Webber," she said. "By courtesy. Sharing the account."

"Oh."

By the sound, I was scalding the milk. By the time I'd salvaged it, Annie Webber was gone. Reesa waved a pinkish hexagon like a foreign coin. "Zach, what's this?"

I didn't even recognize the metal, let alone the writing.

On day three, the original Annie Webber returned. Day four was number two. On Friday both came, not together. Then half an hour after the second, I served a third. Cappuccino, let me put on my own cinnamon. "Do you guys all drink the same thing?" I asked.

"You guys?" This Annie was a woman, with hazel eyes and crooked nose.

"The Annie Webbers."

She licked foam off her lip. "Nature's perfect food."

I caught Pat's elbow. "How many Annie Webbers are there? How long before I meet them all?"

She counted in her head. "Five come in regular. The blond and her partners."

"Partners? Like she's poly?"

She shrugged. "I never asked. Maybe they're a cult."

I groped the pinkish coin out. I'd looked it up online, and couldn't find it anywhere.

Saturday, Annie wandered in around ten. The original in the awful toque, scarf snugged under her chin.

I handed her the cup and cinnamon. It takes just seconds to get a good foam with a commercial machine. "You left this Tuesday." I laid the coin down.

"That should have been a quarter. Sorry." She traded for a dollar bill. "Put that in the jar?"

"Annie. It wasn't you here on Tuesday."

"Wasn't it?"

She winked and turned, leaving the money. I yelled, "Break!" and dove under the counter. Her heels clicked, but this was the smallest Annie. I caught up. Coat flaring, she turned.

"Where do you go?" I asked.

"Excuse me?"

"You. Annie. Where did the coin come from?"

"It was a mistake. I should have looked at the change, but I was out of you—money."

"So you use the free coffees when you've just come back? When you don't have any, what, local money?"

She stared. "I've been coming to that coffee shop since it opened. You're the first to ask."

"You go other places."

"Other . . . *places*?"

"Other dimensions."

"You read a lot of science fiction, Zach?"

"You're what, kind of multiple bodies one mind?"

"*Star Trek*," she said.

"Am I wrong? Why us?" I wondered if I sounded as jealous as I felt.

"Best coffee in the universe." She kissed me on the mouth, with tongue.

∽

I woke itching. My tongue, my hands. The soles of my feet.

When I stumbled to the kitchen, Reesa gave me scrambled eggs, but all I wanted was coffee. Coffee and milk and cinnamon. "Zach?" she asked. I had to bite my lip not to correct her.

That's not my name.

I have to go.

I think I've finally met all of Annie Webber.

The Horrid Glory of Its Wings

"Speaking of livers," the unicorn said, *"Real magic can never be made by offering up someone else's liver. You must tear out your own, and not expect to get it back. The true witches know that."*

—Peter S. Beagle, *The Last Unicorn*

My mother doesn't know about the harpy.

My mother, Alice, is not my *real* mom. She's my foster mother, and she doesn't look anything like me. Or maybe I don't look anything like her. Mama Alice is plump and soft and has skin like the skin of a plum, all shiny dark purple with the same kind of frosty brightness over it, like you could swipe it away with your thumb.

I'm sallow—Mama Alice says *olive*—and I have straight black hair and crooked teeth and no real chin, which is okay because I've already decided nobody's ever going to kiss me.

I've also got *lipodystrophy*, which is a fancy doctor way of saying I've grown a fatty buffalo hump on my neck and over each shoulderblade from the antiretrovirals, and my butt and legs and cheeks are wasted like an old lady's. My face looks like a dog's muzzle, even though I still have all my teeth.

For now. I'm going to have to get the wisdom teeth pulled this year, while I still get state assistance, because my birthday is in October and then I'll be eighteen. If I starts having problems with them after then, well forget about it.

There's no way I'd be able to afford to get them fixed.

The harpy lives on the street, in the alley behind my building, where the dumpster and the winos live.

I come out in the morning before school, after I've eaten my breakfast and taken my pills (nevirapine, lamivudine, efavirenz). I'm used to the pills. I've been taking them all my life. I have a note in my file at school, and excuses for my classmates.

I don't bring home friends.

Lying is a sin. But Father Alvaro seems to think that when it comes to my sickness, it's a sin for which I'm already doing enough penance.

Father Alvaro is okay. But he's not like the harpy.

The harpy doesn't care if I'm not pretty. The harpy is beyond not pretty, way into ugly. Ugly as your mama's warty butt. Its teeth are snaggled and stained piss-yellow and char-black. Its claws are broken and dull and stink like rotten chicken. It has a long droopy blotchy face full of lines like Liv Tyler's dad, that rock star guy, and its hair hangs down in black-bronze rats over both feathery shoulders. The feathers look washed-out black and dull until sunlight somehow finds its way down into the grubby alley, bounces off dirty windows and hits them, and then they look like scratched bronze.

They are bronze.

If I touch them, I can feel warm metal.

I'd sneak the harpy food, but Mama Alice keeps pretty close track of it—it's not like we have a ton of money—and the harpy doesn't seem to mind eating garbage. The awfuller the better: coffee grounds, moldy cake, meat squirming with maggots, the stiff corpses of alley rats.

The harpy turns all that garbage into bronze.

If it reeks, the harpy eats it, stretching its hag face out on a droopy red neck to gulp the bits, just like any other bird. I've seen pigeons do the same thing with a crumb too big to peck up and swallow, but their necks aren't scaly naked, ringed at the bottom with fluffy down as white as a confirmation dress.

So every morning I pretend I'm leaving early for school—Mama Alice says "Kiss my cheek, Desiree"—and then once I'm out from under Mama Alice's window I sneak around the corner into the alley and stand by the dumpster where the harpy perches. I only get ten or fifteen minutes, however much time I can steal. The stink wrinkles up my nose. There's no place to sit. Even if there were, I couldn't sit down out here in my school clothes.

I think the harpy enjoys the company. Not that it *needs* it; I can't imagine the harpy needing anything. But maybe . . . just maybe it likes me.

The harpy says, I want you.

I don't know if I like the harpy. But I like being wanted.

The harpy tells me stories.

Mama Alice used to, when I was little, when she wasn't too tired from work and taking care of me and Luis and Rita, before Rita died. But the harpy's stories are better. It tells me about magic, and nymphs, and heroes. It tells me about adventures and the virgin goddesses like Artemis and Athena, and how they had adventure and did magic, and how Athena was cleverer than Poseidon and got a city named after her.

It tells me about Zephyrus, the West Wind, and his sons the magical talking horses. It tells me about Hades, god of the Underworld, and the feathers on its wings ring like bronze bells with excitement when it tells me about their mother Celaeno, who was a harpy also, but shining and fierce.

It tells me about her sisters, and how they were named for the mighty storm, and how when they all three flew, the sky was dark and lashed with rain and thunder. That's how it talks: *lashed with rain and thunder.*

The harpy says, We're all alone.

It's six thirty in the morning and I hug myself in my new winter coat from the fire department giveaway, my breath streaming out over the top of the scratchy orange scarf Mama Alice knitted. I squeeze my legs together, left knee in the hollow of the right knee like I have to pee, because even tights don't help too much when the edge of the skirt only comes to the middle of your kneecap. I'd slap my legs to warm them, but these are my last pair of tights and I don't want them to snag.

The scarf scrapes my upper lip when I nod. It's dark here behind the dumpster. The sun won't be up for another half hour. On the street out front, brightness pools under streetlights, but it doesn't show anything warm—just cracked black snow trampled and heaped over the curb.

"Nobody wants me," I say. "Mama Alice gets paid to take care of me."

That's unfair. Mama Alice didn't *have* to take me or my foster brother Luis. But sometimes it feels good to be a little unfair. I sniff up a drip and push my chin forward so it bobs like the harpy swallowing garbage.

"Nobody would want to live with me. But I don't have any choice. I'm stuck living with myself."

The harpy says, There's always a choice.

"Sure," I say. "Suicide is a sin."

The harpy says, Talking to harpies is probably a sin, too.

"Are you a devil?"

The harpy shrugs. Its feathers smell like mildew. Something crawls along a rat of its hair, greasy-shiny in the street light. The harpy scrapes it off with a claw and eats it.

The harpy says, I'm a heathen monster. Like Celaeno and her sisters, Aello and Ocypete. The sisters of the storm. Your church would say so, that I am a demon. Yes.

"I don't think you give Father Alvaro enough credit."

The harpy says, I don't trust priests, and turns to preen its broken claws.

"You don't trust anybody."

That's not what I said, says the harpy—

You probably aren't supposed to interrupt harpies, but I'm kind of over that by now. "That's why I decided. I'm never going to trust anybody. My birth mother trusted somebody, and look where it got her. Knocked up and dead."

The harpy says, That's very inhuman of you.

It sounds like a compliment.

I put a hand on the harpy's warm wing. I can't feel it through my glove. The gloves came from the fire department, too. "I have to go to school, Harpy."

The harpy says, You're alone there too.

I want to prove the harpy wrong.

The drugs are really good now. When I was born, a quarter of the babies whose moms had AIDS got sick too. Now it's more like one in a hundred. I could have a baby of my own, a healthy baby. And then I wouldn't be alone.

No matter what the harpy says.

It's a crazy stupid idea. Mama Alice doesn't have to take care of me after I turn eighteen, and what would I do with a baby? I'll have to get a job. I'll have to get state help for the drugs. The drugs are expensive.

If I got pregnant now, I could have the baby before I turn eighteen. I'd have somebody who was just mine. Somebody who loved me.

How easy is it to get pregnant, anyway? Other girls don't seem to have any problem doing it by accident.

Or by "accident."

Except whoever it was, I would have to tell him I was pos. That's why I decided I would sign the purity pledge and all that. Because then I have a reason not to tell.

And they gave me a ring. Fashion statement.

You know how many girls actually *keep* that pledge? I was going to. I meant to. But not just keep it until I got married. I meant to keep it forever, and then I'd never have to tell anybody.

No, I was right the first time. I'd rather be alone than have to explain. Besides, if you're having a baby, you should have the baby for the baby, not for you.

Isn't that right, Mom?

The harpy has a kingdom.

It's a tiny kingdom. The kingdom's just the alley behind my building, but it has a throne (the dumpster) and it has subjects (the winos) and it has me. I know the winos see the harpy. They talk to it sometimes. But it vanishes when the other building tenants come down, and it hides from the garbagemen.

I wonder if harpies can fly.

It opens its wings sometimes when it's raining as if it wants to wash off the filth, or sometimes if it's mad at something. It hisses when it's mad like that, the only sound I've ever heard it make outside my head.

I guess if it can fly depends on if it's magic. Miss Rivera, my bio teacher sophomore year, said that after a certain size things couldn't lift themselves with wings anymore. It has to do with muscle strength and wingspan and gravity. And some big things can only fly if they can fall into flight, or get a *headwind*.

I never thought about it before. I wonder if the harpy's *stuck* in that alley. I wonder if it's too proud to ask for help.

I wonder if I should ask if it wants some anyway.

The harpy's big. But condors are big, too, and condors can fly. I don't know if the harpy is bigger than a condor. It's hard to tell from pictures, and it's not like you can walk up to a harpy with a tape measure and ask it to stick out a wing.

Well, maybe you could. But I wouldn't.

Wouldn't it be awful to have wings that didn't work? Wouldn't it be worse to have wings that do work, and not be able to use them?

After I visit the harpy at night, I go up to the apartment. When I let myself in the door to the kitchen, Mama Alice is sitting at the table with some mail open in front of her. She looks up at me and frowns, so I lock the door behind me and shoot the chain. Luis should be home by now, and I can hear music from his bedroom. He's fifteen now. I think it's been three days since I saw him.

I come over and sit down in my work clothes on the metal chair with the cracked vinyl seat.

"Bad news?"

Mama Alice shakes her head, but her eyes are shiny. I reach out and grab her hand. The folded up paper in her fingers crinkles.

"What is it, then?"

She pushes the paper at me. "Desiree. You got the scholarship."

I don't hear her right the first time. I look at her, at our hands, and the rumply paper. She shoves the letter into my hand and I unfold it, open in, read it three times as if the words will change like crawly worms when I'm not looking at it.

The words are crawly worms, all watery, but I can see *hardship* and *merit* and *State*. I fold it up carefully, smoothing out the crinkles with my fingertips. It says I can be anything at all.

I'm going to college on a scholarship. Just state school.

I'm going to college because I worked hard. And because the state knows I'm full of poison, and they feel bad for me.

The harpy never lies to me, and neither does Mama Alice.

She comes into my room later that night and sits down on the edge of my bed, with is just a folded-out sofa with springs that poke me, but it's mine and better than nothing. I hide the letter under the pillow before she turns on the light, so she won't catch on that I was hugging it.

"Desiree," she says.

I nod and wait for the rest of it.

"You know," she says, "I might be able to get the state to pay for liposuction. Doctor Morales will say it's medically necessary."

"Liposuction?" I grope my ugly plastic glasses off the end table, because I need to see her. I'm frowning so hard they pinch my nose.

"For the hump," she says, and touches her neck, like she had one too. "So you could stand up straight again. Like you did when you were little."

Now I wish I hadn't put the glasses on. I have to look down at my hands. The fingertips are all smudged from the toner on the letter. "Mama Alice," I say, and then something comes out I never meant to ask her. "How come you never adopted me?"

She jerks like I stuck her with a fork. "Because I thought . . . " She stops, and shakes her head, and spreads her hands.

I nod. I asked, but I know. Because the state pays for my medicine. Because Mama Alice thought I would be dead by now.

We were all supposed to be dead by now. All the HIV babies. Two years, maybe five. AIDS kills little kids really quick, because their immune systems haven't really happened yet. But the drugs got better as our lives got longer, and now we might live forever. Nearly forever.

Forty. *Fifty.*

I'm dying. Just not fast enough. If it were faster, I'd have nothing to worry about. As it is, I'm going to have to figure out what I'm going to do with my life.

I touch the squishy pad of fat on my neck with my fingers, push it in until it dimples. It feels like it should keep the mark of my fingers, like Moon Mud, but when I stop touching it, it springs back like nothing happened at all.

I don't want to get to go to college because somebody feels bad for me. I don't want anybody's pity.

The next day, I go down to talk to the harpy.

I get up early and wash quick, pull on my tights and skirt and blouse and sweater. I don't have to work after school today, so I leave my uniform on the hanger behind the door.

But when I get outside, the first thing I hear is barking. Loud barking, lots of it, from the alley. And that hiss, the harpy's hiss. Like the biggest maddest cat you ever heard.

There's junk all over the street, but nothing that looks like I could fight with it. I grab up some hunks of ice. My school shoes skip on the frozen sidewalk and I tear my tights when I fall down.

It's dark in the alley, but it's city dark, not real dark, and I can see the dogs okay. There's three of them, dancing around the dumpster on their hind legs. One's light-colored enough that even in the dark I can see she's all scarred up from fighting, and the other two are dark.

The harpy leans forward on the edge of the dumpster, wings fanned out like a cartoon eagle, head stuck out and jabbing at the dogs.

Silly thing doesn't know it doesn't have a beak, I think, and whip one of the ice rocks at the big light-colored dog. She yelps. Just then, the harpy sicks up over all three of the dogs.

Oh, God, the smell.

I guess it doesn't need a beak after all, because the dogs go from growling and snapping to yelping and running just like that. I slide my backpack off one shoulder and grab it by the strap in the hand that's not full of ice.

It's heavy and I could hit something, but I don't swing it in time to stop one of the dogs knocking into me as it bolts away. The puke splashes on my leg. It burns like scalding water through my tights.

I stop myself just before I slap at the burn. Because getting the puke on my glove and burning my hand too would just be smart like that. Instead, I scrub at it with the dirty ice in my other hand and run limping towards the harpy.

The harpy hears my steps and turns to hiss, eyes glaring like green torches, but when it sees who's there it pulls its head back. It settles its wings like a nun settling her skirts on a park bench, and gives me the same fishy glare.

Wash that leg with snow, the harpy says. Or with lots of water. It will help the burning.

"It's acid."

With what harpies eat, the harpy says, don't you think it would have to be?

I mean to say something clever back, but what gets out instead is, "Can you fly?"

As if in answer, the harpy spreads its vast bronze wings again. They stretch from one end of the dumpster to the other, and overlap its length a little.

The harpy says, Do these look like flightless wings to you?

Why does it always answer a question with a question? I know kids like that, and it drives me crazy when they do it, too.

"No," I say. "But I've never seen you. Fly. I've never seen you fly."

The harpy closes its wings, very carefully. A wind still stirs my hair where it sticks out under my hat.

The harpy says, There's no wind in my kingdom. But I'm light now, I'm empty. If there were wind, if I could get higher—

I drop my pack beside the dumpster. It has harpy puke on it now anyway. I'm not putting it on my back. "What if I carried you up?"

The harpy's wings flicker, as if it meant to spread them again. And then it settles back with narrowed eyes and shows me its snaggled teeth in a suspicious grin.

The harpy says, What's in it for you?

I say to the harpy, "You've been my friend."

The harpy stares at me, straight on like a person, not side to side like a bird. It stays quiet so long I think it wants me to leave, but a second before I step back it nods.

The harpy says, Carry me up the fire escape, then.

I have to clamber up on the dumpster and pick the harpy up over my head to put it on the fire escape. It's heavy, all right, especially when I'm holding it up over my head so it can hop onto the railing. Then I have to jump up and catch the ladder, then swing my feet up like on the uneven bars in gym class.

That's the end of these tights. I'll have to find something to tell Mama Alice. Something that isn't exactly a lie.

Then we're both up on the landing, and I duck down so the stinking, heavy harpy can step onto my shoulder with her broken, filthy claws. I don't want to think about the infection I'll get if she scratches me. Hospital stay. IV antibiotics. But she balances there like riding shoulders is all she does for a living, her big scaly toes sinking into my fat pads so she's not pushing down on my bones.

I have to use both hands to pull myself up the fire escape, even though I left my backpack at the bottom. The harpy weighs more, and it seems to get heavier with every step. It's not any easier because I'm trying to tiptoe and not wake up the whole building.

I stop to rest on the landings, but by the time I get to the top one my calves shake like the mufflers on a Harley. I imagine them booming like that too, which makes me laugh. Kind of, as much as I can. I double over with my hands on the railing and the harpy hops off.

"Is this high enough?"

The harpy doesn't look at me. It faces out over the empty dark street. It spreads its wings. The harpy is right: I'm alone, I've always been alone. Alone and lonely.

And now it's also leaving me.

"I'm dying," I yell, just as it starts the downstroke. I'd never told anybody. Mama Alice had to tell *me*, when I was five, but *I* never told anybody.

The harpy rocks forward, beats its wings hard, and settles back on the railing. It cranks its head around on its twisty neck to stare at me.

"I have HIV," I say. I press my glove against the scar under my coat where I used to have a G-tube. When I was little.

The harpy nods and turns away again. The harpy says, I know.

It should surprise me that the harpy knows, but it doesn't. Harpies know things. Now that I think about it, I wonder if the harpy only loves me because I'm garbage. If it only wants me because my blood is poison. My scarf's come undone, and a button's broken on my new old winter coat.

It feels weird to say what I just said out loud, so I say it again. Trying to get used to the way the words feel in my mouth. "Harpy, I'm dying. Maybe not today or tomorrow. But probably before I should."

The harpy says, That's because you're not immortal.

I spread my hands, cold in the gloves. Well *duh*. "Take me with you."

The harpy says, I don't think you're strong enough to be a harpy.

"I'm strong enough for this." I take off my new old winter coat from the fire department and drop it on the fire escape. "I don't want to be alone any more."

The harpy says, If you come with me, you have to stop dying. And you have to stop living. And it won't make you less alone. You are human, and if you stay human your loneliness will pass, one way or the other. If you come with me, it's yours. Forever.

It's not just empty lungs making my head spin. I say, "I got into college."

The harpy says, It's a career path.

I say, "You're lonely too. At least I decided to be alone, because it was better."

The harpy says, I am a harpy.

"Mama Alice would say that God never gives us any burdens we can't carry."

The harpy says, Does she look you in the eye when she says that?

I say, "Take me with you."

The harpy smiles. A harpy's smile is an ugly thing, even seen edge-on. The harpy says, You do not have the power to make me not alone, Desiree.

It's the first time it's ever said my name. I didn't know it knew it. "You have sons and sisters and a lover, Celaeno. In the halls of the West Wind. How can you be lonely?"

The harpy turns over its shoulder and stares with green, green eyes. The harpy says, I never told you my name.

"Your name is Darkness. You told me it. You said you *wanted* me, Celaeno."

The cold hurts so much I can hardly talk. I step back and hug myself tight. Without the coat I'm cold, so cold my teeth buzz together like gears stripping, and hugging myself doesn't help.

I don't want to be like the harpy. The harpy is disgusting. It's *awful*.

The harpy says, And underneath the filth, I shine. I *salvage*. You choose to be alone? Here's your chance to prove yourself no liar.

I don't want to be like the harpy. But I don't want to be me any more, either. *I'm stuck living with myself.*

If I go with the harpy, I will be stuck living with myself *forever*.

The sky brightens. When the sunlight strikes the harpy, its filthy feathers will shine like metal. I can already see fingers of cloud rising across the horizon, black like cut paper against the paleness that will be dawn, not that you can ever see dawn behind the buildings. There's no rain or snow in the forecast, but the storm is coming.

I say, "You only want me because my blood is rotten. You only want me because I got thrown away."

I turn garbage into bronze, the harpy says. I turn rot into strength. If you came with me, you would have to be like me.

"Tell me it won't always be this hard."

I do not lie, child. What do you want?

I don't know my answer until I open my mouth and say it, but it's something I can't get from Mama Alice, and I can't get from a scholarship. "Magic."

The harpy rocks from foot to foot. I can't give you that, she says. You have to *make* it.

Downstairs, under my pillow, is a letter. Across town, behind brick walls, is a doctor who would write me another letter.

Just down the block in the church beside my school is a promise of maybe heaven, if I'm a good girl and I die.

Out there is the storm and the sunrise.

Mama Alice will worry, and I'm sorry. She doesn't deserve that. When I'm a harpy will I care? Will I care forever?

Under the humps and pads of fat across my shoulders, I imagine I can already feel the prickle of feathers.

I use my fingers to lift myself onto the railing and balance there in my school shoes on the rust and tricky ice, six stories up, looking down on the street lights. I stretch out my arms.

And so what if I fall?

Confessor

Rebecca Sanchez is climbing Mt. Rainier.

Not to the top. Not to the glacier—what scraps of glacier are left—but down at the foot of the rainy side, picking her way between fernbrakes and over the massive, derelict hulks of nurse logs thicketed in saplings and miniature fungal forests until she finds a footworn path ascending.

Somebody has been maintaining this. It switchbacks from left to right, a single-file streak of earth terraced by root-buttresses worn satiny-smooth, the bark polished off by endless boots ascending and descending.

Sanchez settles her pack on her shoulders as she tilts her head back and considers. She slips her thumbs inside the waistband and hitches it up, tightening the strap.

With a sigh, she sets her foot upon the path and begins climbing. Set foot, test foot, kick off the rear toe and rise. Small steps, conserving energy. Pacing herself as if climbing stairs. It's a long way up, and she had no way of knowing if this is even the right path.

Several before it have not been.

The pain starts in her knees. Starts, but does not stay there. First that grinding pressure, and then the ache across the quadriceps. The calves follow, and the arches of her feet.

To distract herself, she contemplates the scenery. It's beyond spectacular. One side of the path ends in the rising mountainside. The other drops off steeply. Dripping evergreen branches like wet green feathers surround her, framing furrowed trunks of Brobdingnagian proportion. The moss lies thick over everything.

Everything except the path her steps laboriously ascend.

The moss is her friend. With a trained, experienced eye, she scans it for scuffs, marks, any sign of damage. Signs of a struggle, in other words. When she finds something that looks right, she uses a sampler device to hunt for traces of DNA, or the signature bacteria colonies that inhabit everyone's skin—and which differ nearly as much as fingerprints.

Once upon a time there were roads here. Once, people came for the day, in cars. They drove from Seattle, Tacoma, Portland. They hiked for a few hours, enjoyed the natural beauty, and then drove home with countless others on smooth-surfaced highways.

That would be prohibitive, now. The roads have crumbled, and the oil that powered the cars doesn't exist. For Sanchez to get from San Francisco to this gig was a week-long journey, starting on the train and concluding on a chargeable bike. But a bike wouldn't bring her up the mountain.

So she climbs.

Around her, birds and small animals rustle and chirp. A Douglas squirrel scolds; something heavier and invisible in the dappled light slides along a tree branch to her right. She turns sharply and catches movement, a hint of camouflage color—greens and browns that would make her suspect a lizard, if there were lizards that big up here. Given the invasives, maybe there are, now. Below, a garter snake whips out of sight, leaving only the puddle of warmth where it sunned itself. For the first time since she almost died in Oakland, Sanchez smiles.

Sweat rolls down her back between the shoulder blades, soaks her hatband, dews her upper lip. She rubs it off her palms onto her shorts. When she pauses, she checks her legs for ticks. She slides one of several water bottles from the net pockets on her pack and drinks, counting swallows. She allows herself five.

The simple mechanics of all of it—leverage, evaporation, the movement of muscle under skin—don't fill up the empty ache inside her. It's strange, she thinks, how strictly emotional damage can feel so much like a physical hole. Like somebody opened her up under anesthesia and took out all the internal organs and replaced them with cotton batting.

She still looks like a real girl. But she's empty inside. And there's no one in the world she can tell why.

The assignment could not have come at a better time. She needs this now, needs to get back on her feet. Maybe it's already been too long. Two months is a long time. *If you fall off the horse—*

When she looks up from stowing the bottle, there is a man in front of her. He wears camouflage and appears unfriendly.

Jackpot, she thinks, keeping her hands at her sides as he closes on her. This wasn't what she was looking for, but she knew it was a possibility that she would find it. It's a start, and it will do. Adrenaline thrills through her, every nerve awake: she's ready to fight, and she tries to look relaxed.

He looks her up and down, drawing himself into a transparently intimidating pose, and glowers. "This path is closed."

"It's a public mountain," she says. Not belligerently, but with certainty.

He comes up on her another step, until she's looking up his nostrils as he tries to stare her down. "What's your name?"

"Sanchez," she says.

It's not a lie, for the duration. When she took the contract, Cascadia Law Enforcement Collective provided ID, gear, a whole identity. They helped with transpo too, which they never would have done if they could have found anybody qualified who lived closer. But this was specialist work. For a gig like this one, you had to be a modern-day Texas Ranger.

And maybe, she thinks, after the mess in Oakland, after everything it cost her—*maybe* this is a good place to start rebuilding her self-confidence. You had to get back on the horse, right? And the sooner the better.

It's a miracle she walked away with her reputation intact. But Cascadia LEC wouldn't have licensed her if they expected to fail utterly, so maybe Doe wound up with the blame after all. Maybe he kept his mouth shut, the way she's keeping hers. Or maybe if he talked they didn't believe him.

She doesn't know. She hasn't seen him since she moved out, though he's called several times. Well, of course. She lied for him, after all. And not the other way around.

Maybe she got lucky, and the long hiatus in licenses was in consideration of her near-death experience. Maybe they were just giving her a rest. Maybe she faked them out, and her reputation is intact.

It's not like anyone would tell her, one way or the other. She'll have to figure it out based on how people treat her. And the long silence has been unnerving. But this case—this complicated case, which may be two cases interlinked, one involving a dead body and the other involving a poaching operation—*this* feels like a vote of confidence.

Sanchez hopes she can do better than fake this one. She wants to *solve* it.

She says, "What's your name?"

He grabs her by the chin, doubtlessly because he's seen it over and over again in movies. It isn't an effective hold. He sneers. "You don't look like a Sanchez."

She's got red hair and hazel eyes, like her grandmother. "I'm fucking adopted," she says. "And you don't look like an asshole."

That's a lie. Whatever assholes look like, at least one of them definitely looks like this guy. But her crack backs him off a little, enough so that there's space between them when she reaches up and rubs her jaw.

"What are you doing here?"

She reaches up over her own shoulder and lays a palm against the orange nylon of the pack. "Hiking."

He snorts. "Then you won't mind me searching your bag."

"You're damn right I mind. Who the fuck are you?" Even as she stands her ground, she's aware of how sharp is the dropoff at her back, how steep is the slope that anyone unfortunate enough to mis-step would tumble down.

She knows who he is. He's Edgewater. Private security solving public problems the old-fashioned way: through force of arms. It drips off him along with his attitude problem.

So she hasn't found a crime scene. But she's found a private security force.

Well, *that's* interesting. Maybe her case *is* linked to the larger system of evil.

"You're trespassing," he says. "On restricted property." Careful choice of words there. *Restricted* makes it sound like something official. "Either I can search your bag here, Miss Sanchez. Or I can haul you inside, and search your bag there, and you can wait in a holding room until the cops come. Which could take days, out here. What do you say?"

She glowers—it's hard to glower, given the amount of information he just let slip—but relents. "I guess you have me over a barrel."

Inside. Holding room. Cops.

She doesn't believe Edgewater is going to call the cops on anybody. She's close enough to being a cop herself to have heard stories. But the mere fact that they're here, defending some secret facility, sends a chill up her spine.

If you start off looking for a murder scene and find something else—

—keep looking.

The hired thug lifts one shoulder in a disarming shrug that doesn't make her forget the chin-grab. "I guess I do."

When the oiled canvas sack in Martha's hand quit twitching and making the honking sobbing noises, she got worried the bird inside was dead. But maybe it was playing 'possum, just waiting for her to loosen the drawstring and give it a peek of sky to fly to. It was still heavy, heavy and a little wet—with what, she didn't like to think—and she tried not to touch the outside while she carried it home.

Matt met her by the gate. She held up the bag, fighting the way her mouth wanted to twist with worry when it didn't kick in response. "Wait 'til you see what I got!"

He bounced on his toes, then winced. She knew—she felt the same pain in her own joints lately, and Matt was older. "What what?"

"Inside," she said.

She let her brother lead her into their tumbledown cabin, up the steep mossy slope to the rocks and the great trees that sheltered it. Daddy's boots still gathered dust by the door. She set the bag on the crumb-covered table, which Matt had pushed out from under the hole in the tin roof. While Matt closed the door latch, she made sure the windows and the chimney flue were sealed. The roof hole wasn't big enough for the bird to get out, she didn't think.

When she came back to the table, she found Matt waiting.

"I never saw anything like this," Martha said, and unknotted the strings on the bag. With a breath of anticipation, she upended it on the table.

And jumped back from a splash of viscous fluid that ran off the boards and splattered the floor, dripping in quick-flowing strings.

"What the heck?" Matt said, pulling back in dismay.

The sack was light, empty. But Martha couldn't help peering into it anyway. One lonely violet feather still stuck, curled and damp, to the inside weave. She pulled it out for proof.

"There was a bird," she said. "In the trap. A kind of bird I'd never seen, all purple and blue and goosey-necked. Fat, like a little turkey, with gooney wings. It had like a feather pompom on its head . . . "

She trailed off, stricken. She held the feather out to Matt silently. Matt took it, sniffed it, touched it to his tongue-tip.

"Salty," he said, and made a face. "Well, there's no bird in there now. You figure it dissolved?"

Of course, he confiscates her camera. But doesn't find or recognize the spyglass concealed inside her walking stick, and he leaves her the sniffer and GPS kit that is far more essential to her mission than any recording device. But she expected that and planned for it. And the end result is as she hoped: Now she knows what part of the mountain to concentrate on.

The GPS is programmed with a dozen likely hiking goals and the address of Sanchez's purported home in Redmond, along with the actual location where she left her actual bike—and it also tracks the sites she's visited and what she found there. *That* information, however, is under password lock.

Sanchez has found, over the years, that sometimes it's smart for a consulting peace officer operating on license, far from support, not to look like a cop. She must have passed this time, because the goon lets her go, after roughing her up a bit, putting what he must consider a good scare into her and quizzing her about her purported hometown. Easier to send a tourist home with another scary story about Edgewater than explain a disappearance to a (fictional) wife and kids.

She hopes she doesn't run into anybody who actually knows Redmond well. She's studied photos and maps, but it's different from being on the ground there.

For now, she trudges on determinedly, admiring the ancient moss-draped trees of the temperate rain forest and remembering the view of Rainier from when she was still far enough away to see it. Here, on the volcano's flank, you could miss its existence: it might just be a virtually endless hill you could keep climbing for a subjective eternity. But from ten miles out, it had floated above the horizon like the ghost of a trillion tons of basalt, like something scraped across canvas with a palette knife. The mountain hadn't seemed to touch the earth, its near-symmetry rendering it unreal.

She wonders how it would look from the treeline. Would it be just too big to see from up close?

Sanchez pauses in the vaulted space under one of the biggest trees and gazes upwards, frowning. Doable, with the right equipment and skills. Sketchy, but doable.

She shrugs her pack off and tucks it among the woody trunks of a stand of rhododendron, scuffing some leaf mould over it to hide the orange nylon and disguise the shape. The boot spikes for her feet and the hook straps for her palms are small, easily concealed. They are tucked inside the false back of the reader that the guy from Edgewater had pried at and returned, its mysteries undeciphered.

The reader even works. Although Sanchez's cover means it's full of hiking 'zines and romance novels.

Sanchez goes up the tree to the lowest boughs in a series of long kick-and-grabs. Dislodged water scatters her hair and drips down her neck.

Moss and damp bark stick between the tines of her hooks. Attaining the bough, she straddles it; the spikes make it difficult to stand on something horizontal, especially when that something was nearly as broad as an avenue.

Okay, a sidewalk, anyway.

A Douglas squirrel berates her from a perch just barely out of arm's reach, its fluffy tail flagging. Sanchez grins to herself and avoids eye contact.

The climb is trickier from here up, because she must spiral and zig and zag to avoid the ponderous branches. As she ascends, the trunk grows thinner and thinner—and eventually, whippy. The claws are a blessing. Sanchez is an experienced climber, but she knows that by the time she had passed the sixty-meter mark on this forest giant, her fingers would have been cramped and sore. Also, the bark is wet and slick throughout, and there is always the threat of it peeling off in her hands.

But the flickering rays of light from above urge her on. When she breaks into sunlight, she can see the last rain steaming off the canopy in plumes and trails of skimmed-milk vapor.

She locks herself to the tree with a length of webbing, the bole now no thicker than her thigh, and leans back on the spikes like a lineman. Gingerly, at first, until she is sure they—and the web belt—will hold. The treetop sways like a skyscraper—gently, with a long period of oscillation. After a moment, Sanchez becomes accustomed. She's climbed the masts of tall ships, working the clipper trade, and this is not too different. The canopy below could be frozen green surf, the vapor misting off them spray.

Oceans didn't smell of clean compost and leaf mould.

The spyglass she sets to her eye could have belonged on a pirate ship too, although it is considerably more high-tech than anything Captains Hook or Blackbeard might have fielded. For one thing, Hook probably would have given his eyeteeth for the autofocus feature. But the glasses are also equipped to register variations in temperature, and it is this feature Sanchez expects to be of service now.

It isn't. She tracks across the forest in a meticulous grid pattern, logging each anomaly, but the variation is never more or less than a few degrees. After half an hour, she bites her thumb in frustration.

All right, then, the facility is shielded. That makes sense; they'd want to avoid detection from the air. But she has a relief map, and she knows what trail she's been prevented from ascending. It's not easy—she's been years learning how to do it, and those skills are a large part of why she's here—but between those things, she should be able to hazard a guess of where you'd build—

She trains her spyglass upslope, on maximum magnification, and begins examining the canopy tree by tree, watching the shadows move. The sun thumps down on her, the shelter of a hat inadequate, and the beads of water that had rolled down her collar are replaced by sweat. She is exquisitely aware of her own vulnerability, the exposure of her position.

She has a birdwatcher's book on her reader, but really, there would be no explaining this.

Then, with the movement of the shadows, she catches sight of a curiously regular line of trees. She leans forward reflexively, the change in angle making her boot spikes creak, and skims along the line over and over again.

Yes. There, behind the trees, a span of camouflage netting.

It would fool an air reconnaissance or a satellite. But it has not, quite, fooled her. With the help of her trusty GPS and her reader's loaded map, she manages to take a bearing without killing herself.

Sanchez smiles softly to herself as she descends.

After the bird vanished, Martha and Matt went out to check the traplines and forage for plants. The fiddleheads were over, but she found a fallen tree full of promising grub-holes, and she and Matt chopped out enough of the waxy worms for supper. Martha loaded them into the pail to take back to the cabin, and Matt went to haul in firewood and bring water.

Martha thought there was still some kindling in the cabin, so she went straight in, tugging the latch string to lift the bar.

When she pulled the door open, a blur of purple feathers nearly took her nose off.

The bird thumped past her, running heavily between wildly flapping wings until one long bound finally lifted it clear of the ground. Martha shrieked in surprise as the thing took off.

Matt turned around, his arms full of sticks. He was just in time to catch the last flicker of purple as the bird vanished into the trees.

"Well, I'll be," he said, sounding exactly like Daddy Corey.

"See?" Martha said. "I *told* you so."

It hadn't been the endangered animal smuggling that originally brought the attention of Cascadia LEC to the slopes of Rainier. It was the dismembered body.

Not a complete body. On the list of reasons one might dismember a dead person, preventing identification of the remains is still high. Even in this era of skin-biota mapping and DNA identification (and forensic DNA reconstruction), it helps to get rid of the teeth and hands. Hiding cause of death is another popular reason, as is aiding disposal of the corpse. Bodies are awkward heavy things.

But not everybody is in a DNA database. And the reconstructive techniques only give an idea of what a person *might* look like—you only have to look at any pair of forty-year-old identical twins to understand that environment and accident have a certain amount of influence over a person's appearance.

Still.

This particular dismembered body—or the portions of it that had been actually recovered here—turned out to have belonged to a University of Washington geneticist, one Darwish by name. Whose DNA *was* on file. And who had not been the sort of person to go casually missing, despite some gambling debts and an incautious affair or two. Which led to a Cascadia LEC operation, which led to the discovery that an Interpol-North America agent was already somewhere on the mountain, engaged in hunting down a poaching operation dedicated to shipping the Pacific Northwest's irreplaceable biodiversity to wealthy collectors everywhere else in the world.

Cascadia LEC would need to send in its own guns to investigate the murder, however. Enter the woman now known as Rebecca Sanchez, who in her secret other life made her living as a licensable peace officer— previously operating out of San Francisco, so local Cascadia crooks were unlikely to know her face or reputation.

The smuggling is the sort of thing you might get off of with a wrist-slap. A body, though—*that* could send somebody to jail for a long time.

Metaphorically speaking, Sanchez has her fingers crossed.

After Sanchez marks the position of the camouflaged facility she continues on until nightfall, making sure that it looks like she's left for real. Somewhere downslope is her contact—the agent licensed by Interpol whose presence on the mountain hinted that more was going on than a random murder, however gruesome that murder might have been.

At the rendezvous point, she makes a cold camp and eats energy bars for supper.

~

It was too hot for the fire, but Martha didn't like to eat the grubs Matt brought home without boiling or roasting them first, so she was piling sticks into the stove. Honestly, she didn't like to eat grubs at all, but they were better than going hungry. And she knew, because Daddy had said, that they were very good for you. Full of protein and amino acids. And easy to collect from under the bark of fallen trees. Much easier than catching a squirrel in a deadfall, for example.

They were one of the best things to eat in the woods, now that Daddy didn't bring them food any more. They didn't taste bad. Like the smoked kippers Daddy used to bring in tins, only wriggly. Unless you roasted them. But they were *grubs*, and Martha did not like them.

Daddy has also said that they were *invasive*, that they came with the palm trees when the winters got warm, and that he and she and Matt were doing a good deed by eating them.

So she was still trying to decide what to do about that—fire or no fire?—when the cabin door banged open and the man came in. He was big and dark, in stompy boots with moss and mud caked on the soles, and Martha's first impulse was to yell at him to wipe his feet. Daddy wouldn't like the mud in the house.

But then she remembered she wasn't supposed to let anybody but Daddy and Matt see her, and she shrank back into the corner by the stove and accidentally kicked over the big pail of grubs. They writhed horribly on the floor, and she danced aside, against the cold iron side of the stove, trying not to squish them.

He towered over her until he crouched down, reaching out a hand. He made himself smile. She still didn't like him.

"Hey, little girl," he said. "Are you Martha?"

"You can't come in here," she said definitely. "Your shoes are muddy."

"Are they?" He looked down. "Well, if you'll come with me I'll go right back outside. And then I won't be breaking the rules."

"I'm not supposed to go with strangers," she said. "Where's Matt? I want Matt."

He'd know what to do. He was older. He always had a plan. And they were supposed to take care of each other. Daddy always said so.

"Matt is outside," the man said. "Come on, sweetie. My name's Doselle Callandar. I'll take you someplace where you can get a clean outfit and something to eat that's better than that." He waved at the grubs. "Cake. You like cake? Kids like cake."

She backed away, wedging herself between the cold stove and the wall. "No."

"Look," he said. "Martha, I know it's you. I saw your picture. Your Papa Corey sent me. I'm going to take care of you and Matt now, all right?"

Now she knew it was wrong. That he was lying. Because if he knew Daddy, he'd know that Daddy was Daddy, not Papa. "NO!" she yelled, very loudly. "Matt, Matt *help*."

"Oh, bother," the man in the boots said, sounding like he wanted to say something else entirely. But even though she screamed, he reached out and grabbed her arm, and no matter how she twisted and wiggled—like the grubs squirming on the concrete—she couldn't keep him from pulling her out from behind the wood stove.

In Sanchez's line of work, reputation is all you have. The new models of distributed policing bear a debt of concept to the U.S. Marshals, Texas Rangers, and Mounties of old. It's a kind of knight-errantry, albeit with better communications technology. But if you work for hire for law enforcement agencies, they like to know what they're getting.

Word of mouth between agencies that have employed her—the personal recommendation—is the only currency that counts.

She's known as somebody who gets results, and gets them in the cleanest manner possible. She thinks of herself as an heir to frontier lawmen of an earlier era, and she's all too aware of the pitfalls of thinking of one's self as Bat Masterson or Wyatt Earp.

All in all, she'd rather be Virgil.

And if she gets away with what happened in Oakland with her nose clean, she swears to herself that she will never step across that particular line again.

There are other cops with other reputations. Some get more work than she does, at higher pay. Some of those are cowboys, some braggarts. Some—like Doe—believe that the way to make an omelet is to bust heads.

Some of those stop being hired by large enforcement divisions after a while—they just find the licenses they're offered getting cheaper, the work getting dodgier. Some of them stop getting licenses at all.

A few of her colleagues, Sanchez considers good cops, and Sanchez passes their names along when she can, confident that they'll do the same for her. And that they'll keep doing that.

As long as Doe keeps his mouth shut.

Man, she hates having to trust anybody that much. Even somebody she used to love. Maybe especially somebody she used to love.

Sanchez sleeps lightly, when she manages to sleep at all. The ground isn't bad—she spreads a tarp, and she has her summerweight sleeping bag, and she's found a good spot: sheltered in a deer wallow among pressed-down ferns.

But she's keyed up and nervous, still full of unspent adrenaline hangover, and as much as she needs rest the restlessness won't leave her alone. Eventually, she gives up tossing and turning and listening to the things move in the darkness and pulls her reader out. *Indigenous Fauna of the Pacific Northwest.* That should be stultifying enough to send her off to dreamland post-haste.

To her surprise, however, she finds it moderately fascinating. She'd still prefer case studies—Sanchez has always been a fan of talking shop—but it turns out that there's something very soothing about the lifestyles of Pacific Tree Frogs.

She wonders if maybe that's what the glossy brownish thing she glimpsed slithering through the trees on the previous day was, though she imagines even tree frogs probably *move* like frogs. They have to hop, right? It's what they're built for.

She's still awake when something big makes a crunching sound in the wilderness. A pass of her hand dims the background on the reader and she blinks, rapidly, willing her eyes to adjust. Okay, so maybe the reader was a bad idea.

Still, it has given her a host a possibilities for the lurker in the darkness. Elk? Mule deer? The wolves that have recolonized these slopes are supposed to be shy of humans. Hopefully it's neither brown bear nor cougar. That would be a little too ironic, getting eaten by one of the species whose exploitation she's come to prevent.

But the crunch is followed by another, and a low and human mutter, so Sanchez does what she supposes any normal hiker would do in this situation.

"Hello?" she calls, drawing he knees up inside the bag so she can move fast if she has to. "Is somebody there?"

There's a pause, and then a male voice answers, "Stand up, miss, and show your hands."

Some cops who can't get licensed anymore go to paramilitary

organizations like Edgewater, but in Sanchez's opinion they're no more than mercenaries to hire to any warlord who wants them, and who won't put too much in the way of limits on their behavior. As the silence stretches, she tries to imagine herself grabbing tourists by the chin, but she's got that too-prickly awareness that tells her that her fight-or-flight reflex is just looking for an excuse.

The man she's come here to meet—the agent originally assigned to the rare-animal smuggling trade in Cascadia—is one Robert Brown, an interviewer of such rare talents he's known in the business as the Confessor. Sanchez has always heard he's a good cop, maybe even a decent man. The latter's more common than the former; power breeds abuse.

But lately—according to the Cascadia ops who handled her briefing— he's become erratic. Possibly obsessed. Possibly confused. Possibly on the take, and it's hard to say which of the three possibilities concerns them more. She has a recognition code to use, but her instructions include feeling him out on other things too.

And even if Brown turns out to be honest—and despite this being the designated rendezvous spot—there's no guarantee that the person or persons who found her have any connection to him. So when Sanchez stands, her hands in the air, the sleeping bag a puddle at her feet that she is careful to step clear of, she doesn't identify herself as a Cascadia op. She just says, "I'm Rebecca Sanchez. I'm hiking through."

The searchlight blinds her. The ground is a carpet of twigs and moss and needles, stabbing her bare soles and prickling between her toes.

"Poaching through, you mean," the voice accuses, while she blinks and squints and forces herself not to shield her face with her hands. Her night vision's shot for the next fifteen minutes anyway.

"You can check my gear," she says for the second time today. "I'm not poaching. Just hiking. All I have is some food and equipment and a reader."

There's at least two of them, because while one approaches, the other keeps the blinding light trained on her face. That could be a bad sign or a good one. Sanchez gives up and just closes her eyes; at least it hurts less, and her eyelids, while translucent, will still limit the dazzle.

Instead of watching what she can't see anyway, she listens.

She thinks the one who crunches over to her is male, by the stride, but she's guessing and she'd be the first to admit it. So she says, as non-confrontationally as she can, "Do you mind telling me who you are?"

There's a rustle as whoever it is squats to go through her stuff. She hears the rattle of food packaging, the slick nylon sounds of her pack. The whisk of the tarp under her sleeping bag as he lifts and inspects it.

"We're nobody you want to mess with," he says, confirming that the first man who spoke is also the one who crouches by her feet.

"Do you live here?"

Personalize. Engage. If they're common thieves, or bent 'on sexual assault, the more of a relationship she can build with them the safer she'll be. If they're Edgewater, and they followed her—well.

"This is our home," he says. There's more rustling, and then an exhale— too soft to call a grunt—as he stands. "Okay, your stuff checks out, Ms. Sanchez."

He must make a gesture to his partner, because the blinding light falls off her face. She lets her eyes open, blinking savagely, and sees nothing in the night except a darkness so intense it sparkles. She knows it's the rods and cones in her retinas firing, trying to make out any shape at all, but it will be minutes before that happens.

His hand must have gone to his belt, because an indirect glow illuminates both their feet and her gear—more or less neatly restowed. Enough light scatters that she can make out the dim outline of his face. He's older, she thinks. Dark-skinned, his hair allowed to run a little wild.

She recognizes him from the images in the briefing.

"I understand," she says. "Do you have a lot of problems with poachers here?"

He holds out the reader, the back open. The tangle of her climbing spikes peers out, visible more through texture and shape than color or shine. "I guess you'd know that as well as I do, Constable."

She looks up at his face again. Of course, he recognized the gear.

His thin lips twist in a smile. "I figured they'd be sending somebody to check on me soon. Welcome to Rainier, Ms. Sanchez. I'm Robert Brown."

He helps her pack the gear and hump it five miles through game trails to his camp. There was no second person, just a mount for the light and a remote. So he's just as smart as she was warned, and she let him get the drop on her.

Not her finest hour, if the reports of his erratic behavior turn out true.

Still, he's perfectly civil the whole dark hike back to his bivouac. He has a tent and a camp chair, which he blackmails her into using by plunking down on the ground. No fire, but a tiny camp stove over which he boils water as they talk. Despite the heat of the day, night has come on with a chill, and the sweat drying on Sanchez's neck makes her glad of the coffee.

"So you found their site?" Brown asks, starting soup as she sips the second cup.

"Spotted the location," she says. "I didn't get a look at it. I met part of their cordon sanitaire, however."

"Charmers," Brown says. "I'm pretty sure they've each got an Edgewater uniform in their closet back home."

"You might be right." She lets the silence hollow out between them. Maybe he'll fill it, maybe he won't.

He lets it sway there until he takes her empty coffee cup away, wipes it out with a rag, and returns it full of soup. "I've never heard of a Rebecca Sanchez on the job. But they wouldn't send a new kid out on a gig like this. So who are you really?"

"Mauritza Aguilar."

He raises his eyebrows in something she could spin to herself as respect, gaunt cheeks illuminated by the can of propellant.

The soup base is dehydrated and reconstituted, but there are fresh things in it as well—gleaned plants, she imagines, hoping he knows his toadstools from his mushrooms—and it's good. She drinks it slowly, to make it last and because it's hot.

"What brought you out?" he asks, when she's had time to get half of it inside her.

"Murder," she says. "I'm not here to bust up your animal smuggling case."

He bites his lip, and she makes a note of that for later. There's something he's not telling her. Of course, she's not telling him that she's here to check up on him . . .

He says, "Murder."

"Portions of a dismembered body were recovered outside of Portland," she says. "It'd been scrubbed down to the skin bacteria, but DNA from a tick head recovered from under the skin led back to Rainier. When Cascadia LEC checked for ongoing investigations in the area, the Interpol link came up. Didn't they tell you that when they signaled that I was coming out?"

"No. Just the flash to expect somebody. I figured it was best to make sure you were who you said you were, in case the bad guys intercepted the flash and replaced you. It'd be too easy to slip an Edgewater op in."

"A lot of them used to be cops."

He nods. "Body," he says. "Was it ever identified?"

She is contemplating a lie versus the truth when he holds up a hand for silence.

"Corey Darwish."

She says, "Should I be suspicious that you know that?"

"Not at all," he says, poking the ground with a stick since he can't stir up the fire. "He was my informant. I imagine his colleagues caught on."

The man hauled Martha down a kind of long, narrow room with doors on each wall. A hall, that's what it was called. She'd never seen on herself before, never seen the inside of any building by the cabin and shed, but she'd heard the word on videos, when Daddy still came to visit them.

Martha had kicked at first, and screamed as the man dragged her, but that just made him pick her up like a sack of vegetables and swing her around until she stopped screaming and wet herself and started to cry. Now she let him carry her, but she stared back over his shoulder at Matt's head and made her small hands into fists. She should kick him, she thought, but she was too scared. She couldn't make her feet move with any force.

Her only comfort was that two of his friends were slinging Matt along between them. Matt was bigger, and the men had tied his hands together behind him and were half-carrying him by his elbows. Matt kept his eyes stubbornly downcast, except when he glanced up to catch Martha's eye. Sweat slid in rivulets across Matt's shiny scalp; Martha knew he was as scared as she was, but he did not say anything.

The hall the man carried her down smelled strange, pungent and musty, like mold and old urine and Lysol. Like snakes. There were sounds from behind the doors, animal sounds. And people sounds, too: Martha was sure she heard a baby crying.

As long as she behaved, the man wasn't rough. Just really in a hurry. He jerked open a door towards the far end of a hall and carried her through, setting her down on a cube-shaped chair with no regard for her wet pants.

The other men pushed Matt in behind her, and one knelt down to untie his hands. Matt turned, ready to hit, but the man blocked the blow easily and stood.

"You be good kids," he said, as the one who had been carrying Martha slipped out of the room behind him. "Somebody will be in to see you in a minute."

The door shut, and Martha heard it lock. "Freaks," one man muttered on the other side.

"Shh," said the one who had carried her in. "They're just kids. They can't help it."

She was wet and the stale urine stank and burned her skin. As if it didn't matter, Matt came over, his hands extended, and reached to put his arms around her. Martha burst into fresh tears.

"Hey," Matt said. "Hey, hey. It's okay. Maybe these people know where Daddy is. Did you think of that?"

It was like he'd opened up a book and showed her something wonderful. "Really?"

"Maybe," he said. She could hear him warming to his own idea. "Hey, how else would they have found us, huh?"

"Oh." She sat up, scrubbing her eyes.

Matt pulled back. "Let me see if I can find you something dry."

As he moved around the room, Martha finally noticed where they were. This one room, alone, was almost as big as the cabin. There was blue carpet on the floor—Martha hadn't seen carpet in person before, either, but she knew what it had to be—decorated with a bright pattern of dots. She liked the dots. You could play hopscotch on them, or they could be islands in a big lake with different kinds of animals and plants on each one. If you had some animals and plants to pretend with.

The furniture in the room was all bright, too—big plastic squares and rectangles. Some had open sides, and some had hinges, and some had plastic padding—like the one she was sitting on. Some were more like tables—child-sized tables, which Martha thought was the best idea ever—and some were more like couches.

The ones that were like tables had other bright things on them. They were toys—blocks and wires and dolls, balls and sticks, round-cornered rectangular objects with screens that looked like computers, only smaller.

Martha was beside herself with curiosity. She got up out of her chair. Her legs hurt where her wet pants rubbed against the insides of her thighs, so she walked in a funny stiff-legged way like a baby deer. That made her knees and hips hurt.

"They have toys," she said. "So they must have clothes, right?"

Matt nodded. He was prying at the top of one of the hinged rectangles, trying to make it open. She heard the ticking sound as he pulled at the lid with his fingernails and they slid, over and over again. "I think it's locked," he said, and kicked it. Not hard, just in frustration.

A second later, the door to the room opened up again, and a new man stood in the doorway.

Martha jumped and turned, her shoes catching on the carpet. She stumbled but did not fall. Matt was beside her before the new man came in.

"Hi," he said. He had a pile of cloth in his arms. "You must be Martha and Matt Darwish. I'm Dr. Klopft. I brought you some clean clothes."

Martha pulled herself up as tall as she could and made her voice big. "Where's my Daddy?"

It didn't sound big enough, when it echoed all around the room. But Dr. Klopft put the clothes down on the nearest table, made his face sad, and said, "Well, Martha, I have some bad news for you. Your Daddy was hurt in an accident. That's why I'm going to take care of you from now on."

If she'd had time to think about it, she would have expected to burst out crying again. Instead, she got very still inside herself. Very still and very certain. If Daddy was hurt, it was because this Dr. Klopft had had something to do with it.

He waited, as if he expected an outburst. But Martha was patient— Daddy always said so, "Martha, you're a very patient girl"—and she just waited back. Eventually, Dr. Klopft reached out and pushed the pile of clothes towards her.

"Here's some clean clothes," he said. "Can you take a bath by yourself? There's a bathroom right through that door."

Martha, who had gotten used to checking traps and cooking on the wood stove since Daddy went away, just blinked at him.

"Right," Dr. Klopft said. "You go get cleaned up. And I'll go see if we can get some dinner, what do you say?"

Sanchez finishes her soup and sets the cup aside. When Brown does not look up, she clears her throat and says, "Home office is wondering how the Klopft thing is coming. Aside from the murder, I mean."

"Klopft thing? Which part of it?"

There aren't supposed to *be* parts. "Trafficking in endangered species for the pet and medicinal trade?"

"That?" Now Brown meets her eyes. He smiles. Half-smiles. "I have enough to hang him, if that's what you're wondering."

"But you haven't called in backup. Or a strike team."

"I haven't," Brown agrees.

"So there's something more you're after."

Gingerly, he drops the lid over the top of the cooking fuel, snuffing the crawling blue flame. The sudden darkness after reveals, a little surprisingly, just how much light that pathetic curl of fire cast. Or possibly it says something about the adaptability of the human eye, because she's as blinded as she was by the dazzle of his lantern, but it doesn't last long. A few blinks, and she can see the shape of his pale khaki shirt-cuffs against the brown of his hands. Not the colors, of course—but her mind fills them in for her.

"So," he says, "who is it you were working for again?"

She carries nothing that could identify her as an agent of Cascadia LEC. Anything that could identify her to Brown could identify her to the quarry. Except, of course, the recognition phrase. Which Sanchez memorized with great irritation, having found it stupid.

Still, she recites it now: "Penelope and Marcia Catoun make of your wifehood no comparison; Hide ye your beauties, Isoude and Elaine—"

The next line of the poem is *My lady cometh, that all this may disdain.* But that's not the assigned response. The assigned response isn't Chaucer at all, but a twentieth century poet.

Brown just sits there in the night, his shirt a paler shadow against the deep darkness of foliage and forest behind him, and his breathing continues low and even. At last, he says gently, "Blue, blue windows behind the stars. Yellow moon on the rise. Ms. Aguilar."

"Sanchez." She swallows.

Sounds tell her he's disassembling the camp stove and folding it up by means of feel, experience, and whatever dim moonlight filters through the canopy. The metallic sounds cease, replaced by rustling.

He says, "You know what happens if we send Klopft up for CITES violations? A couple of years in jail, a fine that's pocket change for an organization that size. And a month later he pokes his head back up in Singapore or Belize."

"You have something else?"

Brown, again, in conspiratorial silence, pauses.

"Tell me."

He sighs. "We'll talk about it in the morning."

Sanchez hears Brown move, sees the shift of his silhouette as he stands.

"Come on," he says. "We have to haul the food up where the bears can't get it."

He walks a few steps through the dark, and now she finds she can see—not well, not at all well, but clearly enough to navigate. If she pays attention to what her eyes are telling her about shape and movement, rather than trying to make out detail, she can follow Brown across his small bare campsite without stumbling over or into anything.

That may be because there's nothing to stumble on, but it doesn't stop Sanchez from a feeling of accomplishment. It doesn't last long, as she's reduced to standing by awkwardly as Brown loads food back into a pack and clips it to a static line tossed over a tree branch some fifteen feet off the ground.

"So what's to stop the hypothetical bear using that as a piñata?"

"Nothing," he answers. "But it won't be trying to climb into the tent, which is the point of the exercise. Speaking of which, I didn't see a tent in your gear."

"Too much weight," she says. "I have tarps."

Long ago and far away, Sanchez had answered phones for a living, and she knew the trick of smiling even when you wanted to strangle somebody, for the change it put in your voice. From *his* voice, she thinks now that he smiles. "Hardcore."

"I was hiking in," she says. "The didn't tell me to expect a long-term stay."

"Right," he says. "I'll help you rig something."

By the time Martha got herself clean and dressed—what Dr. Klopft called *clothes* were just pajamas—the food was on the table. Matt had divided it carefully in half, and set her half aside to wait for her while he ate his own.

The food was grilled cheese sandwiches, which Daddy used to make, and long thin sticks of something white and starchy, but golden and crispy on the outside, slightly gritty with what must be salt. A little dish of ketchup sat beside them.

"What's that?" she asked.

"Fries?" Matt said.

She'd heard of fries, but never tasted one before. She poked it into her mouth and chewed. Her stomach knotted up with nervousness, but she made herself swallow.

"It's kind of boring." She was going to eat it anyway, of course. You didn't waste food.

Especially food that didn't wiggle.

"Use the ketchup," Matt advised. "And drink your milk."

That was good, then. She still didn't trust Dr. Klopft about Daddy. But she and Matt got fed here, and Martha knew Matt would take care of her.

Maybe things would get better again soon.

Brown relents to the extent of using his lantern as they set her camp. He helps Sanchez spread the first tarp and rig a rain sheet from the second one—"It'll rain by morning, never fear"—then goes through her pack for food, which he secures in a second nearby tree. And somehow, Sanchez can't keep herself from talking to him. Especially when he asks, casually, "Why are you a cop? I mean, especially in this day and age, there are easier ways to earn a living."

"You're one too, and you're asking me?"

"I know *my* reasons."

He doesn't sound as if he thinks they're particularly good reasons, right now. Something about the wryness in his tone, as if what he's just said is a confidence rather than a blatant misdirection, makes her want to answer. *That's why they call him the Confessor.* She can identify the confiding tones even as she feels it working on her.

She says, "When you leave people to fend for themselves, the predators come out."

"Somebody's got to play the shepherd?"

"I don't think of people as sheep, mostly." Sanchez hunkers down to unlace her boots. "Well, maybe a few."

He laughs. "Sleep tight, Sanchez. I'll see you in the morning."

"Brown."

He hesitates. She plops her right boot off. "So what was a geneticist doing informing on an exotic animal smuggling ring?"

"That's a good question. Ask me again in the morning."

When he vanishes into the tent, he leaves the lantern. She slips into her bag and clicks it off. The forest night folds down around her again, and for a few moments she finds its sounds soothing. But as she's drifting into sleep, a thought jerks her awake again, heart racing. Curled tight inside her bag, Sanchez shudders, because she's realized that there's another reason a body might be dismembered.

To hide that a portion of the dead person is missing.

Sanchez dozes lightly, when she sleeps at all, but judging by the low snores that drift through the tent wall, Brown isn't having that problem.

Still, she lies curled up small, at least warm and possibly fooling herself a little.

At first light, the clamor of the birds makes further dissembling impossible. She slithers from her bag, finds her jeans—made in San Francisco again, now that shipping them from elsewhere has become prohibitively expensive—and pads across the small camp barefoot. It hurts less in daylight, when she can see where she's putting her feet. After she relieves herself—she finds Brown's latrine pit by the folding shovel stuck in the ground beside it—it's the work of mere moments to figure out Brown's knots and rigging system and lower the food. She roots in her own pack first, finding her small stove, oatmeal, and the cans of fuel. She's got stackable, collapsible pots, so the fact that her stove has only one burner doesn't keep her from making cereal and tea both at once. And that way she's not wasting heat.

There are even tiny boxes of shelf-stable milk to go on the cereal, and she sets out two. Looking at the sparseness of Brown's camp, the milk makes her feel like a tenderfoot wallowing in luxury, but she had planned on being out less than a week and not bringing a tent left her with some extra weight allowance.

Besides, she likes milk on her oatmeal.

Apparently, Brown does too, because when the smell of cooking oatmeal calls him from his tent, he grunts approval rather than making any of the scathing comments she was dreading. Which makes her wonder, exactly, why it was that Robert Brown's good opinion should mean so much to her.

But he eats the oatmeal in trusting—and approving—silence, drinks the tea (black), and finishes off the last few ounces of milk in his package with obvious satisfaction. Having done so, he helps her clean up, and then dusts off his hands and finds his own boots by the flap of his tent. He isn't barefoot, but is scuffing around in camp shoes, so Sanchez takes it as a sign that she should kit up too.

"So that thing you were going to show me—" Her first words of the morning, while the leaf-mould moisture soaks through the seat of her jeans and her boot lace snaps in her hands.

He nods. He is even taller and leaner in the early-morning gloaming, his lined face betraying a sun-weathered seriousness that cracks wide apart when he smiles. "If you want to know what's really going on in there."

She knots the split ends of the lace together and ties it off. She should have used some of her weight allowance for spare laces. Well, you can't think of everything. "It's why I came."

She follows him down a narrow game trail, moving cautiously in the gray light. It is hard to be certain through the trees, but glimpses of sky between boughs tells her that the sun must be about to clear the horizon soon, because the silver-blue is streaked with rose and gold.

They didn't walk far. She starts to ask a question once, but he puts a finger to his lips before the second syllable, and the softness with which he walks soon has her sneaking on tiptoe too.

Finally, they reach a brushy brake that she realizes after a moment or two is a constructed blind. Brown gestures her to crouch down. She hunkers beside him. When he pulls out his binoculars, she's glad she'd thought to slip her spyglass into her hip pocket.

She sets it to her eye and tries to follow the direction of his lenses. Up into the trees—is he looking at a bird?

She misses the nest the first two times her glass skips over it, but on the third one she catches movement. Something stirs inside a bundle of leaves. In the slanted light, Sanchez can see how the movement makes the bundle pulse like a beating heart. Strands of some silvery substance, like the mucilage of slugs, bind the leaves together.

"It's a nest?" she whispers.

Brown nods without lowering his binoculars. "Watch."

His voice is barely more than a breath, so Sanchez holds the rest of her questions and tries to quiet her breathing.

Something slips from the shelter of the leaf-bundle. Something mottled and green-brown, nearly the shade of the leaves, but this thing shines moist-slick and coils like a twisting tentacle. It *is* a tentacle, Sanchez realizes, zooming in her spyglass for a better look.

She presses a button to trigger the glass's internal digital camera as the second tentacle emerges. Now she sees the suckers on the underside of the think, questing sensory organs. Now, the bulbous head, emerging slowly from the leaf-shelter, the one visible enormous eye blinking softly. As it moves further from the leaves, out onto the green of the coniferous boughs that surround it, its color shifts from dappled to a deep, unrelieved pine green.

"Cripes," she whispers.

Brown nudges her, but it's too late. The octopus—the *arboreal* octopus— flashes in pores of dark red against the green, like bloodstone. And then it's gone, vanishing not back into the nest but through boughs, moving away, invisible in moments although Sanchez can track its progress for a few seconds longer by the sway as it moves from branch to branch. But then it must slow, become more cautious, because its progress becomes both invisible and inaudible.

She waits thirty more seconds before she lets her breath out and says, "What was *that*?"

Brown lowers his binoculars. "Pacific tree octopus," he says.

"Those are a joke. They don't exist."

He points up with one long finger, the nail bed strikingly pale in the gloom beneath the trees. "I know."

Dr. Klopft came back in as Martha was pushing the last ketchup around her plate with a French fry. It turned out they weren't any good when they got cold, and she wondered why it was that nobody had told her so. She was also full—really full—for the first time since she and Matt had eaten up all the supplies Daddy had left behind when he vanished. It was almost an unpleasant feeling, like her body had forgotten what to do with that much food.

She put the French fry down when the door opened, and looked around for something to wipe her fingers on. The napkin on her lap (Daddy had always been very insistent about manners) had slipped down to the floor, so she dropped to her knees and grabbed it. When she got back up again, Matt was standing to block her from the doctor.

She wiped her hands and put one on his arm, pushing herself between him and the table until she was standing behind him.

"Hey," Dr. Klopft said. "Did you kids get enough to eat?"

Matt nodded. Martha squeezed his arm for moral support.

Dr. Klopft glanced around and put one hand on a chair-box. He dragged it over and hunkered down it, beside the table-box they had been eating at, even though it was too small.

"Please," he said. "Sit."

It made Martha feel very grown up to be talked to that way. She sat back in her chair, pushing away the cold-fry plate, and in a minute Matt did also. Apparently, it was her job to talk to Klopft, because Matt just bit his lip in that stubborn way that meant he wasn't going to say anything, and his face crinkled up beside the eyes.

"Dr. Klopft," she said, trying to sound respectful, "can you please take us to Daddy Corey now?"

Klopft heaved a big sigh, which Martha thought meant he was tried and frustrated. He steepled his fingers in front of him and said, "Martha, I know this is scary. But I'd like to help you. Can you tell me where your Daddy went?"

She felt a sinking heaviness in her belly. *He* was supposed to know where Daddy was. If he didn't know, how were they ever going to find him?

"I don't know," she said.

"Do you know how long ago he vanished? When was the last time you saw him?"

She thought about it, but the days blurred together. Weeks and weeks. She shook her head.

Matt said, "Three weeks."

Martha looked at him. Was that all? She looked back at Dr. Klopft in time to see his face do something funny.

"That was the last time we saw him too," he said. "You see, your daddy works for me. And we're very worried about him. Now, I'm not angry with him or you, and I won't be angry. I just want to help you find him."

Grownups didn't usually say they wouldn't be angry unless they were actually secretly angry and trying not to show it. At least, that was true about Daddy. And it was true about the people in videos. But Dr. Klopft said *works*, not *worked*. So even if Dr. Klopft was mad, he wasn't going to fire Daddy.

"Okay," Matt said, having apparently reached the same conclusions that Martha had.

But Martha said, "Why did you tie us up?"

Dr. Klopft smiled. "That was a mistake. Officer Callandar and Officer Alison were worried that you would try to get away, and if you hid in the woods you could get hurt or chased by an animal before they could find you. They shouldn't have done it, and I punished them. It won't happen again."

"We live in the woods," Matt said, stubbornly proud. "We wouldn't get eaten by an animal."

Dr. Klopft smiled. "Yes, you're obviously both very smart and knowledgeable children. Now I need you to use those smarts and that knowledge to help me. So think very carefully, please. About the last time you saw your father."

Martha closed her eyes to think better. It wasn't hard to pull up the memory: it was still there, crisp and perfect, just like all her other memories. It shone in her head as if she could reach out and touch it.

She wanted to. She wanted to run into the memory and hug Daddy. But if she tried she knew her arms would go right through him.

Matt was remembering too. She didn't open her eyes to look, but she could tell by his voice. He said, "Dad said he had somebody to meet. And that he'd be home in a couple of hours."

"A couple of hours? You're sure?"

"He was always very—very *punctual.*" Matt pronounced the long word carefully. "He was always where he said he would be."

"Except for that time," Martha said. "He didn't come back."

Dr. Klopft was frowning. "But he was fine when he left you. He didn't seem worried?"

"No," Matt said.

But Martha knew better. She'd seen something while Matt was outside. She said, "He took his gun."

"So that's why you have to involve a geneticist in an endangered animal trafficking ring," Sanchez says, as she and Brown begin packing up the camp. He has more stuff than she does, but he is folding it all away exactly as if he intends to move on and never come back to this little clearing. "Because it's not just trafficking in endangered animals. It's genetically engineering imaginary ones?"

"That's all I've got," Brown says. "Figure the octopus is an escapee. It might be as happy here as an invasive anaconda is in the Everglades."

"But that's not illegal," she says. "I mean, people used to create unicorns by surgically altering goats, didn't they? What's to stop them from doing the same thing with an octopus? I bet plenty of people with more money than sense would buy one. So why do you keep it secret that you're making them?"

Hell, she thinks. *I would buy one. If I had the dosh, because you know something like that doesn't come cheap.*

From the expression crinkling his face, he's thinking the same thing. Maybe even word-for-word. "Because some people will pay top dollar for something when they thing it's unobtainably rare."

"But it's cryptozoology. Who's gonna believe in a *tree octopus*?"

"So," he says. "Do you know what all the weird animals that live in Malaysia are?"

"Oh." She hadn't even thought of that. Whatever somebody will pay for a cool genetically engineered pet, there's some collector who would pay ten, twenty times more for an authentic wild-caught Pacific Tree Octopus. Klopft isn't just *engineering* a cool new pet. He's *forging* a critically-endangered species. "That's fucked up."

Brown smiles again, like he likes her. He reaches out and taps her shoulder, too. "And you know it. Come on, Sanchez. Now that I have you for backup, there's something I want to try."

He won't tell her where they're going, but as they stride along deer trails, having hidden the bulk of their gear, he does tell her to watch out for traps.

"Like punji sticks and tripwires?"

"Like wire loops and deadfalls to kill squirrels." He points, carefully, leading her gaze to a flat rock balanced across a triangle of sticks. It's set just a little off the trail. "They're tricky to set, and it would be rude to trigger them. Not to mention the potential damage to your toes."

"Ow," Sanchez says, feeling the tingle of imagined pain. "So why was your guy setting traplines?"

"Not my guy," he says. "They started showing up about a week and a half ago. But I haven't had the chance to follow them back. Now that you're here—" He shrugs. "Two are better than one."

"I'm not armed," she says.

He gives her a sideways glance. "You've got eyes."

Indeed she does. And because she's looking for traps, and still scanning the trees for signs of a murder scene, she spots the bright gouge in an umbertree-trunk, just a little above head height.

"Brown," she hisses, instinctively dropping her voice.

He hears her and freezes. "Yeah?"

"Look here." She gestures to the tree.

His long face smooths out with surprise. "That looks like a bullet hole."

"I know," she says. "How about that?"

Sanchez doesn't have her camera anymore, but Brown is armed. He photographs everything she suggests, and a few other angles besides, while she examines the scene. There are, in point of fact, *two* bullet holes, though somebody has dug out one of them.

"Why only one?" Brown asks.

Sanchez holds up the second, pinched between a pair of pliers. "Because we're supposed to figure out which gun this one came from."

"And not the other?"

She drops the rifle bullet into a plastic baggy. "Bingo."

She examines the litter along the line between the two scars. Halfway through, she finds a spatter of blood, dark droplets that by chance struck a peeled branch and so stand out, even three weeks later. She calls Brown over.

"Damn," he says. "That looks like a crime scene to me."

"I know," Sanchez says. "Just doesn't it?"

Some of the trails Brown leads Sanchez down are so narrow—so negligible—as to be more the concept of a trail than the actuality. They must be made by deer. The trails wind inconveniently through rhododendron stands, forcing Sanchez and Brown to duckwalk. They plunge down steep clay banks and scramble up mossy slopes. Deer apparently had not yet developed the technology of the switchback.

Leaf-mold compresses spongily under each footstep, except where bare wet earth wants to shed her footsteps entirely. Sanchez and Brown go single-file. She learns to watch where he places his feet and imitate him.

A half-day hike brings them to the edge of a clearing, or at least a gap between the trees. Sanchez's personal idea of *clearing* includes visible sky; perhaps this is more a *glade* by those standards. Whatever it is, the overhanging boughs bower and shade a little ramshackle cabin that—by virtue of its lack of straight lines and shaggy lichen-covered exterior—almost vanishes among them.

Brown holds out an arm to stop her, but she's already paused, one foot still half-lifted, her right hand pressing aside a whippy branch.

"Damn," says Brown. "Do you suppose anybody lives here?"

The door of the cabin is wedged open, one home-made hinge broken so it droops to the ground on the outside corner. They approach cautiously, Sanchez taking point because she is unarmed except for her hiking stick, and if something jumps her Brown has a better chance of taking the assailant out. It's Sanchez's own plan—but that does nothing for the cold prickles spidering up and down her neck—some of which have to do with the ease with which she has found herself trusting Brown.

For all the hammering of her heart, however, the cabin lies empty, humming with a cold abandoned air. An overturned pail beside the woodstove has spilled palm grubs across the rough concrete pad—but they are freshly dead, Sanchez judges, which means somebody brought them in here in the last day or so. A pair of small beds sit against one wall, the covers rucked up into dirty, damp-looking squirrel nests sized for big dogs or human children. There is no place in the cabin that anything bigger than a rabbit could hide.

"Clear?" Brown asks from the doorway.

"Clear," she answers.

He enters, gives the room a once-over, and crouches by the door to examine something. For her part, Sanchez steps closer to the woodstove, drawn by a smear on the floor.

"Partial footprint," she says. "Somebody squashed a grub."

"Pair of men's boots," Brown says. "I'm pretty sure I've seen these on Darwish. Look like they haven't been touched in a while."

"There's a gunrack over the stove," Sanchez says. "There's no gun in it. It's less dusty than some of the other stuff over here. Also, this stove hasn't been well-cleaned in a while—"

"I think there should be a couple of kids here." Brown rattles drawers and a chest. "There's some toys, and kid-sized clothing. Say an eight year old girl and a ten year old boy?"

Sanchez turns. "You have kids?"

"Grown now." He sighs. "Their mom and I split up when they were about this age."

"I'm sorry." She turns her head and studies the peeling bark on the rough and ready doorframe. "I'm divorced, too. My ex is a cop."

He straightens up, tight graying curls brushing the crumbling bough-thatched roof. "Sorry to hear it," he says—the low-key sympathy of somebody who's been there, and knows firsthand the identity-shattering wreck of a failed marriage. "How long?"

"About a year," she lies.

"Any kids?"

She shakes her head.

He twists from the waist to look out the door. "Can you track?"

"You're supposed to know my rep," she says, glad for the diversion. "Do we call in a warrant now?"

He whistles between his teeth. "We have a kidnapping linked to a murder victim who was involved in an illegal animal smuggling ring, and a more-or-less hot trail. Now, or after we track them back to Klopft's compound?"

"You're confident that's where the trail will lead us?"

He shows her a crooked mouthful of teeth. "Be awfully coincidental if it didn't."

"Now," she says. "It will take the squad time to get here, and we'll want them."

The trail, it turns out, is easy to follow. This is a good thing, because Brown's casual personal confidence and her own response to it have left her rattled. Rattled, and thinking about Doe again, when she took this job in part so she wouldn't have to think about Doe.

Something else seems to be bugging Brown, though, because after an hour in which she follows the trail of churned leaf mold and chipped roots, he says, "You're probably wondering why I waited to move on this."

She hadn't been. She shakes her head. "No, I know. If he were holed up in here, you could have scared him off for good, and you needed him. There wasn't any time pressure. What if he caught the scent?"

"What if I led Klopft down on him?"

"Ouch," she says. "Yeah, okay, I see that. So I've been meaning to ask—Klopft must have front offices all over the world, right? Why the hell aren't we partnering this with Hawaii PD? Or Shanghai?"

"We are," he said. "Klopft isn't even the top of the food chain, which is why I haven't moved against him, either, so long as Darwish was feeding me. I've been gathering intelligence so that Shanghai PD could set up a sting. The smuggling syndicate's big man is Laurence Chien—Chien Liáopíng—and he never comes into North America or Europe if he can help it. This complicates matters."

"If you want him, you have to link him unequivocally to this operation."

"It would be best if we could get him into Cascadia. If we arrest him here, if we can link him definitively to the operation and through the operation to your murder, there will be federal charges—in addition to anything China and Interpol can throw at him. We might actually send him up with more than a slap on the wrist. The murder—" he sighs, reluctant as any good cop to say it "—will help."

Sanchez knows this. The fact that Brown knows it too, and is willing to share that knowledge, reassures her. And so here she is, her suspicions keep chasing each other in circles through the moist, bird-mad morning. She's very aware that she's deciding to trust Brown because she doesn't have a good reason to doubt him.

Fortunately for her distraction, it had been a big party—six at least—heavily burdened with unwilling children and moving fast. They left a lot of evidence of their passage. This is even easier to interpret than the crime scene.

And something is bugging her. Brought on by thoughts of Doe, no doubt, and thoughts of confidences.

"Earlier," she says, "when I said I'd been divorced about a year, that wasn't exactly the truth."

"I see," Brown says.

"We've been on the rocks for a year. I moved out six weeks ago. But I just decided to file last week. And I haven't yet, because he's on a license—and I can't tell him until he gets back. He was already gone a week when I packed up. I'm a coward, I guess."

"What's he like?"

Sanchez fights the bitter grin at first, then lets it curl her lip anyway. "He was my partner."

"You mean professional partner. Not just life partner."

"I do."

"So what caused the break?"

She wishes they had a campfire, so she could poke it, busy her eyes and her hands. Instead, she has to look up across the camp stove and meet Brown's steady gaze. "You're a cop," she says. "It would be a bad idea to tell you."

"I'm a cop," he says, like it bothers him. Like he's swallowing the words, *for now.* "And yeah, if it's bad, I probably won't keep it to myself."

She sighs. Presses her knuckles to her eyes, which are already swimming anyway from trying to pick out the tiny details that a fast-moving group of men dragging two children have left in the soil and vegetation. She straightens up, easing her back. "I found out something about him—and something about myself when I was with him—that I couldn't live with. So I left."

"And you still can't live with it."

She huffs. "Yeah. But I can't talk about it either." There—a bright chip of bruised root showing through chipped bark. The pale moist patch leads her another three feet, where she finds scuffed leaf mold further on. Their quarry are sticking to trails, more or less, but the trails themselves are hardly self-evident.

"I cheated," Brown says. Flat-out and even. She looks at him. He shrugs. "It is what it is. I did wrong and I paid for it. It was a long time ago."

What do you say to something like that? "I kind of went the opposite way," she says. "I was loyal over being true to myself, and it turns out that doesn't work out so good in the long run." She gestures at the trail before them, a convenient change of subject to get herself out of trouble. "Look, I'm willing to gamble that they're going back to the compound. What else is there in this direction?"

"Mountain lions." Brown squats to tighten his laces. He slips his pack off and conceals it off the trail, keeping out his hunting knife and his sidearm, worn openly in a hip holster now. When he stands again, his arms swing. "Come on. Let's go."

Sanchez sheds her pack and hides it in about ten meters from where Brown secreted his. Standing, she feels light on her feet, some of the exhaustion stripped away with the load. "Watch for traps," she says, and sets off at a light trot, leaning forward to make up for the slope up the mountain.

Dr. Klopft talked to them for a while, until Martha started yawning. Then he went away. He came back after they had slept, bringing breakfast and more questions. seemed to know about Martha's hearing, but maybe he didn't know enough. Because while he got up, crossed the room, and used the buzzer to get let out, he stood right outside it to talk to whoever he was talking to. Over a phone or an intercom, Martha thought, because she could only make out one side of the conversation. And because before he started talking, he said, "Callandar, get me the box, please?"

Matt was staring intently in the same direction. When she looked at him, he shook his head. He could only hear half of it, too.

"No," Dr. Klopft said. "I don't think there's any mistake. Yes, they pretty much have to be from the first couple of reject batches—no, no. I know Corey was supposed to destroy them all, but I guess he spirited a couple out. Seems to have been raising them as his—yes, yes. No, they don't look any better than you'd expect. No, and apparently before he vanished, the last time they saw Corey he left them alone with some supplies and went out with his gun."

There was a pause. Martha started to say something, but Matt held his hand up. And sure enough, in a moment, Dr. Klopft began speaking again. "Well, obviously if he went to handle it himself, he wanted to hide the reasons from us. Which means it has something to do with the fetuses he stole—

" . . . Yes, I do think it's possible he was being blackmailed. Likely, even. I just wish he'd—yeah. Okay, yeah. I'll look into it. What should I do with the subjects?"

Another pause, and Martha heard Dr. Klopft say, "Are you sure? It's a little different now. No apparent cognitive defects, which is sort of a surprise—no? All right. All right. It'll be a mercy. Good day, Mr. Chien."

Silence followed. Martha looked over at Matt, who was licking sore-looking lips. He must have been biting them.

"We have to get out of here," she said.

Sanchez expects the woods to be riddled with sentries and countermeasures, and she is right. Both she and Brown know what they're doing—they move easily in jackets reversed to show green and brown interiors. The heat-reflective insulating linings of their clothing break up their outlines to any infrared scanners, and loam smeared on their faces reduces reflectivity.

Before they go silent, Brown shows Sanchez his panic button—a small beige box strapped to his wrist with an Ace bandage. If his heart stops, or if he keys a certain simple code, it will alert his control.

"Black helicopters?" Sanchez asks.

He smiles. "Close enough for government work. When I mailed in the warrant and the request for backup, I relayed what we know. I expect we'll have support in a matter of hours, and clear and present danger to a pair of minors is enough for us to move now." He frowns.

Sanchez says, "It'll cost us Chien."

Brown spreads his hands. She's talking about discarding the work of months, and he just sighs. "Somebody else may have better luck. Or maybe we'll get enough out of Klopft for Shanghai or Honolulu to bring him in."

Sanchez meets his gaze. He looks resigned, but calm. "All right then. Let's do this thing."

Brown and Sanchez take to the woods. Their successful infiltration of the compound is a credit to their skill and equipment, and not any indictment of Klopft's countermeasures. Apparently there's significant money to be made in rare-animal smuggling.

At last, they lie belly-down along branches overlooking the compound, peering through camouflage netting supported by the very trees they've made their lair. Men in plainclothes bordering on uniforms—blue shirts, tan trousers, navy berets—come and go, some of them carrying automatic weapons. At the center of their activity—shadowed by the camo net—lies a low building obviously assembled from portable component parts. From above, Sanchez can make out the joints between individual rooms and hallways, the tan tape sealing tan waterproof recycled wallboard together. It's the stuff the U.N. uses to throw up refugee camps in a hurry, repurposed ingeniously.

Somebody is leading two children out of the building. And Sanchez recognizes him.

She can't have done so. He can't be here, but there's no mistaking him. He's broad-shouldered and black-haired and dark and tall, and even at this distance she knows the span of his hands and the ease of his stride in her bones. Hands shaking, she raises the spyglass to her eye, shading the lens with her hand so it won't flash in any stray beam of sunlight.

It's Doe Callandar. She recognizes the curve of his mouth, the shape of his chin, the boyish cheeks, the satiny sheen off his skin. His face is set in a scowl, an expression Sanchez knows a little too well. It's the one he wears when he's faced with a task he finds unbearable.

He's got two kids in pajamas beside him, walking barefoot over hard-packed earth.

Brown must notice something, because the earbud he gave her crackles. "Sanchez?"

"That's my husband down there," she says. "Cascadia LEC is on the job. Except they didn't tell me they had an inside man here . . . "

Or he's dirtier than she ever imagined. And having witnessed a little, like any lover betrayed, she imagined a lot.

When Sanchez's gaze follows his arm down to the little girl on her left, she almost drops the spyglass.

Because the little girl has the face of a woman of sixty. She's slight and skinny, her shriveled apple head bobbing on a stick-thin neck, her thin hair hanging in gray wisps about her face. The boy, too, is wizened and thin and bald. Sanchez can see the discomfort in his expression as he twists his fingers over and over again in Doe's grip, trying to pull his hand loose. Doe holds both children tight, thought, and by the weapon on his hip, Sanchez has a horrible sense she knows what's about to happen.

He leads the children into the woods.

"Brown."

"Copy."

"Hit your panic button, man. I'm going after those kids."

"Sanchez!" A desperate hiss. "Don't be crazy, lady. You don't have a gun!"

"Yeah," she says, already gathering her feet under her, getting ready to move. "I know that."

Officer Callandar dragged Martha and Matt along, away from the bustle of the camp. Nobody would look at them as they passed, and Martha had a horrible feeling that she knew why they didn't want to notice her. Because if they noticed her and Matt, they would have to take responsibility for what was going to happen to them.

Nobody wants to know when something horrible is about to take place.

She screamed and cried, but the big man was stronger than anybody, and he just kept walking. He had a gun—she could smell the gun cleaner, as sharp and green as Daddy Corey's—and his skin was so hot against hers that her palm and wrist were all slicked with sweat. If she could just pull away, she would run—

And leave Matt here alone? Run off into the woods in pajamas, barefoot? Without a knife or a fire?

She wouldn't last the night.

She picked her feet up and hung on the man's arm, trying to drag him to a stop, but he just kept walking. He lifted her up by her wrist, so she dangled clear of the ground, and though she kicked and kicked she couldn't hit him in the face like she wanted. His big body just seemed to soak up any punishment she could dish out. Matt, too, struggled and tried to bite, but couldn't get ahold of the man.

Finally, they were well away from the camp, the big man stopped. He set Martha and Matt on the ground, kneeling beside them, and let go of their wrists. "Go on," he said. "Run."

Martha took a step back. Another. Her bruised hand groped out and clutched after Matt, finding his wrist after two grabs. He slapped his fingers over hers, squeezing.

"If we run," Matt said, "you're going to shoot us. Like you shot Daddy Corey."

Matt was just guessing, Martha thought. But Officer Callandar winced.

He reached down and slowly pulled his gun from the holster. "What do you think is going to happen if you don't run?"

Something moved in the trees behind him. Over the thunder of her own heart, the rasp of her breathing, Martha heard a rustle in the needles. She held her breath.

It was the wrong thing, because the big man noticed. He pointed his gun straight up and fired it twice. "*Run!* You stupid little shits. Get out of here!"

Something big fell from up above.

Martha did not stay to see what happened. She grabbed Bobby's hand and turned and ran, her knees aching with every step.

Sanchez hits the dirt and Doe at the same time. She puts all the force of her leap-and-fall into the stick she swings, bringing it down on his skull. He crumples, the gun he only fired into the air spinning out of his hand to slam into the earth two meters away. Secured by a squeeze safety and a palmprint-lock, it does not discharge.

Sanchez stands over her husband, the bloody stick speckled with a few tight coils of hair in her hands like a baseball bat, like a samurai sword. She breathes heavily—in, out. It hurts.

Doe moans.

She drops the stick and reaches for her cuffs, cursing under her breath when she realizes that in this persona, she does not own any.

The ancient, alien thunder of helicopters rises up the mountainside. The cavalry has arrived.

She must not have hit Doe hard enough—*Pulling your punches? Really?*—because he suddenly scrambles forward, kicking up clods of composting needles. She dives after him, but he rolls and comes up with the gun. Blood trickles stickily across his forehead. He wipes it away with his free hand.

"Mauritza." It comes out as a sigh of relief, startling her. Still, she watches the gun like you'd watch a snake. "Thank God."

"You're under arrest," she says.

He lowers the gun, but doesn't put it away. "What for? I'm legit, love. On a license for Seattle. I replaced some private security goon they busted leaving town. What are *you* doing here?"

She folds her hands. She could lunge for him—she's inside twenty feet, and his gun's not ready. She might be able to disarm him.

But he's bigger and stronger.

She says, "You killed Darwish, didn't you?"

He spreads his hands, leaving the gun in his lap. Intentionally disarming himself. "Klopft killed him. And if you're smart, and you want Klopft to stay in jail, that's the story you'll support." He pauses. "You'll find Darwish's harvested organs and DNA in the freezer here. You've got him dead to rights. Your collar, love."

She meets his gaze. "Like last time?"

He hesitates. And then nods, as if deciding very slowly to be honest.

"In Oakland you planted evidence," she says. "You saved my life, and I covered for you. This time, you framed somebody for murder. For a murder you committed."

"If you send Klopft up for trafficking in endangered species, or for illegal adoptions, he'll serve a couple of years. A few months. I know he killed babies, but I can't prove it. I can prove he killed Darwish. And do you know what Darwish did? Did you see those kids? That's what he was involved in, Mauritza. The first babies they made all had genetic defects. Progeria. They put most of 'em down, but Darwish kept a couple as pets. They'll die of old age before they turn fifteen. These people are *horrible*. Play it my way and you're a hero."

"You can stop me," she says. "You have a gun."

"I know." But he doesn't reach for it.

"You poor stupid son-of-a-bitch," she says. "Darwish was an informer, Doe. The guy you killed and cut up was on our side."

Back at the camp, Cascadia and Interpol's licensed ops and sworn officers bustle about as they hustle men and a few women into coffles. There could have been a firefight—Sanchez is surprised there wasn't a firefight—but surprise must have ameliorated the worst of it.

She hands Doe off to a uniformed officer, dazzled for a moment by the cost in energy, hydrocarbons, fuel cells to bring all these people out here. She tells the woman that they need to mount a search party, that there are two children suffering some form of progeria lost in the woods. That the kids are witnesses against Klopft, and need to be protected.

And then she goes to join the search for them, confident that neither Cascadia nor Interpol had trackers much better than her.

The bole of the fallen tree stretched over them kept the rain off, and the ground underneath was only damp, not soaked like everything else. Martha and Matt had no knives, nor anything but sticks rubbed sharp, but Matt was pulling up the bark and probing in the tunnels underneath for grubs. They chewed them carefully, not wasting anything: food was food.

Martha didn't think the people from the compound—or the other people, the ones who had been fighting the people from the compound—would find them here. They'd run far, and hidden well.

And for a couple of hours, everything was silent except the sounds of animals, and the rain.

Until a boot crunched outside, footsteps approaching, and somebody parted the boughs that fell over them with a pale-skinned hand.

"Hey," said the woman who had hit Callandar and then fought him while Martha and Matt ran away. "You guys want to come out of there? My name's Mauritza. I have a warm dry place for you to sleep."

Martha looked at Matt. Matt shrugged, deferring to her.

How bad can it be?

Gingerly, Martha reached out a cold hand.

Brown waits for her near the outskirts of the camp, his arms folded, letting the official types do their work. He's watching a team carry cages out of the building and line them up in the shade—strange purple birds in polymer boxes with airholes, snakes that seem long and whippy and as curiously jointed as those wooden toy serpents you shake by the tail, octopuses in large wheeled terrariums.

"Look at this stuff," Brown says, when Mauritza walks up to him. "Squonks. Tree octopuses. Hoopsnakes."

She decides she doesn't want to know about hoopsnakes. "What's a squonk?"

"See those purple birds? They were supposed to be able to dissolve themselves in their own tears. These ones seem to be able to convert themselves into an amoeba-like state and back. One of your techs said it was going to set stem cell research forward fifteen years, if they can figure out how to extrapolate the tech."

"They're not my techs," Mauritza says. "This was just a license job."

"Sure it was." He smiles.

She looks away.

"There are a whole bunch of babies inside," Brown says. "That same tech told me they're genetically manipulated. Stronger, faster—"

"You have a way of getting sensitive information out of people."

"I used to have a nickname."

"I heard." She pauses, pressed against her eyes. "If you can build a tree octopus, how much trouble is a superkid?"

"Bet the going rate is higher."

"Yeah," she says. "And so is the cost of failure."

Brown turns to look at her. "You know, my license is up as of five minutes ago. I'm not a cop right this second. I'm just a guy with a conscience."

"Doe's going to walk out of this a hero," she says.

"Unless you tell somebody the truth."

She nods. She can't look at him. She keeps talking. Not because he's interviewing her, but because she has to tell somebody, and maybe if it's him, she can tell herself he got it out of her somehow.

Superpowers.

"The last case we worked before I left him," she says. She opens her mouth. She can't go on.

Brown waits, studying his fingernails.

She studies them too. "Doe planted evidence."

"You have proof?"

She nods. "I have a vid. The same vid that shows me nearly getting shot. I kept it to myself. But that wasn't—" She sighs. "That wasn't murder."

Brown says, "If you come forward with this, *that* will cost you your career."

"And him his." She twists her hands together. "I was a good cop. It's not the end of the world."

Brown looks away. "You are a good cop. You know, I was thinking of getting out of this game—"

"Too much ugly?" she asks, noticing the past tense.

He nods. "They're going to destroy all of these animals."

"I know," she says. "It's not your fault."

"Whose fault it is doesn't change what's going to happen."

She has to force her shoulders out of their hunch. "What about the babies?"

"God only knows. Adoption? Want to raise a superbaby? Somebody will. And Matt and Martha?"

"Group home. After they testify."

"Group home," he agrees. "Until they die of old age."

Her whole body aches with the aftermath of adrenaline. "What about the animals that escaped?"

"Escaped?" Brown glances across at her and smiles. "You think these things could survive in the wild?"

Sanchez looks him in the eye. She looks away.

"Of course. How on earth would anything escape a place like this? It's crazy talk."

She shakes her head, remembering the elegant coil of sticky tentacles through wet boughs.

"Crazy talk," she says. "How on earth would that happen?"

The Leavings of the Wolf

Dagmar was doomed to run. Feet in stiff new trail shoes flexing, hitting. The sharp ache of each stride in knees no longer accustomed to the pressure. Her body, too heavy on the downhills, femur jarring into hip socket, each hop down like a blow against her soles. Against her soul.

Dagmar was doomed to run until her curse was lifted.

Oh, she thought of it as a curse, but it was just a wedding ring. She could have solved the problem with a pair of tin snips. Applied to the ring, not the finger, though there were days—

Days, maybe even weeks, when she could have fielded enough self-loathing to resort to the latter. But no, she would not ruin that ring. It had a history: the half-carat transition-cut diamond was a transplant from her grandmother's engagement ring, reset in a filigree band carved by a jeweler friend who was as dead as Dagmar's marriage.

She wouldn't wear it again herself, if—*when,* she told herself patiently—*when* she could ever get it off. But she thought of saving it for a daughter she still might one day have—thirty wasn't so old. Anyway, it was a piece of history. A piece of art.

It was futile—and fascist—to destroy history out of hand, just because it had unpleasant associations. But the ring wouldn't come off her finger intact until the forty pounds she'd put on over the course of her divorce came off, too.

So, in the mornings before the Monday/ Wednesday/ Friday section of her undergrad animal behavior class, she climbed out of her Toyota, rocking her feet in her stiff new minimalist running shoes—how the technology had changed, in the last ten years or so—and was made all the more aware of her current array of bulges and bumps by the tightness of the sports bra and the way the shorts rode up when she stretched beside the car.

The university where Dagmar worked lay on a headland above the ocean, where cool breezes crossed it in every season. They dried the sweat on her face, the salt water soaking her T-shirt as she ran.

Painfully at first, in intervals more walking than jogging, shuffling to minimize the impact on her ankles and knees. She trotted slow circles around the library. But within a week, that wasn't enough. She extended her range through campus. Her shoes broke in, the stiff soles developing flex. She learned—relearned—to push off from her toes.

She invested in better running socks—cushiony wool, twenty bucks a pair.

She's a runner and a student; he's a poet and a singer. Each of them sees in the other something they're missing in themselves.

She sees his confidence, his creativity. He sees her studiousness, her devotion.

The story ends as it always does. They fall in love.

Of course there are signs that all is not right. Portents.

But isn't that always how it goes?

Her birds found her before the end of the first week. Black wings, dagged edges trailing, whirled overhead as she thudded along sloped paths.

The crows were encouragement. She liked being the weird woman who ran early in the morning, beneath a vortex of black wings.

She had been to Stockholm, to Malmö where her grandfather had been born. She'd met her Swedish cousins and eaten lingonberries outside of an Ikea. She knew enough of the myths of her ancestors to find the idea of Thought and Memory accompanying her ritual expurgation of the self-inflicted sin of marrying the wrong man . . .

. . . entertaining.

Or maybe she'd married the right man. She still often thought so.

But he had married the wrong woman.

And anyway, the birds were hers. Or she was theirs.

And always had been.

"Your damned crows," he calls them.

As in: "You care about your damned crows more than me." As in: "Why don't you go talk to your damned crows, if you don't want to talk to me."

Her crows, the ones she'd taught to identify her, the ones that ate from her hand as part of her research, clearly had no difficulties recognizing her outside the normal arc of feeding station hours.

They had taught other birds to recognize her, too, because the murder was more than ten birds strong, and only three or four at a time ever had the ankle bands that told Dagmar which of her crows was which. Crows could tell humans apart by facial features and hair color, and could communicate that information to other crows. Humans had no such innate ability when it came to crows.

Dagmar had noticed that she could fool herself into thinking she could tell them apart, but inevitably she'd think she was dealing with one bird and find it was actually another one entirely once she got a look at the legbands.

The other humans had no problem identifying her, either. She was the heavyset blond woman who ran every morning, now, thudding along—jiggling, stone-footed—under a cloak of crows.

Things she has not said in return: "My damned crows actually pretend to listen."

Dagmar grew stronger. Her wind improved. Her calves bulged with muscle—but her finger still bulged slightly on either side of the ring. The weight stayed on her.

Sometimes, from running, her hands swelled, and the finger with the wedding ring on it would grow taut and red as a sausage. Bee-stung. She'd ice and elevate it until the swelling passed.

She tried soap, olive oil. Heating it under running water to make the metal expand.

It availed her not.

There are the nights like gifts, when everything's the way it was. When they play rummy with the TV on, and he shows her his new poetry. When he kisses her neck behind the ear, and smooths her hair down.

She felt as if she were failing her feminist politics, worrying about her body size. She told herself she wasn't losing weight: she was gaining health.

She dieted, desultorily. Surely the running should be enough.

It wasn't. The ring—stayed on.

"Cut the ring off," her sister says.

But there have been too many defeats. Cutting it off is one more, one more failure in the litany of failures caught up in the most important thing she was ever supposed to do with her life.

That damned ring. Its weight on her hand. The way it digs in when she makes a fist.

She will beat it.

It is only metal, and she is flesh and will.

Perhaps it is her destiny to run.

One day—it was a Tuesday, so she had more time before her section—she followed the crows instead of letting the crows follow her.

She wasn't sure what led to the decision, but they were flocking—the crows with bands and the ones without—and as she jogged up on them they lifted into the air like a scatter of burned pages, like a swirl of ashes caught in a vortex of rising heat. They flew heavily, the way she felt she ran, beating into the ocean breeze that rose from the sea cliffs with rowing strokes rather than tumbling over one another weightlessly as the songbirds did.

They were strong, though, and they hauled themselves into the air like prizefighters hauling themselves up the ropes.

They led her down the green slopes of the campus lawn, toward the sweep of professionally gardened pastel stucco housing development draped across the top of the cliffs above. They turned along an access road, and led her out toward the sea.

She ran in the cool breeze, June gloom graying the sky above her, the smell of jasmine rising on all sides. Iceplant carpeted both sides of the road, the stockade fences separating her from a housing development draped with bougainvillea in every hot color.

A bead of sweat trickled down Dagmar's nose. But some days, she'd learned, your body gives you little gifts: functioning at a higher level of competence than normal, a glimpse of what you can look forward to if you keep training. Maybe it was the cool air, or the smell of the sea, or the fact that the path was largely downhill—but she was still running strong when she reached the dead end of the road.

Still heavily, too, to be sure, not with the light, quick strides she'd managed when she was younger. Before the marriage, before the divorce. But she hesitated before a tangle of orange temporary fence, and paced slowly back and forth.

She stood at the lip of a broad gully, steep enough to make clambering down daunting. A sandy path did lead into its depths, in the direction of the water. The arroyo's two cliffs plunged in a deep vee she could not see to the bottom of, because it was obscured by eroded folds.

The crows swirled over her like a river full of black leaves tumbling toward the sea. Dagmar watched them skim the terrain down the bluff, into the canyon. Their voices echoed as if they called her after—or mocked her heavy, flightless limbs.

She felt in her pocket for her phone. Present and accounted for.

All right then. If she broke a leg . . . she could call a rescue team.

If she cracked her head open . . .

Well, she wouldn't have to worry about the damned wedding ring any more.

She reads his poetry, his thesis. She brings him books.

She bakes him cookies.

He catches her hand when she leaves tea beside his computer, and kisses the back of it, beside the wedding ring.

She meets his eyes and smiles.

They're trying.

Dagmar pounded through the gully—trotting at first, but not for long. The path was too steep, treacherous with loose sand, and no wider than one foot in front of the other. The sparse and thorny branches on the slope would not save her if she fell, and on the right there was a drop of twice her height down to a handspan-width, rattling stream.

Dagmar wanted to applaud its oversized noise.

Even walking, every step felt like she was hopping down from a bench. She steadied herself with her hands when she could, and at the steepest patches hunkered down and scooted. The trail shoes pinched her toes when her feet slid inside them. She cursed the local teens when she came to a steep patch scattered with thick shards of brown glass, relict of broken beer bottles, and picked her way.

She still had to stop afterward and find a broken stick with which to pry glass splinters from her soles.

The gloom was burning off, bathing her in the warm chill of summer sun and cool, dry sea air. The crows were somewhere up ahead. She couldn't say why she was so certain they would have waited for her.

Sometimes her breath came tight and quick against the arch of her throat: raspy, rough. But it was fear, not shortness of breath. She acknowledged it and kept going, trying not to glance too often at the sharp drop to a rocky streambed that lay only one slip or misstep away.

She actually managed to feel a little smug, for a while: at least she'd regained a little athleticism. And she didn't think this would ever have been *easy*.

"Look at you," he says. "When was the last time you got off your ass?"

Maybe not easy for *her*, but she thought she was most of the way down when she heard the patter of soft footsteps behind her, a quiet voice warning, "Coming up!"

She stepped as far to the inside of the trail—as if there *were* an inside of the trail—as possible, and turned sideways. A slim, muscled young man in a knee-length wetsuit jogged barefoot down the path she'd been painstakingly inching along, a surfboard balanced on his shoulder. Dagmar blinked, but he didn't vanish. Sunlight prickled through his close-cropped hair while she still felt the chill of mist across her neck.

"Sorry," she said helplessly.

But he answered, "Don't worry, plenty of room," and whisked past without letting his shoulder brush. He bounced from foothold to foothold until he vanished into a twisting passage between sandstone outcrops.

"There's my sense of inadequacy," Dagmar sighed, trudging on.

Things she does not say in response: "Look at *you*."

She bites he lip. She nods.

She is trying to *save her marriage.*

And he's right. She should take up running again.

Someone had run a hand-line—just a length of plastic clothesline, nothing that would prevent a serious fall—down the steepest, muddiest bit of the trail-bottom. Dagmar used it to steady herself as she descended, careful not to trust it with too much of her weight. By now, she could hear the wearing of the sea—and something else. Water, also—but not the water trickling in the rocky stream bed, and not the water hissing amongst the grains of sand. Falling water.

She rounded the corner of the gully—now towering a hundred feet or more overhead, to a cliff edge bearded with straggling bushes—and found herself in a grotto.

A narrow waterfall trembled from the cliff-top across wet, packed sand, shimmering like a beaded curtain in the slanted morning light. Its spray scattered lush draperies of ferns with jeweled snoods, hung trembling on the air in rainbow veils. Alongside grew dusty green reeds.

She drew up at the foot of the trail, her throat tightening upon the words of delight that she had no one to call out too. Broad sand stretched before her now, a wide path that led between two final shoulders of stone to the sea. Wetsuited surfers frolicked in the curling waves, silhouetted against the mirror-bright facets of the water. The sun was bright out there, though she stood in mist and shadow.

At the cliff-top, two crows sat shoulder to shoulder, peering down at Dagmar with curious bright eyes, heads cocked.

"Caw," said the one on the right. She could not see if they were banded.

She craned her head until her neck ached stiffly and tried not to think of how she was going to get back up to the top. Loneliness ached against her breast like the pressure of accusing fingers.

"Hey," she said. "This is so beautiful."

The crows did not answer.

Her hands had swollen on the descent, taut and prickling, the left one burning around her ring. Her feet ached still—mashed toes, and she suspected from a sharper, localized pain that one of those shards of glass might have punched through the sole of her shoe.

The ripples beneath the waterfall looked cool. She hopped the rocky little stream—now that it ran across the surface rather than down in a gully, it was easy—and limped toward the pool, wincing.

The crows come at dawn, bright-eyed—how can black eyes seem bright?— and intelligent. The feeding station is designed so that only one bird at a time can eat, and see her. They squabble and peck, but not seriously—and, after a fashion, they take turns: one, having eaten, withdraws from the uncomfortably close presence of the researcher, and the next, hungry, shoulders in.

When they come up to the trough, to pick at the cracked corn she dribbles through the transparent plastic shield that separates her from the birds, they eye her face carefully. They make eye contact. They tip their heads.

She knows it's not good science, but she begins to think they know her.

~

It would be stupid to pull off her shoe—if she did have a cut, she'd get sand in it, and then she'd just have to put the shoe back on sandy and get blisters—so instead she dropped a knee in the wet sand beside the pool and let her hands fall into the water. It was cold and sharp and eased the taut sensation that her skin was a too-full balloon. She touched her ring, felt the heat in the skin beside it. It was too tight even to turn.

Dagmar pushed sandy, sweat-damp hair off her forehead with the back of her hand.

From behind her, as before, a voice—this one also male, but midrange, calm, with an indeterminate northern European accent—said, "Have a care with that."

Dagmar almost toppled forward into the puddly little pool. She caught herself on a hand plunged into the water—the left one, it happened—and drew it back with a gasp. There must have been a bit of broken glass in the pool, too, and now dilute blood ran freely from the heel of her thumb down her elbow, to drip in threads upon the sand.

She turned over her shoulder, heart already racing with the threat of a strange man in an isolated place—and instead found herself charmed. He was tall but not a tower, broad but not a barn-door. Strong-shouldered like a man who used it—the surfers on the water, the soldiers who ran along the beach. Long light hair—sand-brown—bounced over one of those shoulders in a tail as the water bounced down the cliff above. A trim brown beard hid the line of his jaw; the flush of a slight sunburn vanished behind it.

And his right arm ended in shiny scraps of scar tissue four inches above where the wrist should have been.

Iraq, she thought. He might have been thirty; he wasn't thirty-five. *Afghanistan?*

His gaze went to the trickle of bloody water along her arm. She expected him to start forward, to offer help.

Instead he said, "Your coming is foretold, Dagmar Sörensdotter. I am here to tell you: you must make a sacrifice to a grief to end it."

Her name. Her *father's* name. The cold in her fingers—the way the pain in her hand, in her foot receded. The way she suddenly noticed details she had not seen before: that the cliff behind the one-handed man was gray and tawny granite, and not the buff sand she'd been eyeing throughout her descent; that the surfers scudding like elongated seals through the curving ocean had all drifted out of line of sight: that the ocean itself was being lost again behind chilly veils of mist.

She pulled her bloody right hand away from the wound in her left and groped in the pocket of her shorts for her phone.

"It avails you not, Dagmar Sörensdotter," he said. "You are in no danger. When grief burns in your heart, and your blood enters the water, and you run down into the earth at the edge of the sea with your *helskor* on, accompanied by crows—on this my day of all days! Who shall come to you then but a god of your ancestors, before you run all the way to Niflheim?"

He gestured to her feet. She looked down at her trail shoes, and noticed a reddish patch spreading along the side of the right one. She looked up again.

He didn't look like a god. He looked like a man—a man her own age, her own ethnicity, more or less her own phenotype. A man in a gray T-shirt and faded jeans rolled up to show the sand-dusted bones of his ankles. A crazy man, apparently, no matter how pleasant his gaze.

"I have a phone," she said, raising her right hand to show it. Aware of the water and the cliff at her back. Aware of the length of his legs, and the fact that she'd have to dart right past him to reach the beach trail. "I'll scream."

He glanced over his shoulder. "If you must," he said, tiredly. "I am Týr, Sörensdotter. My *name* means *God*. This hand"—he held up that ragged, scar-shiny stump—"fed the Fenris wolf, that he would stand to be shackled. *This* hand"—he raised the intact one—"won me glory nonetheless. Men speak of the brave as Týr-valiant, of the wise as Týr-prudent. I am called 'kin-of-giants;' I am named 'god-of-battle;' I am hight 'the-leavings-of-the-wolf.'" He paused; the level brows rose. "And will that name be yours as well?"

"I've met someone else," he says.

Dagmar lowers her eyes. She slices celery lengthwise, carefully, dices it into cubes as small as the shattered bits of safety glass.

It feels like a car wreck, all right.

She scrapes the vegetables into hot oil and hears them sizzle.

"Do you hear me?" he asks. "I've met someone else."

"I heard you." She sets the knife down on the cutting board before she turns around. "Were you looking for the gratification of a dramatic response? Because you could have timed it better. I have a pan full of boiling oil *right here.*"

"The leavings of the wolf," she said. "Leavings. Like . . . leftovers?" *Dial 911*, she told herself, *before the nice crazy stalker pulls out a knife.* But her fingers didn't move over the screen.

God or not, he had a nice smile, full lips behind the fringe of beard curving crookedly. "It did make a meal of the rest."

She felt her own frown. Felt the hand clutching the phone drop to her side. "You're left-handed."

"Where I'm from," he said, "no one is left-handed. But I learned."

"So why didn't you give the wolf your left hand?"

He shrugged, eyebrows drawing together over the bridge of a slightly crooked nose.

In the face of his silence, she fidgeted. "It would have been the sensible choice."

"But not the grand one. It doesn't pay to be stingy with wolves, Sörensdotter."

Her hands clenched. One around the phone, one pressing fresh blood from a wound. "You said *helskor,* before. What are helskor?"

"Hell shoes." He jerked his stump back at the steep and slick descent. "The road to the underworld is strewn with thorns; the river the dead must wade is thick with knives. Even well-shod, I see you have your injuries."

"I'm not dead," Dagmar said.

"Dead enough to shed your blood on the path to Hel's domain. Dead enough to have been seeking Niflheim these past months, whether or not you knew it."

With his taken breath and the lift of his chin, Týr gave himself away. He gestured to her dripping hand and said what he meant to say anyway. "When you put your hand in a wolf's mouth, you must understand that you have already made the decision to sacrifice it."

"I didn't know it was a wolf," she said. "I thought it was a marriage."

"They are not," Týr says, "dissimilar. Are you going to stand there forever?"

Dagmar raises her left hand. Blood smears it already, the slit in her palm deeper than it had seemed. Still welling.

It palls the diamond in crimson, so no fire reflects. It clots in the spaces in the band's filigree.

She says, "I didn't want to waste it. I wanted to save it for something else."

"A sacrifice," the god says, "is not a waste."

He does not say: What you try to salvage will drag you down instead.

He does not say: You cannot cut your losses until you are willing to admit that you have lost.

He does not need to.

How bad can it be? Dagmar wonders.

She puts her bloody finger in her mouth and hooks her teeth behind the ring.

Damn you, she thinks. *I want to live. Even with failure.*

Bit by bit, scraping skin with her teeth, she drags the ring along her finger. The pain brings sharp water to her eyes. The taste of blood—fresh and clotted—gags her. The diamond scrapes her gums. Flesh bunches against her knuckle.

I don't think I can do this.

"This has already happened," the god says in her ear. "This is always happening."

I don't think I can not.

When she pulls once more, harder, her knuckle rips, skins off, burns raw. With a fresh well of blood that tastes like seaweed, the ring slides free, loose in her mouth, nearly choking her.

Dagmar spits it on the sand and screams.

The god has left her.

Dagmar stands on the strand under the bright sun, her left hand cradled against her chest, and watches the long indigo breakers combing the hammered sea. Red runs down her arm, drips from her elbow, falls and spatters into the shallow play of the ocean's edge. Overhead wheel crows, murders and covenants of them, driving even the boldest seagulls away.

She holds the ring in her right hand. Her fingers clutch; she raises her fist. One sharp jerk, and the ocean can have it. One—

She turns back and draws her arm down, and instead tosses the bright bloody thing flashing into the sky. Round and round, spinning, tumbling, pretty in the sun until the dark wings of carrion birds sweep toward it.

She does not see which claims it—banded or bare—just the chase as all the others follow, proclaiming their greed and outrage, sweeping away from her along the endless empty river of the sky.

"Thank you," she whispers after them.

In a moment, they are gone.

—for SL

↩

The Death of Terrestrial Radio

The first word was meant to be spoken quietly, if it should ever be spoken at all. A dribble of signal. An echo. A ghost. A coded trickle, something some PC running SETI-at-home would pick out of the background noise, flag, and return silently to the great database in the sky, the machine's owner innocent of her role in making history.

I am one of the few who is old enough to remember what we *got*. Something as subtle as a solid whack across the nose with a cricket bat. We couldn't believe it at first, but there it was, interfering with transmissions on all frequencies, cluttering our signals with static ghosts.

Television had largely abandoned the airwaves by then, so the transmissions that came to houses and offices over fiber optic cable were unperturbed. Dueling experts opined with telegenic confidence that the suggestive sequence of blips was some natural, cosmological phenomenon—and not somebody broadcasting to the whole world, simultaneously, intentionally.

That lasted all of about three hours before the first cable news channel produced an elderly man, liver-spotted scalp clearly visible between the thinning strands of his hair. He was a ham radio operator, a lifetime wireless hobbyist who folded his hands before his chest and closed his eyes to listen to those noises straight out of an old movie—exactly like the chatter of a wireless telegraph.

He let his lids crack open again, "It's Morse code; of course I recognize it. It might be the most famous Marconi transmission in history."

He quoted, as if reciting a familiar poem, "*CQD CQD SOS* Titanic *Position 41.44 N 50.24 W. Require immediate assistance. Come at once. We struck an iceberg. Sinking.*"

I was in my office at the ALMA site, surrounded by coworkers, and you could have heard a pin drop. We hadn't exactly gotten the jump on this one—not when the signal was interfering with people's baby monitors. But we had been engaged in trying to track it.

A simple task, given the strength of the signal. It originated in Taurus, and exhibited measurable parallax over the course of a couple of days. Not only was it loud, in other words—but it was close, and moving fast.

A few weeks later, we found the second one. Suddenly, radio signals were blossoming all over the sky. Our own dead signals, our own dead voices—ham radio, *The Shadow*, coded signals from World War I—spoken back to us.

And then they stopped.

When I was fifteen years old, other girls wanted to be doctors and actors and politicians. They played soccer and softball, went to Girls State, marched in band.

I ran SETI and stayed late at school for Math League and Physics Club. Almost nobody really believed in aliens, but I wanted to talk to them so badly I didn't even have words for the feeling, the cravings that welled up inside me.

Other girls and boys—even other geeks—dated. And I guess I tried, sort of. But the people around me never seemed as entrancing as the numbers in my head. I *wanted* to like them—loneliness was certainly an issue—but the gap between wanting and being able seemed unbridgeable.

In retrospect, what I sought refuge in was not too dissimilar from the age-old fantasy that one is adopted, that one's real family will come along someday and rescue one from these weirdos one's been left with. Except I felt so weird I turned to aliens. Maybe someone out there would be like me. Certainly, it seemed like I had nothing in common with anybody else on *this* planet.

Sooner or later, you put aside childish things—or risk being labeled a crackpot. By the time I turned twenty-seven, I had two grad degrees and a tenure-track job at a major research university. I'd gotten time on the VLA and was mining the research for my dis towards further publications.

Radio astronomers get drunk and speculate about extraterrestrial life . . . I'd say "like anybody else," but I guess most people don't actually do that. The difference is, we know on a visceral level how prohibitive the distances and timescales are, how cold the math.

We really *didn't* expect to hear from anybody.

Maybe it's like falling in love. You have to truly stop expecting something to happen before it will.

~

You talk about things that change the world. Usually, it's in hindsight. Usually you don't notice them when they're happening.

Ah, but sometimes. Sometimes there's no way you could have missed it unless you were in a vegetative state.

It's hard to remember now, but we didn't know, then, what the Echoes were or what they wanted. It could have been a passing alien ship, psychological warfare from inbound would-be conquerors (Stephen Hawking would have been vindicated!), or some previously unsuspected cosmological phenomena.

There were new cults; a few suicides. The occasional marriage self-destructed, and I confess I was naively surprised at the number of people who joined or left religions, apparently at random.

I'd never been much of a joiner, myself.

Six months later, our own voices echoed back to us again. This time it was *War of the Worlds* and Radio Free Europe.

With those two datapoints, we could figure out where they were, and how far away, and how fast they were moving.

By the third round, nobody was surprised to receive the signals of early broadcast television—and some clever souls even filtered the signals and recovered fragments of our own lost history: early live episodes of *The Avengers* and destroyed episodes of *Doctor Who*. So *much* entertainment used to be broadcast, carried over public airwaves that now mostly used for cellular calls and more practical things—where great swaths of them are not simply abandoned.

The idea of a cosmological explanation had always been farfetched. Now it seemed laughable. Somebody was bouncing our own words back to us. A means of communication, certainly . . . but a threat or a reassurance? Psychological warfare or reaching out?

How do you know for sure?

It's a little disconcerting to have your cell calls to your place of business interrupted by Jackie Gleason threatening his fictional wife with domestic violence.

Suddenly, after decades of neglect, a new space race rose, phoenix-like, from the ashes of exploration. Except this time we weren't racing other nation-states, but rather the slow motion tumble of what might turn out to be a hammer from the sky.

~

They were slowing down. And by the fourth round, we managed to spot their lightsails—their parachutes—and now we could watch as well as hear them come. Hailing them produced more echoes, and as we sent them new, specific signals they stopped reproducing our old ones.

The sources further away from Earth were braking harder; some had paused entirely (not that anything really pauses in space, but allow me the conceit) and at least one—the initial signal, the strongest Echo—seemed likely to pass very close indeed. We had a betting pool. My money had it making orbit.

I figured they weren't here to blow up the planet, enslave us, or kidnap our nubile young men away to Mercury. For one thing, if they were hostile, the easiest thing in the world—*out* of the world—would have been for them to sneak up on us and drop a rock on our heads from orbit, which would pretty much soften up any useful resistance right then and there. Alien invasion movies aren't usually written by physicists. For another thing, sending back our own voices . . . it seemed kind of friendly, somehow.

My work friend Carl pointed out that it was something bullies did, too, mocking what you said by repeating it. I looked across a plate of gyros at him and replied, "They do it in funny voices."

The constellation of radio sources strung out against the sky seemed to me to be relay stations, signal boosters. I guessed they were sending messages home.

I won the betting pool, which was a strange sensation. Carl, who shares my office and sits at the desk next to mine, knew better than to tease me about it. He'd tried when we were first thrown together, but I think he caught on that I was faking engagement with his jokes.

Rather than being offended, though, he just backed off of them.

Carl was a good guy, even if he wasn't funny. I was so young then; it was so amazingly long ago. Sixty-three years: a human's productive lifetime, under pretty good circumstances.

He was also the guy who thought enough of me to forward me the links to the breaking news articles on China's emergency manned mission to the Echo.

"Crap," I said.

"Easy, Courtney," he responded, without looking up from the rows of numbers scrolling his desktop. "We've still got their trail to chase back up the sky."

I was still frowning. He was still looking at me.

He said, "Look, it's seven. Let's get some dinner and you can vent all you want."

"Thanks," I said. "But I need to work tonight."

The U.S.A. was outraged, and loudly said so to everyone, whether they would listen or not. But there wasn't much America could do about it, having sacrificed our space program on the altars of economic necessity and eternal war. I found the prospect of China getting first crack at the Echo frustrating mostly because it meant that my odds of getting near it were exponentially smaller. And if I could have itched—I mean physically *itched*—with desire . . .

But as it turned out, we didn't have to go to the Echo.

The Echo came to us.

It separated into a dozen identical—we later learned—components, which settled themselves near population centers scattered around the globe. China got one; so did India.

It will surprise no one that I read a lot of science fiction. Read and read—one spelling, two pronunciations, two tenses. There's a subset of the genre that fans call the "big dumb object" plot: basically, *2001*. Intrepid human explorers meet up with an abandoned alien artifact—a probe, a relic—and have to decide what to make of it.

This wasn't a single big dumb object so much as a web of little ones. I spent some time thinking about it—well, who didn't?—and what I realized was that whoever built it had allowed for the fact that it might make landfall at a world where the sentient life forms had not yet achieved space flight. If we couldn't come to them, they would have to come to us.

The component that drifted down in New York City wound up at JPL, and a number of xenologists—a new specialty pretty much as of that morning—were invited to examine it.

And so I became one of the vanishingly small percentage of humans privileged to hold in my hands a disc of metal originated on another world. It was pristine, a perfect circle electroplated with gold, the surface etched with symbols and diagrams I forced myself not to try to interpret, just yet.

Carl leaned over my shoulder. He put his hand on it and gave me an excited squeeze. "Damn," he said. "It's just like Voyager."

"I guess good ideas tend to reoccur." Through the nitrile gloves, I felt the slight irregularities of its surface. "You don't suppose this one is a phonograph record too?"

To human ears, their voices sound like the layered keening of gulls.

You know who I am because I'm the one who found their star. It's a small, cool red sun about 31.5 light years away.

If you can name something that already belongs to someone else, I named it Hui Zhong, for my grandmother.

We've never actually seen Hui Zhong—it's too small, too cool, and washed out behind a brighter neighbor—but we know where it has to be. Hui Zhong burns at about 3000 degrees Kelvin—half the temperature of Earth's own sun. It's a Population II star, and poor in heavy elements. Its spectrum is recorded on the discs, and so we know that it is a first generation star, one of the early citizens of the thirteen-and-three-quarters billion-year-old universe.

Hui Zhong is nearly immortal. The convective structure of such dwarf stars offers them stability, constant luminosity, and a lifespan in the hundreds of billions of years. Our own Sun, by contrast, is only some four and a half billion years old—and in about that same amount of time, will become a red giant as its nuclear furnaces inevitably begin to fail.

We'll die with it, unless we find someplace else to go.

One of the tracks on the record the Echoes sent us is a voice counting, and one of the diagrams on its surface is of a planet and primary—so we have a sense of their homeworld's orbital period—a mere fourteen Earth days or so . . .

The Echoes, in other words, could have been planning their approach to other civilizations and sending out probes in likely directions for a very, very long time. The probe was a sublight vehicle; we couldn't know exactly how long it had taken us to reach us . . . but "millennia" wasn't out of the question.

We returned the call.

Not as one strong, unified signal, but as an erratic series of blips and dashes—governments and corporations and research institutions. There was an X-Prize. Groups and mavericks, answering the stars.

And we kept answering. We've been answering for almost seventy years now. I've gone from hot young Turk to eminence gris in that time, from sought-after expert to forgotten emeritus. For sixty-five of those years, I think I must have been holding my breath. Waiting for the word across the void. Waiting for these people who reached out from their ancient world, circling their ancient, stable star, to hear our reply and start a slow, painstaking dialogue.

On Turnaround Day they dusted me off. I found myself standing at a cocktail party next to the President of East America, wondering how I'd gotten there, wondering what was in the brown paste on the glorified cracker in my hand.

I turned around to say something to that effect to Carl before I remembered he'd died eighteen months before, predeceased by his wife of forty years. After he died, he used to call me every week, like clockwork.

His jokes still weren't that funny. But I could feel him waiting, lonely, on the other end of the line. As waiting and as lonely as me.

The world really did hold its breath. And our silence was met by an answering silence . . . and after a pause the world moved on.

It's not just Carl. Most of my other colleagues are gone. I live alone, and the work I can still do goes frustratingly slowly now.

Sometimes I think waiting to hear the answer was what kept me going this long.

I don't expect to hear an answer anymore.

Maybe the Echoes forgot they'd called out to us. Maybe they never really expected an answer. Maybe they moved beyond radio waves, the same way we have. Maybe—even more so than us—they no longer listen to the stars.

Maybe, despite their safe old world and their safe old star, something horrible happened to them. Maybe Fermi was right, and they blew themselves up.

Maybe we'll blow ourselves up someday really soon, too.

But they reached out once. They let us know we weren't alone. We heard them and reached back, and they haven't answered—or they haven't answered *yet*.

Maybe they live a lot longer than we do. Maybe they don't have the same sense of urgency.

We do keep trying. And maybe someday they'll send an answer.

But it will be a slow conversation and I won't be here to hear it. (Two words; one pronunciation.)

Too late, I think I figured something out. It's everybody, isn't it? It was Carl, too, and that's what he was trying to tell me. That we could be lonely together, and it might help somehow.

The silence stretches loud across the space between us. And I can't decide if knowing they were out there and that they reached out in friendship, with a map and the sound of their voices, is worse than imagining they were never there at all.

Acknowledgements

"Introduction" © 2012 by Scott Lynch. First publication, original to this volume.

"Tideline" © 2007 by Elizabeth Bear. First published: *Asimov's Science Fiction*, June 2007.

"Sonny Liston Takes The Fall" © 2008 by Elizabeth Bear. First published: *The Del Rey Book of Science Fiction and Fantasy: Sixteen Original Works by Speculative Fiction's Finest Voices*, ed. Ellen Datlow (Del Rey/Ballantine).

"Sounding" © 2006 by Elizabeth Bear. First published: *Strange Horizons*, 18 September 18, 2006.

"The Something-Dreaming Game" © 2007 by Elizabeth Bear. First published: *Fast Forward 1: Future Fiction from the Cutting Edge*, ed. Lou Anders (Pyr).

"The Cold Blacksmith" © 2006 by Elizabeth Bear. First published: *Jim Baen's Universe*, June 2006.

"In the House of Aryaman, a Lonely Signal Burns" © 2012 by Elizabeth Bear. First Published: *Asimov's Science Fiction*, January 2012.

"Orm the Beautiful" © 2007 by Elizabeth Bear. First published: *Clarkesworld*, January 2007.

"The Inevitable Heat Death of the Universe" © by 2006 Elizabeth Bear. First published: *Subterranean, Issue #4*.

"Love Among the Talus" © by 2006 Elizabeth Bear. First Publication: *Strange Horizons*, 11 December 2006.

"Cryptic Coloration" © by Elizabeth Bear 2007. First publication: *Jim Baen's Universe*, June 2007.

"The Ladies" © 2007 by Elizabeth Bear: First publication: *Coyote Wild*, December 2007.

"Shoggoths in Bloom" © 2008 by Elizabeth Bear. First Publication: *Asimov's Science Fiction,* March 2008.

"The Girl Who Sang Rose Madder" © 2008 by Elizabeth Bear. First publication: *Tor.com*, 11 September 2008.

"Dolly" © 2011 by Elizabeth Bear. First published: *Asimov's Science Fiction,* January 2011.

"Gods of the Forge" © 2011 by Elizabeth Bear. First publication: *TRSF: The Best New Science Fiction*, ed. Stephen Cass (Technology Review, Inc.)

"Annie Webber" © 2008 by Elizabeth Bear. First Publication: *Nature,* January 11, 2008.

"The Horrid Glory of its Wings" © 2009 by Elizabeth Bear. First publication *Tor.com*, 8 December 2009.

"Confessor" © 2010 by Elizabeth Bear. First publication (audio): *Metatropolis: Cascadia*, ed. Jon Scalzi (Audible Frontiers).

"The Leavings of the Wolf" © 2011 by Elizabeth Bear. First publication: *Apex*, November 2011.

"The Death of Terrestrial Radio" © 2012 by Elizabeth Bear. First publication, original to this volume.

～

About the Author

Elizabeth Bear was born on the same day as Frodo and Bilbo Baggins, but in a different year. The author of over a dozen novels and a hundred short stories, she has been honored for some of them with the John W. Campbell, two Hugos, and a Sturgeon Award. Her hobbies include rock climbing and cooking. She lives in Massachusetts with a giant ridiculous dog and regularly commutes to Wisconsin in order to spend time with her step-cat—and his human, author Scott Lynch.